Death Piled Hard

Death Piled Hard

A Tale of the Confederate Secret Services

W. Patrick Lang

iUniverse, Inc.
New York Bloomington

Death Piled Hard
A Tale of the Confederate Secret Services

iUniverse books may be ordered through booksellers or by contacting:

iUniverse
1663 Liberty Drive
Bloomington, IN 47403
www.iuniverse.com
1-800-Authors (1-800-288-4677)

ISBN: 978-1-4401-2388-7 (sc)
ISBN: 978-1-4401-2391-7 (dj)
ISBN: 978-1-4401-2389-4 (ebook)

Library of Congress Control Number: 2009923045

Printed in the United States of America

iUniverse Rev. 03/23/2009

For

George Henry Sharpe

Major General, United States Volunteers

"So now the Confederacy,
Sick with its mortal sickness, yet lives on
For twenty-one falling months of pride and despair,
Half-hopes blown out in the lighting, heroic strokes
That come to nothing, and death piled hard upon death."

"John Brown's Body"
Stephen V. Benet

Foreword

(Just After Gettysburg)

The spy plodded forward in the dripping rain. His black broadcloth coat and trousers held back the wet at first, but within a few minutes water began to run in tiny streams down his legs. The long skirt of the frock coat defined a precise line of separation between cold wetness below and relative warmth above, but he knew it was only a matter of time before his waistcoat and shirt soaked through. He shivered convulsively.

How cold a summer day could be.

The cortege stretched back through the mist for blocks, back all the way to the church. The black, rectangular bulk of the artillery caisson rumbled along on the cobbles just in front of him. His brother's casket rode high, its length filling the space between the wheels. The brass handles and waxed ebony gathered beads of rainwater.

He had protested the military symbols of grief, insisting that his brother had not been a soldier, had never served in any army. Edwin Stanton, the Secretary of War insisted. He said that the brother had been a valued friend and counselor of the president. Stanton said that his brother had died on the field of honor in the moment of triumph, had died at the rebels' hands.

Had died at the rebels' hands...

It was possible. Fire had swept the hill. There had been fire from all sides. *Who could know?*

The rain poured down. On the horizon he saw the flicker of lightning. The street became dirt and grew softer in the rain. Mud coated the iron tires. A spot of brown appeared on the side of the casket. He wiped it away with a pocket handkerchief.

Behind him, in the carriage with his parents and wife, his sister-in-law began to weep. His mother's soft, foreign voice was there.

The gate of Saint Mary's cemetery stood open on the left.

He looked at the dirty handkerchief in his hand, and started to put in a coat pocket.

"Give it here, Mister Devereux. I'll take it," Joe White said from his left. The footman's pale brown hand drew the cloth from his fingers. White put the handkerchief in the black top hat which crowned his somber costume. Joseph White looked exceptionally grand today. Devereux's mother had fussed for hours over the smallest details of the funeral, taking refuge in that from the pain of acceptance. He remembered that she and Betsy White, Joe's mother, had brushed Joe's coat several times, fretting over invisible strands of lint.

The company of infantry leading the procession reached the gate. The company commander ordered the turn. The troops marched into the cemetery, tramping firmly down the muddy lane between the tombstones. The six horse team drawing the limber and caisson swung left at the same place.

Devereux followed. His ankle failed to function in the turn. It seemed not to have any bone in it. His knee entered into the same conspiracy of weakness. Pain flashed in all direction from the old trouble of his ruined leg.

Father Willem Kruger caught his elbow, pulling him erect. "Just a little further, Claude!" he whispered. "Just a bit, and then you can rest."

White gripped the other arm tightly.

Devereux felt within himself for his legs, sought the inner metal that sustained him. Over Kruger's shoulder, across the sodden white of his confessor's surplice, he stared down the line of vehicles. There were many, all filled to capacity with friends, family, and those who wished to be thought friends. Behind the immediate family there were two army carriages. The second held a clutch of blue uniforms.

The first was an old black buggy. Abraham Lincoln sat on the seat next to the sergeant driver. The president wore a black rubber army rain cape, the logical outcome of a soldier's concern for the commander-in-chief.

Their eyes met across the distance.

Lincoln inclined his head gravely.

Claude Devereux had sought a way to keep him from the funeral, but the president's genuine solicitude for the family of Patrick Devereux made that impossible.

Patrick's wife raged at the thought of Lincoln's presence at her husband's requiem mass, but to no effect. Now she wept in mute grief with his parents and her sons.

Kruger turned enough to see what held his attention. "You must not hate him, Claude," he whispered. "It is not permitted to hate him. He is not a bad man. He is merely our enemy."

Devereux looked into Kruger's eyes. In the black depths of the other man's pupils, the Jesuit saw emptiness without limit.

Devereux struggled to focus on his face. "All right, Willem..." he said after a moment. "I hear you." Pulling away from his friend's grasp, he started forward, through the gate, onto the gravel path that led to the open grave.

As he neared the waiting pit, Frederick Kennedy came to his mind. He wondered where Kennedy was now. He and Patrick were, had been, of an age. Why had he sent Kennedy to New York?" What a senseless thing to do... He felt dizzy. Everything had happened so fast in the last days. He tried to remember the last time he had seen Kennedy.

It has been a week!

He remembered now, remembered the camp behind Cemetery Ridge, the night after Lee failed in his final attack at Gettysburg.

Chapter 1

Homecoming

(3 July, 1863)

"Why do you think they will believe us?" Bill White had asked.

Devereux had ordered him and Sergeant John Quick to cross into the Confederate lines to describe to General Lee what Meade's intentions were for the next day. This was a sentence of death. The chance that they might survive the experience in the midst of the unfinished battle was very small.

The foolishness of this was like the order with which Lee had sent an army corps forward that day to certain ruin.

Devereux had not answered White. He could not answer. He was, for the moment, a dumb beast.

My brother is dead? Is it possible that Patrick is truly gone, never to return? Is it possible?

He sat on the ground, cross legged, staring at the little fire on which they had set a can of water to boil for coffee. With one hand, he worked at arranging the burning pieces of wood to his satisfaction. The sticks hissed and popped as the heat drove out water. The other hand held the open silver case of his watch. "Tell them you come from me, from Hannibal," he told Bill, "Tell them you come from me."

Bill studied his friend in the unsteady, yellow light. Nearby, Fred Kennedy and John Quick sat with their backs to trees. They knew this was not a conversation in which they would be welcomed.

"Now, why would they take the word of a strange black man and an Irish deserter?" Bill asked. "You know them, Claude. You know how bad this may be." White's eyes held no pleading, no expectation of a reprieve. In his heart he knew that Devereux would not relent, could not make a different choice.

"I must go home." Claude said as though the statement would explain everything. Patrick's body lay ten feet away, wrapped in a rubber army ground sheet. His boot soles protruded from one end of the covering. It was unacceptable that he was gone, unacceptable to them all.

Bill understood that. He had caught himself making a mental note to tell the dead man that one of his heels was broken.

"I cannot cross the lines," Devereux continued. "The risk to our mission is too great. I probably could not get back."

"And Lieutenant Kennedy?"

"I have something for him to do in New York, something that will not wait." He looked at Kennedy. "Johnston Mitchell. His time is come. You will not forget?" Kennedy shook his head. He was not really listening, but that did not matter. He knew what was wanted.

Fifteen minutes later White and Quick disappeared into the night, headed for the gentle rise of Cemetery Hill. Beyond the rise lay Gettysburg and the Army of Northern Virginia.

The next morning Devereux sat silently with Kennedy on the wagon's seat as they left the battlefield.

The provost guards let them pass without comment after looking at Devereux's credentials from the War Department.

They decided that they would go to Baltimore to seek preservation for the body and transportation to Alexandria.

Before they left Gettysburg, Claude asked George Sharpe to have the news of Patrick's death sent to the family with their probable route. Sharpe had not heard of Patrick's death and went to find George Meade after saying that he would see to the message.

Devereux managed to avoid shaking Meade's hand, turning his back to him slightly as if to hide his tears.

Sharpe thanked Claude profusely for the help that his brother had given the army's order of battle study in the previous days.

Finally, the hypocrisy of his acceptance of Yankee condolence ended.

Union cavalry was spread across the rear of the army.

Meade had said that he was not sure that Lee would move away. For that reason the army still sat on the "fish hook" of hills, waiting to be sure that the Confederates would not attack again.

Near Hanover a cavalry officer, sweating in the heat, looked at the boots sticking out from under the tarpaulin in the wagon bed and suggested that there was an ice house in the little town. The trip to Baltimore would take two more days. Claude paid the ice house a dollar for enough cracked ice to cover his brother's body a foot deep. Two men broke the ice with sledgehammers while another shoveled the ice on top of Patrick's body.

The long ride down to Baltimore and the railroad was endless in the steaming weather of July. The countryside was so pretty and green that it was hard to believe in the reality of what they had seen, heard and smelled. Birds sang. Insects buzzed and Mennonite farmers stood at the side of the road watching gravely as they passed. Most removed their round brimmed hats when they saw Pat's boots sticking out on the lowered tailgate.

They reached Baltimore around four in the afternoon on the sixth, and went to the telegraph station. There they found Joseph White and John Everly, the undertaker. They had come in the belief that the body would surely pass through Baltimore. They had divided their time among the railroad stations and the telegraph office.

Claude went in with Joe to talk to the telegraph people.

Everly looked in the wagon and asked how often they had filled it with ice.

"Three times altogether, we bought more every time we found an ice house," was Kennedy's reply.

"This was a good idea. We can cover up water discoloration... I think we should find some more ice." He looked up the street at likely businesses. "I'll ask the telegrapher," he finally said and then, unaccountably, laughed.

Kennedy looked at him in surprise behind which something else grew. He seemed to get bigger standing there in the heat and horse dust of the unpaved street. His normally florid complexion darkened.

"No, no," Everly said, holding up his hands to ward off the growing menace. "I'm as torn up about this as you are. I was just wondering how my sister is going to take this." He glanced at Pat's body under the ice and canvas and shook his head. "There was a time when the two of them were pretty sweet on each other. Then he took to courting Robert Lee's girl. It damn near killed her. Then, he married someone else yet. I don't think Clara ever truly got over him..."

Kennedy nodded, remembering this small town drama, remembering that Everly's rather pretty sister had never married. He remembered her growing up around town, part of the background of daily life. "Tell her I will come to see her when I can," he said. "I.. I.." He suddenly realized that this expression of his interest was inappropriate to the moment and said no more.

Everly did not know what to say. It had not occurred to him that Fred Kennedy might be attracted to his sister Clara. "Aren't you coming with us," he asked to change the subject?

"No. You and Joe can take everyone home. Joe will get the team back to my stable. They're my horses. I rented them out to Claude for this trip north. The family doesn't have horses heavy enough for this. Theirs are too fine bred. These are some lucky animals. Neither has a scratch on him. I'll ask Joe to load them and the rig into a car together for the trip."

"We'll put the body in there too when I find a box. Joe can ride with it."

"Claude won't let you do that," murmured Kennedy. "He'll want to sit with Pat."

Devereux came out of the telegraph office with White.

They told him what they wanted to do. "Please put my brother in the baggage car," Claude said, confirming the depth of Kennedy's understanding. "Joe and I will ride with him. The rest is fine."

Everly looked surprised at that, surprised to be told that his company was not wanted. He thought about it, then remembered how close the Whites were to the Devereuxs and just accepted it, and nodded.

"Thank you, John," the haggard, dirty man in black said and then held out a hand. "Thanks for coming up here. There was a telegram waiting here from General Halleck. There will be a military escort waiting at the station in Washington City..."

For Devereux and Kennedy, two officers of Confederate intelligence, this should have been a moment of triumph, but it was not. Three of the four men present understood the irony of the situation. The guard of honor would receive the body of a man who had wanted nothing more than to destroy the Union. This meant nothing when weighed against their grief.

Devereux looked down at his feet. "You are going to New York City?" The question was for Kennedy.

"You told me to go..."

Devereux was confused, torn between his need to hold his family close and his resolve to kill his most dangerous enemy,

This was Major Johnston Mitchell of the National Detective Bureau. He could still "see" Mitchell in Colonel Lafayette Baker's Pennsylvania Avenue office. Mitchell had done a wonderful job of hunting Claude and his brother, Patrick. It had been a very close thing. Fortune had played a major role in evading Mitchell's traps. Claude thought of his parents, of his wife, of the Whites. Only luck and quick thought had prevented disaster, arrest as spies and disgrace. Mitchell lost that "round" in the game and was exiled to New York, but, given the man's competence and dedication it was only a matter of time… "Yes. Go to New York. Stop by in Newark and talk to this man." He wrote a name and address in his notebook, tore out the sheet and handed it to his lieutenant. "He will help you..."

Devereux's face worried Kennedy. It did not seem focused. He looked down and saw that water dripping from the bottom of the wagon was running together in little streams that wet his dusty boots. Turning, he could see that there were wet patches in the dirt street back along the way they had come. He turned to face the dead man's brother. "Do you still want him gone?" he asked.

They both knew who was meant.

"Yes, gone." Then after a second he said, "Do what you think best."

"I will," Kennedy said. "I'll leave tomorrow. Now I am going to find a hotel and a bath."

Chapter 2

The Irish

- August, 1863 -
(Washington)

"That was not like you," she said. The words seemed unusually clear in the space left vacant by the waiter's retreating form.

Devereux ignored a sudden urge to peer about the room in search of those who might have overheard his angry outburst.

The Willard Hotel habitually filled its dining room for lunch. Today was no exception. Army and Navy officers sat crowded at tables intended by their makers for fewer diners. The noise was appalling. Only his name and long acquaintance with the *maître d'hôtel* had secured a table without a reservation.

He glanced across the table at his wife. Her features were set in the expression of slightly embarrassed disappointment which usually greeted his occasional lapses in self control. "I am sorry, my dear. Forgive me... I am impatient today. I don't want to sit at table endlessly waiting for the man to take our order. It is bad enough that these… people will question our lunching out so soon after…"

She considered that. A small frown spread around the corners of her mouth. As he watched her, he discovered an impulse rising in him to lean forward to kiss her pretty lips.

Hope Devereux wore her mourning well. A high necked, navy blue dress of watered silk set off her ivory skin, blue eyes and golden hair perfectly. Half the men in the room seemed in danger of injuring their necks in attempting to get a better look. Devereux had doubts about the rest.

"You are normally so kind to waiters and other…" she began, trailing off doubtfully.

"Inferiors?"

She stared stonily at him. "You know very well what I mean!" Exasperation filled her voice. "A gentleman's obligations toward servants and those, in service, are clear." Irritation with him merely accented her beauty.

Devereux rubbed his nose, using the gesture to conceal a small smile. "Don't you recognize him?" he asked softly.

Her eyebrows knit in concentration. "That's the same man who served us twice before in this room," she announced after a moment. "I particularly remember him at lunch with the Nevilles.

He nodded. "You've got him. I'm sure he must be one of Baker's hounds.

"I see. Then, you should be particularly nice to him."

Devereux grinned, delighted with her.

Any of the numerous observers in the room would have said that they made a somewhat odd looking couple. Claude Devereux had never been thought a handsome man. Strong, distinguished, well dressed; these were terms more likely to be used in speaking of him. The last few years had not been kind to him. A double life leaves its mark. His hair was greyer than it might have been had life and history taken a different course.

"This means that he is still having you watched."

"Of course, did you think otherwise?"

She tilted her head slightly to one side in the mannerism he associated with real introspection. Hope seemed to inspect the decor of the far wall somewhere above his head.

The Willard's dining room fit the popular taste for opulent clutter. Ferns littered the floor, giant stag horn ferns, wispy Boston ferns, exotic, vaguely threatening ferns that looked appropriate to one of the odd paintings so common in books concerning Darwin's theories. Dark wallpaper with a chocolate hue, and walnut wainscot dominated the scene. Heavy velvet draperies nearly completed the task of keeping out the light. The soggy misery of a summer day pervaded the room. There was a small, but ominous water stain in one corner of the plaster ceiling.

The guests steamed. The more newly arrived brought with them the heat of the street.

Devereux could feel a tiny rivulet of sweat forming slowly in the small of his back.

He wondered how it could be that his wife never seemed to sweat *in public*. His mother never really appeared discomfited by hot weather either. How did they manage it in these high necked, heavy dresses? He began to run through a series of images of women he knew in a rapid survey of their perspiration potential.

Victoria Devereux, his sister in law took shape first.

An image of his dead brother came to him. How long before the sharp edges of Patrick's features would no longer live in his mind? Hatred for the blue figures around him welled up.

Elizabeth Braithwaite. No, she made other people sweat.

Amy Biddle. Amy Biddle. Stereoscopic pictures of the woman circulated in his imagination. He found one in which a faint sheen of moisture glistened on her temple. He recognized the setting. It was the funeral. His mother and Hope had stood at the graveside with Victoria, holding her elbows in fear that she might not manage. The rain had stopped. The umbrellas had disappeared, leaving all those present to suffer from the humidity. There hadn't been enough rain to cool the air, just enough to create an accurate imitation of a Turkish bath. The Biddle woman had been in black. The dress stuck in his memory as too severe, exactly the kind of monstrosity which he expected of her wardrobe. He could see her profile, just beyond Hope's.

She looked at him.

He saw that nothing had changed for her. She did not flinch from him. Her features were rigid, but he knew that she was his, knew the depths of her gratitude that he too, had not been taken at Gettysburg. She turned away, bending her head to listen to the priest's words. Her bosom rose and fell a little faster. Devereux thought of her breasts. They were white and large, larger than Hope's. They had never seen the light of day. Milk white they were with pink nipples and areolae. He knew there must be tiny beads of sweat forming in the deep, warm pocket between her breasts.

Hope brought her eyes down to his. "Surely his only remaining concern with you is as a rival for Stanton's favor."

He remembered the subject of their conversation. "Yes. Except that I fear the other interest in me will never quite disappear."

She looked skeptical.

The waiter in question made his way to them, carefully threading a path between the tables, watchful for sudden movement, a small tray carried aloft on one brown hand. In one, smooth, rotating motion of the wrist, he brought the tray down to the level of the white linen surface of their table. Steam rose from the dishes. "Turtle soup, ma'am! Turtle soup! Our famous turtle soup!"

Lieutenant Kennedy arrived in Newark, New Jersey on the 7th of July. He found the city to be untidy and an unappealing place. It was not the buildings that bothered him. The three and four storey structures were familiar. They were the shabby brick construction common in big cities. It was the general layout of the town that disturbed him. Around the business district of banks and commercial establishments were packed neighborhoods in which wooden tenement buildings were everywhere. There did not seem to be a lot of indoor plumbing in these buildings. There were outhouses in the alleyways behind. Kennedy found that to be "unprogressive." Alexandria had long had piped household water and sewage systems. Kennedy had grown up poor and Newark made him imagine bitterly that there must be other parts of this town or parts of some other town where the "decent people" of Newark lived, the people who owned the banks and businesses.

There were saloons and churches scattered throughout the tenement areas. The saloons seemed to have more customers than the churches. Factories loomed on the horizon and along the river bank. This was an industrial and commercial city and evidence of that pre-occupation was everywhere. There were signs painted on the buildings. One sign advertised a brewery, another was for a haberdasher. A particularly large collection of buildings looked like an iron foundry. The smoke stacks were taller than any he had seen before.

It had been an easy train passage from Baltimore. He was in funds from Devereux, came north in the best car the train possessed. He dined on oyster stew washed down with cold pilsner.

Every sizable American town had a hotel called "The American." Newark was no exception. To his surprise there was no shortage of rooms in the hotel. He asked the porter who carried his bag why that was.

"We jest opened last month, sir," was the response. "Lots of new hotels in Newark, we had some army people a week back, but they all left yesterday." The young man shrugged in puzzlement over that, and pocketed his tip with a nod.

The room was clean, the bed as firm as he liked. Dinner in the empty dining room was acceptable.

The next day, he began to carry out Devereux's task. To do that, he needed to find a saloon called "The Volunteer." That was the address on Claude's scrap of paper.

The desk clerk looked at him curiously when he asked for directions. The man glanced at the hotel registry, saw his name, smiled and wrote a note.

He went out into the street, and walked to the nearest corner where he looked at the paper. At the top of the small page was written "*Na Fianna Eireann.*" Fred Kennedy was Virginia born and raised. The words meant nothing to him. His knowledge of Ireland was largely the product of fireside discussions with his father and mother. The Kennedys had left Ireland in a search for farm land and freedom from Protestant domination. In America they had found both. Ireland rapidly diminished in family memory. There was nothing like an Irish neighborhood in Alexandria, and Frederick Kennedy grew up with a sense of self in which Ireland was a minor factor. America, Virginia and Alexandria were far more important for him.

He walked the streets until he found "The Volunteer." This took an hour. His destination was down a narrow, dirty side street that he passed several times because it looked so unpromising.

From across the street, the saloon was quiet and somewhat sinister even in broad daylight. The windows were opaque and black. The sign over the door displayed a painted carving of a man in 18th century clothing carrying a musket. A harp rested incongruously next to this figure in a green meadow. He crossed the street and entered, stopping inside the door for a moment to let his eyes adjust to the dimness. From behind a dark, wooden bar a mustachioed man in the professional dress of a bartender inspected him. There was no one else in the place. "Whut can I do for you, sor?" the barman asked.

"I am looking for the owner of this place."

"Do you not know his name," the barman asked. A quizzical look spread across the face.

Claude had given Kennedy a name. Devereux's banker "friends" in Baltimore knew men in New York who cooperated with the South. The bankers had arranged a meeting with these men during a trip which Devereux and his wife had made to New York a few months earlier.

"Joseph Fahey," Kennedy said.

"And who wants to speak to him? Yourself?" The barman seemed to think that was amusing.

"Yes. I do. Are you Fahey?"

The man said nothing.

"I was sent by a man who met Fahey here in Newark in a carriage driven by a black man last..."

"And how is she, the beautiful blond lady who loves her husband?" Fahey the barman asked. "What is her name? I would know her name, just her Christian name, just that. It is a rare thing to meet a woman so beautiful and so... dutiful." The voice was pure "auld sod" laid on with a trowel.

"Hope. Her name is Hope," Kennedy responded, "and she is what she seems."

"Hope, Hope," Fahey seemed to relish the sound and the taste of the name. "And what does Hope want of me?"

"Not her." Kennedy was disturbed with the emerging "bogtrotter" fraud. "Her husband sent me."

"The lucky captain, yes. I remember the leg. It should have come off..."

"He showed you that? Yes, it should have come off… He has sent me to New York to hunt a man and kill him."

The hands disappeared beneath the counter.

"Not you, a Yankee major, a policeman, a traitor in fact. He is from Kentucky..." Kennedy wished he had not said so much. This man would never understand.

"Ah," Fahey grinned, "Johnston Mitchell. It would be Johnston Mitchell. The man just transferred up from Washington? Baker's man? Is that who it is, *Mr. Kennedy*? You want him? Well, we want him as well. Were you in the captain's regiment?"

"The desk clerk told you… Yes, I was in his regiment."

Fahey's head chin moved down ever so slightly. "Yes, and we have been waiting for you half an hour. You were slow."

"We?"

Two more men emerged from a back room to sit by the door. They looked him over in search of a reason to be hostile. There was a big, slow looking black haired man who avoided looking directly at him. The other was much older and bent. He had grey hair.

"Mitchell has been here but a short time," the old one said, "and he is already a great nuisance... Much too interested in our connections... Want some help, do you?"

"Yes. That's why I am here."

"Were you at Gettysburg? The big one asked.

"I came from there. The captain's brother was killed there. He was doing our work... We took his body to Baltimore to send home. I came after that."

The three were looking at him.

"Did you know him? I mean the brother," one of the men by the door asked. His grey head was badly scarred and most of an ear was missing.

"We grew up together. He was a brother to me as well."

The older man considered him, and then nodded to Fahey. The barman drew a beer and put it where it was clearly within Kennedy's reach.

"Empty your pockets," the grizzled one whispered hoarsely.

They pawed through his belongings. "Frederick Kennedy?" You own a livery stable... How did you manage that?

"The captain helped me buy it. He owns a bank."

"Is he Irish?"

"No idea... Maybe." He had never thought about this. Now that they had mentioned it, he could see that the Devereuxs must be Irish in some way.

"Are you Catholic?"

"More or less. Why do you care?"

They laughed.

"We want to know who our newest "friend" from Richmond might be," growled the grey haired man. "Send him to John Hughes," he rasped after a pause. "Hughes likes rebels like this one. Hughes is more or less Christian, but, altogether Catholic," he remarked to Kennedy smiling evilly the while. "What do you know of the Draft Lottery," he asked?

"We have a draft, but it is not a lottery," Kennedy answered.

They thought about that.

"The lottery for this abomination begins in three days," the grizzled one commented.

"Ours will be by lottery," Fahey said. "and you can buy your way out if your name is drawn. Can you buy your way out of yours?"

It was Kennedy's turn to laugh. "Yes. If you are rich enough you can buy your way out of anything." After a minute he said. "I was not drafted. I volunteered."

They saw the joke.

"Are you an officer?"

"Yes, but just for the war. I started by carrying a musket."

They nodded.

"Good," said the grizzled one. "We will take you to see Hughes. He will give you shelter. You should not stay in a hotel. We will have the record here erased. We will bring you to kill Mitchell and then we will get you out of town. Agreed?"

"Why don't you do it yourself?" Kennedy asked.

Fahey sighed. "Unfortunately, the swine in the Detective Bureau office here know us well. They might recognize us. We want Mitchell done in but.... You are a "godsend.""

They all looked pleased with that.

"Why don't they arrest you? You must have broken some law..."

"We have friends," the grizzled one said. "Friends, political, and others..."

"Who is Hughes?"

"Ah, 'Dagger John Hughes'. That's what your Yankee "friends" in the 'Union League' call him."

Kennedy looked blank.

"He is the archbishop of New York."

Kennedy was silent for a minute. "Jesuit?" He was thinking of Father Kruger at home.

"No, no, just another damned priest. Don't tell him specifically what you are going to do."

Kennedy looked blank.

"You know... with Mitchell, don't be specific about it. Do you understand? Tell him you are a deserter and seeking, seeking... Oh, we'll think of something you are seeking. We are all seeking something."

"What are you going to do about the draft," Kennedy asked.

"We will fight. We will fight. We don't much like you Johnnies, but we like the draft even less. We will fight."

"Who will you fight?"

"Anyone, everyone..."

"Ah, yes. I have seen this before. My uncles are like that..."

"By the way, your lovely captain, husband of the even lovelier Hope, he lied to me," Fahey laughed.

"How's that?"

"I called him colonel, and he did not correct me…"

"Why would he tell you the truth?" Kennedy laughed.

They were all grinning now.

"Where is Mitchell to be found?" Kennedy asked.

Chapter 3

The Auction

-August, 1863-
(Alexandria, Virginia)

Heat and humidity loomed over the throng of hopeful buyers. Whitewashed brick walls surrounded scarred pine floors that glowed with the energy collected during weeks of tiresome heat.

It was a large room, filled in its upper parts with a complex pattern of beams and structural iron fittings. It was a renovated warehouse. Young Negroes lined the side aisles, sitting on boxes and three legged stools, operating in relays the mechanisms which drove the ropes and pulleys of rotary ceiling fans.

Indecently bright early morning sunlight intruded through tall grimy windows along one side of the building. Dust particles billowed in slanting shafts of light.

The residents of Alexandria; locals, occupiers, and new people alike, had hoped for the last week that the break in summer weather which regularly announced the approach of Autumn would show itself, revealing its arrival in the cool, blue light of dawn.

Sadly, the sun had risen this morning in a haze of orange fire, climbing higher and higher over the green Maryland hills beyond the river.

In the hall, row upon row of scroll backed wooden chairs filled the front with benches crowded in behind. The auctioneer started the morning's business slowly, his gavel rising and falling at a pace which might have mirrored the level of alertness of many of those seated before him. Unaccustomed to early morning hours, they huddled in their seats, searching with sliding eyes for the trays of tiny coffee cups with which ushers sought to appease the crowd.

Claude Devereux sprawled across two front row places, his legs thrust out before him, an empty cup occupying the caned seat of the chair upon which rested one arm. He had arrived early, indeed, had awaited the appearance of the employees of the house. Watching him, one might have been attracted by the thought that he was not really listening to the steady drumbeat of the auctioneer's voice, so absorbed was he in the conversation of two Federal officers seated beside him.

These were so similar in the face that their true relationship as brothers was immediately clear.

The three men were preoccupied with some subject of great interest to them all. The sale of property taking place before the crowd did not seem to be important to them.

Joseph White sat alongside one of the dark young men who operated the levers driving the air circulating mechanism above. Corduroy trousers, a cotton jacket, a clean shirt and string tie gave him an appearance to which some of the white men gathered on benches in the back should have aspired. He listened intently to the business of the auction.

From time to time he held up, chest high, one of a variety of pasteboard squares marked with obscure symbols. These signals always brought Devereux's attention fully to bear on the progress of the business at hand. The relaxed figure in black broadcloth then bought the object in question. Competing bids met with friendly glances and casual gestures of the hand or head to the auctioneer. These steadily drove up the price until Devereux bought the piece in question.

The morning passed, and the auctioneer more and more grasped what was expected of him. As bids rose on a given lot, he would watch Joe White closely. The flash of a pasteboard card riveted his attention upon the man in black seated in the front row. He appeared to be slightly confused by the way in which Devereux pursued his adversaries' offers without mercy, driving the game relentlessly, talking and chatting the while with his two neighbors.

White recorded each acquisition painstakingly in a large ledger which rested on his knees.

The sale went on.

After a while, a pattern emerged. Devereux was buying old silver, linens, paintings and furniture. From time to time a signal from Joe White caused him to sweep the room with his eyes, seeking the identity of a bidder. Now and then, he abstained from participation in the contest. In three cases, he bought specimens of the same Hepplewhite chair.

Commander Richard Braithwaite watched this performance thoughtfully. At last, seeking a respite from his brother's insistent pursuit of Devereux's help in arranging capitalization of one of his railroad schemes, he asked why the Virginian wanted all these things.

"Well, I have a lot of friends. And a host of relatives in various places, including my mother's people in France..." The exchange had hardly interrupted Devereux's purchase of an eighteenth century sideboard.

The sale went on.

Ten rows back a small group of men sat together. The clothing of several suggested a decline from previous levels of prosperity which characterized many of the old time residents of the town.

The auctioneer's helpers carried the previous lot away as one of these men spoke to another. "I don't quite understand this. Young Devereux sitting there with these, people, and buying up all these things! Surely, he must know that the government has seized all this in houses taken for non-payment of property taxes, surely he knows that! You are his father's partner! What is this?"

Harrison Wheatley meditated on the question. "I can see the way of it. You are right, Philip... Claude is too well known. He should not do this again. We must have a larger group of, buyers." He turned to look directly at the men near him. "We think that you all will do nicely."

Another of the elderly men spoke. "We have no money."

Wheatley said nothing. His silver hair and bodily beauty made him stand out in a group to which he naturally belonged. A small smile played at the corners of his mouth.

"Where are you keeping it all," someone asked? This was the tallest of the group, a man so advanced in years that his great height was partially hidden by an unavoidable stoop.

"We have a warehouse in Washington City, just by the Navy Yard," he smiled. "Some years ago Charles bought the structure so that Clotilde might offer the use of it to charitable activities in which she played some part. Over time we have used it for a variety of purposes. These things will never fill the place. We have them sorted and marked by family."

On the platform the auctioneer's helper held up a deeply carved crystal punch bowl. On the side, an oval cartouche held initials.

An army officer in the second row offered ten dollars. A civilian in the same row raised the bid to fifteen. A third cried "Twenty"!

Joe White raised a card marked with an outline drawing of a horse.

Devereux turned to see the bowl. He opened his mouth.

The tall old man raised his head. "Twenty Five!" He bowed slightly as Devereux turned to see.

The younger man smiled, and nodded back.

"Well that's one you won't get Claude," the army officer beside him said.

"You're right, Frederick. In fact, I think I've had enough of this. Shall we go?"

Chapter 4

Balthazar

-September, 1863 -
(Paris)

A certain aura surrounds buildings which have seen events which shaped the fate of nations. One such place is the Palais d'Orsay, the home of the foreign ministry of France. This magnificent building has stood for many years on the left bank of the Seine near a broad esplanade which extends from the river to the Hotel des Invalides.

In the era of the Second Empire, Paris was at the height of its beauty. Its reputation as the capital of the civilized world was unchallenged. The Palais d'Orsay served as a perfect setting for the diplomacy of Louis Napoleon's government. Its elegance and glittering decor gave a certain tone to the business conducted within.

The reception room was magnificent. It seemed a place made for gods, not men. Sunshine poured through vast windows along one side. Crystal panes glittered in the morning light. They reached almost to the towering height of the carved plaster ceiling. Through the windows, one could see and sense directly the vitality of the city. Carriages and wagons rumbled in endless profusion of type down the Quai d'Orsay. Beyond the traffic, the Seine flowed by on its way to the Channel. Steam tugs pushed barges forward, passing slowly beneath the stone bridges. The light had the lovely clarity and slightly golden tone that early autumn often brings in illuminating our memories of better days.

A man stood alone at the center of the wall of windows. His back to the room, he seemed to contemplate the heart of France. Framed against the brilliance outside, he made a striking picture. Red, baggy pants and a thigh length blue black tunic marked him as a soldier. His rank was conspicuous in the gold and silver rows of narrow braid forming elongated Austrian knots on his coat sleeves. They reached from the cuff to a point just below the shoulder seam. On his breast was hung the red glory of the Légion d'honneur. His white gloved hands grasped each other firmly in the small of his back. In truth, the solidity of his posture did not reflect the state of his mind. The watcher looked out on the passing crowd with hope, but only that. He felt that this morning's summons must hold some special meaning for his future, something better than his present situation. He hoped for a sign. As he inspected the scene below, a river boat hand looked up at him, holding his eyes for a second. The sailor raised a hand and the officer bowed slightly from the waist.

A tall, slight young man entered the room, crossing to stand just behind the soldier. Clearing his throat, he spoke. "Bonjour, mon commandant".

The blue and red figure turned to look at him. Jean-Marie Balthazar d'Orgueil looked down his long, high-bridged nose at the man who addressed him. An expression of studied disdain was almost hidden behind a fixed stare and long, waxed mustaches.

The contrast between the two men could hardly have been greater.

D'Orgueil stood five foot, ten inches tall in regulation shoes. He possessed the figure characteristic of his Gascon heritage. It is said of the men of Languedoc that they are "as wide as they are tall". His broad torso and bull neck supported a head that looked like a tree stump. Between the open lapels of his coat there was a wide expanse of blue sash partly hidden by a black waistcoat with small brass buttons. A curved Zouave saber hung at his side.

The other man wore grey morning clothes. He carried himself with the air of confident correctness so common in career diplomats. "I am so pleased that you could join us," he said. "General Druot is in with the minister now. Would you like coffee?"

An aged footman of immense dignity stood to one side waiting for orders. The stooped, white haired man wore black formal dress. Across his stomach a gold chain closed the front of his coat.

"Yes, why not", laughed D'Orgueil. "I suppose we will wait for the great ones to finish their little chat.. I assume that you have no Turkish coffee hidden away in the depths of this mausoleum?"

The old man shook his head. "You would assume incorrectly, sir. We have many foreign visitors."

"Wonderful! Medium sugar. I hear from your voice that you are from the Southwest. Where?"

"Albi."

D'Orgucil strode across the room to one of the artfully arranged seating areas. He warily lowered his considerable bulk into a Louis XVI chair and looked up to inspect the tapestry hanging on the wall before him. It depicted a mythical scene of uncertain origin. The center of the piece was commanded by a banquet table at the center of which sat Janus, the two faced, two headed god of beginnings.

"Nice town, Albi," d'Orgueil remarked without taking his eyes from the god. "Although I can't say that I care much for the cathedral. Too much painting for my taste, too much painting of death, too much judging of, of, everyone really." He looked at the waiter. "How long have you been in Paris, in the North?"

"Thirty years, sir."

D'Orgueil frowned, the brown eyes disappearing in the general contraction of his deeply tanned face. "A long time, I have never lived in the north. I was in Africa. My wife wanted me to take this post. She wanted to leave the 'bled.' She thought it would help my career. Now she is gone, and I am here..." The pain crept up close to the surface for a moment.

The waiter looked away. "I will bring the coffee, sir." He bowed, and limped away toward a door.

The seated man glanced about, seeing with relief that the diplomat was no longer there to hear what he had said.

In the next room, the minister of foreign affairs and the chief of staff of the Imperial Guard met to decide his fate.

"Forty years old, and still a major! Does that tell us something?" the minister asked, looking up from the dossier before him.

General de Corps D'Armee Henri Druot picked an imaginary thread from his tunic while suppressing an impulse to say that such things did not properly concern the foreign ministry. "Only that he has a pronounced distaste for service in higher headquarters, and a preference for his beloved Africa," he said. Resplendent in gilt epaulets and buttons, he felt himself obliged to defend the army's indifference to the opinions of the civilian government.

The minister looked doubtful. "And why would he feel that way?"

Druot began to be uncomfortable. He had approved d'Orgueil's selection for a special mission. He now suspected that the minister mocked him.

"He is a fighter," the general said, surprised at the words.

"Aren't you all?"

"Yes, we are, but some really cannot live without it." Druot had to admit to himself that what he had said was true. "His whole family is this way," he continued. "They, fight. They always have." He looked moderately confused.

The minister lowered his gaze to search in the papers on his desk. "D'Orgueil," he read. "The family first appears in recorded history in the 11th century as protectors of an area of infertile plateau on the south bank of the River Lot 150 kilometers east of Bordeaux. There, they constructed a fortress around which a considerable town grew up. Liege men of the counts of Toulouse, they were strongly suspected of adherence to the Cathar heresy in the early 13th century. As proof of this, the Inquisition pointed to their evasion of service in the crusade against the Cathari. Several parties of Inquisitors who ventured into their lands to search for Cathar Perfecti who might be hidden there were never heard of again." The minister peered at the general over his pince-nez.

Druot shrugged. "Ancient history," he laughed.

The minister looked down and continued. "This development, and their firm profession of the Catholic faith after the fall of Carcassonne to the crusaders, caused the attention of the church and the king to be directed elsewhere."

"Where did you find all this?" Druot demanded. "We do not have such information in army records!"

"I am so fortunate as to have the benefit of the help of my young friend, the baron, who sits behind you."

Druot turned to see the slight figure in grey, seated by the door which led to the ante room. He turned back to the minister. "And does this matter?"

"Perhaps not, but I wish to know precisely with whom I am dealing. May I continue?"

"Of course!" Druot looked baffled.

"At the commencement of the Hundred Years War, the Seigneurs d'Orgueil pledged themselves to the Duke of Aquitaine, who was also, of course, King of England."

"A common enough thing among the ancient Gascon nobility of the sword," the general remarked defensively.

"Quite so. Quite so. Their castle was taken by storm in the course of the war. It, and the surrounding town, were utterly destroyed by the French forces."

"Really? Destroyed?" Druot was astonished.

"Yes, destroyed, and most of the family executed on the site," the baron remarked from behind him. "Unusual. I take it to be indicative of the grave injuries which they had previously done to the cause of France."

"And what then? What happened then?" the glittering general asked, taken up in the story despite himself.

"They fought on," the baron said softly. "They led a "Free Company" which was directly in the pay of the English king. It seems to have been recruited from Englishmen, Spaniards, and the peasants of their former lands. The final defeat of the English was the occasion for further executions. The male survivors fled to Britain and Spain for a time, returning only when there came an opportunity to take service with the Catholic forces in the Wars of Religion. This, of course, accomplished their, rehabilitation."

"And the women?" the general asked.

"The d'Orgueil women have always married well enough to insure the persistence of the family," the baron said.

His master, the minister listened attentively and motioned that he should continue.

"The blood is widespread among the minor nobles of the Southwest, as well as in several prominent merchant families of Bordeaux, and London."

"London!"

"Yes, their alliance dates back to.."

"The Hundred Years War?"

"Just so," the baron said. "It should be mentioned that the men have devoted themselves to the military profession with astonishing perseverance. They have cultivated the soil on the same stony heights, and they have followed the drum, all these years. Surprisingly, there are not many priests among them." He discovered that no one was listening and fell silent.

Druot ruminated for a time. "His wife was English," he finally said. "A lovely woman, so blond, so refined. A great tragedy, her death last year, so unexpected."

"She was a distant cousin," the baron said. "The d'Orgueils are connected to some of these families in almost every generation." The baron seemed to relish the idea. "They all speak English easily. It is a family tradition."

The minister appeared thoughtful.

"And, the American connection?" General Druot asked.

"Ah!" The minister exclaimed, searching through the papers. "Our friend's grandfather was the brother of the grandmother of Monsieur Devereux, the secessionist agent at Washington. Colonel Jourdain's friend," he added.

"This was part of the pattern of their alliances?"

"The Champagne military family of Berthier is well known, I believe?" the baron asked.

"But, of course! Ah! Yes! It is the pattern." After a moment Druot spoke again, suspicion in his voice. "Jourdain asked for d'Orgueil by name."

"Devereux suggested him when the colonel raised the question of an observer," the baron said.

"It is only natural," the minister commented. "They are cousins, and know each other slightly."

"How is that?"

"Their little bank has a branch here, just by the Bourse," the baron replied. I believe that Devereux aided his kinsman in some small affair of farm finance several years ago when he was the director. Actually, I think Devereux visited the place."

"What place?"

The minister searched.

"Cabanac, in Quercy." the baron said. "It is hard by the site of the destroyed castle. The church still stands. 13th century Romanesque, I am told, very picturesque. He was baptized there, our Comandant d'Orgueil. His parents are buried in the churchyard."

"What do they grow there?"

"Grapes, and goats. Nothing else will grow on those stony heights."

"Are they loyal?" the minister enquired of the general.

Druot held up his hands in a gesture of helplessness, and waved one at the baron. "As he says, they have been an enduring presence in the army for as long as anyone can remember. They adhered to the late Emperor's cause early and fought all the way to the end. One of them died at Quatre-Bras. They seem always to seek the enemy's presence on the battlefield. Their losses were terrible." His voice trailed off.

"In fact, he is the last," the baron added. "He has no children, and there are no other men with the name."

"I will ask you, Henri," the minister said addressing his aide. "Is he loyal?"

The baron hesitated a moment. "He will do whatever he tells you he will do. When he accepted a commission in the army, it was a personal commitment. He will not betray a trust."

"You don't like him, do you?" the minister asked softly.

The baron looked away in silence.

"And you know him well after all this digging," the minister commented thoughtfully. He turned to Druot. "Is he competent for this task?"

The general grimaced. "Do you imagine that we have given him a battalion of the Imperial Guard Zouave Regiment because we think otherwise? No! This officer spent 15 years in the Kabyle Mountains with his precious Arab riflemen. He was responsible for the pacification of a group of Berber villages that no one else could approach! In the Crimea, he was on the staff for a while. He did very well there, but escaped to rejoin his Algerians in time for Magenta. At Solferino.., but you see how it is with him."

"You have asked him if he will go?"

"No! One does not ask a man like him such a question. He would be offended. You tell him that he will go."

The minister looked weary. "Our observer must be willing. He will have none of the protection offered by our uniform."

Druot held up a hand. "He will do anything to escape from Paris. In my opinion he will go mad here. If this had not come up, I would have sent him back to Africa."

"Very well. Henri, bring him in."

A minute later the massive form appeared in the doorway. He bowed slightly, his red-topped kepi under one arm, the saber scabbard clutched in the opposite hand. "Minister! General! Good morning."

The foreign minister rose to his feet to come forward, a broad smile on his face, his right hand extended. "D'Orgueil, how good of you to join us! Do come in! I believe you know General Druot?"

Druot nodded, unsmiling.

"We have a proposal for you," the minister continued. "I think you will find it attractive."

Chapter 5

The New World

- 25 September, 1863 -
(New York)

Standing at the rail, D'Orgueil searched among the faces on the quay for someone. He was not sure there would be anyone. There had been very little time. The foreign ministry assured him that a letter preceded him in the diplomatic bag. To improve the odds, he had written his cousins, but nevertheless there had not been much time. He was aware of the ease with which such communications go astray when they are most needed. None of the upturned faces looked promising.

The harbor smell and litter of the pier were familiar, but the city behind was like nothing he had seen before. There was a raw quality about the place, a look of not being quite completed. The buildings looked wrong. There was something alien in them.

While the tugs moved the ship up the channel and against the pier, he searched the skyline for reassurance. It had not been there. Paris, Rome, and London were large cities, but this was something different, something new, something gigantic.

A steward brought up the bags, struggling with them. He was followed by a helper with yet more bags. The Frenchman smiled and raised a hand, halting the steward's progress toward the rail for a moment to give him an envelope. The young man felt it discreetly, murmuring his thanks. The vessel's master waited at the head of the gangway for goodbyes with his passengers. His ship had cabins for only a few and he believed he had made friends of them all during the passage.

D'Orgueil started down the gangway, following the steward toward the customs and immigration officials at the bottom. A uniformed policeman stood to one side, a few feet from them. He was engaged in conversation with a short, sandy haired man. This second man was dressed plainly, but well. D'Orgueil imagined that he might be the policeman's superior.

"Good Mornin', Sir" beamed a portly man with "U.S. Customs" in brass on his cap.

"Good Afternoon." d'Orgueil replied without any particular expression in his face. He handed a second blue suited figure his passport in the belief that the usual distribution of labors must prevail. This man thumbed through the pages in the customary way, searching for a visa. Finding it, he turned back to the first page. "Mister Balthazar?"

"Yes," d'Orgueil answered. "Jean Balthazar."

"You sound English, Mister Balthazar," the customs agent said. "Why is that?"

D'Orgueil knew at once from the tone that this was not an advantage. He looked at the two officials. They had the map of Ireland in their faces. "I am not English," he said. "I was educated in England." He saw hostility and suspicion begin to gather in their faces. "I have never come to this country before this. The English speak this way. I am French."

The two uniformed men whispered together. "Why does your bag there have the letter "O" in the leather?" the customs agent asked.

"Are you sure you're this Balthazar?" the immigration inspector asked. He was looking at the largest of the cases; the one his late wife's mother had given for Christmas five years before.

"I am not English," he repeated, "not at all." He considered a bribe, and rejected the thought as too risky. He thought of bringing out his various letters of credit. Perhaps the fraudulent papers naming him North American representative for his brother-in-law's wine business might help. None of these seemed good ideas. He began to think of the embarrassment of returning to France on the ship.

The two policemen approached.

"Whut's the trouble, Flaherty?" the uniformed one inquired helpfully.

"This gentleman may not be what he seems," the customs man laughed.

"Are you Balthazar?" the man in plain clothes demanded after looking at his passport..

"Yes."

"This is the man we are seeking," he said.

The immigration inspector shrugged, stamped the passport, and handed it to d'Orgueil without looking up.

The customs agent chalked a strange little mark on the bags. "Welcome to America," he said.

A carriage waited. Inside, they spoke for the first time.

"Claude sent you?" d'Orgueil asked coolly, unsure of his ground in the wake of the scene in the wharf shed, but careful not to show emotion.

"I work for him," the blond little man said. "They all sent me. Your aunt wants to see you."

"And, you are?"

"Frederick Kennedy. Colonel Devereux wanted me to collect you, sir. He was afraid there might be some trouble."

"Why did that happen, back there?" d'Orgueil asked, puzzled and worried at his inability to deal with something as simple as a border crossing.

Kennedy sat looking at him for a moment, and then he grinned. "It's your voice," he said. "These Paddies hate that voice. If you think they would have put you back on the boat if they could, you're right."

"You are a banker?"

"What?" Kennedy was visibly startled by the question.

"You said you work for my cousin."

"Oh!" He threw his head back and laughed so loudly that conversation on the driver's bench halted momentarily. "No, I own a livery stable in Alexandria, but I've known Claude all my life. It's not the bank I help him with." He fell silent, staring out the window at the passing scene. He frowned.

D'Orgueil looked out to see rows of burned buildings standing together, their shattered walls and windowless openings gaping into the street. "What is this?" he asked.

Kennedy laughed again, this time with a touch of regret. "This, sir, is what's left of a nigger neighborhood, burned out in July in the riots against the draft. I was here. *Where was it? Somewhere along here? It was somewhere along here, somewhere...*

How do you want to be called?" he asked suddenly. "Not very many of our people are going to be able to say your name." He was smiling again.

"I will use the name on my passport. Actually, I will begin to think of it as my true name from this moment."

"John Balthazar?"

"Certainly. Now tell me where we are going."

"We have one hour to cross this damned city. A train leaves for Washington at 3:00 P.M.

"You were here during the, the revolt?" Balthazar asked.

"Yes." Kennedy was still looking out at the widespread destruction. "Claude sent me up here after Gettysburg. I saw all this."

These streets were worse than Gettysburg.

He remembered the bodies hanging from lamp posts. He remembered a black man running down a street with a howling mob in pursuit. He looked at Balthazar. "I believe you've come to be with our army."

"You are a soldier, I think," the Frenchman remarked still looking at the ruined buildings. "You did this?" he demanded. The tone of voice was unreadable. He saw with satisfaction that Kennedy's eyes came around from the window to blaze with outrage at the idea. The fire subsided after a moment. "No, no, this isn't my work. I wouldn't mind killing a few of these folks, but, we don't do this down home, not like this."

"Which folks?"

"Oh, bankers, lawyers, maybe a few ministers, the people who won't leave us alone."

"No priests?"

"No, no priests. We have no reason to kill priests."

Balthazar thought about that. "Are you Catholic?"

Kennedy was somewhat taken aback at this. Questions about religion were not asked this way in his world, but, then he remembered that the Fenian killers had done the same. "Yes."

"That is why you know the Devereux family so well?"

"No. Is Europe like that?"

Balthazar nodded.

Kennedy shook his head. "Alexandria is a small place. There are not many Catholics. Religion don't mean all that much, not in that way. Just about all the real Alexandrians are for the South, including the priest."

"But, you are a soldier?"

"No. I own a livery stable." He looked stubborn about his answer, but then changed his mind. "Yes, I'm a soldier, for the last three years in fact."

"And you would not do this?" A grey gloved hand waved compellingly at the desolation.

Unhappiness showed in Kennedy's face. "I was sent here to talk to those who wanted to resist the draft and to help them." He did not think he wanted to tell this stranger of his mission of murder, not yet. "The Micks got completely out of hand. They have their own leaders," he concluded bitterly.

"What did they do?" The elegant, stocky figure examined him closely.

"They fought the police,"

"To be expected," murmured Balthazar.

"They fought the army, the Union Army," Kennedy said. "To be expected, I know. Then they killed, or tried to kill every civil official they could find." He looked at Balthazar.

"How many?"

"A few hundred."

"Still acceptable."

"They caught a few volunteer Irish officers in the streets, men home on leave, one just back from Gettysburg. They beat them. Two died."

Balthazar shrugged. "And, what, exactly, was their objection to the conscription, merely a dislike of military service?" He fished around in a vest pocket, and retrieved a rosary of blood colored beads with a red silk tassel at one end.

"What is that?" Kennedy inquired.

"I've given up smoking. It is bad for the heart. My Mussulman friends find this comforting." The beads clicked. "You did not answer my question."

The cab rumbled along. Loud talk penetrated the carriage from above. Kennedy listened.

"Who is the second man, the big one who waited with the cab?" Balthazar asked.

"One of ours, John Quick." Kennedy wanted to get out of the enemy city. The place always made him uncomfortable in its sprawling, ordered, enormity. The Frenchman worried him. No one should be this self possessed in the aftermath of a near disaster like the one on the pier. He searched for the thread of the conversation, and found it. "Ah!" he exclaimed. "The Irish have discovered that this is not their war."

Balthazar looked puzzled.

"They now think the Yankee war against us is the same old war against them, the war of the English, and their money. The priests told them this first, and their leaders in Ireland took up the same song."

"You believe this also, Mister Kennedy?"

"Yes, it's true. The bastards drove my grandfather off his land in Meath, but I have a home here, something new, something I am not going to lose."

Balthazar looked like he wanted to say something.

Kennedy held up a hand, wishing to continue. "The Yankee draft allows commutation."

Balthazar looked blank.

"You can buy your way out."

"How much?"

"Too much."

"And what is it that your Irish friends did here, in these houses?"

"They burned these people out, the colored people. They hung the men from the trees all along here. The worst was the coloreds orphanage about four blocks from here. The mob torched the building, and then shot the children as they ran out."

And I shot Johnston Mitchell as he tried to stop the rioters. God help me. The Micks knew that he would come to this place and they walked me up to his back… God damn you, Claude. God damn you. When I went home you told me maybe it wasn't a good idea to kill him. God damn you. Your wife heard that. You said that to me in front of her. She wept. Maybe it was me she cried for. Damn you…

The Frenchman's chin dropped to his chest. "No. That is not acceptable. You are an officer?"

"Lieutenant."

"Ah, yes. You seem the infantry type to me. Is this so?"

"Used to be. Signal Corps now."

"Is this Signals work?"

"It is in our army."

"I see. What sort of leaders would send them against orphans?"

Kennedy nearly choked with emotion. He leaned out the window to hide his feelings. He could now see the railroad station. He sat back on his seat and faced the Frenchman. "You met one."

"Who?"

"The policeman on the pier, the man who saved you... Here we are. Stay in the cab, sir. We'll handle the bags."

Balthazar enjoyed the ride south. He had much to think about, and the train itself was an object of curiosity.

The passenger car conductor clearly found his accent to be interesting, but in this case it seemed to inspire a kind of reverence which was almost as disturbing as the enmity of the two Irishmen in New York.

The furnishings of the cars were roughly what Balthazar would have expected in Europe, but there were subtle differences in design, textiles and color. The car was filled with blue uniformed men, and their families. Mixed among them were well dressed citizens whom Kennedy explained to him as commercial travelers. He watched Kennedy closely. The man was unconcerned, chatting amiably with their fellow travelers. In particular, he seemed to find fascinating a youthful engineer lieutenant colonel seated across from them. The young man was newly appointed to command a battalion of that arm. He was "en route" to his regiment who were somewhere in Virginia. Listening to the chatter, Balthazar was lured at first into assuming that Kennedy had seized an opportunity to drum up business for his stable from this officer. Slowly, as he half listened, half watched the countryside slip by, he changed his opinion. With amused admiration, he heard Kennedy skillfully extract from the young man the strength, location, and history of the 2nd Massachusetts Engineers.

A Negro waiter walked the length of the car ringing a chime in a universal signal which announced that lunchtime had come. The young officer asked them to join him in the dining car. They begged off, pleading a late breakfast.

"What do you eat for breakfast?" the Frenchman asked after he left, wanting to know if this, at least, was predictable.

Kennedy thought Balthazar distractingly homely. The big nose, walrus mustache, and brown eyes framed a face which was warmly pink under the tan. He grinned in spite himself, wondering if the man knew how much he looked like a caricature of a Frenchman. "Eggs, generally fried," Kennedy answered, " but sometimes boiled, bacon, ham, the like, potatoes, also fried, maybe grits, stewed apples, things such as that, that's what we eat."

Balthazar had been reassured at the start of this list, finding it to be English. As Kennedy rattled on, his heart sank.

"What's the matter?" the lieutenant asked, alarmed at the expression on his charge's face.

"What are 'grits'?"

Kennedy explained.

"And, you eat potatoes with this?"

"No, usually either grits or potatoes, and then we cook the spuds in the same skillet the bacon was in. You can throw in some onions if you have any."

The heavy head bobbed on its massive support. "That sounds tasty; this is something one could cook in the field?" The brown eyes looked hopeful.

Kennedy began to feel good about this man, seeing in the foreigner a welcome figure, the kind of officer who liked to sit by a wood fire, watching while other men ate. "It sure is! Snake Davis, and Jim make the best home fries in the whole army. My mother don't make better."

"Snake Davis?"

Kennedy chuckled. "Our cooks in my old company, they're two black men from Alexandria."

"Slaves?"

Kennedy stared at him, and then searched his memory. "It's been a long time now that I've known them as free. Oh, I guess they were once, but not for years. They work for the army."

"The Confederate Army?"

Kennedy looked around to be sure no one had heard. "For Christ's sake, Major!" he snapped.

Balthazar held up a hand. "I am sorry! I am seduced into carelessness by your mastery of this situation. I must say that I am a little startled to learn that there are black men with you of their own will, but then, we have many Algerians who take our side against their own. They think we are their own," he said reflectively.

Kennedy shook his head. "I don't know about all that, but Snake, Jim and Bill belong to us, to the regiment I mean."

Balthazar waited. When it was evident that there would be nothing else, he started to speak.

Two Union naval officers passed, chatting and laughing over the promotion of an acquaintance. He hesitated long enough for them to pass.

"Which regiment?"

Kennedy was now irritated, fearful of the risk run by talking too much. He began to look sullen.

"I want to know," Balthazar whispered patiently. "Come, come, there is no one."

"17th Virginia Infantry."

Balthazar had hoped for more. "Is there something unusual about this regiment," he prompted, a little impatiently. Having judged Kennedy to be a true man and old veteran, he expected that this question would force a reply.

"You'll have to ask Major Devereux. Is there something else you'd like to know?"

"You referred to him as 'colonel' before."

Kennedy did not reply. He had decided to say nothing more.

Balthazar sighed. "Who is Bill?" he asked hopefully.

Kennedy searched back through his memory to find the reference in their talk. "Bill White, our chief teamster. Good man, one of the best, his 'pa' is the Devereuxs' butler. You'll meet him."

"Black?"

"More or less."

"Mulatto?"

Kennedy nodded. He looked down for a minute, then up. He hesitated. "It's none of my business," he said at last. "You can talk to Claude about it, if you want."

The volunteer engineer officer entered the car. He walked, smiling up the aisle toward them.

"No more of this!" Kennedy warned.

Balthazar nodded.

The boy colonel took his seat. "You fellows missed a great meal, Porterhouse steaks!"

Balthazar smiled, turning back to Kennedy. "The 'home fries' potatoes?"

Kennedy raised his eyebrows in surprise. "Yes?"

"You say there is onion in it?"

"Yes."

"What sort?"

"Generally wild onions."

Balthazar seemed doubtful, and then shrugged. "Well, perhaps. We will see. A touch of garlic may be delightful in this."

"We don't eat garlic," the young engineer said with a small air of superiority.

The Frenchman was shocked. He looked at Kennedy.

The Virginian winked with the eye invisible to the third man, smug in spite of the fact that he, also, could not imagine eating garlic. "And then there's red eye gravy."

"Yes?"

He explained that the salty, peppery ham of rural Virginia should be slow fried and then eaten with a sauce made in the de-glazed pan with an infusion of strong, black coffee.

A smile lit Balthazar's homely face. "This becomes more interesting, my friend," he said.

Claude Devereux met them on the station platform in Alexandria.

Balthazar saw him as the cars rolled to a halt. Momentarily disoriented by the uniform, he wondered who this ramrod straight figure might be. The face of his cousin, beaming up at him brought everything back into focus.

Devereux waved and started for the door of the car.

Balthazar was surprised to see the terrible effect which a few short years had made in Devereux. The hair was nearly all grey now. Wrinkles showed around the eyes. He tried to master his shock, and had nearly banished it from his mind as he reached the end of the car to step down on Virginia's soil.

Devereux grasped him firmly by the hand until Balthazar seized him by the shoulders to pull him into a tight embrace. "I won't kiss you Claude," he said. "I sense that your countrymen would have as difficult a time with that as our English relations, but it is good to see you again." The burly Frenchman held the other man at arm's length. "Blue becomes you," he said finally. "The eagles suggest that you are a colonel, I believe."

Devereux's features froze. "I thought someone would have told you."

Balthazar shrugged expressively, a gesture full of acceptance. He smiled widely, brown eyes lighting up the big face.

Devereux relaxed. "I have found it necessary to accept their offer. I am, in fact in the office of the Secretary of War as a volunteer," he said.

"The bureau of the minister of war, you are in the bureau of the minister of war?" The audacity of the thing and the immensity of the opportunity bemused him.

Devereux nodded.

"Mon Dieu!" Balthazar looked up and down the platform, examining the building. "What a lovely little station! Come! Let us go, I would see my aunt, and your splendid town. You could speak of nothing else in France. Now, I would see it for myself." A spring wagon waited in the station yard. The cousins passed arm in arm through the crowd, with Devereux smiling and nodding in reaction to the greetings of several men.

A lovely brunette stood against one wall, a ticket in one gloved hand. Brown silk became her. She pointed the end of her parasol at Claude in recognition.

Devereux paused to speak. He removed his kepi. "Elizabeth. Going into the city today?"

The beauty beamed at him. "Claude, you have been so cruel!"

He cocked his grey head to one side. "Pardon?" he asked.

"You know," she said. "We have not had you for weeks! I have been to see your mother, and Hope, but you are just so, 'occupied', and now you are a colonel. La! You have no idea how jealous some people are! So sudden!" she said and then turned her light upon Balthazar.

Devereux looked relieved at the diversion of her conversation to someone else. "Elizabeth," he said. "May I present my cousin, John Balthazar. John, Mrs. Frederick Braithwaite." She extended her hand.

Balthazar scooped it up, raising the russet kid glove to a precise inch from his lips. "Enchante', Madame," he breathed.

Her eyelids fluttered. "My, goodness, Claude. One of your French relations?"

"Yes," he said. "John has come over to seek a market for the family's wines."

"What sort of wine is that Mister Balthazar?" she asked.

"Bordeaux, or more precisely, Cahors, a land to the east of Bordeaux. We have lived there a long time." He still held her hand.

She looked confused.

"I apologize for my accent. I did not learn English here." He released her hand.

"Whatever for!" she laughed, "a French gentleman who sounds like the British ambassador. You just keep right on talking that way, Mister Balthazar! You'll do well here, exceedingly well"

"What do you think?" Devereux asked when they were seated in the carriage.

Balthazar looked back into the station.

Elizabeth Braithwaite watched them from the same spot, beside the ticket window.

Balthazar held her eyes across the distance. "A bit of a tart, a light woman of good family, but very pretty. Is she of this place?"

Devereux grimaced. "Only moderately good family, her husband is with the military railroad, and a damned nuisance he is!"

"Ah, the lady of a brother officer!" The Frenchman smiled more broadly, bowing in her direction.

She dimpled prettily, fluttering an ivory fan the while.

The carriage began to roll across the cobblestone yard of the station, turning out into Columbus street through a clattering confusion of military traffic.

"Why, 'a nuisance?'" Balthazar inquired, craning his neck to inspect the passing multitudes.

"He's a railroad engineer in civilian life."

His cousin still looked blank.

"He wants our financial support for his post-war schemes, wants to become wealthy in the boom to come after they finish us off."

Balthazar said nothing, thinking it over.

"And we'll give it to him. He probably will become rich, and we might as well make money right along with him! I just wish he would shut up about it for now!"

"And with regard to the lady?"

"Elizabeth?"

"Yes. You haven't been..?"

"No! No! Nothing like that!"

"Good."

"Why would you think that?"

Balthazar threw back his head and roared.

People on the brick sidewalk turned to look.

"Come now! Your exploits in Europe were the talk of the family! The officers of my regiment thought you one of the greatest swordsmen in France."

"I am reformed. Hope and I are reconciled."

Balthazar slapped his cousin on one blue knee. From long observation of mankind, Balthazar knew that a rake was likely to remain a rake. He had seen his cousin's need for the love and devotion of women. "Splendid! These houses are not, in fact, Georgian, are they?"

"No, they are all a bit different."

The carriage rumbled along Washington Street, passing the Grecian facade of the Lyceum, and then turning left into Duke Street. They rolled downhill, toward the river.

On the far side Balthazar saw green hills. "That is Maryland," he commented, proud of his grasp of local geography.

"Uh-huh." Devereux seemed lost in thought. "Jean-Marie, I want to get you out of here and across the lines as soon as possible, before you become a remembered part of the local scenery."

"Good! Excellent again! How will you do this?"

"We run a secret line of communication across the Potomac farther down. I can send you across at night, perhaps this Tuesday."

Balthazar calculated. It was difficult to keep track of the days during a long trip. "That is four days from now", he finally announced.

Chapter 6

Family

The music of women's laughter rose from the front sitting room like a golden cloud, drifting up the stairwell to Balthazar's bedroom.

He woke in a state of mild confusion, uncertain of his situation.

The pale, dying light of an autumn afternoon glowed behind the lace curtains.

He began to feel confined by the tight envelope of bedclothes around his legs. Shaking a leg, he managed to extricate one foot from the clutching sheets. He contemplated his toes, wiggling them happily.

Masculine footsteps climbed the carpeted stairs. They paused before his door.

"Jean-Marie. Are you awake?"

"Yes, Claude. Are you waiting for me?"

"Whenever you are ready, the family would like to meet you."

"I'll be right down."

The footsteps descended.

A momentary hush greeted his cousin's return to the salon.

As he rose, searching for his trousers, Balthazar heard the music begin again. Stretching beside the bed, he realized how tired he still was. Looking at his watch, he understood that he had slept eight hours, nearly all the day. His legs and lower back were stiff. He stretched against the cramped muscles. For one hesitant moment, he wondered what his American cousins might wear for dinner. Claude's polished image rose before his eyes to decide the question. He searched in his trunk and grunted in satisfaction at the state of his clothes.

"Clotilde, will you have another cup of the Oolong?"

The baritone voice reached his ears as an almost unintelligible murmur as he descended from the second floor. The chestnut of the banister slid voluptuously beneath his fingers. He focused on the long runner beneath his feet. The excellence of the piece caught his eye.

Khotan, he thought. I wonder how many snobs in London could believe that. Turning the corner, he came upon them all. They were arranged across the sitting room as though for a family portrait.

Claude stood by the black marble fireplace in evening dress, one arm draped across the mantle. A beautiful blonde sat by his side. Balthazar recognized his cousin's wife from the miniature painting which Devereux had carried in France.

Charles and Clotilde were seated on a high backed settle. The red silk of its upholstery made a frame for them. Balthazar was struck by the lady's physical familiarity. She was so much like his aunts that he felt vaguely guilty at his inability to remember her particular face. He bowed to the enthroned couple. "My dear aunt! I have so looked forward to this meeting! Uncle!" He bowed again.

Clotilde beamed up at him, immensely pleased to see a member of her own family beneath her roof.

Charles rose and gripped his hand. "So good to see you, major. I hope you will be able to spend some time with us before my son sends you away."

To Charles' right a Catholic priest sat. His white hair and ruddy complexion contrasted starkly with the starched purity of his collar and the utter blackness of his cassock.

He stood. "Willem Kruger," he said while offering his hand.

Balthazar's big fist slowly enfolded the smaller man's hand, taking possession of it. "A pleasure, Father."

A butler stood beside a mahogany tea cart, his grey hair and composed features almost a part of the room's decor. "Good evening, sir," he intoned in a deep voice.

A footman brought Balthazar a cup and saucer.

Balthazar searched the room for the widow.

A woman's knees could be seen beyond the footman's left arm. He glanced at the face of the servant. It was the same man who had carried his bags upstairs from the street.

Joe White somehow sensed that he was in the way and with the good sense that God gave him realized what was wanted. He stepped back far enough to let the visitor see Victoria Devereux. She was looking at an embroidery ring in her lap. The crown of her coppery head was what he saw at first, that and the black dress. Her hands held the wooden ring. A finger traced the pattern of colored thread, counting stitches. She raised her head.

Balthazar D'Orgueil knew he was a romantic. He actually thought it one of his better qualities. He had known and admired many women in the days before his marriage. "Loved" would have been too strong a word.

He was not prepared for this woman. His world changed when he saw her. He told himself that he must not walk across the room to her.

She looked at him in a friendly, welcoming way into which there gradually crept something different. Her eyes shifted slightly from him and she looked a little puzzled. She focused on him again, and smiled.

He began to feel foolish. There was nothing especially striking about her. She was pretty in a healthy, buxom way, but she did not look like his ideal of an American lady. He glanced at Claude's wife.

Hope Devereux was a great beauty, dazzling in her perfection. The radiance of her filled the space by Claude's side. She had leaned forward to speak to Clotilde. The line of her neck deserved a sonnet.

Victoria Devereux's round face was a little too full, her nose a little too short.

"Madame, I have not the words," was all he could find to say.

She smiled a little, her head bobbed once in acknowledgment. "Thank you, major. Patrick often spoke of the visit he had with you and Claude." She frowned just a little, trying to remember. "Three years ago it is now, I suppose."

He bowed, too overcome by emotion to speak again. Crossing the room, he took refuge in conversation with his cousin's wife. Hope was so lovely. There was a flawlessness in her physical being that demanded attention. Balthazar discovered that the beauty was also a wit. Her command of anecdote concerning the court of Louis Napoleon surprised him.

Claude looked on with pleasure, occasionally offering a comment, quite relaxed and at ease, beaming to see them together.

Balthazar remembered his manners and did his duty in circulating among all those present. The butler followed him around the room, insisting that his cup should be full. There was something interesting about the man. Balthazar could not quite put his finger on what it might be. The footman followed the butler, assisting with the tea service. The Frenchman noticed that Claude and his father had stopped drinking tea. They held small glasses of some brown liquid. "I will have that," he told the butler. The old Negro gestured to the younger servant. A cut glass decanter appeared from which an inch of liquor was poured into a tumbler.

"What is your name?" Balthazar asked the butler.

The pale eyes looked right at him for the first time. "George White. This is my son, Joseph."

Balthazar inspected the footman.

The mulatto grinned at him.

"And what is this that I am about to drink?"

"That, sir, is the finest sour mash Kentucky whiskey, twenty years old," White replied, a small smile at the corners of his mouth.

Looking at him, Balthazar knew there was no meanness in it.

Claude came to him, his own glass in hand, "You don't have to drink that," he said. "It is very much an acquired taste."

The guest took a sip, holding it under his tongue for a moment. He swallowed. "That is not whisky," he announced.

They all looked disappointed.

"But, it is very, very good. One can get this in the field?" he asked Devereux.

Laughter shook their end of the room, causing the others to listen.

"Sometimes nothing else. You will do well, very well indeed!"

After a time, Balthazar found it possible to place himself in the chair beside Victoria. He asked about her needlework. She showed him what she was doing. The faces of George Washington and Jefferson Davis looked up at him from her lap. He glanced about the room, realizing how privileged he was to be included. He asked of her sons, asked of his godson.

She looked relieved.

That disturbed him, afraid that his attentions were unwelcome.

"He would be so glad to meet you! Charlotte was always so good about sending him little things!" She glanced at him shyly. "I know you were always in some place like Africa, or Russia..." She put a hand over her mouth. "Oh! My! We haven't said one thing about your loss. How can you forgive us?"

The memory of his beloved wife flooded back into him. He fought against tears.

Seeing his distress, Victoria put her hand on his sleeve. "Dinner will not be for a few minutes. We are waiting for friends. "Our house is in the next street. Come meet my sons. They will be so pleased!"

Clotilde Devereux saw them to the door, telling them to return quickly, and reminding that Colonel Jourdain would be among the guests.

George White held the door, closing it behind them.

Walking back from her house in the cool of the night, she took his arm.

Seeking an explanation for this blessing, he thought it could have been the evident pleasure which he and the boys had taken in each other.

It was moderately dark. The gas lighting flickering high atop the metal posts cast small pools of light outside which the darkness waited. The glass enclosures did not look very clean.

He had held out an elbow without thinking.

The pressure of her hand made him a little light headed.

He reminded himself that this lady's husband had died violently in July.

It did not work. The evening was crisp and clear. The air smelled of leaf mold and horse.

A blue uniformed Union Army lieutenant walked down the street toward them. As he passed, he tipped his cap to Victoria. "Evenin' Ma'am," he murmured.

She turned her head from him.

The young man looked as though he had been slapped. He hurried away.

Balthazar was a little shocked. "Was that necessary?" he asked.

The auburn head snapped around. "If they want to be treated nicely, they should get out of our country!" The fire in her burned brightly before him.

They stopped on the brick sidewalk. The bricks had an interesting pattern of entwined leaves molded into some of them.

Victoria looked at him waiting for a reaction. She wore a woolen shawl with a long, tasseled fringe. "They are no good, major, no good at all!" she said.

"If they are your enemies," he replied, "then they must surely be without virtue." He grasped the fringed edges to either side of her neck, and tugged it higher. His knuckles touched her throat for a second. "You must not catch cold. The two young men we left in your house just now need you. Do not provoke your enemies. They are so strong, and they are everywhere."

She shrugged. "We are going to lose, and then nothing will matter, nothing!"

They walked on in silence, away from the river, up the rising breast of the street to the glowing windows.

Dinner proved to be something less than a joyous occasion. Balthazar could think of no decent way to place himself near Victoria. He was not, in fact, sure that this would have been welcomed. Then there was the matter of his countryman, Colonel Edouard Jourdain. The man did not like him. That much was miserably clear. Balthazar knew instinctively what the problem was. Jourdain did not like that Balthazar represented something older and deeper in the French Army than Jourdain could become. Jean-Marie Balthazar d'Orgueil was a man of the soil. He came of a race wedded to the stony plateau of their dreams, the goat pastures of their destiny, a place in which they clung to their own people and their way of life. War came to them as their calling not as an alternative to the soil, but rather as an expression of their acceptance of nature's plan.

The colonel wanted nothing like that. He was a modern man. He did not think of himself as a Bonapartist. In truth, he was republican to the core. His wife, Helene, claimed descent from one of the great baronial houses of eastern France, but he insisted that the title of "bourgeois" should be thought the noblest of all. He did not think Balthazar a Bonapartist either, but he saw in him something worrisome. Jourdain had passed the years of his career in a miscellany of postings throughout metropolitan France. He had endured the pitiless weather of Lorraine and the Pas de Calais for an eternity. The petty backbiting of garrison politics had worn at the corners of his soul. At last he had escaped to the General Staff and to Paris. The romantic "posturing" and "juvenile adventurism" of the Army of Africa was to him an evasion of duty.

What right did these madmen have to think themselves better? They should try some real soldiering!

The younger felt the elder's disapproval. His perception of it had grown throughout dinner. At first he simply ignored the feeling of oppression that came with this empathy. It seemed unimportant. Claude introduced them in the salon, and brought them together in the music room for a few minutes, believing that they would be happy to see one another. The three men found themselves in the center of the room, standing closely enough that whispers would suffice. The heavy window hangings made it impossible that anyone would hear them in the street. A fire spat and hissed in the brick hearth of the white, wooden fireplace.

Jourdain wasted no time in small talk. "Welcome!" he whispered. "Your arrival here comes a little late, but that is no fault of yours. Claude has delivered you to us with his customary dispatch and competence. As your superior officer, I wish to be certain that you understand what is expected of you..." The tall, grey haired and elegant figure peered at him with something in his face that looked like suspicion.

Irritation began to grow in Balthazar's heart. He knew from long experience that the men of southern France were thought to be not quite "right" by some Frenchmen. They were thought to be a little too "uneven" for tasks requiring qualities of calmness and persistence. He saw that the military attaché of France might be one of those who held such opinions. "I am to attach myself to General Lee's army, conform to its movements, and to render such reports to you as will enable the Emperor's government to formulate its ultimate policy with regard to the Confederate States of America." The last words were spoken in English. The sound of them struck suddenly home to him. There was something in them that brought foreboding.

"And what of your communications, D'Orgueil?" the colonel demanded. "How will you send me these reports"?

"What is your regiment, mon colonel?" Balthazar asked, unwilling to be dragged around by the man.

"6th Hussars," Jourdain responded with satisfaction.

Balthazar did not relish cavalrymen. He found their jumped-up air of superiority unacceptable. "I will send you reports through the responsible officer of General Lee's staff..." He looked inquiringly at Devereux.

"That would be either Marshall or Charles Venable."

"When I meet these gentlemen, I will have a better idea..."

Jourdain examined him closely.

The evident lack of friendliness was clear to Devereux. He cleared his throat. "Ah, we'll deliver these dispatches to you, Edouard. Never fear. I'm sure that Jean-Marie can handle that cipher machine that you gave us as well as we can. Actually, I'll leave the room if you'd like to discuss this sort of thing."

Jourdain raised a hand in protest. "Pas du tout! You are a subject of the Emperor, one of us!" He turned back to Balthazar. "If it is not possible to send letters to me through the Confederates, then you should seek the aid of the Papal Nuncio here. He has been instructed to offer you the hand of the church in friendship. I believe you are in funds from the foreign ministry?"

"Yes."

"If you should run short..."

Devereux gathered up the two men, holding each by an elbow, guiding them toward the door. "Not to worry, Edouard. My cousin will not lack for means in my country... Let's go in. The ladies are waiting."

Like most Frenchmen, Balthazar liked to talk at table. An animated discussion of life's minor incidents, and the events of the day, ranked high among his expectations at table. He found this gathering to be captivating. The Devereuxs and their Alexandria friends were among the most engaging people he could remember. Their conversation was both frank and amusing. Regrettably, he found his own people, as represented by Colonel and Madame Jourdain, to be less interesting. His attention kept wandering back to Victoria. He was pleased to see that she took part in the spirited occasion, in fact, seemed at the center of it.

In the midst of the fish course, a sensation of touching against the side of his face caused him to glance to the left.

He found himself looking into her brown eyes. She smiled and looked away.

George White and his son had just removed the remains of several fowl when Balthazar sensed that there was some disturbance at the back of the house. There was a persistent knocking followed by muffled exclamations of surprise. He had not seen the kitchens, but the general logic of domestic architecture told him that the commotion must be there.

Clotilde appeared not to hear, but Claude excused himself, returning after a moment. He took his place, responding to his mother's inquiring glance with a small shake of the head. The incident did not interrupt the smooth progress of service.

Hope stared at her husband.

He eventually looked at her, and in reply to her mute demand formed a word with his lips that to Balthazar looked impenetrably to be "smood".

She looked surprised. Her eyes widened in shock.

Claude grinned at her confusion.

She covered her mouth with her napkin, turning to listen to the man at her right. A moment later Balthazar heard her laugh a silver laugh, evidently in approval of some witticism. A little later, after making what seemed to Balthazar a rather weak excuse, she left the table.

Finally, mercifully, Clotilde, Charles, and Victoria shepherded the other guests into the salon.

Claude led him through a swinging door. The butler's pantry bulged with the debris of the meal. An inner door opened into the kitchen. Over Claude's shoulder, Balthazar could see four people seated at a large, wooden table. Hope, and a pretty white haired mulatto woman sat across from each other. Lieutenant Frederick Kennedy occupied a third chair. At the head of the table was a stocky, sun tanned man in his mid-thirties. His rough clothing made you think of a farmer. A bright, new scar ran down one side of his face, down from his forehead, across the eyebrow, into the cheek, disappearing in the red-brown beard. At the sight of Claude, he put down his fork to stand.

Devereux crossed the room to seize him in his arms. "My God, Isaac!" he cried so loudly that Kennedy went to the pantry door to listen. "I thought we had lost you forever!"

The recipient of this attention squinted at Balthazar with growing alarm, unable to place the face. He gently detached himself from Devereux's embrace. "Good to see you, sir! I wasn't too hopeful m'self. I just thought to drop by for some of Betsy's apple pie. It's as good as ever."

The older woman smiled at him.

Devereux looked puzzled at the expression on Smoot's face.

"Claude," his wife prompted. "They haven't met!"

Devereux did not answer. He still seemed absorbed in the other man's presence.

"Major Balthazar, this is Sergeant Isaac Smoot, 43rd Battalion, Virginia Cavalry," Kennedy offered.

"Here?" Balthazar could not believe his ears. "We are in President Lincoln's back garden!"

"An Englishman?" Smoot rasped in surprise.

"No! No!" Devereux said. "This is Major John Balthazar of the French Imperial Forces. He will visit our army. I have written Richmond about him. He is expected. What are you doing here, Isaac? I have a sudden presentment that you have not come to rejoin us.

Smoot still watched the stranger with guarded attention. He did not reply.

Hope reached up and held one of his hands.

Smoot looked down at her.

"He is our cousin, Isaac," she said.

Hope Devereux had the gift of attracting affection.

Isaac Smoot loved her more than a little. He squeezed her hand, and then let it go. "The major and young Dulany have decided that Pierpont must be silenced," he said, "and an example made for Tories..."

"They are coming in?" Devereux's eyes flashed.

"Tonight. They sent me on ahead to warn you, so you could stay clear."

Hope saw a look of bewilderment spreading across the Frenchman's face. "Francis Pierpont is a misguided fool," she said. "He is also Governor of Virginia in the view of Lincoln's government. None of them care that we already have a governor, and legislature, whom we elected, and who sit in Richmond, where they are supposed to be. Francis lives and has his 'capitol' over on Prince Street about four blocks from here. Oh!" She smiled up at him. "French Dulany is with Mosby. He is an Alexandria boy. His father is Governor Pierpont's military aide, and a volunteer colonel."

"Yes, rather like myself", Devereux suggested.

"Not exactly like you, dear," Hope said sweetly.

"And Mosby, the partisan leader, I have read of him in France. What has he to do with this?" Balthazar pressed.

"He is 'the major,'" Kennedy said somewhat impatiently. The 43rd is his battalion."

"Ah! Mon Dieu! I understand now! Why did you not say so at once? Ah, but all of you know these things. I must not forget! They are coming here tonight! How splendid! But Claude, this solves your problem of my movements. I will leave with them!" The elegance and simplicity of this arrangement so appealed to Balthazar that a wide smile animated his face as he turned from one to another, expecting approval.

Devereux watched Smoot for an indication of his opinion.

"He won't like it," the sergeant decided aloud.

"But, why not?" Balthazar demanded.

"He doesn't like to be taken unawares like this, especially when he's in the midst of something serious."

"Ah! But this is only to be expected! The temperament of leaders of 'guerilleros' is a well known thing. I have encountered it elsewhere. Not to worry."

Smoot looked at the big foreigner with growing interest. "Well, maybe."

Chapter 7

Mosby

The streets of Alexandria teemed with Union military men. The army's somber blue mixed everywhere with the dark jumpers and colorful neckerchiefs of the crews of ships at anchor in the river.

Devereux stalked along the sidewalk, the very picture of a purposeful senior officer abroad on the nation's business. He and his large companion chatted amiably, evidently forgetful of their surroundings. The soldiers parted before them turning to watch the two men after they passed. Ahead of them, Joe White led two horses, turning as he went to greet passers by and to lift his hat to ladies out for an evening's walk.

The little procession went south along Fairfax Street passing the well lit houses of substantial citizens, then a firehouse five blocks from the Devereux home, and finally a roaring bawdy house overflowing with soldiers of the garrison. A provost officer stood in the road with three of his men. His hands clasped behind him, he studied the place purposefully.

Devereux came upon him unseen. "Evening Dodge, from your expression I'd say that you are going to break up the fun."

The captain spun on his heel, and straightened to attention as he recognized the voice as a colonel. "Good evening, sir! The neighbors have complained three times tonight. One of those damned Pennsylvanians from the new artillery on Shuter's Hill broke into a house over there, and raped a servant girl! At least she says it's rape. You never know... They're apt to say anything to make difficulties for us. I wouldn't give you ten cents for all the Alexandrians who ever liv..." He clearly had forgotten to whom he spoke. He looked abruptly at Balthazar and Devereux. "Oh! I am sorry, sir! I was not speaking of loyal men!"

Devereux waved vaguely at him in passing as he walked away. "Of course! Of course! I know exactly what was meant. Carry on." Balthazar kept out of the light, passing behind the group of soldiers while inclining his head in an apparent salutation which hid most of his face. They walked on in silence for a time until Balthazar could contain himself no longer. "Claude, I have not much time... I would ask your permission to, to write to..."

"To me? My word, Jean-Marie! Why of course you'll write to me!"

Balthazar said nothing for a minute, trudging along quietly until he glanced at his cousin.

My God! The vile creature is grinning at me!

"What is so damnably amusing, Claude?" he demanded.

"You! You're just off the boat, headed off for God knows what and asking me for permission to correspond with my recently widowed sister-in-law." Devereux scratched the side of his face. "You should. We, none of us, have time to fool around with the niceties. Go ahead! Write to her. She needs some other interest than the boys. She needs to think about something other than Pat."

"I had not thought I was so, obvious. My apologies, your brother..."

"We all miss him of course, she most of all... He was standing at my side when he was killed. He never should have been there of course. We chased him up the hill. You'd never think a man on crutches could move that fast, and there we all were, Pat, me, Fred Kennedy, Bill and Quick. We reached the top just in time to watch the whole thing, the whole damned thing. Pickett's attack, you know." Devereux coughed into a closed fist. "You write her, Jean-Marie. I insist. Send letters with your dispatches. I'll see that she gets them."

"Colonel Jourdain?"

"To hell with him! He doesn't have to know everything about us. We don't belong to him, do we? Actually, I believe that is something of a family tradition?"

"Yes, we give ourselves with some discrimination."

Devereux laughed deep in his chest, laughed from emotion, filled with the anticipation of what must come soon for his cousin. He stopped walking, standing quiet, listening.

"What now?" the French soldier asked.

"Here we are. Smoot and Joseph are waiting in the shadow of the barn across the street."

Balthazar held out a hand. "A bientot."

Devereux gripped the hand hard. "You were not obvious," he said. With that he turned on his heel and walked off down an alley, limping in the chill night air, disappearing almost at once in the darkness of the shadow cast by the houses.

Balthazar crossed the cobblestones, going directly to the barn door.

It stood slightly open, inviting him.

Ingrained caution stopped him three feet from the blackness. He inspected the featureless opening without enthusiasm.

"Go on in, mister," Smoot's voice suggested.

"Yes, do," someone urged from within. The voice had a curiously flat quality about it.

Balthazar remained where he was, unwilling to jump into the unknown.

"Whoever you are, we don't want you standin' out there in the street!" a third man whispered loudly. The tension in his voice was plain to hear.

"Devereux looks well, even in his costume," the flat voice remarked. "You must come in, and tell me who you are. Smoot!"

"Yes, Major."

"Walk the man in."

Isaac Smoot's stocky form came around the corner of the barn.

Balthazar held up a hand to stop his forward motion. Satisfied that he had paused, Balthazar strode directly into the darkened interior of the barn.

The door closed behind, making the blackness yet more complete.

Feet moved about in the straw. The odors of horse and soldiers hung all about.

A match was struck, revealing a tall, dark man engaged in lighting a candle. With the light in hand, he came close to Balthazar, staring in his face for a moment. "And, who the hell are you?" he finally inquired.

"You are not Major Mosby," Balthazar stated with certainty.

"No? Look, fellah... I'm whatever I say. We don't need no Englishmen stickin' their noses in our business." The candle moved from side to side passing perilously close to Balthazar's considerable nose.

"You are not Major Mosby," Balthazar said again without much interest.

"No, I am," the flat voice declared. A small, slender, smooth shaven man walked into the light. His thin lipped, narrow face smiled without warmth. "You are?"

"Devereux told me to give you the story." Smoot spoke from a place somewhere by the doors.

"Good! Good! At least there is a story." The sharp face divided in a white toothed grin. "Tell us, Sergeant Smoot."

"Very well," the little man said when the story was told. "I see that I have no choice. Devereux should not have done this, but, I'll take you along when we're through. We may be moving pretty fast. Are you sure you can keep up?"

A rustle of amusement ran from man to man around the unseen presence.

"I will do my best."

Mosby leaned forward to scrutinize more closely a man who did not meekly accept what he gave him. He frowned very slightly. "We will have one or more prisoners. You will not speak in their presence."

Balthazar bowed a little. "As you wish, I shall wait here?"

"Smoot will stay as your 'nurse'."

The whispering started again in the corners of the barn.

"Did you hear, Sergeant Smoot?"

"Yes, major. I heard."

The door opened and closed. Dimly defined figures crossed the square of greater illumination, leaving the two of them alone in the yellow, flickering light. In the silence, the shuffling, breathing noises of horses was loud.

"Don't pay him any mind," Smoot said evenly. "It's his way, that's all."

After a little, Balthazar asked the question which had formed in the part of his mind reserved for professional rumination. "How is he with wounded, with those who are truly inconvenient?"

The animals shifted and stamped. The sound of a horse staling filled the emptiness of the space around the French soldier. "I thought as much," he finally said, judging Mosby with a finality that would lie heavily on them both.

"He doesn't have much time for such things," Smoot commented at last. "But, he's a great man..."

"Where did you receive the wound on your face?"

The talk hung in the dark between them. Smoot did not reply.

"Did he leave you?"

"No! No... I had a letter from Claude. I had to be carried to General Lee... He couldn't leave me..."

Balthazar shook his head silently in the sheltering darkness. "And what of my cousin?" he demanded. "You have been under his orders?"

"He's a fine man, your cousin. There's no better. The whole family is nothing but the best, nothing but the best, especially.... and that's all I'll say about it." With that he could be heard settling into the straw of an empty stall.

The raiders came back after midnight. With them they brought a man in Union Army blue. The Rebel soldiers gathered in one corner of the barn, surrounding their prisoner.

Balthazar watched from a discreet distance.

After a time, a young man left the group to speak to Balthazar and Smoot. Whispering to them in a corner he gave them the news, laughing the while. "We went to Pierpont's house," he began. "Snuck up on it real good, we did! I went in the back door since I know their cook and maids and such real well."

Smoot held up a candle to see the man's face.

"And who are you my young friend?" Balthazar inquired softly.

"I'm French Dulany," the handsome youth responded in surprise. "I'm from here. You're the Devereux cousin, aren't you?" Satisfied that this was correct, he continued his story. "He wasn't there. He's gone to Washington

City for the night. I'll bet he's sleepin' snug as can be in one of the Willard's big beds." He chuckled agreeably at the thought.

"So, what did you do, French?" Smoot wanted to know.

"Oh, we went over to my pa's house, and collected him instead. He was right surprised to see us, I believe. That's him there in the Yank uniform. He was real impressive to see, stood up to the major, told him he wasn't welcome in his house, but said I ought to take a pair of boots before I left. Of course, they were old boots. I took them, and we took him as well." The soldier looked across the barn at his father who appeared to have a lot to say to the partisan leader.

"Do you have a mother?" Balthazar asked.

The beautiful young man turned to face him. "My mother is with us!" he said forcefully. "She knows we won't hurt him. He'll be in Richmond in a couple of days and then we can trade him for an important person that we want back. I won't let anything happen to him, she knows that. He's just wrong, sidin' with Lincoln."

"He does not know who I am?"

"No. The major aims to keep it that way. He sent me over to tell you to stay away from him. Ah! Here we go. You bring up the rear with Isaac."

Mosby's men collected their animals and now began to lead them out the back side of the barn, heading south; angling for a place by the river where they could pass out of Union held territory.

Balthazar followed them in the maze of moonlit alleys. From time to time he looked back to be sure that Smoot was still there leading his own horse and the pack mule that Devereux had given for baggage. A gleam of silver made him look to the left, where the Potomac River was visible between two houses. The buildings became fewer, the spaces more frequent and threatening in their openness. Up ahead he could see a belt of thicker vegetation.

A stream, he thought.

The tiny column slowed. The men spread out, entering the brush in a line parallel to the vegetation. Several halted on the edge. They gathered the reins of others who pressed forward through saplings and vines.

Smoot tied the animals to a tree. They followed the line into the scrub. Balthazar felt with his toes for sticks that might snap. He found none. He came to the edge of the growth and looked out across an open space at a stream. It did not seem to be more than thirty meters wide. Four of Mosby's men were half way across in waist deep water. In the middle distance a Union soldier lay on the ground, a huddled lump of darkness and indistinguishable details. Only his boots made him recognizable as a human being.

Balthazar and Smoot stood at one end of the line hidden in the brush.

Several Confederates were within a few feet.

"The major will wait until the scouts clear the other side, and then we'll all go over together," Smoot muttered.

Balthazar nodded, not listening very closely, engrossed in watching this small affair, hoping for early understanding of his host's competence.

Brush crackled to the right.

Balthazar turned his head and watched another Northern soldier emerge from a clump of small trees.

The man tripped on a root and fell heavily to one knee. He grunted loudly in surprise. Regaining his feet, he rubbed one hand on the knee and peered about. He held a cavalry carbine in one hand. In the other he held some sort of container. "Evan! Evan!" he called. "Where are you? It's me, Henry! I brought you some coffee." Henry straightened up seeking his friend in the open space near the stream bank. The broken figure lying nearby was so unacceptable a possibility that he seemed not to see it. On the far bank one of the scouts was a poorly defined human shape. "Evan! Is that you?" the cavalryman called. He removed his cap waving it above his head.

To either side of Balthazar, rebel guerrillas shifted perceptibly in their stance, gathering themselves to spring on the unsuspecting man before them.

Balthazar considered the possible outcomes. A messy, botched killing might involve noise. The reserve force for Evan and Henry must be somewhere nearby. A fight inside Federal lines would mean the end of his mission. With his left hand, he pushed back the lapel of his coat, reaching into the small of his back for his knife.

The soldier to his right began to move forward.

Balthazar gripped his sleeve, and stepped past him, walking quickly toward the man named Henry. The unsuspecting victim still had his hat in hand, waving it above his head. As he came closer, Balthazar could see the details of the man's dress.

Henry wore a long, blue overcoat with a short cape. Two small brass buttons were sewed on at the waist, in the small of his back. It was a copy of a French Army coat.

Balthazar held the *khanjar* in his left hand. The familiar, dry comfort of the bone grips filled his consciousness. He had not formed any specific plan as yet. He knew that in matters of this sort it was better to let instinct and the body's habit decide. The long hair on Henry's head attracted his attention. With his right hand he grabbed a handful of hair, yanking the man's head back and to the right, tipping his chin up until his eyes must have been filled with the quarter moon. He could see the spot he wanted in the side of the soldier's throat. The knife went in easily. The point was made for such work. Its narrow blade was fearfully sharp on both sides for the first few inches. A slight resistance assured him that he had found the windpipe. The tip grated on something which he knew must be the uppermost vertebrae. Balthazar forced the point higher, feeling for the hole in the bottom of the skull through which the spinal cord emerged. Resistance to the progress of his dagger ceased suddenly and the knife moved on an inch. It then wedged solidly against the walls of the *foramen magnum*. With a sharp twist of the wrist, he severed the man's spinal cord from his brain. All life instantly disappeared from the body. What had been a sentient being became dead weight. He kept his grip on the hair, feeling the oily mass between his fingers. The weight of the body was suspended for an instant from his right arm. He withdrew the blade, being careful not to damage the man more. The body fell to the ground.

Several men appeared at his side. "My God!" one whispered. "I never saw the like."

Balthazar looked at the knife, and the hand that held it. The blade was dark with blood, but his hand was clean. He reached down and took the dead man's hand, holding it as though in friendship. He wiped his weapon on the blue sleeve.

John Mosby came to his side. "That is quite a knife..."

Balthazar handed it to him, hilt first. "It was made for me in Fez. It fits my hand exactly."

Mosby held it up to the moonlight. The blade rippled with the watered silk loveliness of Damascus steel.

Balthazar took it back.

Two soldiers finished tying Evan's body across a saddle. Two more approached.

Balthazar gave one of them Henry's hand, then picked up the carbine, examining it in the moonlight.

"We should be off," Mosby said. "Others may arrive unexpectedly." He began to walk away.

"One moment, major."

Mosby turned back to face him. "Yes?"

"I am alone among you now. My government has given me an important task, important to you as well. I find that you have a droll sense of humor. In most circumstances I would find it amusing to indulge you, but I can not afford to be an object of ridicule. If you do it again, I shall be forced to take notice." This was said in a whisper that allowed an illusion of privacy, but which was heard by all nearby.

Mosby said nothing for a long moment. "Understood," he finally responded. Mounting his horse, he led his troops across Hunting Creek.

Balthazar watched him go, and then turned to find his animals.

Smoot waited at his elbow with all three. "I've got these two. You just keep up with him. He's not happy."

The others were nearly all across.

As they urged the horses into the water, Smoot's voice came to him. "You're not alone. I'm right behind you..."

Chapter 8

Rappahannock Station

-November 6th, 1863-
(Somewhere Near Culpeper, Virginia)

Jubal Early chewed reflectively. “If I understand correctly,” he said. “You met everybody of importance in Richmond. You must have been a busy man.”

He and Balthazar lounged in camp chairs built of tree branches. The weight and bulk of the two of them made those watching wonder if the interview would end in a general collapse of the furniture. They sat with their backs to the open end of a tent. You could see General Early’s field desk and camp bed inside. The chairs were angled toward each other so that discussion was easy but not too intimate. A bottle and two glasses stood on a small table.

The weather was clear and warm in an Indian summer display of generosity to those who lived in the forest. There were still birds singing in the trees.

Balthazar noticed a brown bird with a crest and an orange beak. As he watched a second arrived to sit beside the brown creature. This one was brilliant red in color. *Ah, the mate,* he thought. *I must ask of these birds.*

"Where've you been since then?"

"With General Lee's headquarters."

"And you're an officer of our army?" Early held a collection of official papers in a large hand. His morose features darkened in a frown. The reddish whiskers added to the effect. He spat a stream of brown liquid onto the green grass out in front of his boots. The stain lay there among others.

Balthazar liked him. The Gascon formed impressions of people at once. Sometimes these were quite wrong. He thought of Early as similar in character and physique to the mastiff that one of his English cousins once kept. As a boy, he feared the dog, but then came to know the kindness which the beast hid in his heart.

The general poured a couple of fingers of brown liquor into each glass.

Balthazar tasted his, expecting the silk, smoky sweetness of his first experience of American whiskey.

Raw, hot power slid down his throat.

He felt the warmth all the way down into his gut. "General Cooper thought it best that I should become a 'volunteer,'” he said. “I understand you have a number of these?" He looked quizzically at Early who spat again.

"Not enough!"

"No?" Balthazar shrugged. "In any event, he reasons that there will be fewer unanswered questions if I am taken by the United States authorities, and am truly one of your own...”

"The United States authorities..." Bitterness appeared in the other's slow, sharp edged speech.

Balthazar tried to remember what he had been told of this man. "You are a graduate of the military academy at West Point?"

Early dropped his chin in acknowledgment of it.

"But, you did not follow the profession of arms?"

The big, slope shouldered man heaved himself erect in the chair, and spat again. "No, never intended to, always wanted to be a lawyer. I left the army when I could and took up the law. I was Commonwealth's Attorney in Franklin County for a long time." He saw the lack of understanding on the other's face. "That's the state prosecutor. Was a militia officer as well, went to Mexico in fact." He laughed. "You probably haven't heard this, so you might as well know it from me first. I led the fight to keep Virginia in the old Union. Charles Devereux and I, we fought to the end at the secession convention. We only lost by one vote, one vote. It was that bastard Lincoln that caused our defeat. He wanted us to help him fight South Carolina! They were right all along, the secessionists were. The Yankees have always meant to rule us. This war proves that. They'll stop at nothing to have their way with us." He saw that Balthazar's glass was empty and poured.

"And you think you can win your independence?"

Early stared at him, looking for signs of mockery. "Yes... I do. We've hurt'em bad, killed'em in droves. They're not all crazy. If we keep on hurtin'em, and don't give up, who knows? The main thing is to wear'em down." He saw the doubt in Balthazar's face. "Not in material things!" he said quickly. "There are more all the time countin' those they're enlistin' in Europe. And then, there're the niggers, our own niggers by and large, since they don't have any to speak of." Early looked up at his orderly.

The uniformed black man stood a few feet away.

"Don't pay me any mind, Justus. You know who I mean..."

"I do gen'rul. You mean them trech'rous nigguhs goin' to the Northe'n side." He looked at Balthazar. "Them Yankees don't give a dam' for us cull'ed people. They jus' usin' us. We not fooled. After the war it'll be bettuh here."

Early continued to look at Justus for a second, and then turned back to his visitor. "He's right. The old way is dead. It was gonna die soon anyhow." He inclined his head toward the black man. "We'd be finished by now without their help. We're gonna be somethin' different afterwards, somethin' interestin'..." He spat again, wiping his lower lip with the back of a hand. "You look comf'table in that uniform," he said inspecting Balthazar's new clothing. "You want to paint those stars dark, or not wear'em. A lot don't. Sharpshooters are somethin' awful up in the line. They shoot better than they used to."

"You do not follow your own advice, my general." Balthazar smiled looking at the faded, corroded, three stars and wreath on Early's collars.

"Well, shit! They'd be crazy to shoot me. The Congress might make a mistake, and appoint somebody worthwhile. Besides, I'm not pretty enough to be taken for a general from a distance. Thomas Jackson was my only rival for shabbiness, and he's gone now. No, I'm safe enough. Well, you suit yourself. What'd you think of Cooper?"

"A deep subject."

Early smiled broadly. "That would be fair."

"I assume he is the chief of military information."

"What! Who said that? He's the Adjutant-General!" Early looked around to see who stood nearby.

"No one." Balthazar replied, pleased to know he had guessed well. "But, Seddon and Benjamin take him so seriously in my own case… And then, there is the way in which the British deal with these matters. The Adjutant-General is the responsible person for such business... One of his assistants brought me to you."

"You mean that red headed fellah, Jenkins?"

"The very one, a serious man."

"What about that one?" Early glared across the open space in front of the tent at Isaac Smoot.

Smoot sat on a stump twenty yards away staring back at him.

"I asked for the services of Sergeant Smoot. General Cooper was kind enough to honor my request. This is all so strange to me."

"Yes, you need a guide, but one of Mosby's men?"

Balthazar was surprised at the tone. "You do not care for them?"

Early grimaced, still looking at Smoot. "I don't like cavalrymen much. I don't like anybody who can get on a horse and ride away from a fight they started." He glanced at Balthazar. "They're good at that, and they ride off and leave my infantry at the same time! What's so funny?"

"My general, I think I used nearly the same words a few days ago, but I believe Sergeant Smoot to be a good fellow."

"Well, he don't appear to be afraid of me," Early muttered, still peering across the clearing. "That's somethin' in his favor."

"No, he does not fear easily. He is not afraid of Major Mosby..."

"Well hell! In that case... Sergeant!"

Smoot stood up.

"Come over here!

Smoot stood before them.

"I understand you've signed up to look after our visitor?"

"He can look after himself," Smoot replied.

"You know what I mean."

The partisan nodded.

"Sit down."

Smoot dragged another of the flimsy chairs up to face the two officers.

"So, what do you want to do, major? What are you after?" The soft brown eyes gleamed in a weathered face.

Balthazar mentally fingered the edges of the general's disbelief. "I must see your troops in the field. I must feel them; see for myself what they can do."

Early said nothing for a moment, then grinned and spat again. "You want a chaw, Sergeant?" he asked politely.

Smoot accepted the plug, worrying at the tobacco with a clasp knife to get an acceptable piece.

"I'm gonna send you up to Harry Hays first," Early said. An odd smile played at the corners of his mouth. "He has my Louisiana brigade. You may find them more familiar than the rest. I find them peculiar enough!" He chuckled, amused by his own words.

Balthazar was pleased. "But, that is marvelous. I have read of the 'Tiger Infantry.' It is they, I hope."

Early chortled, laughing aloud until the staff looked at him in alarm. He began to cough, hacking dryly for a moment until he managed to get the spasm under control. He sat there heaving silently, red in the face, a bandanna held to his mouth. "Sorry, I've had a cold. I'm really too old for this." He lowered the cloth from his lips. "Yes, it's them! There's another bunch of'em in the Stonewall Division, but they're all the same so far as I can see. They're not like these," he said, waving a hand at the surrounding camp.

"How so?"

"Oh! These are citizens in uniform. But, the Tigers, they started out with a lot of men that had been in other armies; Europeans, Walker filibusters from Nicaragua, Americans like Jim Wheat who had gone around the world lookin' for a fight, and found it.

"I may know Wheat," Balthazar said thoughtfully.

"Could be," Early opined, "but he's been dead for some time now. They added on Irishmen from New Orleans, a lot of Creoles, some Cajuns, farmers from upstate, and some fellahs who are said to be white as a matter of courtesy since they want to fight and are somebody's cousin, if you take my meanin'. It makes a rich stew. At Sharpsburg I found two of'em on the field after the last Yankee assault. They were goin' around lookin' for gold teeth in enemy heads, knockin'em out with rifle butts. Had pockets full of teeth, they did. One of my staff told'em to stop. They said he should 'go fuck himself'. They went right on with what they were doin'."

"Do they fight?"

"Always. They fight with ferocity and devotion to our cause. They also are infamous for desertion and crime against civilians, often against our own. You'll find that this is unusual in this army. These boys," he waved at the camp again, "are just home folks. But not the Tigers, they're somethin' real special.. Hope you like'em. Let's have another drink before you go! Sergeant, find a glass."

-10:00 A.M. 7 November – (The Rappahannock River)

In the morning sunshine, the chill of the previous night's sleep on the ground began to leave Balthazar's bones. He had a comfortably full belly. Smoot had made breakfast in the camp fire while Balthazar watched and offered advice. The sorrel mare between his knees moved with a rolling gait that had become comfortingly familiar.

He remembered that Joseph White had given him the reins while they waited for Smoot in the Devereux stable. "Mister Patrick's animal, sir," he said. "Miss Victoria wants you to have her. She has a tender mouth, sir."

Balthazar had wanted to see the man's face, but it had been hidden in the shadows. Then Joseph had led the horses away, following Smoot into the night.

Now, he leaned forward in the saddle to rub the neck just behind an ear. The head turned to look at him with a large, brown eye.

Balthazar and Smoot followed an infantry soldier down a dirt track toward a pretty river half hidden by overhanging trees. He thought there must be a bridge up ahead. Familiar sounds from that direction made him certain. Alongside the dusty road, a group of faded, weather stained tents stood under tall trees.

The trees reached out to him with slender branches. He looked at the leaves. They were of a kind unknown.

Then they waited in front of the tents.

Balthazar's inspection of the landscape was interrupted when a young officer came out of the biggest tent. An orderly held a horse while the man mounted. Balthazar stared in disbelief at the many rows of braid on the uniform sleeve.

"Here he is, colonel!" the escort soldier sang out, turning from the colonel to the major, watching to see what would happen.

Nothing happened.

Balthazar saluted the young man, who returned the greeting with solemnity.

The infantryman looked disappointed. "He speaks French," was offered hopefully.

The young colonel looked annoyed behind a wall of military courtesy. "Thank you, Higgins", he said to the rifleman. "My compliments to Major Lafleur." The man nodded and turned glumly away, and walked back up the track.

The colonel cleared his throat. "A courier brought news of your coming, major. Unfortunately, General Hays is absent as president of a court-martial. So, it is my pleasure to welcome you to Louisiana in Virginia, and the brigade. Wherever we are is Louisiana. My name is Davidson Penn. Welcome again!"

To Balthazar, he was something new, a senior officer who appeared to be so young that he might have no need to shave regularly. His immaculate uniform made an interesting contrast in the memory with Jubal Early's shabby dignity. "You are most kind, mon colonel. In General Hays' absence you command the brigade?"

"Yes."

It seemed impossible. Brigades of veteran infantry were not playthings for children. Perhaps something of this sentiment showed in his expression or tone of voice.

Penn grinned at him. "Actually, I am the senior colonel of the brigade."

"Et, vous etes Louisianien?" Balthazar asked in a moment of forgetfulness.

"Virginien en origine, mais j'etais avocat et commercant a New Orleans avant la guerre."

Balthazar was touched at the young man's willingness to speak French, but did not wish to push it too far. "And you are a West Point man as is General Early?"

"No, VMI."

Balthazar looked to Smoot.

"The state military school."

"Ah, yes. I have heard something of this place. General Jackson."

"One of my teachers," Penn replied.

"There are many of you from this school in the army?"

Colonel Penn shrugged in a curiously Gallic fashion. "There are several among the Louisiana troops, but in the Virginia regiments, they are everywhere. A number are in the ranks."

Balthazar found that astonishing. "But, they are needed as officers!"

The shrug came again, this time accompanied by a frown. "You have to understand, Major. A lot of us really insist that we are fighting for the kind of country Jefferson wanted. The VMI men in the ranks, they think that officers are European hogwash, tending toward aristocracy, and beneath the dignity of a gentleman."

Balthazar thought of Early. This fit. "But, this is completely Jacobin."

Penn's grin grew wider. "Without a doubt! I, obviously, only partly agree with these 'purer' spirits.

Smoot listened to this talk and decided to explain. "There's a whole crowd of these fellahs in Mosby's command, Major, more all the time. None of them want to be officers. The major, he doesn't like them much... They judge him, but, they're real useful."

Colonel Penn waited for Smoot to finish. "Look here, I need to go out to the vedette line. The cavalry sent word just now that our 'friends' are restless and are moving around. Want to come? We can continue our talk on the way."

The Rappahannock gurgled softly behind him.

Balthazar thought it the prettiest river he had seen in America. Steep, wooded banks crowded close to the water and covered the cool depths in shade. Beyond the stream, a low ridge climbed away into the distance.

The three men rode to a pontoon bridge across the stream.

Engineer troops clung to the sides of the structure, helping comrades in small boats repair some invisible defect in the cables which bound the pontons together.

As they clattered onto the planking of the bridge, Balthazar looked at the boats.

An officer stood in one of them. He wore grey trousers and a red and black checked wool shirt. A battered kepi rode on the back of his head. He raised it, holding it in one hand to shade his eyes and inspect the horsemen.

"Morning Cartwright!" Colonel Penn called out. Hear anything up ahead?"

The engineer grimaced as though in pain. "A little carbine fire half an hour ago, nothin' since. Let me know if we have to run! Me and the boys don't plan to be out on this dam' bridge with the Yanks tryin' to get on the other end!"

Penn smiled at the thought.

The Negro Pioneers in the boats did not seem impressed by his confidence. One of them raised his voice. "Don't you be laffin' 'bout this now, Cunnel! You go up theah and keep them folks away so us hones' so'jers can get on wif ouah wuk!" General laughter followed among the engineers.

Penn waved a hand in greeting as he rode through them.

"Come on boys!" a white sergeant said. "We've got them bad-ass Loosiana fellahs up front. Let's get these lashed back up so we can go get some grub!"

The little cavalcade clattered off the end of the floating bridge. The track sloped uphill between two swelling hillocks.

A deer appeared unexpectedly ahead. Its wide eyes filled with terror at the sight of them. Turning to flee into the forest, it heard the sound of soldiers above. The animal hesitated, swung back to look at them.

Penn stopped his horse.

The three sat quietly for a few seconds.

The doe gathered herself and leapt into the brush. The sound of her going receded along the bank of the Rappahannock.

The horses drove upward, passing below the crest on the left. The raw, red scar of trenches crowned this hill.

Colonel Penn waited for Balthazar at the top of the little pass. "There's another redoubt on a hill over there to the right." A sweep of his arm pointed the way. "You can just see it."

The red earth made it easy to see.

"The line runs around beyond that."

"What about this way?" Smoot asked, his meaning clear as an arm swept in the opposite direction.

"It goes southwest for half a mile and bends back to near the river." Penn spurred his horse forward.

They burst from the woods, cantering downhill across a grassy plain toward a small copse ahead.

Balthazar turned in the saddle to see the extension of the lines to the west. The ditch curved following the shape of the hills, disappearing behind the shoulder of one in the distance. A thin line of infantry lounged in the grass forward of the trench line. *This will be a force of tirailleurs,* he thought.

Cavalry waited in the grove.

Penn dismounted. He left his animal with them and stalked forward through the vegetation.

Balthazar nodded to a bearded, roughly clothed soldier while tying Patrick Devereux's mare to a tree. He and Smoot followed the Louisianan into the little wood. The same golden light shone before them through the brush.

Penn stood just inside the tree line on the far side with several others.

Balthazar avoided the group and placed himself a few yards away in the shade of a large tree.

Smoot came up beside to find him turning a leaf over in his hand.

"What is this?" he asked "It appears to be a species of oak, but the shape of this is..."

"Strange?"

"Yes."

"It's a White Oak."

"I see..." His gaze shifted back to the scene before them and to the enemy soldiers massed in the open ground. "This is intriguing. I suppose that this could be a reconnaissance, but I think we have approximately three thousand men before us."

Smoot stood silent.

The little group of cavalry officers around Penn bent toward the infantry colonel in animated description. "There were none an hour ago," one said. "Then they came through the oaks over there all at once. I lost half a dozen men who didn't get out from in front of them quick enough..."

"What do you think is behind?" Penn asked.

"No idea!"

Balthazar pondered the scene. Union infantry filled the vast meadow. They stood in long lines of battalion length. Their leaders gathered in little clumps to chat. They did not even look at the Rebel scouts only a short distance away. There were no flags.

"Major Balthazar!"

"Yes, my colonel?"

"Your opinion, sir?"

The stocky figure turned toward the cavalry leaders. "I have not had the pleasure..."

Penn smiled slightly. "This is Captain Anderson, and his officers."

Anderson nodded, "Cobb's Georgia Legion," he said. "How're you?" He held out a large, hard hand. While they shook hands he pointed to a lieutenant of cavalry in the group. "This fellow is named Faver, and this is my brother-in-law James Rawlins. He's our battalion adjutant."

Balthazar's hand made the rounds of the family circle. He found the thought so charming as to almost take his mind from the professional problem at hand. He remembered that Penn waited for an answer. "They follow our thinking in matters of tactics?"

"As slavishly as we."

He said nothing for a moment, looking around at the bright sunlight, the red-gold of the leaves and the earnest faces.

The circle of enlisted soldiers grew closer. They watched him skeptically, hoping a little, for what they knew not.

"My colonel, there should be fifteen thousand more back in the forest, just there..." he said pointing. He turned to Captain Anderson. "Have you seen more?"

The Georgian nodded, laughing a little. He indicated the south. "Just before you turned up, there was a column of dust beyond the trees over there. You could hear the guns. They were goin' south." He looked at the stocky brown figure.

"The wheels? You could hear the wheels?"

"Yes."

"How many?"

The brother-in-law spoke. "'Bout eighty by my count, mebbe a few mor'er less, mebbe.."

Balthazar turned back to Penn. "May I assume that this *tete de pont* is intended to prevent a crossing elsewhere?"

Colonel Penn bowed slightly from the waist.

Anderson was clearly fascinated by the discussion. "The fords are good below," he offered, hoping for a renewal of the talk.

"Too dam' good!" the brother-in-law growled. "They'll go over Kelly's Ford like shit through a goose!"

"General Lee expects that our presence will slow their advance there..." Penn spoke without looking at Balthazar directly. His eyes were fixed on the blue host.

"Ah! I see the strength of this position, the two *redans*, and first rate infantry within... I assume there is a battery? Yes?"

Penn nodded.

Balthazar waved a massive arm and shrugged. "Well, let them come! It will be a memorable affair. The ground is well chosen. General Lee's reputation as an engineer is sound. He fished in a jacket pocket. A short, black cheroot appeared in his fingers. He lit a match with one hand, puffing the little cigar to life and then looked around. "Ah! Mon Dieu! I forget everything in the tumult of the moment! You must pardon me!" He handed cigars around. He looked at the Union troops again, then back at the entrenchments, then at Penn. He glanced at Smoot.

The partisan's eyes were fixed on the Rebel officers. His face grew steadily grimmer. He avoided Balthazar's eyes.

None of the Confederates uttered a sound.

Balthazar sighed. "Ah! What is wrong? You know something that is not evident to me, a stranger... What could it be? I can see the enemy, and the ground. I can see our works, but I can not see all our strength. I can not see all..." He spun on a heel to look at the line of riflemen lounging on the grass outside the entrenchments. "No more than that?" he breathed. "This is not wise, my colonel. Not wise. Why has General Lee done this?"

"Unavoidable," Penn muttered. "It couldn't be helped. We lost too many men at Gettysburg, then more at Bristoe Station. Pickett's Division is in Carolina rebuilding. The rest of First Corps left for Georgia a couple of weeks ago.. Unavoidable. The other choice was to withdraw still further south. That was unacceptable."

After a second's thought with his head sunk on his breast, the Gascon looked up. "May I ask of your arrangements?"

"I will bring the rest of the brigade across the river, three companies..." Penn smiled at the thought.

Balthazar bowed slightly in acknowledgment of the joke.

"And, I will inform General Early of the... coming crisis in our affairs."

Balthazar bowed again. "You will excuse me? I would join your troops, to become better acquainted. Good day, gentlemen." He strode away, back through the oaks.

Smoot flipped his cheroot away, shook his head and followed.

A galloper bound for the pontoon bridge passed in a cloud of dust as they led their mounts across the red dirt road and up the gentle slope toward the Pelicans.

Some stood up, waiting to greet them, and hoping as soldiers always do for some interruption in the boredom of their lives.

Pat Devereux's mare picked her way through the deep grass, seeking the choicest, sweetest clumps. The hobbles kept her feet fairly close together, but she knew to move carefully, and did not seem unhappy.

Balthazar sat a few feet from her on the ground. He had made a small fire and was brewing Bedouin coffee. A boxlike contraption lay in the coals. The smell of roasted Mocha beans filled the air.

Smoot watched from a supine position off to one side, his head propped on a hand. "Need some help?" he asked.

The half dozen Louisianans with whom they had been conversing watched with interest to see if this might be true.

Balthazar found a small mortar in his saddle bag. He handed it to the American telling him to fill it with beans from the copper “shoe” lying in the hot coals. With the mortar in hand the Frenchman began to beat the beans into powder. The ringing bell-like sound brought more soldiers to their fire.

Soon several small brass coffee pots lay in the coals. Balthazar sat cross legged in front of them, chatting with the men and fussing with the pots. He sniffed one and poured its contents into another. He added a pinch of something from a small leather bag. Finally, he produced a stack of thimble size china cups. They had no handles. Holding them in one hand, he went around the circle of soldiers pouring a half inch of jet black, steaming liquid in each and waiting for the recipient to take it off the top of the stack. When each had his, Balthazar waited proudly, pot in hand.

They all stood motionless, watching him. He frowned. "But, my friends, you must drink it, a little at a time. It is quite strong." He made encouraging motions with the pot and his free hand. "Please!"

A swarthy captain held up his little cup in a hand missing two of the fingers. "Votre santé, mon commandant." He then tasted the brew. A smile creased his weathered features. "*Mais, c'est merveilleux! Il faut boire, mes enfants*! You must drink boys! My gran' maman she do'nt make coffee so good! You learn this from the Arabs?"

Balthazar nodded happily as he watched the diminutive cups empty before his eyes. He stepped forward to fill them again, but Smoot took the pot from his hand and made the rounds himself. Balthazar's saddle and other belongings were on the grass a few steps from the fire. The Sharps carbine that he had inherited from Henry was propped up on them.

A gaunt sergeant with three faded blue stripes on his jacket sleeves picked up the weapon, hefting it in his hand. "Where'd you get this, major?" he wanted to know.

"From a friend..."

"It's the latest model. I've only seen one other like it. That was off a fellah we caught up near Bristoe last month. You shot this yet?"

"No." Balthazar found the bandolier that Henry had worn. He held it out. "Show me, please."

The sergeant opened the chamber by levering the trigger guard down. Opening a pouch, he extracted a cloth covered cartridge. The lead bullet showed at one end. He slid this into the exposed opening of the chamber and raised the trigger guard to its original place. "When you pull it up like this the block comes up, closes the breech and cuts off the end of the bag." He looked at Balthazar to see if the foreigner understood.

"The bag burns when it is fired?"

"Yes, altogether," the Creole captain answered joining in. He watched as the sergeant examined the small pouches attached to the bandolier. "What are you doing, Roarke?"

The sergeant had opened another, smaller pouch, fishing in it with his large fingers. "That what's new about these, Cap'n. They use these caps now, not those dam' paper tapes. He held out a copper pellet, flat on the edges and rounded in the middle.

Balthazar rolled it between thumb and forefinger.

The sergeant cocked the carbine, pointing with a cracked fingernail to a small opening behind the nipple. "There's a magazine of those beneath. When the hammer drops, one goes on the nipple, and that's it." He lowered the hammer to the half cocked position and gave the gun back. "That's a sweet piece, Major, real sweet."

Balthazar held it at the balance. With his free hand he raised the leaf sight. It was marked for ranges up to a thousand yards. He looked off across the sloping grassy meadow at the Union skirmish line, visible in the distance to either side of the group of trees.

The Rebel cavalry had left the copse an hour before, riding back down the road to the pontoon bridge and the river.

Behind him, Balthazar heard Smoot curse. Looking back he watched the Virginian carefully pour the remains of one batch of coffee into a pot with a new brew underway.

Smoot was sucking the ends of several singed fingers of his left hand.

"But, you have learned so quickly, my friend," Balthazar said. "Soon I will be unnecessary. If someone could hold our horses it would be helpful." With this, he strode away from the fire, searching for something on the ground. Some distance off, he found a place to his satisfaction. It was flatter than most of the hillside. Holding the Sharps in one hand and bracing himself with one hand behind, he carefully lowered his massive torso to the ground.

As the soldiery drifted up behind him, they saw that he had seated himself at an angle of forty-five degrees to the Union line. Elbows braced against the inside of the knees, cheek against the stock, he peered at the blue line through the aperture of the tall sight.

A sandy haired private knelt beside him. "You gonna shoot sumbuddy or jus' scar'em?"

Balthazar did not reply.

"I never saw nobody sit like that to shoot," the soldier said, "an' I been shootin' all my life."

Balthazar did not raise his head from its place with a cheek alongside the stock. "I was taught that a comfortable seat is essential for long work. Bone to bone support between elbow and knee makes for steadiness. What do you suppose the range to be out to their line?"

A motion to his right made the Gascon look up.

The sergeant with black hair, three stripes and a full beard laid his own rifle down on the grass a few feet away. It was the man named Roarke. A telescopic sight ran almost the length of the rifle's heavy barrel. Roarke produced a small brass device from a vest pocket. It was made of two parts that slid together. Etched lines and numbers ran along one side. He held the tool up so as to look through an aperture in the center between the two sliding halves. He made a sound of discontent and removed his round, high crowned felt hat, finding it to be a problem. He then adjusted the opening until a blue soldier just filled it from his boots to the top of his forage cap. He looked down at the scale on the range finder, and smiling through his black beard said, "nine hundred yards, sor!"

Balthazar turned back to contemplate the Northern host. He ran the muzzle of the Sharps across their ranks, searching. He found a group close together. They must be officers. Even at that distance their posture proclaimed their rank. He chose the tallest. The knob on top moved the slide of the sight up to "900".

Placing the Union officer in the notch of the sight, he took a breath, held half of it, and squeezed, thinking of Victoria Devereux, thinking of the texture of the skin of her arms, thinking... The carbine jumped in his arms. You could almost see the heavy bullet in flight, the long, arching, ballistic curve, the descending angle.

The group of Federals prostrated themselves on the ground. The soldiers in ranks to either side leapt back, some joining the officers flat down and others shaking their fists across the distance.

"Merde! I have missed!"

"Where'd you aim?" the sharpshooter demanded with professional curiosity.

"But, at the knees! I was certain that this would place the bullet somewhere in the chest...

"Should have..."

Behind the lines of enemy infantry, the trees shook with the coming of the guns. Out of the forest in a thunder of iron shod wheels and hooves, a dozen batteries charged.

Balthazar watched with admiration.

The columns of artillery advanced at the gallop through the gaps between brigades of foot. A hundred yards to the front they spun in the lethal dance which would bring them into "battery", each with its six guns in line, prepared to fire.

"My, my!" the sharpshooter muttered.

Balthazar followed his pointing finger.

The federal infantry, frightened momentarily by Balthazar's shot had taken heart from the presence of their artillery friends, and resumed their places in the ranks. Behind the lines two men knelt beside a still, dark figure.

With a grimace, Balthazar returned to watching the gun drill unfold each battery into a line of pieces behind which stood limber and caisson at precise intervals. The separate columns of equipment and animals extended back away from the trail of each gun. Cannoneers and drivers took their places. The horses waited patiently, mercifully unknowing of what might come.

The right hand gun in one of the center batteries fired a solid shot. It sailed across the meadow, striking the hill a hundred yards away and bounding over the crest to smash and shatter the small trees beyond in its downhill progress to the river.

Patrick's mare reared and shook her head in alarm at the sounds.

The Louisiana infantry turned as one man and walked calmly up the gentle slope toward the trench line above.

Smoot began to gather their belongings into a pile through which he sorted quickly.

Balthazar took his saddle bags from the pile, stuffing the pockets with the speed of long practice. "Sergeant, will you take the horses and our equipment back to our bivouac, and wait for me?"

"The hell I will!"

The French officer looked at him with interest. "No?"

"No!" Smoot returned his scrutiny defiantly, continuing his hurried preparations without turning away.

Balthazar smiled at him. "You are a good man, Isaac Smoot, but I would not lose my cousin's mare. I might not be forgiven... I ask you to accommodate me in this, please. I am not your commander. I can not order you..." He knew that these words would compel obedience in someone like Isaac Smoot.

Smoot handed him the Sharps, the bandolier of ammunition and tools that accompanied it and then, while the stocky officer watched, he saddled the two horses.

The single cannon coughed again. A round shot grew spectacularly from a black point to something resembling a billiard ball. It arched across the sky, struck the ground below them and bounded up the slope, spinning and turning as it came.

Smoot stepped back out of the space it would occupy.

They watched the thing bounce once between them.

The horses threw back their heads in terror of the hissing black death.

"Go now!" Balthazar demanded. "They have no one but us to shoot at!"

Smoot swung up into the saddle, took the mare's reins from Balthazar's hand and kicked his mount into a trot, headed for the high ground and the bridge beyond.

Balthazar looked once more at the blue army below.

A tiny figure mounted on a tall, black horse waved his kepi across the distance.

Balthazar took off his wide brimmed hat. With the hat held to one side, he bowed deeply. Then, with his back to the enemy, he plodded up the long green slope with the carbine reversed and held on a shoulder and the muzzle in one hand. As he walked, the ammunition belt settled more comfortably across his chest.

At the top of the hill, the Rebel infantry watched him come. Several smiled at his gesture to the Yankee officer.

"Armand!" cried the Creole captain who had so enjoyed the coffee.

"Oui, chef!" said a man standing beside the soldier who had been helpful to Balthazar in knowing the range.

"You must shoot me that officer, the one who made the bow! The noble Jackson, you remember his words to us at Kernstown?"

"But, yes, *mon capitaine*! He said that we should always kill the brave, that they must die that we may live to welcome the rest as visitors to our country. Roarke!"

The big Irishman held the heavy, telescoped rifle in his arms as a musician holds his instrument. "Yes, First Sergeant!"

"Come! We shall slaughter this gallant gentleman..."

Together they walked to one side, climbing out of the trench to find a comfortable spot.

Balthazar saw them go. *"Go, mon vieux... Go now!"* he said in his inner heart.

As he came to the red lip of the entrenchments, he looked down to see friendly faces upturned.

A corporal reached up for the Sharps with a brown-sleeved arm. "Let me he'p yeh, majuh.."

The sniper rifle banged.

Balthazar tried to remember the last time he had seen artillery deployed with such perfection of formation and drill. He thought he remembered that the Russian guns on the Alma had looked something like this

If we had a few more guns of our own, they would not escape... he thought. *They could not then stand before us so boldly in all their glory.*

As if in response to his thought, the four rifled "Parrots" of the Louisiana Guard Light Artillery spoke from within the redoubts, the shells bursting over the gun line, bringing down men and animals in sprawled disorder.

The Grand Battery below then opened fire from right to left in one long, rippling wave of smoke and fire, the guns jumping in recoil before their report could be heard, the smoke hiding each piece in turn. Shells shrieked over the ridge. The crash and flash of the explosions in the river valley below rolled back over the crest.

Balthazar looked at the men around him.

A few inspected him, watching for a reaction to the barrage. A number leaned on the parapet of the trench, elbows spread, chewing slowly, contemplating the enemy. Most sat in the bottom, lining the sides, knees almost touching. Several seemed to be asleep. Most of the rest managed to look bored.

Balthazar smiled, knowing that he was among his own kind.

The bombardment continued for an hour. Most of the projectiles went over the top, clearing the crown of the hill by less than six feet. After a while, the men began to show the effect of the strain of the close passage of so much death. The whispering, sibilant sound of solid shot and shells seemed the very voice of the devil, of Satan himself.

Soldiers gathered in little knots in the places where communications trenches and traverses came together. Occasionally, a shell burst somewhere above spewed hot metal into the huddled bodies.

In the midst of the shelling, word was passed from man to man that help had come.

From the mouth of a trench leading down to the river a steady stream of "Butternuts" began to emerge. They turned right to pass just beyond Balthazar's toes.

"Who're y'all?" a man beside him inquired of the newcomers.

"54th North Carolina," a soldier rasped in passing. "You fellahs got enough Yankees up here?" he asked and was gone.

The Louisianan scratched the side of his face, glanced up at the sound of rushing metal above, and back at the French officer. "Hoke's Brigade, good fighters. We'll be all right now..." He looked confident.

At the tail end of the column of Carolinians, Jubal Early appeared at the mouth of the ditch which ran up from the river bank. He stopped at the trench junction, straightening his back and peering about.

A solid shot struck the earth and bounded over them.

Early crouched slightly for a moment; a look of annoyance crossed his face.

Balthazar raised his hat in greeting from his seat in the bottom of the entrenchment a dozen feet away.

Early came to squat beside him. "Whut d'yuh think?" he asked without ceremony.

The Frenchman grinned back at him. "I think you should not put any more troops into this bridgehead..."

"No?"

Balthazar shook his head. "I do believe we are about to be overrun. You should leave, my general. Now!"

"What about you? A foreign fellah like you, no need for you..."

Balthazar laughed aloud. He was looking down the length of trench to the next traverse.

Four riflemen were peering back at him with interest.

"How many friends have you brought us, sir?"

"About five hundred. They're filling holes in the line over on the left... It isn't enough, and I can't pull you out." Misery showed in the big man's eyes.

"No," Balthazar replied. "The river looks to be too deep, and there is only the pontoon bridge. This appears to have been a miscalculation."

Early nodded. "They're across the river at Kelly's Ford. General Lee won't let me withdraw. You'll have to fight it out. Have you seen young Penn lately?"

"He's down 'round this tr'verse, Gen'rul", one of the four riflemen sang out.

The general lurched to his feet.

Balthazar grasped him by the sleeve. "Do not be so foolish as to stay, my general!"

Early looked down at him.

"You must not!"

The bearded figure nodded once, and walked away, disappearing around the corner.

The sun slid toward the far horizon. It guttered orange and red to the West.

After an eternity of dissonance, the cannonade stopped abruptly.

The Confederates hesitated a few seconds, crouched in upon themselves, and waiting for it to start again.

Balthazar was among the first to raise his head. He felt his way up the trench wall with his fingertips until he could see over the top.

A solid wall of blue filled the grassy space below.

He rubbed his eyes to get the grit out of them. He had tried to keep them covered during the shelling but, nevertheless, tiny, hard edged objects had found spaces between his fingers.

"Damn you! Damn you! Damn you!"

The man beside him had climbed up on the parapet, and stood shaking his fist at the advancing multitude.

"God will curse you, you Yankee bast'ids! And, if he don't we're gonna do you right here!"

"Get down, William, you damned fool!" an officer bawled, "and start in on sendin' 'em to hell where they belong!"

The Second Corps of the Army of the Potomac marched to the bottom of the slope and started up the long incline.

Guns of the Louisiana artillery opened fire with canister from the *redan* to Balthazar's right.

Considerable holes opened in the blue mass, torn by the well sighted fire of the four guns. The gaps closed with a terrible constancy as the mass of federal troops pressed on up the hill.

"At will! Commence firing!" a bearded young man wearing the two stars of a lieutenant colonel yelled from nearby.

One rifle fired, then two or three, and then many rifles fired all at once with the ripping, ragged noise that meant everyone was shooting. Ramrods rattled for reloading while those late in the first volley shot at specific people in whom they had developed an interest.

Balthazar got the Sharps up onto the parapet and flipped up the sight. He looked at the marksman, Roarke, a few feet away.

"Three fifty," the Creole sergeant, Armand said from behind. "I will give you the ranges, *mon commandant.* I suggest the one mounted so well on a grey behind the center division..."

"Ah yes!" Balthazar willed himself into a state of indifference to the oncoming throng. Again he thought of Victoria...

The grey horse ran wildly to the rear, scattering men, dragging a boneless sack of blue from a single stirrup.

"Three hundred. Perhaps a color sergeant of the center regiment?"

"Which?"

The roar of musketry and the metal clamor of the infantry's loading filled his head.

He thought of their own artillery, and looking that way, he saw the barrel of one Parrott lying atop a broken wheel outside the redoubt. Two of the Southern guns were still in action. These remaining pieces were trading blows with the whole artillery force below. Fire from two dozen guns descended in converging trajectories searching, searching.

"Will they go? Will they leave us?" he asked pointing with his chin at the remaining Confederate guns.

"No," Armand replied. "We are their countrymen. They will not go. Two hundred!"

"I know the range now."

The Federal infantry came up the hill leaning forward against the bullets as though they were hail.

Balthazar fished in his ammunition pouches and lined up a handful of cartridges on the lip of the trench. Methodically he loaded and fired at the blue figures that grew rapidly in size, detail and individuality before him.

A hundred yards away they broke out of the measured step that had brought them this far behind their flags and drums. The front line charged at him. It seemed that every man along a thirty yard stretch of regimental frontage was looking directly at him. The beards and red, straining faces grew and grew as he fired into them. They reached the *abatis.*

He shot a corporal in the head that was in the act of tearing at the interwoven branches.

The man fell heavily, wailing and clutching at himself.

To either side, the Tigers raged at the Union infantry, raged and fired in a blinding fury. Men howled and emptied their weapons at their enemy trapped for a moment in the embrace of the bony arms of the dead trees in the *abatis.*

Roarke, Armand and their captain scrambled out of the trench, and ran forward to grapple with a color party in the obstacles.

Seeing them go, the Tiger infantry scaled the earthen barrier to join them. Rumbling deep in their chests, they cleared the top. On their feet, in the forest of deadwood, the Rebel yell ripped from them to echo across the darkening land.

Balthazar found himself in their midst. He pushed between two riflemen to reach the front of the moving mass. Behind him he could feel the charge of the Tigers as he raced to the fight around the colors.

Armand lay writhing on the ground.

His captain held a U.S. flag in his arms and stood astride the soldier from which he had taken it.

Roarke fought with clubbed rifle to make a space around his friends.

Balthazar shot an officer with the Sharps carbine.

The blue lieutenant fell across Armand's legs.

The Frenchman drew his pistol with a free hand. The big Lemat jumped in his grip taking a man full in the face at a distance of four feet. He then killed two more with the scatter barrel as they reached to tear the flag from the Creole officer's hands.

The Tiger onslaught passed them by.

In the shadow of their ranks, he looked across the brightness of their courage into the fading light of the orange dusk. Across the backs of the fighting line, he peered down the endless distance to the woods.

A bullet hummed past his cheek. He brushed his face with the back of the hand that held the pistol, too intent on what he saw to pay much attention.

The Union assault began to give ground, driven back by the ferocity of the assault.

Across the distance, he watched the Grand Battery limbered up.

They will move closer in case the infantry needs more help in finishing us, he thought.

In the middle ground, in unending ranks of blue black uniformity more Federal infantry advanced. On they came, on and on, at the "double-quick", pounding up the grassy slope.

The earth was suddenly, overwhelmingly full of Union soldiers.

Roarke went down, stabbed through the body as the lines came together again.

Balthazar shot the victor in this little fight as he stood above the Irishman with a foot on Roarke's chest, trying to pull out his bayonet.

Roarke crawled away, moving on his belly toward the river.

The sun set.

Nightfall came on the hill with a suddenness that broke the combat into a crowd of invisible, but clearly audible fights.

A Union officer came at him from the left swinging a heavy sword in a powerful, descending blow aimed at the juncture of neck and trunk.

Balthazar brought the Lemat up and fired full in the face.

The head snapped back. The dim figure slipped to the ground, holding its face, screaming with an oddly muffled sound from behind the fingers.

Behind the dying officer, more riflemen appeared. Their bayonets filled the night, searching for him.

Confederate infantrymen grappled on all sides with their enemies. They were dark forms swinging clubbed muskets. In the midst of the fight Balthazar was surprised to hear them curse and scream, transported with feeling.

Next to him a Tiger beat a Yankee's head against the ground, and then battered the man's face with a stone to finish the job before turning his attention elsewhere.

Union soldiers fell before their wrath to left and right, but their places were filled by the blue tide flowing in through the *abatis*. The Yankees were everywhere, surging, pressing, cheering as they reached the trenches and swept past.

Abruptly, he was alone. He looked for his comrades, but they were not to be found among the still forms nearby. He backed away up the ground that led through the *abatis*. He stepped on something that moaned. He bent to see who it was.

An enemy soldier lunged through the darkness.

He clubbed the man with the barrel of the Sharps and then kicked him in the head to be sure.

It was now very dark.

He was a strong man. The blood of ancestors bred for the burden of chain mail and the weight of edged weapons was full in him. Grunting with the strain, he put Roarke across a shoulder and made his way to the rear, picking his direction cautiously through the deepening blackness, avoiding the sounds of victory that meant danger. He leapt the trench and moved to the right, seeking a route down the back of the hill. Below and to his left he heard a metal ringing, a clamor of voices, and the staccato crackle of small arms. Through the trees, he saw that the bridge was in flames. The last remaining artillery piece from the bridgehead was on the bridge. It was wedged between two pontons. One wheel was off the treadway and hanging down in the river. Around it the crew fought with sponge and rammer staffs against the Federal troops who had caught up with them. The bridge had been fired from the southern side of the stream. Flames spread along the planking and among the boats toward the combat in mid-stream.

Balthazar turned away. Settling his burden with a shrug of the shoulders, he went on down the slope. Holding the Sharps by the barrel, he used it as a walking stick to brace himself on the steep and treacherous ground. At the bottom, he found himself standing unexpectedly in a foot of water. The far bank was almost invisible, hidden by rising mist and drifting smoke. Behind him the brush shook and snapped ominously.

He waded out into deeper water. The current pulled at his legs. The cold felt at him, reaching with icy fingers for his groin.

Roarke groaned.

Balthazar looked down.

The wounded man's hand trailed in the black water, his fingers recoiling from the chill.

Balthazar pulled him around in front of his body so that Roarke's mouth was against his chest. He stepped farther into the stream, wading out until the cold water reached his arms. Holding Roarke under the chin, he pushed off, swimming for the other side with powerful scissor kicks. Intent on finding his way across the fast running river, he hardly noticed the rifle fire and drifting clouds of gun smoke from the banks.

The raging fires consuming the bridge lit up the surface.

Bullets splashed in the water nearby.

He kicked harder. The bank was close.

Surely the Christ of my fathers, the living Christ, will not leave me now. There is so much left to do.

The sheltering darkness of the shadow of the bank hid them.

Men splashed into the water. Hands took Roarke's weight from the leaden paralysis of his right arm.

Someone gripped his body around the chest to drag him up out of the killing numbness.

He tried to make his feet operate. Stumbling into a tiny "run," he grabbed at tree roots and low hanging branches. He used the massive muscles of his back to haul himself up onto solid ground five feet above.

An encircling arm braced him in his ascent.

Standing in the brush with the fiery light of the bridge on his face, Balthazar turned to see Smoot. He straightened his back, arching the curve in the spine to ease the stiffness. "I asked you to wait at our bivouac."

Something passed on Smoot's face which could have been annoyance, or perhaps amusement. "I brought a couple of blankets. I'll get you one." He turned toward the road that Balthazar knew must be close by.

Two men carried Roarke noisily through the brush beside the river.

Balthazar followed, shivering uncontrollably in the wintry cold.

In the road there was a party on horseback, a dark, huddled mass of shifting men and snorting animals. Two were apart, deep in conversation. The others waited quietly.

The unknown benefactors carried Roarke into the open, laying him on the ground where he rolled slowly from side to side clutching his hurt.

Smoke drifted by. It reeked with the acrid, creosote smell of tarred wood.

Balthazar knelt by the side of his new friend. He took a blanket from Smoot's hands and tucked it around the big man. "You will be fine, do you understand?" he said. "You will live to fight again."

Roarke reached up to grasp Balthazar's lapel with a bloody fist. "Find the boys, major. Find them that's left. You belong with us. I'll see you..."

A stretcher party took him away.

"I'll take that, major." Smoot whispered while prying the barrel of the Sharps from Balthazar's frozen fingers. Leaning the carbine against a tree, he wrapped another blanket around the shivering man's shoulders.

Jubal Early dismounted and came to stare into his face. "My Gawd! it is you! I thought you were gone for sure."

Lee walked his grey horse to them, looking down in the dimness, saying nothing at first.

Smoot stepped back, took off his hat. "Evenin' Gen'ral Lee," he said softly.

Lee nodded, pausing in his inspection of the Frenchman to look at the ranger. After a moment, he smiled. "I remember now. You came from Washington last spring with information. Turn your head, sergeant," he said and after he had looked said, "I am happy to see that you heal well."

Smoot looked away, his eyes filled with tears.

"Your men fought well, mon general," Balthazar rasped. "They are a credit to their people, and to you." His teeth chattered uncontrollably as he forced the words out. "In particular I would wish to commend the young Colonel Penn. A brave soul!"

"A pity," Lee muttered. "A pity!"

Early said nothing. His face was hidden as he stared at the far shore and the burning remnants of the bridge of boats.

Gripping the blanket tightly, holding his elbows against his ribs, Balthazar drew himself up to his full height. "May I ask a favor, mon general?"

"What do you want, John?" Early rasped invisibly.

"I would stay with the Tigers. You were correct. I find them..." He searched for the word.

"I am sure General Early will have no objection..." Lee said.

Jubal's laughter rang in the woodland, loud enough to cause the Yankee troops across the stream to yell at them in derision. "Glad to have you, John, glad to have you! Come see me tomorrow. Got somethin' in mind for you. Smoot, go thaw him out. Get!"

The saddle horses waited deep in the forest where Smoot had tied them.

Balthazar rubbed the mare's nose, and then mounted to follow through the trees. He rolled from side to side for a minute, thinking of the animal's owner, thinking...

Smoot looked back, surprised by the gentle snoring.

Balthazar slumped in the saddle, his fingers clenched in the mane, the blanket hanging from one shoulder.

The Ranger tucked it around him more tightly, and then led the mare toward the embers of their fire. He could just see it now through the sycamores.

Chapter 9

The Battalion

In the silver light of dawn, Hays' Brigade formed for muster in a clearing south of the river. First sergeants called the roll. Officers searched in the ranks for familiar faces. This led to questioning of those present and ended in the shaking of many heads.

They had come back to this place in the night. They came in small groups, groping their way through the dripping forest, carrying their wounded, shocked with the suddenness of their defeat at the hands of the hated and despised enemy.

Hays stood before them to watch his adjutant assemble the returns. He faced the thin ranks with hands clasped behind his back, unspeaking, fearful of the fact of his losses, knowing, but not wishing to know the truth.

Jubal Early waited with him. He had nothing to say. In one hand was a tin mug of something steaming.

The morning was cold. Men's breath hung in the air about them. The water poplars loomed over their small numbers.

Behind Early, Balthazar stood with Smoot. A little sleep wrapped in a rubber ground cloth had returned him to life.

"Four hundred and ninety-seven, sir," the adjutant reported, his saber hilt at his lips. The blade swung down until the point neared the frost rimmed earth.

"Sweet Jesus!" Hays cried out, unable to hide his emotion.

"Six hundred missing," one of the staff muttered.

Hays faced the division commander to make his report.

"All right, Harry," Early grumbled. "Don't brood on it too much. It's never as bad as it seems at first... We may get some back. More will come from Louisiana. They always do, somehow,"[1]

Hays' features showed that he took little comfort from these words.

Early's hard, bearded face watched him with concern. "It wasn't your fault, Harry. We all know that. *He* knows it. We're goin' back 'bout ten miles, back in front of Culpeper. You lead... Be ready in an hour."

"Yes, general," Hays said as he walked away.

Early beckoned.

Balthazar crossed the grass, saluting with all the dignity he could summon from stiff joints.

"Oui, mon general?"

Had Coffee?"

"No."

"Justus!" Early pointed with his mug to Balthazar and Smoot.

---

1 500 came back of their own volition, exchanged a month before the Wilderness.

Justus brought an enameled pot from a glowing heap of coals at the edge of the grass.

They stood together savoring the warmth and aroma of the brew.

"I would like your help," Early began. He glanced at Balthazar, looking for a reaction.

The Frenchman swirled his coffee around, and around.

"The troubles we've been havin'..." the general continued, "A whole lot of regiments beaten up.., bits and pieces broken off..." He looked at Balthazar again.

Nothing showed in the foreigner's face.

Early frowned. "I've got some Texans, Marylanders, Virginians, even some Louisianans, 'bout two hundred and fifty in all."

Balthazar was looking at him now.

Early smiled, looking more confident. "I'd appreciate it if you'd take 'em in hand for a couple of weeks. These fellows have lost all their officers, some of 'em are new people, from home. Some are..." His voice trailed off.

"What? Some are what?" Smoot demanded.

Balthazar held up a hand.

Smoot looked at it and cleared his throat.

"You were saying, sir?" Balthazar asked.

"Well, they need trainin', they need organization, they need..."

Smoot blew his nose on a big, red bandanna.

Balthazar waited.

Tell me, mon general, he thought. *Just tell me.*

Early stopped talking. He drew in a breath, letting it out slowly. The white fog of his exhalation seeped from his lips. He sighed. "John, we've had a number of Northern soldiers come over in the last few weeks. Some are foreign, others are real Yankees, but most are our men who joined the enemy to get out of prison. Their own don't want some of 'em back. I don't want to take official note of 'em... The law, you know the law about, deserters. General Lee... Will you take this whole lot?"

Smoot snorted in disgust, opened his mouth to say something, and then thought better of it.

Balthazar was immersed in thought.

Early waited for a moment hopefully, then sighed and threw the remnants of his coffee to one side. "I'll find someone else. I know you're not here to do this, but I don't have anyone who can do what I think you can do, and after last night... Well, I hoped you could help me out with this for a few days..."

Balthazar waved a hand in deprecation. "I am pleased that you would make me such an offer. I am, after all, a stranger, but I have found over the years that it is not a good idea to have one officer train a *bataillon de marche* and another lead it in battle. Such units are inherently unstable and a matter of personalities. Therefore I would ask that you allow me to retain command so long as my conduct is satisfactory."

Smoot stared at him in amazement.

Balthazar reached into a pocket. The string of red stone beads appeared in his fingers. "As I said, I had hoped to stay with the Tigers."

Early bit a chaw of tobacco from a twist. He chewed reflectively for a moment, settling the plug in one cheek before speaking. "It's yours as long as you want, if you'll keep it, I'll see that you get all these strange folks as they come along."

"Not just the Yankee deserters?" Smoot wanted to know.

"No, all of them"

The partisan nodded, comforted by the thought.

"I will, of course, continue to report to my government."

"Of course."

"One more thing."

"What's that?"

"Smoot will be second in command."

"He belongs to Mosby."

Balthazar said nothing. The beads clicked.

Early spat. "What do you say?" he asked the cavalryman.

Smoot felt his scar, smiled and said, "John Mosby has a lot of men."

Early laughed, tilting his head to one side as he did so. "He's yours. Mosby will raise hell, but I'll ignore him. He's yours. What'll you do with them?"

"I will make of them a *Corps D'elite.* They will be your personal reserve."

"Thank you. Thank you. Major Hale will show where they are." He shook their hands, and walked away.

Justus held his horse by the embers of the cook fire.

He took the reins from the black man, and mounting rode into the woods, going south, away from the Rappahannock.

All through that cold and windy day, the army fell back along farm roads to the southwest. The rear guards held the enemy at arms length without much trouble.

The Yankees seemed disoriented by their success. They did not push hard and the greatest menace was the frost.

At one point a company of Carolinians looked back from a low ridge near Brandy Station to see an astonishing thing. Coming across the vast plain east of the station were Federal troops in line of battle behind their cannon and flags. Their front was a mile and a half wide.

The ragged Southerners stopped to watch in admiration.

On they came in unending precision, the lines expanding and contracting around obstacles in the ground.

The Rebels turned from them to continue their retreat to the south.

Balthazar took charge of his new command the next day.

The division provost marshal was happy to give them up. They were an embarrassment. These men said they wanted to fight for the South, but what could one believe of some of these? Among them there was little common ground.

The soldiers who had lost their regiments did not want to be with the Northern deserters. No one knew what to think of the Confederates who had come back wearing blue.

The Frenchman got them all together around a big fire in a crossroads settlement outside Culpeper. It was dark and cold. Men stood silently, shivering and beating their hands against their sides. Some still wore Union Army overcoats, but that was not unusual in Lee's army. A number had wrapped blankets around themselves to keep the heat in. Too many breathed raggedly and coughed with a sound that made you know they were on the edge of sickness from exposure.

The fire burned huge in the night. It was so big and hot that some moved away from it to get relief. Because of this, the circle around the hill of flame was large enough to hold them all.

Balthazar stood facing them in a brown mackinaw coat, a smile on his face. In one hand were the red beads.

At first they could not see his eyes under the brim of his hat. He noticed that and looked around for a place to lay it down. In the end, he gave it to a soldier in a blue coat who stepped forward to take it.

They had eaten well. Smoot knew people in the neighborhood. Smokehouses were not as empty as the commissary department thought.

Balthazar began to speak. It wasn't much of a speech. He told them that he was glad to meet them, and that the circumstances that brought them together were remarkable. He said he knew that they must feel very much alone in this new place and with these new people. He said that he was as much alone as they, that he had come to America to see the war, and now knew that it was not right to stand to one side and watch. He told them that he had been at war for a long time. He mentioned the places where he had fought, and the men with whom he had served. He introduced Smoot. He said that Smoot would be the only other officer for a while, but that the most experienced among them would be made leaders for the time being.

Smoot's faded chevrons made some frown in puzzlement, but they said nothing.

A red faced soldier in butternut wanted to know why he sounded like an Englishman.

Another, a young man in grey with a Louis Napoleon beard, asked him a question about Zouave drill, a very technical question.

A third asked if they could go back to their home regiments, if they could find them.

"Certainly. I will be happy to help any who wish to do so, but for the moment General Early asks that we make a 'battalion of demonstration' to see what is the good of applying the methods of training which I have used in the Army of the French."

He was pleased to see that Early's name meant something.

"What's that mean?" a soldier asked. His voice was empty of Dixie's music.

"It means," said the young man in grey, "that you are going to work your ass off."

Balthazar smiled at him. "Quite so. We will all 'work our asses off'. Company and battalion drill, route marches, battle drill of a kind I have myself devised, much time at marksmanship practice..."

Several laughed derisively.

"We know you boys can shoot," Smoot said from nearby, "but you ain't never seen this man shoot."

"And what do we get in return?" a man with a New England accent wanted to know.

Silence ringed the fire under the stars. The wind whistled in the bare trees, sweeping down on them, pushing the flame far out over their heads for a second. The wind was a knife between the shoulders.

"You will have whatever it is that you came for," Balthazar said in a voice so low that they leaned forward to hear, "You will have whatever it is that you have stayed for, or have come back for. That is all that you will have. Now! We are so lucky this night as to have the use of the buildings of this lovely little village." He swept the dimly seen outlines of the houses with a gesture. "The inhabitants have left for the time being. They, quite understandably, do not wish to offer their hospitality to our Yankee friends. I would ask you to remember that the absent villagers are *our countrymen*. Good night."

The words hung in the air among them, an emblem of their shared purpose.

They drifted away to the buildings, some looking over their shoulders, their faces indistinct in the darkness.

Smoot brought the soldier in grey to Balthazar.

The young man stood at "attention" before the battalion commander. He looked as though he might be twenty-five years old. He was darkly handsome and clearly something of a dandy by his dress.

In the flickering light of the log fire, Balthazar saw the red braid on his trousers and a metal cap badge. It was a pelican. Looking at the uniform he thought to himself, *This man has private means.*

"What is your unit?"

"The Louisiana Guard Artillery, sir. I was at Rappahannock Station..."

"In the redoubts?"

"Yes, major. My piece was dismounted by fire... I believe you were there as well?"

Balthazar nodded. "You are professionally trained?"

The man grinned. He had a lot of white teeth in a deeply tanned face. "I was dismissed from West Point in December of '60 for making insulting and disloyal statements about the president-elect. I went home and joined the militia."

"You are a cannoneer?"

"No. I am a sergeant gun captain. I've never gotten around to sewing the stripes on."

"In most armies that would be reason to reduce you to the ranks."

The gun captain smiled.

Balthazar looked around at Smoot.

The Virginian seemed busy pushing things around in the fire.

The French soldier returned his attention to the man before him. "Your name?"

"Harris, Raphael Harris."

"You are from New Orleans?"

"Yes, sir."

"Sergeant, I would like you to accept the position of acting adjutant of this battalion. Lieutenant Smoot and I will need your help in this matter. There is little time. We begin to make order and to train in the morning. Do you accept?"

Harris opened his mouth, closed it, looked at Smoot, and said yes.

"Good! Bring your kit to that farmhouse. We must talk of other appointments. Do you know anyone who might make an *adjutant-chef*, a sergeant-major?"

Harris seemed rooted in front of him. "Sir," he began. "I am not seeking advancement..."

Balthazar's face contorted in irritation. "Yes! Yes! I know. You do not wish to be an officer. Smoot has told me of this divine madness which infects you gentlemen. I find it fascinating, perhaps enchanting. Seductive might be a better word. We can discuss it later. I will force this on no one, but I need your help. D'accord?"

"D'accord, chef."

- 9 November - (Washington, D.C.)

John Wilkes Booth was in exceptional form. He was not hoarse. His tendency to declaim was under control. His voice could be heard throughout the room. Ford's Theater was not very large and Booth's tenor filled the hall. "The Marble Heart" seemed to have been written with him in mind.

Charles Devereux and his family had seats in the middle of the orchestra section about half way back to the overhang of the balcony. They made an attractive picture. The beauty and style of the Devereux women were well known in the city. Claude's Army Blue figure seated among the ladies made a pleasing contrast. His mother had decided that they would not wear mourning colors any longer. She said that there was "just too much sadness" and that they should not contribute to it

Claude tried to avoid this evening's entertainment. Lincoln was certain to attend the Washington opening of the play's "run."

He did not want to spend any more time with President Lincoln than he could avoid. He felt, beyond reason that Lincoln would see into his soul if they were too much together. He knew that was foolish and that his secret work demanded that he seek Lincoln's company but could not force himself to do it. The man's face haunted his dreams. There was no escaping him. His annoying mid-western twang filled the corridors of the War Department building on 17th Street. Devereux's office was a few doors from that of the Secretary of War. He was lodged there in a row of rooms occupied by, John Hay, William Davenport and Nikolay, the president's secretary. The four of them often gathered in the afternoon for a glass of Claude's excellent whiskey and a chat. Devereux's little suite of rooms was the favored meeting place

Lincoln's voice haunted the building. He spent much of his time reading reports in the War Department telegraph office on the fourth floor and had developed the annoying habit of "dropping in" on groups that interested him. Devereux dreaded the day that the president would discover the afternoon meetings.

Seated on the main floor of the theater below the presidential box, Claude felt that someone in the box above was looking at him. He was certain it must be Lincoln. He had stood with the audience to greet the arrival of the presidential party, but avoided looking directly at them. He knew that people are more likely to remember those with whom they have made eye contact. Nevertheless, the feeling that he was watched had grown in him for some time, and the faint, ghostly pressure on the side of his face was becoming so strong that he knew he could not ignore it much longer.

On the stage Booth delivered a line with exceptional force and then turned to point at the president. Devereux had not listened closely enough to remember the line, but he instinctively turned to the box.

There, seated just beside Mary Lincoln, was Amy Biddle staring down at him with a face heartbreakingly devoid of the guile that would have been needed to disguise her love.

Lincoln and the rest of his group were focused on Booth.

Devereux turned to his left to look at his wife. She seemed to be absorbed in Booth's performance. He then turned back to the box.

Abraham Lincoln was looking first at him and then Amy in turn, first one and then the other. He nodded very slightly to Devereux, and then shook his head in the slightest of gestures.

In their carriage on the way home, Hope said nothing for half the trip and then remarked, while looking out the window, "if she is going to moon at you in public then you will be attending events without me..."

"I have no control over her actions or yours. I do not encourage her."

Now she looked at him. "Swear that is true?" She looked incredibly beautiful in the lantern lit interior of the carriage.

"Yes."

She made a small face and then turned fully toward him. "What did you think of Booth this time?" she asked.

He was at a loss for words. The magnitude of his lie to this woman who loved him so pressed down on him even as he knew that he would persist in the lie.

"Are you going to answer me?" Her face was unreadable. Her face was often unreadable lately.

"I have mentioned him to our people."

Will they use him for something?" She looked impatient now.

"I imagine so. He travels widely without anyone questioning the need. That must be useful."

"Should we invite him for dinner? He would seem a "catch' for the kind of social set we are creating..." He looked at her speculatively contemplating the thought of Hope and Booth as a couple, and then dismissed the idea.

"Certainly. He should be amusing. Have we received an invitation to the Chase girl's wedding to Sprague?"

"It came a few days ago. I wouldn't miss it for the world." Now she looked mischievous.

"Why?"

The beautiful blond creature laughed aloud. "She is such a nitwit and can't shut up to save her soul. You didn't hear her lecturing Senator Sumner last Sunday at his wife's tea?"

"I missed that. I suppose that since her father is Treasury Secretary and her fiancé is also a senator she can say what she pleases."

She sniffed and lifted her little chin.

Looking at her, he decided that he had not been spending enough time at home.

The Army of Northern Virginia halted its retreat just north of the little town that was the seat of Culpeper County. Lee would not have admitted that he stopped his retreat there for other than military reasons but in fact he could not yet compel himself to abandon the loyal Virginia people of this town, and so the army turned for a few days to face the Northern forces that followed.

The troops fanned out in the shops around the old court house. Some found old friends. Some bought whatever Confederate money could still buy. In this third winter of the war, it was surprising how much it would buy. Perhaps the buyers' faded, shabby uniforms had something to do with the money's value.

After a few days they moved on again, filing out through the streets in silence, leaving women, children and old men standing in their doorways watching. Many held small flags. When the troops had passed, the townspeople went indoors to wait for the enemy. They went on south, beyond the Rapidan to a line Lee believed they could hold.

Throughout the army, soldiers started to construct their winter quarters. They had lived so long in the forest that they could build solid little houses of sticks and mud if they had a couple of weeks in which to work. Small towns rose in the woods, filling the forest that stretched south from the foot of Pony Mountain.

Smoke drifted in the wind, eddying and streaming, bringing an acrid bite of wood to the nose. Oak and hickory, maple and poplar, the smoke carried with it the smell of the little communities, these villages so like those that the ancestors of the soldiers had made in the beginning of their life in America.

The men thought of Thanksgiving; and some reached out beyond that to remember Christmas.

Balthazar watched his troops build their winter town. He had never seen soldiers do such a thing. In Europe, soldiers on campaign lived under canvas or in requisitioned houses.

He thought their skill a marvelous thing, and told them so.

He and Smoot and Harris kept them occupied throughout the shrinking hours of daylight.

They began with "The School of the Soldier". The training began with the manual of arms and bayonet drill. That lasted a week.

Then they moved on to company drill under the men he picked to command the four companies.

One had been first sergeant in a Union New York regiment. His name was Seamus O'Brien. Short, robust in physique with a "bull neck and black hair, he was the very type of a "Gael." He said that the Draft Riots in July had been too much for him. There had been too many Irish killed, far too many. He said he would not fight to free "the niggers," and that was what it came to now. Balthazar watched with interest the discomfort with which Smoot and Harris listened to this. O'Brien had been a laborer before the war, first in Dublin, then in New York City. He said he had voted for Breckinridge in 1860. He received command of "A Company."

Another was a former Confederate officer, reduced to the ranks in a re election. He said his name was Taylor Randall. Blond, blue eyed and slim, he was from Tennessee, a quiet, soft spoken man who led by example. His unassuming manner won friends easily. "B Company" looked pleased at the news that he would lead them. Balthazar was not surprised. In his experience the men really did "love a gentleman."

- 12 November –
(Kate's wedding)

"We seem to be moving in similar circles, Colonel Devereux," the voice said. Lincoln had a distinctive voice. It was throaty, but also nasal in a Midwestern sort of way.

Claude turned to see the smiling face and looming black figure surrounded by the usual group.

Stanton stood slightly to one side and a step behind.

John Nicolay was at the president's left hand as a good secretary should be. Stanton was beaming. His round steel glasses reflected one of the gas lights. His ragged, long spade beard was as unsightly as usual.

Nicolay looked serious, but not harried.

Things must be going well today, Claude thought.

He looked around for his wife and found her. She had walked away from him to stand with his parents. They were at the other end of the room chatting with the bride by the big black marble fireplace. The gaslight sparkled on the women's jewelry. His father did not seem as morose as usual in this situation. Charles Devereux rarely came into Washington City from Alexandria anymore. He left that to Claude and the bank's employees. Today seemed different for him. He was actually smiling.

He has known Salmon Chase for many years and the senator's residence is a familiar place. Perhaps that is the reason, Claude told himself.

Kate Chase was a beauty. On her wedding day she managed to seem almost as pretty as Hope. The white silk of the dress shimmered in the flickering light.

Senator Sprague, the groom, appeared resigned to several more hours of conversation with official Washington. He did not look really happy with that, but he could be forgiven for wishing that he was somewhere else alone with his new wife... He was a rich man, rich enough to have given his bride the diamond tiara that she wore for the wedding. His attention kept shifting back and forth between Hope Devereux and his bride. Claude recognized roving lust when he saw it.

Not a good omen, he thought while watching Sprague.

You would know about that, a voice in his head reminded him.

"You have been hiding something from me, Colonel Devereux," Lincoln persisted.

A wave of fear swept the spy. Then reason assured him that the president of the United States would not confront and arrest him at a society wedding.

"Sir?"

Nicolay says you and several of your friends are conducting an afternoon "Lyceum" on the war?

"Yes, sir. We are doing that. Just a few friends talking over the day's events…"

"Might I be invited?"

Devereux carefully avoided looking at Nicolay. He knew that the mask would not hold firmly in place if he looked the man in the eye. At the same time, he also knew that the president's desire to be included in the group discussion was the greatest gift that Nicolay could have given the South. Claude's instinctive desire to avoid Lincoln warred with the needs of his mission in Washington. He continued to be both repelled and drawn to the man. "We would be honored, sir. I had no idea that you would be interested."

"Oh. I am. I am. John, please tell me when the group sits together."

Nicolay nodded faithfully in a "nice doggy" way...

Lincoln moved toward the bridal group, perhaps to go and take his leave, but after a few steps returned to speak to Claude again. I forgot," he began. "You were at the theater a few days back." It was not a question. "I did not care for the play and you did not seem to either. What do you think of Booth as an actor?" The subtle reproof was clear to them both.

Claude shrugged. "He is over rated. There is too much marching up and down. He is too loud and it is all in the same tone."

Lincoln smiled, "Mary likes him. She wants to invite him to a luncheon..." He did not seem to relish the thought. "I am taking the cars to Gettysburg in a few days for the cemetery dedication. If Edwin can spare you I would like you to go with me. I have to write something to say at the ceremony. I have seen some of the papers you draft for the War Department. Perhaps you could help me with this? I need to talk to someone who was there about the battle, chiefly concerning the last day." He glanced at Stanton who bowed slightly in the inevitable assent.

The "C Company" commander was an English corporal from Manchester. He deserted his regiment in Canada and made his own way from the border near Detroit to Lynchburg, Virginia seeking a place to enlist. He arrived at the "Camp of Instruction" there wearing a cloth cap, corduroy pants and a canvas coat. He had about him the air of an "old sweat," one of the sort of men who had made Napoleon's *Grognards* earn their pay.

Balthazar asked where he had served and in what ranks. "Royal Marine Infantry, sir! Fifteen fucking years! Was up to sergeant-major twice, and back down as fast! I reckon I was in a hunderd little fights with the 'Jollies.' Then I hit a officer, a little poofter of a leftenant. It was in India outside Lucknow, the Mutiny, you know..." He looked at Balthazar to make sure he knew.

The Frenchman nodded.

"He was a ass," the Englishman offered in way of explanation. "So I run from the hangman, run all the way to Goa, where the Portugee run things, and shipped out on a merchant ship to Montreal. I knew a lot about ships from the marines. Was rated 'able, I was. I took the King's shillin' there again, in Montreal." He was watching Balthazar for a reaction. "I didn't know what else to do... This looks a good fight..." He looked at Balthazar again in search of an opinion.

The captain who had given him the oath in the little Piedmont town that he finally reached in his long trip from the border had no right hand and a patch on one eye.

The Britisher, William Fagan was his name, grasped the officer's left hand firmly afterward, thanking him for the chance to serve.

"You'll do," Balthazar told him. "But, a word of caution... From what I have seen thus far, I would say that if you strike one of these..." He waved at Smoot and Harris. "They will probably kill you."

The fourth company commander was no one in particular. He was a beefy, brown haired man of medium height. They all just liked the look of him and the way he had of getting other people to help him. He would not tell them where he came from, and insisted that his name was John Smith. There were endless arguments about this man. He would not even tell them from which army he had emerged, and no one seemed to know. After two weeks of indecision, Balthazar took Smoot's advice and asked "D Company" to vote. Smith won hands down.

They moved on to battalion drill after two weeks.

Balthazar taught the battalion things they shook their heads at, muttering threats of disobedience if ordered to perform such foolishness. Many complained bitterly to their new leaders.

Sergeant Harris listened, shrugged and walked away.

The Britisher, Fagan, laughed at them, saying that at last they were really learning to soldier.

Balthazar set Smoot to the job of finding them all bayonets.

A grindstone was set up in a farm yard. There, they sharpened the long sword bayonets, grinding them to a fine edge.

Edwin Stanton was not a generous man. He hated anyone who might possibly prove to be a rival for power and position. He worked late and alone, brooding constantly on the threats presented to him by wartime Washington.

On a particular November morning he reflected on his enemies. He believed that Washington was filled with enemies. The Confederate underground was not among his pre-occupations. He reckoned that Colonel Lafayette Baker would deal with them.

Stanton was more concerned with his rivals within the Lincoln Administration. *They are all jealous,* he thought. *There are so many, so many from before the war. They are waiting for a sign of vulnerability, a political weakness, a chance to make me look inept before the president.*

On this day he had something new to worry about. He was not happy with Lincoln's invitation to Devereux to accompany the official party to the cemetery dedication. This man worked in Stanton's own office and because of a presidential whim, would have several days with Lincoln.

Who could say what sort of foolishness the man might speak to the president? He looked out the grimy window of his office. Leaves fell and rattled against the cold glass. A hopelessly lost cardinal landed on the sill and looked in. It pecked the glass hoping for food, hoping for anything.

Stanton looked away.

The bird flew on.

Stanton brought his attention back to the matter at hand. It was his way. The need to survive and prosper was always foremost in his mind.

After all, he thought *he is still a Virginian, even though a loyalist. How much can you ever really trust these people?*

Nevertheless, innate caution made him carefully consider Claude Devereux.

In civilian life he is a merchant banker. What sort of schemes will he press the president to support either now or after the war? After the war...

The Devereuxs were rich, rich beyond the dreams of most Americans.

Perhaps it would be a good idea not to antagonize him... I wonder if he has political ambitions. Let him talk to the president. I should talk to him now...

He sent for Devereux.

"Have you thought of politics, perhaps a senate seat from Virginia, once this war is... over?" Stanton's question seemed normal in the context of conversation with the elegant figure in dark blue before him. The silver eagles inside rectangular gold braided shoulder straps looked very natural on his uniform tunic. Salt and pepper hair added to the air of restrained dignity and discreet power that hung comfortably about the shoulders.

Claude smiled, basking in the comfort of Stanton's uncertainty and insecurity. "No, sir," he replied. "I have been planning to take my wife to Europe to live in Paris and to run our company's office there. We have kin in France. She has never lived in Europe. My father does not intend to retire and we are hoping that my brother, Joachim, will come to his senses and soon appear at home where he can be of help to father. My mother misses him deeply, as do we all."

Stanton looked blank, and then remembered. "Ah, the rebel, he is an officer now if I recall correctly from...

one of Baker's reports on you Devereuxs.

The last phrase was unsaid but the obvious source of the knowledge lay between them on the Turkey carpet covered table. "I heard…"

"I believe that is true," Claude interrupted, "although we seldom get news of him." *What do you want to tell me?* Devereux thought in the space inside his breast that was now filling with fear of family disaster. *What would I tell father? He despises me for leaving Jake behind with the army. What will he think if I bring him news of his beloved son's death?*

Stanton changed the subject. "I think it is a good idea that you should ride up to Gettysburg with the president and help with his speech. You write well… You can tell me what his intimate thoughts are on the War Department. He does not talk to me very much. I wonder why…" He smiled. The smug superiority that he felt toward Lincoln was visible for a second. Then it was gone, replaced with his usual, unreadable facade.

I write well? Devereux thought.

I am a credit to my people? Thank you, master. Perhaps Yale had something to do with that.

Stanton was intimidated by Devereux. He did not like that. He reacted to such feelings with murderous hostility. Somewhere down inside him he knew that Devereux laughed at him, detested him, and thought himself superior in every way.

I hate this man, Stanton thought. *I always have. Why did I take him into the office? Ah, the bank. Now, I remember. His father knows everyone who is anyone. These damned slave beating "gentlemen," how dare they talk down to me? How dare they?*

Devereux's uniform showed the difference in class between them. The fine broadcloth fit perfectly without being tight anywhere. The double row of gold buttons had a suspiciously soft glow. The shoulder straps were definitely bullion.

Bullion?

Stanton seethed. Looking down at Devereux's feet, he saw black half boots that spoke of a London maker. Small, rounded silver spurs without rowels were built into the back of the heels. Mastering himself, he smiled. "I hope you have a nice trip."

Devereux did not like the implication. "Are you not coming, sir?" He did not take pleasure in the thought of days on end in Lincoln's company.

What on earth will I say to him?

"No. I have not been invited. Let me know how it went..."

Watching Devereux's retreat through the office door, he gloated over the conviction that no one liked Claude Devereux, no one at all.

Stanton was a good judge of people, but this time he was wrong. Abraham Lincoln liked Devereux very much. Claude's graceful presence, fine wit, and unshakable calm re-assured him. He had liked both the Devereux brothers. He was hurt in a personal way by Patrick's death. The loss came at a bad time. He had been open to new hurt because of the sudden death of his son, Willie. And there was always the matter of his wife, her perpetual illnesses and physical weakness. She blamed him. She blamed him for everything evil that happened.

There were so many deaths in the war and he felt responsible for all of them. The statistics of combat deaths injured him personally. He could not absolve himself of feelings of guilt for Confederate deaths. He still thought of the rebels as fellow Americans temporarily gone astray and yearned for their repentance. The guerrillas for whom he approved death sentences in Missouri did not affect him the same way. He believed that these were evil men who had injured the innocent, but the death of soldiers, any soldiers, wounded him.

Unfortunately for all concerned, Claude Devereux increasingly liked Lincoln as a person, and as someone who unaccountably was worried about Devereux's own state of mind and well being. Why the president would take a personal interest in him was a mystery to Devereux. He had no idea of the cause, but the feeling of being appreciated was strangely comforting. Devereux's father remained a distant and disapproving figure whom he had never been able to please. The knowledge of the dangerous and demanding mission that Claude had accepted for what they both saw as their country had done nothing to improve that. Devereux had seen Lincoln in the company of his father several times.

The contrast in feeling toward him was painful.

On the 18th, Devereux settled into a big parlor car chair reserved for him on the president's train. Mercifully, someone had placed him two cars away from Lincoln. Sgt. John Quick rode with him to the station in Washington, and then boarded a car for orderlies farther back in the train.

Black smoke surrounded the engine and cars as the train left the station. The city looked terrible in the early morning light. It was sooty, rundown, overly rich, and vulgar. Thankfully, the Maryland countryside was still green. He could concentrate on that as the train rolled north. His welcomed solitude lasted until the Baltimore station.

Then, John Hay came walking back through the train looking for him. "The chief wants you," he said in his usual pleasant way. "He says he needs help with the draft remarks he has been writing." He frowned a little, seeming to find that odd.

Devereux sat across the carpeted aisle from Lincoln with the notes of the speech in his right hand and a pencil in the other. "It's too long," he said looking up at the bearded face.

It's not too long he thought to himself. *The damned thing is perfect. Perfect. His reasoned arguments will carry the people even farther in deciding that we are criminals. This will be in every newspaper in the country tomorrow. It is a perfect piece of preaching for their cause.*

The president squinted at him. The red and black curtains draping the windows swayed behind and around him. "I thought it was rather good," he said. He seemed puzzled. "Senator Everett will speak at length. He wrote last week to give me the skeleton of his remarks. It will be most elegant, dignified and written to be something like that fellow Pericles' funeral speech." Lincoln always risked ridicule when he attempted classical reference in his rural Kentucky voice. The high pitch of his speaking apparatus only made it worse.

"Sir, that is why I think you must concentrate on the elegiac quality of a lyrical and poetic expression, something that will sing in history rather than to preach of politics. We Americans need to be reminded of first things, of the founding principles that have made us the one people that the rebels are trying to drive apart..."

Not too far. Don't go too far. Let us see if he will ruin it by over reaching. His ego may do that if you don't push too hard.

"Think so? The tall man contemplated him. "Tell me what it looked like from the ridge when Lee attacked the third day? I need to see it in my head to finish this, to make it sing."

Can I do this? Claude asked himself. *I pushed Joe Hooker into sending this man a telegram that got him fired. Can I hope to do that now and strike a subtle blow against them, or will I over reach rather than he?*

"...the graves of our brethren beneath our feet call out to us. It is with hesitation that I raise my poor voice to break the eloquent silence of God and Nature. But the duty to which you have called me must be performed; — grant me, I pray you, your indulgence and your sympathy."

Everett sounds good, Devereux thought. *He is in fine form, just as Wilkes Booth was when we saw him. Last week was it? Booth, Hope sees something in him, something that I do not. If Everett keeps this up, he is bound to make Lincoln look bad...*

It was cold, cold in a confused, Pennsylvania November way.

"A day so fair and foul."

Macbeth.

Claude felt momentarily happy with himself over the line. It was freezing cold on the platform. The wide, wooden structure faced south, toward the length of what had already come to be called Cemetery Ridge. He could see the little patch of tall trees where his brother Patrick had died and where Devereux would have shot George Meade if only the man had been closer. Lincoln sat at the middle of the platform, near the bombast, Everett.

A thought came over Devereux;

I could shoot him from here...

Claude's service Colt was in its holster at his side. It would be an easy shot. The pistol was a custom order from the factory in Connecticut. Old man Colt owed "Devereux and Wheatley" money. This was a special gun. It would be a very easy shot. Claude contemplated the back of Lincoln's head.

Why not do it now?

For some reason Abraham Lincoln turned, looked at him, and then smiled. It was one of those moments when staring at someone for a while becomes a kind of spectral touch. The expression on his face told Devereux that Lincoln was bored and frustrated with Everett's speech.

In that moment Devereux knew several things. Most importantly, he knew he would never kill Lincoln himself. He had killed before. He had killed many and except for the death of George Dangerfield, a friend who had died by his hand in a foolish duel, he had little difficulty in living with the memory of the rest. He had come to understand that Lincoln would have to be removed from government if the South were to live as an independent state. Unfortunately, he now saw that Lincoln was both the best and the worst of things for him personally. Devereux searched all his life for acceptance and friendship. Something in him demanded it, screamed for it, but some other part of his being kept him from finding that friendship, that brotherhood. He had sought and found what he wanted in the Confederate army. That was taken from him by the Confederate government. He had not wanted to be sent away from his regiment. Judah Benjamin forced his exile from his friends. He had sought real intimacy in his marriage. His wife tried so very hard to give it to him. Even now, he thought of her flesh and her warm bed with longing. It was not enough. This man was the father he had always needed. He was unlike the distant, cold man who lived on Duke Street in Alexandria.

Devereux knew that someone else must act for him. Someone else must strike the tall, bearded man. He could not do it.

The women in his family circle suspected something hidden in Lincoln's nature. They hinted at something unnatural in the president's deep interest in the Devereux brothers. Claude did not think that Lincoln had a "lavender streak," but this was of no great importance to him. He was as secure in his own sensuality as any man who ever lived. Lincoln might be whatever he was. That had nothing to do with Devereux.

The increasing difficulty of dealing with his two women was of much greater importance. Hope did not believe him faithful to her. Nevertheless, the memory of her sweet and passionate self called him home even now as he sat in the cold Pennsylvania wind. At the same time, Amy Biddle's body had become something which he could not imagine giving up. Her sad and needy devotion to him was matched by the heat of the newly discovered sexuality that he had awakened in her. The foolishness of his reckless philandering impressed him in his soberer moments. He was certain that the triangle he had created would end in emotional disaster, but he was powerless to help himself, a prisoner of the very qualities and characteristics that made him such a formidable spy.

The clouds came over fast, soaring across the sky. They colored those listening below with a harlequin succession of light and darkness.

Must be something symbolic in that... I ought to be able to think of a quotation... He could not. Everett droned on. There were a lot of people in the audience, all sitting on those round backed chairs often seen in cafés or church basements. There were graves everywhere. The work of reinterring the Yankee dead went on. Across the field where Pickett's men had attacked there were open holes. The bodies had been buried there just after the battle. The fresh dirt on a lot of the graves looked grayish brown. Yankee dirt. There were caskets along one wall of the new cemetery.

Across the new burial ground, Claude could see the red brick arch on the road leading into the town's burial ground. "Evergreen Cemetery" was inscribed on the arch. He remembered that Bill White and he had taken refuge there when they arrived with Howard's Corps on the first day of the battle. He remembered the Sanitary Commission wagon they had ridden. He looked down the ridge again. A red bird settled on a branch in his line of vision to the group of trees.

What the hell are you doing here this time of year? he thought and smiled. *Is that you, Pat, come back to visit us on this day of days? What should I do? Tell me. Is it my task to kill this man? Is that what you are here to tell me? Surely not? I have no taste for murder. Tell me I have no taste for blood.*

Do I?

Everett's voice rose to a closing note. "But they, I am sure, will join us in saying, as we bid farewell to the dust of these martyr heroes, that wheresoever throughout the civilized world the accounts of this great warfare are read, and down to the latest period of recorded time, in the glorious annals of our common country, there will be no brighter page than that which relates the Battles of Gettysburg."

The applause was polite but less than deafening. Devereux was struck by a moment of doubt as he thought of the last draft of Lincoln's remarks. The copy that Lincoln had given him, written in Devereux's hand and covered with Lincoln's notations, was in his breast pocket.

I should keep this as a souvenir of the occasion he thought.

The tall bearded man approached the speaker's rostrum. He began by putting on his spectacles and after looking at the crowd, spoke these words.

> "Four score and seven years ago our fathers brought forth on this continent a new nation, conceived in Liberty, and dedicated to the proposition that all men are created equal. Now we are engaged in a great civil war, testing whether that nation, or any nation, so conceived and so dedicated, can long endure. We are met on a great battle-field of that war. We have come to dedicate a portion of that field, as a final resting place for those who here gave their lives that that nation might live. It is altogether fitting and proper that we should do this. But, in a larger sense, we can not dedicate—we can not consecrate—we can not hallow—this ground. The brave men, living and dead, who struggled here, have consecrated it, far above our poor power to add or detract. The world will little note, nor long remember what we say here, but it can never forget what they did here. It is for us the living, rather, to be dedicated here to the unfinished work which they who fought here have thus far so nobly advanced. It is rather for us to be here dedicated to the great task remaining before us—that from these honored dead we take increased devotion to that cause for which they gave the last full measure of devotion—that we here highly resolve that these dead shall not have died in vain—that this nation, under God, shall have a new birth of freedom—and that government of the people, by the people, for the people, shall not perish from the earth."

Applause was sustained and thunderous. With lead in his heart Devereux knew that he had failed. He had made the speech better. He had encouraged

Lincoln to make extravagant claims of the justice of the Union cause in the belief that any fool would see the irony of such claims for a cause so patently aggressive and revolutionary. He had been wrong. The Yankee fools accepted the words at face value and felt the better for them. This speech had wings for them.

Lincoln looked at him amid the applause and nodded in gratitude.

Devereux knew then that he could never escape responsibility for what this president would do to the Southern people. He did not want that responsibility but it was his portion, and not to be avoided.

The little red bird flew away toward the other side of the valley, toward Seminary Ridge.

Jubal Early came to Thanksgiving dinner. He sat on a saw horse in the barn where they ate, a tin plate of venison and wild turkey in one hand, a tea cup of whiskey beside him.

The troops sat in the hay eating happily.

Balthazar had taken charge of the cooking; supervising the half dozen black cooks that Harris recruited in Hays' brigade.

The day the cooking started, he was pleased to have several men volunteer to help. Among them was Smith, the "D" Company commander. After watching his creation of an admirable kettle of turkey soup, Balthazar was sure that Smith, like Harris, was professionally trained.

Early complimented them on the stuffing, said he had never had anything quite like it, and accepted a second helping.

He had a chaplain with him, a French Jesuit who worked in the military hospitals in Lynchburg.[2]

The priest and Balthazar chatted in their own language during dinner. The men listened to this with interest, turning from one to the other, examining their commander, seeking assurance of something they could not name.

After dinner, the priest offered his thoughts on the meaning of such a remembrance in wartime and the injustice of the war being waged against them by the North.

The soldiers listened politely.

When the chaplain finished his talk, Early stood up and announced that General Ewell was gone on sick leave for his old wound, and that he would be

---

2 Louis Hippolyte Gache, S.J.

in command of the Second Corps until Ewell came back. He said that they would be attached for now to corps headquarters.

You could see from the soldiers' faces that they were not sure if that was good or bad.

The priest offered to say Mass if there were Catholics present. A number raised their hands and he moved off to a corner of the barn with them.

Balthazar asked Early if he wished to attend the service. After a moments thought, the general shrugged and said he could not see any reason not to do so. "After all," he said, "the Pope has taken note of us. He, at least, recognizes us."

After Mass, the Jesuit asked if Balthazar wished him to hear his confession.

The answer was no.

A courier came at four o'clock that morning with the news that Meade was across the Rapidan, marching southeast through the Wilderness.

Balthazar had found among his men a soldier who had been a bugler in a regular U.S. cavalry regiment. "Reveille" sounded sweet and compelling in the darkness of the camp.

Chapter 10

Mine Run

Early formed his command for the march with his own division in the lead. He gave Harry Hays charge of it and Hays, of course, put what was left of his "Tigers" up in front.

Balthazar arrived with his men at headquarters by five, falling in behind the staff and provost guard on the road.

They all went down the Orange Turnpike together, Harry Hays' division in front, followed by those commanded by Robert Rodes and Edward Johnson. All of Second Corps moved off in a long snake of steaming men and horses.

The soldiers looked like bears in their earth colored clothing. White crystals grew in their beards. The heavy brogans kicked the surface of the macadamized road free of hoarfrost that had settled on it overnight. Soon there were black grooves in the white, formed as the men passed in their fours.

Time settled into the endless pattern of long route marches. Talk died out after the first hour. The cold gradually released its iron grip on their feet as warm blood reached the extremities. With faces flushed, the riflemen shifted the load across their backs. Ten minutes in each hour they rested by the side of the road, rifles stacked in the center. Early had learned this lesson from his hero, the martyred Stonewall. The men would always get their scheduled breaks so long as he commanded. Four hours passed in the winter morning. A freezing drizzle descended on them. The troops marched doggedly down the road into the unknown. They held their arms as close as possible to their bodies to keep in the warmth of their vitals.

The head of the column reached the hamlet of Locust Grove at one in the afternoon. They found Yankee pickets taking their ease under tarpaulin shelters in the heavy growth around the junction where the Plank Road led to the southeast.

Colonel William Monaghan[3] shook out his five hundred Tigers in line of battle and swept through the Federal outguard like the wind rattling leaves on a cold day. He drove them east for ten minutes, and then halted astride the turnpike to wait for Hays and Rodes to come up.

A mile back down the column, Balthazar moved his men off the road to make way for a battery which drove straight up the highway to reach the

---

3 Third commander of 6th Louisiana Regiment (The Irish Brigade). This unit had the highest percentage of foreign born of all the Tiger regiments (54%). It was said of them that they "were turbulent in camp and requiring a strong hand, but responding to kindness and justice, and ready to follow their officers to the death." Monaghan, who like most of his men was Irish born, was killed August 25th, 1864.

"Tigers." The horses breathed fog and clattered onward without the urging of the drivers. The road was slick and animals scrambled to keep their feet beneath them.

Smoot stepped up on a stump to see as far down the road as possible. He looked at the battery pushing its way through the hurrying troops ahead. He could see up the tunnel of trees and slash a long way.

Several hundred feet ahead, Early's mounted staff and cavalry escort towered above the infantry. As Smoot watched, this body of mounted men kicked their animals into motion, and followed the battery toward Wilderness Church, disappearing around a bend in the turnpike.

The sound of firing around the crossroad ahead died away.

Half an hour passed beside the turnpike. Men began to stamp their feet impatiently in the snow, waving their arms and yelling at each other with fog drenched voices.

The "D" company commander, Smith, built a fire around which his men gathered.

Seeing this, other companies started looking for wood.

Balthazar stood at Smith's fire, his hands outstretched to the heat. He held the Sharps carbine under one arm, the muzzle pointing at the flame. In his brown clothing, he might have been a country gentleman out for a day in search of rabbits.

The men around the fire kept looking at him sideways, talking to each other, but studying him all the same.

Behind him, to the north of the road, the open ground of a meadow filled with the wagons of the corps' trains. Horses and mules stood patiently, turning their heads to see as others of their kind came to stand beside them, shivering and miserable in the weather.

A rifle shot rang in the trees beyond the gathering trains, and then another. A ragged fusillade ripped through the wood. White smoke rolled out in clouds.

Amongst the wagons, the drivers struggled with animals that reared and stared wildly about.

Bullets hummed and cut canvas.

A mule went down, kicking and screaming in pain.

The drivers leapt for their seats, turning the teams and whipping them with the slack ends of reins. With a remarkable show of unanimity they ran their wagons off the field in a clamor of wheels and ringing tires. On a front of two hundred yards they careened through the battalion.

Men dodged from side to side, seeking shelter behind trees, laughing and throwing rocks at the animals to turn them away.

With a rush the onslaught passed by into the woods south of the road.

All were gone from the field except for a Negro teamster alone with the task of cutting a dead mule out of its harness. The bullets kept coming to kick up dirt all around him. He finished up with a big clasp knife and pulled the live mules around to follow the others. Half way across the snow covered grass he met Balthazar's advancing battalion.

They came on in open order, spread across most of the clearing. The four man fighting teams picked their way over the ground, looking for the nearly invisible folds in the earth that would mean survival if the fire grew heavy.

The teamster slapped the back of his beasts, urging them through the hole which the infantry made for him.

The men waved as he passed. "Uncle, you go now. We'll take care of this..."

He waved back.

"Fire at will and then halt in the tree line!" Balthazar yelled loud enough to be heard along his front.

A scattered volley swept the battalion front as the fours moved ahead, the soldiers taking turns loading, and moving.

The rolling advance was more than the Federal skirmishers had expected. As the battalion came near, they ran. They did not seem real people. They were blue backs, dimly seen in the winter sun, disappearing quickly in the obscure shadows.

Balthazar blew a silver whistle that he wore on a chain around his neck.

Some of the troops, especially the old timers, had objected to its use in training, saying they were not dogs, but he insisted and now they halted as one man just inside the trees.

An odd silence settled over the wood to their front. Just occasionally, the crisp snap of a stick came to them through the grey wetness of the underbrush.

At his post behind the left of the line, Smoot wiggled his toes, feeling the cold damp in his socks, wondering how long they would stand still while their feet froze. He noticed soldiers looking back over their shoulders at the road and turned to see Johnson's division coming into sight, marching like a dun colored river into the meadow, forming a wall along the ground over which the battalion had advanced.

After a minute, the long lines rolled forward stamping over the snow slick grass, to pass Balthazar's men, smiling and nodding in a hearty way as they went by.

Smoot looked at a battle flag as a colonel and the color sergeant behind him brushed past.

"33rd Virginia Infantry" was embroidered on the heavy cloth.

Stonewall Brigade, he thought[4].

In the battalion men looked at each other and smiled. They visibly began to relax, secure in the belief that the irritating skirmishers in front of them would soon be gone.

Behind the center of the battalion line Balthazar stood quietly watching the backs of Johnson's men disappearing in the gloom, listening to the receding sounds of crackling and spitting.

Smoot watched him.

They all watched him.

Smoot saw a grin break out on the dark face of a corporal who stood beside him. The man was staring down the line at Balthazar's bulky form.

"What's so funny?" Smoot asked.

"The major," the soldier replied. "He's something special..."

Smoot turned from him to look at Balthazar again.

The silver whistle shrilled in the heavy winter air. The French soldier looked to right and left and waved them forward.

The battalion followed Johnson's moving line of infantry through the wood. Mist hung low among the trees. Grey snow lay in miniature drifts against the trunks, climbing the bark, reaching toward the branches. It was early for snow, but there it was.

They halted at the far side of the wood. Surprisingly, it was only about two hundred yards wide. Beyond the edge of the trees was another meadow, perhaps a quarter mile across.

Ahead of them, Johnson's division advanced in line against a rail fence in the middle of the open space.

There was a blue presence behind the fence. It was not clear how many there were.

Red flags dotted the moving Southern line, outlining the regiments and brigades, marking the skeleton of the division.

A blue mass rose behind the fence. It stood elbow to elbow to elbow, a solid mass of Yankees. The rifles came up. A wall of dirty grey-white smoke rolled out, covering the Union troops, making them invisible.

---

4 The 2nd, 4th, 5th, 27th and 33rd Virginia Infantry were together named by act of Congress, "The Stonewall Brigade". These regiments were raised mainly in the Shenandoah Valley. They were part of the command which Stonewall Jackson assembled at Winchester in 1861 to defend his district. This command, including the brigade, made up a division in Jackson's 2nd Corps. The division came to be known as the Stonewall Division in the way that military nicknames seem to spread.

The bullets struck the Stonewall Division, staggering the ranks, dropping men in the slush.

The *whhzzz* around their ears made Balthazar's battalion pull in their necks like turtles.

The volley's crash hit them like a blow. It rang in their heads as their minds grappled with the moment.

Balthazar turned to Raphael Harris beside him. "Johnson is overmatched! He must come back quickly!"

As though intent on making him a prophet, the Federal infantry began to climb over the fence.

Out in the field, Major General Edward Johnson waved his cane, swinging it in frustration at the frozen tufts of grass. He cupped one hand to yell at a man far to his left.

The tiny figure waved an arm in understanding.

Another, on the right held up a hand.

In front of the fence, the Union troops gathered themselves up, straightened their lines, and stared into the faces of the brown death facing them.

The Rebel infantry began to retire, coming back in leap-frog bounds, grudgingly backing away from their enemy. A volley ripped along their line, a demonstration of their unyielding hostility.

Smoke hid them from the battalion, dropping a curtain across the landscape, drifting toward Balthazar's men in the edge of the woods.

Out of this acrid fog a rank of Johnson's men emerged, coming halfway across the grass, turning to face the Federals hidden in the billowing grey.

Flashes of orange marked another exchange of fire within the smoke. Bullets passed through the ranks knocking several men flat, sending one kicking and rolling about, staining the white as he writhed on the ground.

The whirring Minie balls reached the battalion.

Randall, the "B" Company commander spun on a heel, grabbing his shoulder, dropping to a knee.

Smoot knelt to look in his face. He always worried about shock in a newly wounded man. "William? You're gonna be with us, aren't you?" he asked.

Red stained the brown fabric between Randall's fingers. He worked his arm in a small circle, showing his teeth in a grin of painful cheerfulness. "Still works... Help me up, will you?"

Smoot pulled open Randall's jacket and shirt to inspect the wound. It was small and round, with blood seeping around the skirt of the bullet just below the skin. "Spent round, William. Must have bounced off a rock. We'll get you to Johnson's surgeons. They're by the pike."

Fagan, the Britisher peered around Smoot. "I can get at that," he said, pulling a long-handled tool from a black leather pouch at his side.

Two riflemen from Randall's company gripped their leader while Fagan held a match to his instrument. He then reached into the hole for the bullet, spreading the jaws inside the puncture to get a grip on the rings of the conical projectile.

Randall groaned. The sound came out slowly, seeping through his clenched teeth.

Smoot held his hand, pressing hard against the pain.

Fagan whistled a tune unknown to the Americans. The sound rose at the end as he pulled the forceps from Randall's shoulder, clutching the bullet in its bloody grasp.

The company first sergeant, standing anxiously behind Fagan reached forward to hand Smoot a clean shirt to pack in against the wound.

Smoot buttoned the jacket over it, and looked Randall in the eye. "Go to the rear, William! Sergeant Mathieu here will take over. Go to the rear!"

The two soldiers tightened their hold on Randall's arms, looking around to mark their path back to the road.

Randall shook his head. "No. This is my company, I believe." There was a question in his voice.

"Yes".

Randall drew himself up. "Mathieu, you stay by me. Thank you for your assistance gentlemen..."

"Smoot!" It was Balthazar. He had his red beads in one hand, silver whistle in the other. "Look there!" he cried, waving with the beads.

Beyond the flank of Johnson's long fighting formation, a Yankee line of battle had come out of the forest, standing at a right angle to the Confederate force.

The sweet, pure sound of the silver whistle pierced the air again. Balthazar swung an arm at the shoulder indicating a path through the wood that led to the flank of the new enemy.

The men turned in their fours, turning and breaking into a trot all at once, two hundred acting as one.

Out in the field Johnson spun around to stare at their disappearing backs. Blood suffused his cheeks. He shook his cane at them, enraged to see his suspicions confirmed.

Balthazar had never been good at running. His massive torso and short legs made him lumber along when forced to run.

Because of this, Smoot and the men were surprised to see the speed with which he overtook the head of the column, tearing through the brush, leaving behind a trail of split branches and turpentine oozing from a hundred wounded trunks.

Pounding along through the trees, the battalion kept an eye on the Federals out in the snowy field. Between the pines they watched the end of the line seem to rotate as they passed.

A few of the blue soldiers spied them passing among the trees, heard the thunder of their brogans. They pointed at the forest to their right, begging their officers to turn their eyes from Johnson's men.

The whistle called, its music keening through the ranks, stopping them suddenly, all together, heaving with the exertion of the run, filling the spaces between them with the fog of their ragged breath.

Three short blasts followed by two long faced them to their right, moving from column into line, facing into the end of the Union force.

"Battalion! Forward! March!"

They came out of the tree line a solid mass of butternut, bristling with the steel of their rifles and bayonets, the two long lines staggered so that every weapon would bear. They halted ten yards into the meadow.

Out in front of them the Northern commander tried desperately to pull his flank around to face them. Drums rolled, officers shouted commands. The end of the line began to swing back.

"At my command!" Balthazar's baritone rang across the field, clearly heard by the enemy as well as his own men. "Present!" The wall of Enfield muzzles came up to stare unwinkingly with its tiny black eyes at the Federals. "Fire!"

Flashes of orange and sudden, dirty brown smoke hid the battalion from the Union division ahead. Out of the smoke came the crashing voice of the volley and its burden of leaden lightning. The swinging wall of blue soldiers fell to pieces before it, chewed by the .577 caliber teeth into dead, dying or despairing humanity. Through the smoke the Union men heard the rattle of the ramrods, then the strangely accented words.

"Present! Fire!"

The scythe swung among them again.

"Load!"

The ramrods chattered again.

Edward Johnson watched first in amazement, then with a spreading smile as his situation was transformed. All fire ceased from the force on his left flank. They were fully occupied.

The original Yankee phalanx to his front seemed uncertain and confused. He could see men looking around.

"Drummer!" he called out.

"Sir?" a Black musician spoke from nearby.

"Beat the advance! Now!"

The drumsticks came up smartly to parallel the ground at the level of the man's nose. His brown sleeve glistened with slick, freezing mucous. The sticks came down in a staccato roar which straightened backs across the Stonewall Division.

The Rebels looked at their enemy, seeing them in a new light.

The charge started at a walk.

Their officers counted cadence to hold the formation together.

They started to shuffle after a few steps. The sound in their chests came out of them at first as high pitched laughter. This had nothing to do with humor. There was something hysterical in the sound. As they broke into a trot across the dirty snow and clumps of grass, it changed to a scream, carrying with it the sobbing anger and unqualified murder which they held deep in their hearts.

The Union infantry watched them come for a moment, then broke and ran for the woods behind them. Officers tried to hold back the rout until they realized that they would be left alone to face the Johnnies.

Johnson's men chased them all the way back to the fence over which they had climbed, and then pursued them into the trees beyond.

The people in front of Balthazar saw their comrades run and found in this an excuse to do the same. Suddenly, the only blue soldiers in the field were prostrate in the snow, or standing in clumps with their hands in the air.

O'Brien, the "A" Company commander yelled across to one group. "Hey! You lot! Get your arses over here before som'un shoots yuh!"

His Irish voice made Balthazar smile.

"He sounds like my grandfather," Sergeant Harris said beside him.

"The Paddys are everywhere," Fagan commented from his post nearby behind his company.

"You too, sor!" O'Brien called to a captain who held an injured arm with a free hand.

The blue soldiers looked at each other and at the wounded officer, and then trudged over to the battalion.

General Johnson rode up as Balthazar, Smoot and Sergeant Mathieu knelt around Randall, re-dressing his wound with another piece of clothing. It wasn't bleeding much anymore, but he was beginning to look blue around the mouth.

Balthazar stood and saluted.

Johnson looked down at them. His long nose seemed a monument in a clean shaven face. A stiff leg stuck out strangely in front of the horse's chest.

"I am in your debt, sir!" he said to Balthazar. "These fellows of yours saved the day for us here!"

Balthazar had his red beads in one hand. *"La shukr 'ala waajib,"* he replied.

Johnson was puzzled.

"No thanks for duty done," Smoot translated. "Its one of his favorites."

"What language?" the general asked.

"Arabic," Balthazar replied.

Johnson shook his head gravely. "Well, major, you can give me lessons in Chinese if you keep these men fighting this way. What's the matter with him?"

Randall raised his head, smiling palely from the ground. "A little disagreement with one of their Minies." With his unwounded arm, he waved in the direction of the enemy's departure.

Johnson squinted. "Randall, my god is that you?"

"Yes, general. It is my humble self."

"I thought you had gone home! I have been writing to get you to come back for a place on my staff..."

They all turned to look at the man on the ground.

"Kind of you, General, but I believe I'll roost with these folks for a bit."

Johnson blinked at them. "Snowing again," he said, brushing at his cheek with a gloved hand. "Major Balthazar, take your men back to the road, sir, and I will make my surgeon aware of Captain Randall's wound. How many other casualties do you have?"

"Three, general," Raphael Harris reported. He was standing beside Johnson's horse.

The general looked him over. He shook his head again, turning his horse away.

They watched him go.

"Fine man," Harris said. "No foolishness in him."

"You West Pointers always hang together," Smith remarked.

Harris looked startled by this comment.

Balthazar watched Smith closely.

My, my, where did that come from? What unknown history lies there?

"Thank you, gentlemen," he said ending the discussion before someone took offense. "Let us carry *Captain* Randall and the others to the surgeon and find our wagons. I do not wish to see our men sleeping in the wet tonight. Mister Harris, I would like you to talk to these prisoners. See if there are any among them who might interest us..."

"Oui chef."

After the repulse of this Sixth Corps attack on his line of communications, Lee withdrew ten miles to the west and dug in astride the Orange Turnpike with his left on the Rapidan.

Meade then tried for several days to make his army do his will. He searched for Lee's right flank to the south of the turnpike. He thought he had found it, but could not bring his greater force to bear in a turning movement. After a while he gave up this effort to gain a fairly bloodless victory through maneuver and marched west down the turnpike straight at Lee's position on Mine Run. He should not be blamed for this lack of subtlety. The politicians in Washington were hard at his heels.

"Meade isn't the man for facing down Robert Lee," Devereux said. "As you British would say, he hasn't the stones for it. I saw him in action at Gettysburg. He is a good man, but too careful and civilized to deal with Lee. You need a real bulldog for that, someone who either does not care about the amount of abuse that Lee will heap on his army or who will just put his head down and suffer and suffer and then go on. I hope they don't find that man. Maybe George Thomas would do, but they would never trust him that far, after all, he is a renegade Virginian." Claude looked satisfied with that thought.

Major Robert Neville, late of the "Rifle Brigade," thought that over in silence for a few seconds, and then took a sip from his glass of whisky. "I still have not recovered from the first sight of you in that uniform, old boy," he said. "A brilliant move, but, from what you just said, have I guessed correctly that they do not trust you fully...yet? Oh, I almost forgot. What do you think of Ulysses Grant?"

Devereux provided weekly "feedings" of information for this member of the military attaché's staff at the British embassy in Washington. In general, he gave Neville enough material from the War Department's files to keep the relationship alive, but only that. He did this because the connection might someday be needed. In return for present help, Devereux had received assurance from Her Majesty's Government that help with escape and protection in a new home would be given if needed. That might or might not be a realistic pledge but it was worth having.

The paneled bar of the Willard Hotel made a good place for a meeting so long as the conspirators were watchful for Lafayette Baker's "helpers" among the staff.

Looking at him in the bar's muted light, Devereux considered the Englishman. Neville was slender, erect and immaculate in a beautiful grey frock coat. Claude remembered that his wife had said that she thought Neville was the handsomest man she had ever seen. He wondered if he had reason to be jealous.

"No, "Devereux replied. "They do not trust me fully as yet, not yet, but I continue to work on it. I expect your help in building my position with them whenever you get the chance. You ask my opinion of Grant. What is it that you know of Grant? I saw him last month when he was here for a meeting but did not speak to him. I hear he drinks too much. I hear mixed comments on his talents as a commander."

Neville nodded. "Will he be appointed to succeed Meade?" he asked.

"It seems likely, but a decision has not yet been made and much depends on what Meade can do against Lee in the next few days. They are looking for the same thing that I mentioned, that is, some sign of whether or not Meade has "the stones."

"If that is the case," Neville replied. "I think Grant will have a new job. Let's have oysters for lunch. Waiter!"

Claude made a mental note to visit Colonel Jourdain the next day to compare notes on this matter of Grant's possible appointment.

Cain Comfort went to his death blessing his old friends. He was twenty-one years old, and a rifleman of the 6th Louisiana. Born in Cork, he came to America at fifteen to work with his uncles on the New Orleans waterfront and found employment there as a newsboy.

Years passed and Comfort came to love his new home beyond the possibilities available to truly stable men. Secession gave him the chance to show it.

This "Tiger" had the misfortune of being captured by the U.S. Sixth Corps at Bristoe Station in October. From his point of view there hadn't been any point in rotting in a Union prison waiting for exchange that might not come, better to take the Oath, join the Union Army and desert back to his own side when the chance came.

He was captured by his own company in the fight in which Balthazar's men first drew blood. A field court-martial listened to his story, condemned him to death and recommended clemency. He wasn't the first to have followed this route home. Balthazar had many in his ranks. They had been luckier.

Hays and Early endorsed the court's finding, adding their weight to an appeal for mercy to the commander of the Army of Northern Virginia.

General Lee approved the sentence of death without comment.

The Army of the Potomac closed on the Confederate defenses in a drizzling, freezing rain. In their rubber raincoats they looked like seals glistening blackly across the landscape. They filled the ground as far as anyone could see.

The Johnnies had cut a two hundred yard wide strip of land clear of trees and underbrush to open fields of fire to their front. The ground sloped uphill from the bottom of the valley of Mine Run. The rising earth rose gently, slowly, to the first line of stakes, abatis and chevaux-de-frise. There were rifle pits and trenches behind the obstacles. Finally, there were log revetments for artillery, but those could hardly be seen from the bottom of the valley.

The "seals" stopped at the bottom of the slope, riveted in place by the scene at the top.

A six foot stake stood outside the obstacles.

Two condemned Louisiana deserters had been allowed to escape execution by Stafford's Brigade the day before. They had let them run away, and then had turned an indifferent face to the Judge Advocate General's demand to know who had done this. Lee's renewed order for Comfort's execution was then impossible to avoid.

Jubal Early gave Balthazar the task of shooting him.

The Confederate Second Corps stood to arms in their fighting positions. Rank on rank of warriors in brown. Cold water dripped from the brims of their hats as they stared through the rain at the "seals."

The firing party marched Comfort out through the *abatis* to the stake.

Balthazar had thought to do this thing himself, but Raphael Harris said that it was his to do, his to do for another "Pelican."

Tied to the post, Comfort looked like any other Southern soldier. Someone had found him some clothing so that he would not have to die in the enemy's uniform.

Father Sheeran, the brigade Catholic chaplain, stood beside him.

"I fergiv' yuh all," Cain Comfort cried out from the stake. "Yer ony doin' yer duty, all uv yuh. You too, Sergeant Harris. Yer a good man. I wish I'd known yuh!"

Harris walked down the line of the firing party, passing behind them, whispering a few words to each.

"In the heart, in the head, in the heart..."

Having finished his walk, he took his station at the right of the firing squad.

The priest moved away.

"Shoot straight boys! Don't let him hurt!" Harris said. He looked up, into the eyes of Balthazar who nodded slightly.

"God bless our country!" called out the man at the stake. "God bless the Confederate States! God bless Louisiana!"

"Present!

Aim!

Fire!"

The volley crashed on the wintry air, the smoke billowing and rolling.

Comfort sagged, collapsing in on himself, hanging in his bonds.

Harris drew his revolver, and walked to the stake. He looked closely at the body, and felt for a pulse in the side of the throat. Thumbing back the hammer of his pistol, he fired the grace shot into the brain.

Among the Union troops, a mounted group of senior officers watched. Shivering from the cold, Major General George Gordon Meade, turned his horse to ride back along the turnpike, back to a building he had passed, where he could get out of the rain.

That night, the Army of the Potomac began to withdraw from the south bank of the Rapidan. They crossed on their excellent pontoon bridges, departing unmolested from the presence of this enemy from whom they had yet to seize a victory.

The Confederates stood to arms in the freezing rain and sleet. In the morning their patrols followed the Yankees' trail of abandoned equipment and broken down animals, followed it all the way to the river bank. That afternoon the Rebel infantry left their trenches and started back down the roads to the west, back to their winter camps.

After this withdrawal, Lincoln decided to bring Ulysses Grant east to take command.

Chapter 11

Snowballs

- 3 December –
(The Office of Colonel Lafayette Baker)

"When will Grant arrive," Baker asked. He had one hand in his curly black beard for the purpose of scratching his neck. This "tic" was familiar to all those who knew him well. It showed up whenever he was ill at ease and feeling threatened by unexpected events. His impassive face and well controlled body rarely betrayed his feelings in other ways. Just now, he was uneasy because of the sudden and unexpected arrival of Edwin Stanton in his Pennsylvania Avenue offices.

"Damned if I know," Stanton said. "The matter is out of my hands. The president and that group of young men around him are all afire to have Grant take over the Army as soon as possible. I wanted to give Meade another chance, maybe even bring back Hooker, but Lincoln just ignored me, just ignored me..."

The clatter of traffic in the street beneath the windows obscured some of Stanton's words. Baker leaned toward the Secretary of War, knowing that it would be dangerous to miss the import of whatever it was that Stanton had come to say. It must be something that Stanton did not want overheard. Otherwise, he could have summoned Baker to 17th Street. The two offices were only a mile apart.

Watching Stanton closely, Baker estimated the level of his rage. The red face and throbbing temple vein told him much. From long association he knew that Stanton's internal "temperature" had brought him close to an explosion. "So, Grant is going to take command of the Army of the Potomac?" Baker asked.

"No! God damn it! He is going to be Commanding General of the whole US Army. They are going to renew the title of Lieutenant General for him. He will be the first to hold that rank since Washington. I tried to tell the president that this is not a good idea, that he will have the idea that he really is in charge of the Army, that..." His voice trailed off.

"What about Halleck? What about Meade?" Baker whispered.

What about me? He thought.

"I don't know about Meade. Grant wrote to me to ask to that Halleck stay on as some sort of Chief of Staff to 'look after the Army's business in Washington.' The message was clear. I am to stay out of his business. This wretched drunk has the audacity to tell me that I should stay out of his business!"

Ah.

Baker glanced away from the darkened face. His offices were very simple. Austere would not be too strong a word. The white walls were without adornment. He and Stanton sat in straight backed chairs around a cheap table, something a soldier had bought for him in a local store. "He wins battles," was all he could find to say.

"Yes! Yes! That is what I am told every time I try to raise some point about the rashness of these steps. He wins battles."

A sly smile crept over Baker's regular features. "He hasn't met Robert Lee yet." A thought came to him. "Did he know him… before?" The wartime volunteers like Baker often seemed almost furtive in asking about the ties that still bound the officers of the old Regular Army to each other.

"Not that I know of," Stanton said. "A drunken failure of a captain would hardly have known Lee either professionally or socially." He clearly relished the thought.

"Was there something else, Mr. Secretary?" Surely Stanton had not come to visit just to complain of Lincoln's fickle nature.

"No. Yes. There is this man, Devereux…"

Baker's predatory instincts now held him in suspense waiting for some sign that he might yet capture his lost prey. He said nothing, waiting for a cue.

"You are still watching him and his family?"

"Yes, and mighty expensive it is. Why is he of renewed interest?"

Stanton blinked and shifted in his chair. 'I am not convinced of his loyalty. There is something about him, something… unrepentant. He has an attitude of unspoken superiority."

"I see."

Yes. I see. He makes you feel like a buffoon and a fool. Well, he makes most people feel that way.

"You did appoint him to a position in your offices…"

Stanton looked trapped. "A mistake. Many people recommended the appointment. I thought it was a good idea, but now I see that his influence grows constantly. His friends at the French and British embassies sponsor him."

"Assistant Secretary Davenport in your offices explained to me in this room that Devereux was your instrument in feeding the French what you wanted them to hear."

"Yes. Yes, but I am not sure that I am using him and not the other way around… He now has virtually unrestricted access to the president. Lincoln sends for him to discuss all kinds of matters concerning the rebels."

"What would you have me do?"

"Watch him. Watch everyone connected to him. Perhaps you should bring back that major from Kentucky, the one who accused him before."

"He is dead. He was killed by the mob in New York during the riots in July."

Stanton was silent at the news. "What about the one armed captain who was his helper?"

"Ford? He went back to the artillery, to Hunt's staff. Someone told me recently that he was brevetted to major after Gettysburg."

"I will have him brought back," Stanton said.

"He will not be pleased. He does not like the work."

My God, I do not want that man back here.

"I do not much like him. He is a regular officer. You know how difficult they can be."

"That is your problem. I will have him made a lieutenant colonel of volunteers, no, a colonel. That will make him Devereux's equal in rank. Yes. That is what I will do." Stanton seemed satisfied with the thought, and having decided what to do about Claude Devereux, he rose and left the room without another word.

- 15 December -
(In Camp Near Orange, Virginia)

It snowed hard the night of the fourteenth. Big, white flakes came floating down in the windless darkness. A new moon did not bestow enough light to see well, but if you left your hut to stand alone in the forest, you could feel the snow in your eyebrows and on your cheeks. You could smell the smoke from the chimneys, and hear the gentle sound of the flakes landing all around. You knew from the sound that it would snow all night, and that there would be deep, heavy, new snow in the morning.

Dawn brought with it the still, shimmering brightness that makes a winter's day seem full of new promise. It was the kind of day which gives men back their childhood for a time.

The snowball battle began about ten A.M. in a skirmish between some Alabama men and a wood cutting party from Coppens' Zouaves. The Louisianans had worked hard since breakfast with two man cross-cut saws, dropping trees for their division's saw-mill. The rasp of the saws and the ribald French songs of the detail could be heard across the surrounding fields. Men stood outside their huts to listen. They scratched and spat while making comments on the singing.

It was probably the obsessive nattiness of the Zouaves that set off the attack, the grey baggy pants and the embroidered red vests. Perhaps that was it, or perhaps it was nothing in particular. Maybe they just happened to be there, looking the other way while they worked, and not seeing the stealthy advance through the trees.

The opening fusillade of snowballs smeared white across the red vests. More than one Zouave combed snow from long hair with his fingers. The trunks of oaks and pines suddenly bore snowy circles. Coppens' men reacted with the ferocity that was their pride. The gaudy red and grey figures chased the brown men back through the woods into the meadow from which they had come.

The spectacle of the "Tigers" in hot pursuit drew the attention of all. Men laughed, clapped hands to thighs and yelled encouragement to the Alabamians who had made the attack. No one liked the Zouaves much. Their finery and rough behavior with the country people were irritating to many. This was an opportunity to pay them back.

The raiding party's friends came rushing across the open ground. The snow was calf deep. The Alabamians ran awkwardly, unused to this strange impediment. Nearing the "enemy," they scooped up handfuls of snow to pack into ammunition. In "line of battle", they laid down a withering fire which drove the Zouaves back to the wood line. Seeing the "enemy," in retreat the Alabama men ran on through the trees and out into the sunshine beyond. In the open, they looked around, realizing that they had pursued the Zouaves into the very heart of Harry Hays' division camp. The attack lost speed. A run became a walk. The walk slowed to a stop. Then, they began to back away, turning toward their own huts.

Across Hays' division, drums began to beat the long roll.

Over their shoulders the retreating men saw company streets fill as officers formed their units.

All the rest of the day, the fight raged through the woods and fields around the camps. Three times the heavy masses of men from the Deep South drove the Stonewall Division's Virginians and Hays' Pelicans before them, drove them back through the camps, driving with the force of their numbers the men who had followed Old Jack when all who knew him had thought him mad.

About three o'clock, Brigadier General Jim Walker arrived up to take charge of the Stonewall Division. He stood in the snow laughing and talking with Leroy Stafford and the other senior officers on the scene. Balthazar stood beside him listening to the discussion of tactics with a broad smile. He was a chaos of snow from head to foot, and resembled a snowball more than anything else. They all looked like that, all the hundreds and hundreds of soldiers.

A jug appeared and passed around the circle of officers.

Behind them, Smoot had the battalion in line, a central piece in the defensive position holding off an attack during the staff conference.

"Yer not gonna' thrink all that?" an Irish voice questioned from Balthazar's ranks.

"Shut up ye scut!" roared O'Brien from his post. "The gentlemen will have yer need for liquid sustenance in mind, I'm sure."

Walker sent them the jug.

"Major Balthazar, perhaps you could advise us at this critical moment?" Walker said across the six feet between them.

Balthazar looked pleased, scuffed a foot in the snow, and peered around the group of officers to see if they were watching.

Their friendly faces reassured.

He looked in the snow for a stick, found one the right length, and after breaking off a few twigs, knelt to draw on the white surface.

Roars of triumph shook the trees, as the opponents of the Stonewall Division watched in puzzlement, and not a little disappointment as nearly half their "enemies" threw up hands in disgust and simply walked away, turning their backs on the fight, passing quickly from the scene, striding over a fold in the meadow to disappear from view.

Coppens' Zouave Battalion remained in the center of the now shrunken line of the Stonewall Brigade. Upon their colorful heads a thousand snow balls fell. The Zouaves stood their ground manfully, backed by all the weight of "fire" available to the Virginians on either side of them, but it was not to be. The effect of numbers made itself felt and soon the center of Walker's line began to bow inward as the Zouaves were pressed back. The Virginians moved back to straighten the line, and a howl of victory swept the ranks of the men of the Deep South as they pressed forward.

"*Sauve qui peut*!" cried someone. There was an instant's hesitation, and then the Zouaves turned and ran, carrying with them the inner flanks of the units to either side. Walker's "line of battle" disintegrated in a flash as men sought escape from the humiliation of capture. They fled along the way that their friends had gone, over the rise in the ground, headed for the distant shelter of the trees.

The foemen followed, pausing only to manufacture new stocks of ammunition. Every few yards they halted momentarily to rain down a barrage on the backs of the defeated.

They chased Walker's soldiers at least three hundred yards, and were beginning to think of giving it up when they saw Jim Walker himself come to a dead stop in the middle of the fleeing mob, holding his walking stick up high over his head, waving it back and forth and yelling, "Rally, Boys! Rally!"

The refugees turned to form their sodden ranks. They stooped to scoop up snow, piling up missiles at their feet.

Their pursuers came to a ragged halt, confused by the suddenness of the change. They looked to their leaders for some indication of what should be done.

A cheer rose over the wood lot to their right. Out of the trees, shoulder to shoulder, marched Stafford's Pelicans, each man cradling an armful of snow balls. At the left, extending their line was Balthazar's battalion.

"Brigaade, Halt!" roared Brigadier General Stafford from his place in front of the advance. "At my command!"

A thousand arms cocked back.

"Fire!"

Arrows darkened the sky at Agincourt. Snow balls did the same this day.

"Fire at will!" Stafford commanded. He was laughing and out of breath from dodging the dozens of balls thrown at him from the other side.

The Georgians and Alabamians tried to re-form facing in both directions.

They were halfway through this intricate maneuver when Balthazar judged the moment to be just right and yelled "Charge!" He ran right at the "enemy" line, dropping his ammunition as he went.

The battalion surged ahead, sweeping forward behind him like a pack of dogs. They covered the thirty odd yards in an instant.

Balthazar hit the line like the old Rugby boy he was. He shouldered men to either side, driving through, and out the other side. Brushing aside staff officers who sought to shield their chief, he tackled a tall, mustachioed man who had clearly been the directing force on the other side.

They rolled over and over in the snow, pelting each other, and stuffing the cold whiteness down collars and up shirts.

"All right! I yield!" the victim of this attack said at last.

They climbed to their feet, helped up by the cheering mob of soldiers.

Major General Robert Rodes brushed snow off his sleeves and stuffed his shirt back into his trousers. "My God, Balthazar, I had no idea you were so upset about that Poker game..." He was grinning.

Balthazar smiled back. He had come to admire and like this man, so young for his rank, so upright and unpretentious.

Rodes reached into an inner pocket of his coat, retrieving some papers. "General Early gave me these last night. He had to go away, and knew you and Smoot are coming for dinner today." He looked up, and around, searching. "Smoot!" he called. "Come over here!"

Smoot saluted as he reported.

Rodes' hand came up to return the greeting. He looked odd with the snow still caking his long, blond mustaches. Opening one of the papers, he said, "Isaac, this is your commission in the Confederate States Army. Congratulations, Lieutenant!"

Smoot shook hands all around, and then read the paper. He looked up. "This must be a mistake."

"Why?" Balthazar asked.

"This is a commission in the Regular Army. I'm just in this for the war. There are commissions for the others as well..."

They both looked quizzically at Rodes.

He shrugged. "Yes. Cooper and Lee like what you've made of these men. They aim to keep it. It has no state identity so they have decided to add it to the small list of regular units." He looked at another paper. "It will be... Here it is. 2nd Infantry Battalion, Confederate States Army, but I suspect it will always be Balthazar's Battalion."

"Why this?" Smoot demanded holding up his commission.

"Regular troops are commanded by regular officers," Balthazar answered for Rodes. "Always." His face flushed red beneath the tan. He seemed distracted by something off on the horizon. Taking out a red bandanna, he blew his nose loudly.

"Yes," the general said looking at the Frenchman. "And as you've guessed, you are appointed a lieutenant colonel as well." He smiled. "Congratulations, Colonel," he said, holding out a hand.

Balthazar hesitated only a second before taking it. There were two pieces of paper in the envelope. The second was a certificate of naturalization.

"Yes, that's right also," Rodes said. "With a regular commission comes citizenship, colonel. Now you are fighting for your own country. Now you belong to us..."

A cheer went up.

Balthazar looked up into the eyes of his men. They had crowded forward, elbowing their way through.

A member of Rodes' staff handed him a triangular, oilcloth covered packet. "Your battalion flag, sir", he said diffidently. "It came with the papers."

Balthazar held it up for them to see.

They carried him back to their camp.

Chapter 12

Victoria

- 18 December -

"When you come back, I'd dearly like a few days to see the family..." The words stayed in his mind, slowly dissolving with the passage of the miles and the song of the rails. Smoot's face stayed longer, lodged in the brain, appearing again and again when he turned to the dirty, cracked window. He couldn't get it out of the back of his head. The wooden seats were hard. Sleep was not a possibility.

Soldiers sat on the floor; their backs against the vertical walls, their possessions were piled among them.

His rank got him a place above, among the women, and convalescents. The train carried them southwest to the junction with the Virginia Central.

It was cold outside. The windows were frosted around the edges. A pot bellied stove glowed red in a box of sand at the center of the car, tended by an elderly black man.

Balthazar waited an hour and a half at Gordonsville, moving restlessly back and forth from the platform to the little station's only room. The stationmaster and telegrapher waited with him, surprised and pleased to have a foreign gentleman volunteer with whom to visit. They walked up and down the platform talking about Europe and the war.

A freight train came at midnight. There were twenty-two slat-sided cars filled with sides of bacon and livestock. The conductor swung down to stand in conversation with the stationmaster. The two faces were golden in the lantern light. The conductor finally looked at Balthazar, and raised a gloved hand to beckon.

He played poker with the trainmen on the way to Hanover Junction They sat at a table built into one wall of the caboose. Poker wasn't really his game. He had taken it up in America to amuse the senior officers who often invited him to play. In these games, he lost a fair amount of money at first until Sergeant Harris explained that the game was largely a matter of bluff. After that, he began to break even over the course of an evening, his heavy winning balanced with streaks of suicidal plunging. He seemed more interested at such times in watching the opposition than the cards.

From Ashland the train rolled south through flat, wooded country broken with open fields. At one crossing there was a battered wooden sign lettered with the words, "Yellow Tavern." It hung from one nail, swinging in the wind. Behind the sign post stood a rundown, rambling structure. Half a dozen horses were hitched at a rail outside the front door. Balthazar wondered if this was the tavern. The building was really more white than any other color.

After another hour, the countryside changed as the train entered a substantial town. Destitute shanties housing crowds of Negroes crowded close against the track. They watched the moving machine. Children waved.

He waved back. This seemed to amuse the trainmen.

The freight rumbled up Broad Street to the Richmond, Fredericksburg & Potomac depot.

Balthazar examined the buildings to either side of the tracks along the avenue. He decided that their state of repair had declined in the last few months and then, having seen what there was to see, he paid them no further attention.

The station was in the heart of Richmond, three blocks from the capitol of the Confederate States. A Signal Corps lieutenant waited on the platform. Telegrams from Lee's Headquarters had brought him to meet each of the last three trains from Hanover Junction. He stood impatiently in the cold, stamping up and down, swinging his arms, and striking one fist into the palm of the other hand from time to time. Tall and blond, he was perfectly dressed in the prescribed uniform color, French Grey. His overcoat was of the finest English wool. Its brass buttoned half cape was thrown back negligently over his shoulders.

The freight train groped its way to a screeching halt beside all the other lines of cars.

The lieutenant leaned on a baggage cart to see down the line of boxcars. He did not think his man would be on a train like this,

but one never...

Then, he spied a burly, mustachioed figure climbing down from the high step of the caboose.

As he strode down the *quai* toward the newcomer, the signal officer watched the new arrival shake hands with a brakeman and wave at others inside. He then picked up a carpet bag with one hand and carrying a cavalry carbine at the "balance" with the other, walked away from the caboose. A sword rode comfortably strapped to the bag. As they approached, the lieutenant found his probable "guest" more and more interesting. He wore a brown leather mackinaw coat lined in fleece. A round felt hat, canvas pants and a red and black shirt completed his uniform. His face was ruddy with outdoor living. A black bandanna around his neck was tied into a neckerchief. It looked like silk. The signal lieutenant had some knowledge of the theater. The closer the other man came, the more he looked like Cyrano de Bergerac. A smile transformed the lieutenant's expression. He stopped and stepped aside to let a group of railroad men by.

The newcomer approached to within a few feet.

Drawing himself up the lieutenant saluted gravely. "Harrison, Signal Corps, sir. Major Jenkins sent me to receive you."

The visitor looked at him. Grounding the carbine butt in front of him, he leaned its muzzle against his belly and held out a hand. "John Balthazar, 2nd Infantry Battalion. Awfully good of you to meet me... You must have been here all day? Very grateful!"

Harrison pulled off a glove to shake the large fingered hand. He had not been warned about the English accent, and was so surprised by it that speech deserted him.

The freight's locomotive hissed mercifully, covering his confusion. It spouted white steam from somewhere in the depths of the machinery. The whistle blew with shrill force from beside them as the train began to back from the station.

Harrison replaced his glove, took the carpet bag and led the way to the street. "Yes, well, we got Venable's telegram last night... You didn't waste any time coming back," he commented while peering around for their vehicle and driver.

Balthazar looked sideways at him. "No. A summons to meet a courier from my embassy is something I will treat with some urgency."

Hearing the tone of this statement, Harrison's confusion increased. "I meant no criticism, colonel."

The other nodded.

They reached the sidewalk and Harrison peered around for the driver. "It looks as though that black ape has taken himself off somewhere. Damn! I asked for one of our better drivers, but he's sick. I've never seen this nigger before in my life! What do you say we walk? It's only a few blocks."

They started off down Eighth Street together, turned on Franklin, passing in front of the Mechanics Hall, the building which housed the War Department's main offices.

Striding along beside Harrison, Balthazar soon began to feel himself the poor relative come to visit his city cousins.

Women on the street found opportunities to peek at Harrison whenever they could.

Soldiers saluted the lieutenant, not seeming to see his superior until so close that the two corroded gold colored stars were impossible to miss.

"Did you bring some other clothes, sir?" Harrison asked after watching the street's reaction.

Balthazar thought that reaction both odd and sad. He contrasted in his mind's eye the winter camps of the Army of Northern Virginia with the scene which now surrounded him. This situation was something new to him, a war fought by a volunteer citizen army so close to its own capital. "Yes. I have the civilian suit in which I first came to Richmond. It is in the bag you carry."

"Would you like a service dress uniform in grey?"

"No."

They said nothing for a block.

Balthazar looked up the hill to the left, at Jefferson's capitol. "You are a staff officer?" he asked.

Harrison's head came up. He was stung by the implied disparagement. "No. I've been a scout mostly. I worked for Longstreet a lot. Now, he's sore at me for something that happened last summer. It looks like I may be going out to the Trans-Mississippi... I'd be glad to get out of here. Richmond is beginning to depress me."

"Why?"

"You'll see."

"Do you know my cousin, Claude Devereux?" Balthazar asked seeking to repair the atmosphere between them.

"My God! You're his cousin?" Harrison whistled a few bars of something unfamiliar. "Yes, of course I know him, a phenomenon. He brings to mind Melville's description of Captain Ahab, 'a grand, ungodly, godlike man'. And that wife of his! Don't wrap her up! I'll take her just as she is!" He glanced at his companion to see if he had taken offense at that, but the Frenchman was smiling at some private joke.

Actually, Balthazar was thinking of Smoot and the feeling that the man obviously had for Claude's wife. Smoot had done his best to conceal his emotional attachment for Hope but the depth of his feeling had become clear in the course of Balthazar's constant association with him. How that would end was a worry for Balthazar, but in the context of the war…

Encouraged by a lack of reaction to his mention of Hope, Harrison went on. "But then, you know the courier. It's his sister-in-law, the widow." He stopped, halted by Balthazar's hand on his arm. Swinging around to make some light comment on the lady, he knew from the other man's face that to do so was to make an enemy.

"Where is she?"

"The American Hotel. You are staying there. We expect that she will pass on to you whatever it is that Colonel Jourdain gave her. The note she brought from Devereux made it clear that we should stay out of this..."

"How did she come?"

"Across the lines at Fredericksburg. She had some very fancy papers. Signed by Edwin Stanton himself they were. It seems she has an aged maiden aunt in Henrico County who has reached her last days... She'll be here a week, colonel, a week." Harrison continued down the street, stopping in front of a big building with a marquee. "Here it is! Let's go in and get you registered. She's in room 224." He paused in the space made by a door held open by a liveried Negro. "Jenkins told me he would like to talk to you sometime tomorrow."

Balthazar looked at him seeking guidance on the urgency of that request.

Harrison stopped smiling. "You do what you want, sir. They're all scared to death that you'll write something bad about us. You do whatever you want, and then escape from this God damned place!" With that he waved Balthazar through the door, and followed him in.

At the reception desk, Balthazar stood with pen in hand signing the register while a clerk searched in a cabinet for his room key. Having finished, the Frenchman waited quietly. He was not really thinking of anything. The night had been long and cold. He looked at the cubbyholes behind the counter. The rectilinear framework held a variety of envelopes and notes. Eight or nine keys hung on hooks in front of the openings. "You have the custom of asking guests to leave their keys when they are away from the hotel"?

The frock coated clerk found it. It had a paper tag attached to the copper disk from which it normally would hang.

Balthazar could not read what was written on the tag from where he stood.

Behind the counter, the hotelier stood irresolutely with the key in hand. Frown lines of confusion showed between his eyes. "No, sir. We don't ask that. Perhaps in London..."

Harrison reached across to take the key from him. "We thought you might want a suite, colonel. We have several here that "belong" to Jenkins' office."

They moved away to stand under the chandelier in the middle of the lobby.

Well groomed men and women passed around them. A middle-aged woman in a fur trimmed cape drew in her skirts to pass Balthazar. She saw the two stars and smiled.

"Perhaps I should find something more suitable to wear" Balthazar said.

Harrison laughed silently. "I'll send my tailor. He's an oily little fellah, but he'll take good care of you." Picking up the carpet bag and the Sharps, he looked around. "Porter!" When the bellman came, he handed the gun and bag to a grizzled old black man who lifted the carbine to look at it. "Take the colonel's bags upstairs, Room 226. Thank you." He tucked the key into the pocket of the man's flowered waistcoat.

"By your leave, sir". He said to Balthazar, and with a slight bow he was gone.

The American was a fine hotel. The blockade had bitten deeply into the way people were able to live in Richmond, but the staff there still took pride in the quality of their efforts. A copper tub came out of a closet to be filled with hot water by a series of waiters pushing carts covered with steaming buckets. A barber shaved him and cut his hair. Someone took his civilian suit away to clean.

The Italian tailor arrived, took his measurements for several uniforms and left promising to return for a fitting in the morning.

Balthazar managed not to smile in disbelief.

He showed the tailor out, thanking the man for his promptness, and was standing in the doorway wearing the hotel's monogrammed dressing gown when Victoria Devereux turned the corner at the head of the stairs and walked down the hallway toward him between the potted ferns.

Joe White was behind her. He looked sideways at the tailor as the man went by ducking his head and lifting his hat to the lady.

Balthazar became aware of his bare feet. The carpet fringe between his toes seemed thick as rope.

She stopped in front of him. Her brown eyes were filled with mischief, but they resolutely focused on his face. She offered her hand.

He raised it to his lips. She had that quality found in some women of not needing artificial scent. Her skin had a warm, healthy fragrance beyond the ability of human skill to imitate.

With some reluctance he released her hand. Lifting his head, he saw, or hoped to see, something for him in her expression.

"I *am* in luck," he said. "Out of the field for a week in the dead of winter, and the privilege of your company as well! It is too much!"

She smiled a little. "John, I think Claude has more to do with it than luck. I have enjoyed your letters..."

Now, he knew that he had not hoped too much. He took her hand again.

Behind her, Joe White cleared his throat.

Balthazar looked at him over her shoulder.

Joe looked expressively up and down the corridor.

"Ah, Yes! Thank you." He returned his attention to Victoria. "May we have dinner?"

She nodded. "Actually, I have two tickets for the theater tonight. Lieutenant Harrison left them in my room. Would you join me?"

Balthazar automatically felt for a watch in his missing trousers.

"Ten after five, colonel," Joe said.

"Thank you, again. "I see that my secret new status is not very secret..."

"It's surprising what Claude knows," Victoria said seeming pleased with the thought. "He told us of your appointment before we left."

"Would six-thirty in the dining room be good?"

She was nodding and about to agree when Joe spoke once more.

"Major Jenkins said that the two of you should not be seen in public together, sir..."

"Yes, Claude said the same thing..." Victoria added.

"But the theater?"

"Box seats, sir. May I suggest dinner at six forty-five in Mrs. Devereux's rooms? Is someone doing your clothing for this evening? Good. I'll find them and come around to help you dress."

"I can dress myself."

Victoria's face was a study in wordless communication commanding him to obey, to give Joe what he wanted.

Balthazar looked at Joe. "Very well... Be here at six, I should like to talk to you..."

"Yes, sir."

She lowered her chin slightly to hide the smile, and was gone down the hall to her door.

He went back into his sitting room and sat for ten minutes with a tumbler of Bourbon in one hand facing the connecting door

"And what was he like, my cousin Patrick?"

Joe seemed puzzled by the question. "But, I believe you knew Mister Patrick, sir..." The Black man stood before him in a pose of respectful attention.

"Of course. He visited us in Soturac. I was on leave. My wife thought him easily the most charming man she had ever met..."

"Not Mister Claude?" Joe inquired.

Balthazar studied him and then spoke. "Claude, she believed to be a genius perhaps, but not someone she would wish to be close to."

Joe nodded solemnly after a moment's thought. "Mister Patrick was a fine man. They all are fine men, but the ladies are the finest of all. Madame Clotilde..."

"I know, Joseph. I had only a few hours with her, but..." Words left him in the confusion of the memory of his own childhood.

"She is another mother to us all, sir."

Balthazar looked around at the room, at the wallpaper with its English design, and the stain from a rain leak around the casing of a window. He turned back to Joe, now busy with his shoes. "I see that you want something, Joseph," he said. "What do you want of me?" he asked. "What is it?" They had been talking for fifteen minutes and a growing sense of the other's unspoken question had built in Balthazar.

"War is a cruel thing, sir, a cruel thing."

Balthazar waited in his chair.

"I want you to be kind to her, sir. That's what Mr. Claude wants, that is what we all want..."

"You presume a good deal. There are many who would think that..."

"No. You know the truth, I think."

"Do I?"

Yes, I can see the truth. It is surprising that there are those who do not.

The French soldier and the mulatto footman faced each other wordlessly across the empty place between them. The carmine *misbaha* clicked in his fingers.

"Those are mighty nice beads, colonel," Joe said at last.

Balthazar rose from his seat to rummage about among his things, searching.

Joe watched him, puzzled until the massive figure turned to face him, a broad smile on the strong features.

In his fingers, Balthazar held another string of beads. These were black with silver tracery on their surface. Three small coins trailed from them. "Joseph, I would give you the red, but they are a gift from a true friend..." He handed the ebony beads to the black man.

Joe looked at the coins. They were inscribed in a language which was both beautiful and alien. The beads were smooth to the touch with just the suggestion of the heads of the silver pins which made the inlay.

"A rosary?"

Balthazar nodded, pleased. "Just so! Very good, but they are for the mussalman!" Balthazar looked around searching for his jacket, turning back to find Joe holding it.

The courting couple chatted amiably through dinner.

Balthazar could not recall afterward what it was that they ate. There was much to say of family life in Alexandria, much to say of what had passed with him since their brief encounter. He was careful not too speak too much of death.

It did not seem to matter that they had been together so little. There was between them an instinctive recognition that they somehow meant something special for each other. He talked to her of the battalion, of Smoot. She seemed to think of Smoot as yet another member of the family. She told him that his second in command was a favorite of Hope's, and that to have Hope for a friend was a powerful asset in the world of the Devereuxs.

He told her how much he thought Smoot cared for Hope.

She frowned a little at that. "Perhaps it is better that he is here with you..."

Joe stood out in the hall while they ate, knocking to admit waiters, waving them out when they had served a course. Finally, he entered to find them deep in conversation, and reminded that the curtain would rise in fifteen minutes.

Balthazar helped her into a coat. His hands held her shoulders from behind. She smiled over her shoulder, patting his hand and walked to the door.

They descended the grand staircase to the lobby. A few heads turned to look.

Among them was Harrison. He stood by the porter's desk with another man. Both wore civilian clothes. Harrison bowed slightly to Victoria.

She nodded in recognition.

The signal officer and his companion followed them up the street at a discreet distance.

The lobby of the "Richmond Theater" was spacious but not impressive to a European. They swept through it without a glance. Balthazar afterward remembered a few potted plants and some marbleized paneling. To his surprise only a handful of army and navy men were present in the foyer. Evening clothes were very much in evidence. Some of the fashions worn by both men and women were things that he remembered to have been this season's creations in Europe.

A Black usher in tails and white tie saw them up narrow stairs, held the door for Victoria and seated her.

For just a second, seated by her side, he felt they were alone and began to relax, absorbed in her profile. Then he remembered, and turned to look out into the auditorium. It was surprisingly grand. There was a lot of gilt, a lot of dark red velvet, and many chandeliers glittering with facets and candlelight.

The show was not a drama. It was a collection of musical selections, of songs that were mostly by Stephen Foster. Balthazar loved music but it was Victoria who really interested him that evening. His inner self drifted steadily toward her as the singing went on.

Nevertheless, the music was compelling. He found the melodies to be something that felt for a place in the heart. There were several comic sketches, many of them satire of the political life of the capital.

As he watched, it became clear that while politicians were fair game, the army and navy were not. Lincoln received a fair amount of humorous abuse and the stereotype of the New England Puritan hypocrite appeared several times to the universal amusement of the audience.

His attention drifted back and forth from the performance to the woman by his side. He did not want to lose this chance to talk to her.

She was acutely aware of his attention. It told her something she wanted to know, something she had crossed enemy lines to learn. She thought of her sister-in- law, Hope. She thought of the essential faithlessness of Claude Devereux, of the worthlessness of his love for any woman.

His father has much to answer for she thought. Isaac Smoot is a better man. She needs to know that he loves her. I must tell her. It will help, but Isaac must stay with John...

The family grieved for Hope's devastated life. It had seemed for a time that Claude had reformed, but now, it was clear that he had not. Victoria did not wish to bring another family tragedy into the house on Duke Street. She needed to be sure about this nearly unknown man beside her.

She leaned close to whisper. "Watch the show!"

Feeling foolish, he concentrated on the audience. There were men in the theater whose presence he could not understand, young men, well dressed and formed, sitting and laughing with women, women who did not look to be better than they should be. *Why aren't they in the military?*

The curtain rose on a new group standing before a painted backdrop depicting a sylvan scene. There were three characters in the group. All of them were instantly recognized by the audience. The balcony hooted derisively. Balthazar looked up and was relieved to see that this part of the theater was filled with soldiers. All of them were enlisted soldiers, many of them with arms still in slings. Canes were propped on the balcony rail.

He looked down at the stage, and listened for a few minutes. It was a parody of war profiteers. There was a Jewish merchant in dark clothes with a silly nose. A second was a large and pompous man who proved to be a grasping transplanted Yankee industrialist. The third was a British blockade running captain.

All were favorites in the balcony. The convalescents reacted with spirit to every line spoken on stage.

The three characters engaged in a lively discussion of the risks and profits provided by the war.

"When can I haff dose bolts of zilk you brought me from London?" the Jew asked rubbing his hands together. Balthazar noticed that the actor wore a strange conical cap of the kind that Jews wore in cartoons in Punch.

"To hell with your fripperies, Mose!" the industrialist roared. I need those stamping dies you have on board from Germany. There's no way I can keep up with the demand for new carriages in Atlanta and Savannah! Some people have made a little money in all this, and they want their barouches!" The factory owner smiled with deep satisfaction at the thought. The twang of his Yankee voice sounded very authentic. The gallery roared with catcalls and rude noises. "I've sweetened up the railroads to haul them for me 'priority freight" the factory owner announced.

Another cacophonous clamor descended from above.

The "English Runner Captain" was dressed in such high style that he could have just arrived from his club on Pall Mall. "I saay, old thing," he drawled. "You will just have to contain yourself until after the week-end. I cahn't possibly do anything about unloadin' the ship till then, don't you know? Been invited up to the country for a spot of grouse shootin'."

"See here, Percival!" the carriage maker pleaded. "I have customers waiting. I'll give you a thousand dollars Confederate to unload your damned boat today!"

The "Englishman" yawned behind a hand gloved in suede.

"Dat will do no good, Hiram," the Jew declaimed. "Dese vellows make zo much in gold that ze money iss nutting to dem."

In the orchestra seats many backs were rigid and heads did not turn in response to catcalls from the balcony.

The scattering of military men among them, mostly officers, laughed openly, clearly in sympathy with the convalescents.

After a while he looked at her. "Do you agree with this?"

She grimaced. "The Jewish thing is wrong and unfair from everything I know but probably inevitable. The remaining two are exactly correct."

The convalescents continued to hoot.

Mercifully, the skit ended and the musical review began again with a song about a log cabin performed by several men in blackface. After listening to several more selections, Balthazar found paper and a pencil in his pockets and began to make notes, asking Victoria for the names of pieces he particularly liked. This proved to be a pleasant way to learn. As she leaned toward him he caught the scent of her skin. She smelled wonderful.

The performance ended in a finale of massed singers and "My Old Kentucky Home." The "Jew", the "Yankee", and the "Runner" were on stage with the "Puritan" and "Old Abe." Applause was hearty and the performers returned for an encore and several bows.

They left the box to find Joe waiting for them.

"Did you see the show?" Balthazar asked.

"Yessir. I watched from up behind the second balcony seats, behind the soldiers..."

They reached the lobby, and passed through double doors into the street. It was cold and Balthazar was wondering if she would accept his overcoat around her for the walk back when he heard loud voices behind them. He turned to see one of the convalescents sprawled on the sidewalk, a crutch beside him.

The man's friends began to help him up.

Facing the group of soldiers were three of the dandies from the orchestra seats. All were flushed and appeared upset. Of the three, the man in the center was clearly the angriest. He moved restlessly, shifting from foot to foot, waiting for the soldier to get back on his feet. "I'll teach you your place, damn you!" he said to the wounded man who was now on his feet. With that, he raised a walking stick to strike.

They made an arresting group in the yellow gas light. The wounded man raised a hand to protect his head. Cavalry chevrons covered his upper arm. He had lost his hat and from the blood beginning to ooze through brown hair, it was clear that the dandy's cane had been in use. The man with the cane wore an exquisitely tailored Chesterfield coat. It had ridden up as he raised his arm, and hung open in the front. Beneath it there could be seen a waistcoat of dark, flowered silk. He was shorter than the soldier and had to look up at him. From the look on his face it was easy to guess that he did not like that.

Harrison stepped through the circle of wounded to seize the civilian's wrist. Outrage showed in the man's face as his attention shifted.

One of his friends felt in an inside pocket for what could only be a pistol.

The cavalryman was unrepentant. "You blood-suckin' limey bast'rd! I'd shove that stick up your aiss if I didn't have this laig!," he snarled.

Balthazar opened a path for himself by gently pulling men apart. "Actually, it is *their* place; you know..." he said in a conversational tone to the little man.

His cultivated English voice confused the other man. The Britisher focused on him. "I will not be spoken to in this way by a common soldier! These bloody Americans *will* learn respect for their betters!"

"I rather doubt you are *better* than they," Balthazar remarked, "and I have found them to be anything but common..."

"Colonel, we'll handle this," Harrison said. "Why don't you take the lady and go back to the..."

The Englishman stood on his toes to see over the crowd. A sly grin came over his features. "Yes, *colonel.*" The sarcasm was unmistakable. "Why don't you take the *lady...*"

Balthazar's left hand slipped under his coat and around into the small of his back. The cool, dry bone of the *khanjar's* hilt fit comfortably into his hand.

The Englishman's associate began to draw his pistol from within his garments.

One of the convalescents hit him with a cane in the angle between neck and shoulder. He screamed and sank to his knees holding his injury.

Balthazar stepped close to the Englishman. "Listen to me, my friend," he whispered in the ear. "This officer is about to release your arm. If you strike this soldier, or anyone here, I will kill you... Do you hear me, sir? Do you?" He could feel his breath shuddering as the blood heat; the death hunger, came over him. He knew his words trembled, but could not help himself. In his bones and guts he could feel the blade going in under the last rib, knew in his soul just how much force to use. He could see an inch of point protruding through the back of the beautiful coat.

Fear came into the other man's face. Knowledge of the closeness of death came to him. "Yes, yes, I hear you. Let me go, please."

Balthazar nodded slightly.

Harrison released the wrist.

The silver headed cane slowly descended. The Englishman stepped back, away from Balthazar.

Several uniformed men arrived, pushing and shoving their way through the crowd that had gathered until they saw Harrison. Their leader was in civilian dress. He held up a hand for his men to stop. "What is this, Lieutenant? What has happened?"

Harrison looked at Balthazar who glanced at the soldier who had been struck.

The man shrugged.

Balthazar brought his two hands together in front of his stomach.

"Nothing," Harrison said. "Nothing at all..."

The three Englishmen turned away, quickly disappearing in the dark.

The Provost Guard followed them down the street, their breath steaming in the cold.

"Thank you, cunnel!" the cavalry sergeant said. He held out a hand, which Balthazar took for a moment.

The group of convalescents boarded a waiting horse drawn omnibus. Harrison and Balthazar helped several onto the step.

"It would be pointless, sir, to make a complaint," Harrison began. "No court would act against these men. We need them too badly..."

Balthazar nodded in agreement and sought Victoria. He found her a few feet away, waiting with Joe. Grasping her arm, he walked toward their hotel.

Nothing was said, but half way back she took his hand and held it until they reached the American Hotel's door.

At her door he kissed her hand before she went in.

He saw that Joe waited at a discreet distance. "Where are you sleeping, Joseph?" he asked.

"In the servants' quarters, sir." Joe looked puzzled.

"You can stay with me. There are two bedrooms and you should be near your mistress."

"Perhaps the hotel may object, sir."

"Provincial nonsense! Do not trouble yourself. I will tell them you are *my* valet. Get your kit and a bottle of whisky from the bar."

You see, I do understand.

"Yes, sir."

Behind the door, he could hear her laughing softly.

The next day they went to see her aunt. Joe drove the rented carriage and they sat in the back and chatted. The ride out to Henrico County was not long. The old lady proved to be truly ill. Balthazar had begun to doubt the reality of her sickness. She proved to be quite feeble, but not so much that she did not find the strength to flirt shamelessly with the French gentleman.

On the way back to town, Victoria took his hand again. He could not find words, but covered her hand with his.

The tailor brought his uniforms in the afternoon. They were made of the finest blue-grey woolens with two gold colored stars on either side of the collar. The Austrian Knots that his rank required were sewn on the sleeves.

Joe was immensely pleased with the effect.

After a moment's thought, Balthazar searched in his saddle bags and found his *Legion d'Honneur*. He pinned it on the left breast of his tunic. The scarlet ribbon lay in its accustomed place making a pleasing contrast with the grey cloth.

He went next door to show Victoria his new clothes. She stood by the window looking at him for a long time. The light of a winter day framed her figure, shining through the edges of her auburn hair. He could not see her features very well because of the halo made by the light outside.

"Grey becomes you, John," she finally commented. "I don't think I have seen a sword like that before."

He had put on his Zouave saber. Its curved, slender scabbard hung to his knee. He drew the sword and laid it on the fringed, lace cloth which covered a round table in the center of the room.

She came to look down at it. "Where was this made?" she asked with an inclination of her head.

"At, Fez, in Morocco, for me."

"And the other, the one you had under your coat last night?"

He reached with his left hand into the small of his back to retrieve the *khanjar* from its place beneath his sword belt. He laid it on the table with the saber. "Also made for me in Fez."

She ran her fingers over the leather covering of the sword's scabbard, and looked at him in surprise.

"Shark skin. It does not slip."

She drew the knife, and looked at the blade. It was engraved in a language she did not recognize. "What does it say?"

"*La ghalib ilaa Allah*... 'No victor but God.' It is a reminder to us all from the devout."

She placed the dagger on the table. "What shall we do with the rest of this day?"

"What would you like?"

"I'd like to go for a walk so that I can show you off, and then we should have dinner in this hotel's admirable dining room, which I think can still do rather well by guests. But, then Major Jenkins might not like that..."

"Ah, yes. I have a *rendezvous* with him after dinner. But we shall go for our walk. In Richmond I am merely another officer on leave. Poof! What do we care for his opinion?"

She dimpled nicely in a way that made him feel a little giddy. He now saw that her widow's weeds had given way to lighter shades. He put on the tools of his trade and held her coat so that she would be warm.

Outside the door Joe waited with his overcoat.

He found his interview with Major Harry Jenkins to be a difficult, somewhat confusing thing. They sat together for a long hour in a drafty, bare little room in the Mechanics Building.

Not surprisingly, Jenkins remained focused on Balthazar's mission on behalf of the ministry in Paris. He held his peace while Balthazar deciphered and read the letter that Victoria had brought, but then could contain himself no more. "From what Devereux tells us your Colonel Jourdain is pleased with the reports you have made..."

Balthazar agreed. "Yes, he is happy. I shall continue to send him my thoughts, but now..."

"Ah, yes." Jenkins looked thoughtful. "Now you have to decide how much you want them to know, and what you want them to think... We actually did not plan this. I wish I could take credit for such cleverness, but your own actions and the opinions of your friends..." He saw the question in the other's face. "Oh, Early mainly, but also John Mosby. Ah! You are surprised! *I am not surprised.* I heard of your 'discussion' with him in Alexandria." The intelligence officer looked pleased. "An unpleasant little bastard, isn't he? No matter! He has his uses... He does indeed! He was quite complimentary about you, and made no trouble about giving you Smoot. Actually, I think he was seeking a way to rid himself of Smoot. Someone who has served with Claude Devereux is unlikely to make a good foil for Major Mosby. Whatever his defects, Claude encourages his people to bow to no one." Jenkins stood up, holding out a hand. "Well, enjoy your leave. Unfortunately, spring is coming. God know what will happen then. Please give my respects to Victoria."

Balthazar stared at the man, seeking the meaning of these words.

Jenkins still had him by the hand, and did not let go. "No. No," he said. "Her husband was my classmate at the Military Institute. I remember dancing a waltz with her at a ball when we were cadets. You are like him in some ways. Good luck, colonel. You are in many respects a fortunate man. Good night."

The following day they walked up to the capitol and sat in the gallery to listen to Congressional debate on a number of subjects including an army pay bill in which Balthazar found he now had more than a passing interest. After a while his interest in this faded and they went back to her rooms.

Seated beside her for tea, he glanced up in the midst of their conversation and decided to take the plunge.

"I know it is not right to speak to you of my feelings... It is too soon, but these are exceptional times. I do not know when I will see you again. I, I must tell you. I love you, and would be deeply honored if you would be my wife. To care for you and my cousin's sons would be, for me, all that life could promise. Please do not be offended."

He looked at her anxiously, hopeful for something, something…

Victoria inspected him silently for a few seconds. A *knight from a girl's dream… Of course I want you,* she thought.

"Yes, John," she said at last. "It is too soon, and I will still grieve for my husband, and love him forever, but you are right. These are not normal times.

We do not have much time, perhaps no more time at all." While these words rattled in his head, she walked to the door, turned the key in the lock, and returning sat in his lap with her arms around his neck. "I asked Claude to come as courier so that I could know if my heart had deceived me, if your letters were just cleverness. Now I know. We will go see Bishop McGrath in the morning." She kissed him, warmly, sweetly and then with the insistent passion of a mature woman.

He wrapped his arms around her, settling her in a more comfortable position.

She laid her head on his shoulder as his lips found hers.

Even at this moment his soldier's instinct listened for danger. Outside the door he heard Joe murmur to someone. "I don't think so, sir. Colonel Balthazar is out and will be back in the morning."

The Bishop of Richmond married them in Saint Peter's Cathedral at noon the following day. Harry Jenkins and Harrison stood up with them. The bishop, as good a Confederate as Jefferson Davis, abandoned any number of strict interpretations of canon law to get the job done in the interest of wartime romance and his long friendship with the Devereuxs.

The only awkward moment in the church was the suggestion by the new Mrs. Balthazar that her husband should have his cross blessed by the bishop.

After a small hesitation he opened his tunic and removed the silver chain on which this object hung against his chest.

Bishop John McGrath held it in his hand. He rubbed his thumb and forefinger over the surface.

"It is so beautiful," Victoria gushed, caught up in her happiness. "I've never seen anything like it."

Jenkins and Harrison peered over the bishop's shoulder.

It was only an inch high. There was no cross; only the living *Christus* suspended from the top of the head, fully robed with his arms held up in greeting and his legs separated so that he looked like an animate "X". The bearded face was slightly oriental in its features with the mouth open in a warm smile.

McGrath looked at Balthazar.

The bridegroom appeared ill at ease. "It is very old," he offered somewhat uncertainly.

"How old?" Jenkins asked.

"Ah, perhaps six hundred years... It is passed in my family from father to son."

He looked hopefully at the bishop.

"You are from the South of France, my son?" McGrath asked.

"Yes, your grace."

"This is Albigensian I believe. I studied them in Ireland, at Trinity College. It is a beautiful thing. They would not accept the thought of Christ's suffering. They said it was, too much... You *are* Catholic, aren't you my son?"

"Certainly, your grace, it is a memento of my family... Only that."

McGrath and Balthazar faced each other, then the clergyman nodded, moving to the font where he blessed Balthazar's ancient Cathar symbol of resistance to tyranny.

The lovers passed the rest of the week in a dream of peace and repose. There was so much to say. Things could be said now that were impossible to say before. There was so much of family history and secrets to share. She told him everything she could think of. She talked for hours about the Devereux and the Whites, of the ties among them all. She told him of George White, Junior's service in the Union Army.

"Not surprising, given the family history," he said.

In her arms he found that she was, in many ways, the lover he had always wanted. She was passionate, untiring and affectionate. He was a little ashamed to admit that his beloved wife had not been so ardent.

The night before he had to return to the army, he invited Joe in for a drink at her suggestion. Glass in hand they stood at the round table.

"John, Joseph has something to tell you." She waited for Joe to speak.

He raised his chin. "Sir, I have decided to stay with you as your valet. Mrs. Balthazar agrees that I should do this. I would hope that you could make the necessary arrangements at the War Department for my employment."

Balthazar inspected the bottom of his glass, and reaching for the decanter poured Joe another shot. "Are you sure about this? Is this your fight? You will be with me in the front line."

Worry lines appeared on Victoria's pretty face.

"We are free men, sir," Joe answered. "I am sure that slavery will end no matter who wins the war. This is a family matter and we stand together, all but my brother who has taken his own path. I hope you accept my offer."

Balthazar took him by the shoulders. "Of course, of course I accept. We will speak of it no more. Now, I wish to have Christmas dinner with this lovely person...

Cold filled the R.F. &P. shed as the train backed away in the grey morning light.

Balthazar stood on the platform in his beautiful grey uniform with Joe behind him. Soldiers passed, saluting respectfully, but he had no thought for them.

Victoria leaned from the window, one hand pressed to her bosom while she waved with the other. A smile was fixed on her face in what he knew was a heroic attempt to send her soldier back to the war with that picture in his mind.

Balthazar felt some comfort in knowing that Harrison would see her back to the Northern lines. Claude's name would insure her safety after that. In spite of that, he felt a great echoing emptiness opening in his chest. With tears in his eyes he saw her small figure slipping away. Her hand was still at her throat. The Frenchman took out his handkerchief to wipe his eyes. He knew why she held her hand so. Between her beautiful breasts lay his ancient cross.

He turned to find Joe holding two carpet bags. One had his saber strapped to it. "Well, Joseph, we must find our freight and return to the battalion. Your friend Smoot is waiting for our return..."

Chapter 13

Winter Quarters

(Orange, Virginia)

The seemingly endless time of cold darkness crept past in a succession of grey days and long nights.

In its camps, the Army of Northern Virginia once again experienced the religious fervor that came to them when they were not busy. At such times, men of all faiths sought solace in prayer and gathered in revival meetings where many found the inner peace that war denied them.

Families came to the winter camps to spend the season with their men. Most boarded with local families. Bearded warriors held in their arms for the first time tiny folk who had not yet been seen. The children brought joy to them all, but in the evenings the soldiers brooded over their families, their thoughts unreadable in the light of the fireplaces.

Amateur theatrical productions were a natural gift of this army, something so familiar from home that the men expected them. Wooden theaters sprang up in the snow and frost caked mud. These were crude structures of field sawn boards, each with its glowing pot bellied iron stove. The programs were filled with familiar plays, but some of them were only a year or so old in London or New York. One of these was entitled "Our American Cousin."

Balthazar was fond of the theater. At school in England he had been prominent in Christmas pantomime and Shakespeare alike. Now, he did all a commander properly could to interest his men in this activity, thinking it a healthy diversion from the boredom of the winter. The Stephen Foster songs he had heard in Richmond appeared on the boards as renditions by his battalion chorus. Soldiers' singing groups were a tradition in the French Army. He followed the custom in America. The foreigners in the battalion made up the backbone of the soloists and Joseph White played the piano to accompany. His skill was yet another of Clotilde Devereux's gifts to the Whites. Balthazar played the role of Falstaff in a Second Corps' officers' production of "The Merry Wives of Windsor." His English accent and baritone were praised around sentry fires for weeks after the play's run.

At Christmas Balthazar's battalion chorus presented a program of carols. His rendition of "Oh Holy Night" in French was well remembered.

Food was short that winter, but the Commissary Department managed to deliver just enough to give everyone a chance to rebuild strength worn down by years of deprivation.

Sick and run down horses and mules were sent to the big veterinary hospital at Lynchburg. Cynics laughed at the possibility of seeing them again, knowing that the army supply system would somehow send those beasts who recovered to some other home. Well-loved mounts and the odd artillery horse lucky enough to have a friend were nursed in secret by men who hid them from the veterinary service.

Smoot came back from leave bringing with him his family. He had found that life in western Prince William County had become too hard. They could not be left behind. The Yankee army had learned of his new rank and his wife could not stay with her people any longer.

Balthazar was surprised by Smoot's wife.

In the crucible of war Smoot had become a worldly person, a man at home in all surroundings and circumstance, a man who looked natural with his feet under Clotilde Devereux's table.

His wife was not like that. She remained the simple country woman he had left at home in 1861 when he joined Turner Ashby's cavalry. Balthazar could not but wonder how she would adapt to the life of an officer's wife if they managed to gain the South's independence.

Balthazar now understood that Isaac Smoot's personal world had been forever altered by life in the Devereux household and that the memory of Hope Devereux was lodged in a special place in his inner being. How that would end he could not imagine.

All winter Balthazar trained the battalion, working them hard the whole day long. In the time available he did what he could to transfer to them the knowledge he had gained in a lifetime of active soldiering. Everything he had to give, he gave them, for he felt deep in his bones that the fight coming in the spring would be the greatest fight of the war, perhaps the greatest fight of all time. He continued to teach them battle drills of various kinds, seeking through the inculcation of rote reaction to command to make them into a force more effective than mere numbers would suggest. He also continued to receive reinforcement in the form of individuals that no other command was well suited to absorb. After interviewing them he decided whether or not they were acceptable for inclusion in what he was building. By the middle of February, he had three hundred and fifty men in the battalion.

In the evenings he devoted many hours to instruction of his officers. He found that many of them had soldiered a great deal but there were bad habits to be undone and his own way of doing things to impress on them.

In early March the army began to think of the possibility of spring. It was still cold. The wind howled miserably some nights, but just occasionally, you could feel a hint of something different in the air, something almost warm.

At that time there occurred one of those events which seem momentary in meaning but which later can be seen to have been truly important.

On the first of the month yet another big Union cavalry raid reached the outer defenses of Richmond. Raids of this sort had been made by the Federal horsemen with some regularity throughout the war. They never accomplished very much, but the Union cavalry appeared to think them necessary as a justification for their existence. The price in men and beasts was always high.

The current commander of one of the divisions of the cavalry corps of the Army of the Potomac led this expedition. He was called Judson Kilpatrick, a young man vaguely remembered by old soldiers among the Confederates as a junior officer of no great promise in the "Old Army."

The Richmond garrison of War Department clerks, Virginia Militia and convalescents kept Kilpatrick outside the city by pretending to be more than they really were. They made him think they were too strong and that he could not break in. This was foolish. He could easily have entered the city, but he did not believe he could and that was the end of it. As is often the truth in such events, a lack of confidence was equivalent to a lack of capability. In Kilpatrick's mind, there was then nothing to do but go home. The mounted blue horde turned away from the Confederate capital.

The long ride to the safety of Union lines north of the Rapidan was hard and bloody for they faced the resistance of Jeb Stuart's men all along the way. The road home was richly marked with the blood of yellow legged troopers and the hundreds of dead and dying horses shot at Kilpatrick's order as they broke down in the forced marches needed to escape. The horse bodies and wounded beasts were everywhere along the dusty roads.

Cavalrymen from the Carolinas and Virginia cursed Kilpatrick and swore they would give him no more mercy than fate allowed them to give his animal victims. For these men, the unavoidable destruction of those poor creatures which tried to join the Confederate columns of march brought tears of rage. Wade Hampton, the Low Country grandee who commanded one of Stuart's brigades, said he would follow Kilpatrick to hell itself to make him pay.

With the Union cavalry's departure from Richmond, the militia defenders came out through the trench lines to search for the enemy's leavings. Near Mantapike Hill they found the body of one legged Colonel Ulric Dahlgren, killed while leading 500 of Kilpatrick's raiders in a flanking column. He had been ambushed while trying to enter the city of Richmond from the south. Dahlgren was twenty-four years old, the son of a Union admiral and himself a fervent abolitionist. He lost a leg at Gettysburg. In his pockets they found papers which he had used to brief his men. According to these notes, his troops were ordered to free Union prisoners of war, capture and hang Jefferson Davis and his cabinet without trial and burn the city.

The resulting furor in the newspapers in both the United States and the Confederacy was impressive.

General Meade denied any knowledge of such orders. His denial was accepted by Davis and Lee. They had known him too well in the old days to think he would have been behind such a thing. He was too sober, too sensible a man for such foolishness no matter what the present political disagreement might be.

Judah Benjamin, the Secretary of State, and Samuel Cooper, the Adjutant General, eliminated this feeling of reassurance by explaining that there was a separate line of political communication that ran from Dahlgren to Kilpatrick to Edwin Stanton, the Secretary of War and on to the radical wing of the Republican Party in Congress.

The implication was clear. Meade's disavowal meant nothing. He might not have known what Kilpatrick's real instructions had been. Lincoln might not have known. Men who would have died kicking at the end of a rope, and whose families would have been driven from their homes by fire brooded long over this development. Gradually, the sound and fury of the columnists died away, but the damage was done. The belief was established in the Confederate government that their enemies had marked them for death without trial. What the consequences of this might be no one could have said, but the idea was established in Richmond that old, unspoken rules no longer applied and that political murder was acceptable in the North.

Balthazar read of this in the newspapers, and tried to learn more from recent visitors to Richmond. He wrote Colonel Jourdain a report in which he said that the Republican leaders had made a terrible mistake, that now the Confederates would stop at nothing.

In the middle of the month Ulysses Simpson Grant took command of the armies of the United States. He came east to receive his commission as Lieutenant General, came to Washington, to a city which may have held more of his enemies than Richmond. Neither the radical Republicans nor the deeply imbedded Confederate underground meant him any good.

Grant and Lincoln did not appear to like each other much. They were rarely seen together. This was noted by all concerned, but the new generalissimo made a quick start in planning for the spring campaign and that made a good impression.

Devereux suggested to Stanton that it might be a good idea for the War Department to be represented by an observer in Grant's planning staff. Stanton liked the possibilities in this, liked the thought of keeping Grant "in his place," but Colonel George Sharpe and Devereux's old adversary, Lafayette Baker, talked him out of it, pleading that Grant would think that a War Department "spy" showed a lack of confidence in him. These arguments probably would not have dissuaded Stanton but some unknown also raised the matter in private with the president. He sided with the "naysayers." This meant that Devereux had to settle for the information which Grant's staff chose to give the War Department concerning his plans. From these tidbits, Devereux learned that Grant would seek to employ the armies of the United States simultaneously in the belief that the Rebels would not be able to deal with all of them at once. He did not find this to be surprising. The man's record in the West pointed to the likelihood of such a campaign.

Devereux continued to live a life which pulled him in many directions. His wife held his devotion and was the object of his deepest desires. She was a woman beyond praise. He could not explain to himself why he could not rid himself of the desire for Amy Biddle. His hunger for her only grew with the passage of time. He found himself spending ever more time with her in the little room behind her office at the "Soldier's Rest" convalescent camp. He wondered what her staff thought of their association. To compound his foolishness, he asked for and received the assignment of Amy's nephew, now a captain, to his office staff as an assistant. The young man occupied an outer room and guarded Devereux's door with the immense sergeant, John Quick.

The nephew's presence was a convenience. Colonel Edouard Jourdain, the French military attaché, had become a nuisance in the last months. Devereux had known for some time that he was using Biddle as a source of information. With the young fool just a few feet away it was much easier to use him as a conduit to the French embassy.

Jourdain himself was a difficulty. He reacted with outrage to news of Balthazar's promotion, saying "This rogue is like all the wild men of Africa. He is without discipline!" The marriage reduced him to smoldering impotence, unable to speak out in this family matter, but certain that his authority had been flouted in some way. In February he showed Devereux a dispatch freshly arrived from the Quai D'Orsay, saying "I would not have you read this under normal circumstances, but..." In the letter the Foreign

Minister praised Balthazar's reports, congratulated him on his command and offered best wishes on the occasion of his marriage.

Devereux looked up from the paper. "Perhaps Jean-Marie will choose to remain with us after the war. He would have a place of honor in *our* army."

Jourdain said nothing, but made a note on the margin of the dispatch. Sour disapproval of his loss of control over Balthazar warred in his face with the need to stay on good terms with Claude.

Turning his naked back to her Devereux rolled away from his wife's embrace and began to dress while sitting on the edge of the big walnut bed. "I'll be home early, home in time for dinner," he said. "I have to talk to Fred Kennedy about something he must do tomorrow for, our work." Behind him, she contemplated the possibility that this statement might be true. She was still flushed prettily from the intensity of her passion and not sure that she had heard him correctly. Her blonde hair was spread across a pillow and the perfection of her creamy skin and pink nippled breasts were a reproach to any man who would leave her bed. "Where are you going?" she asked again.

"I'll be back in an hour." With that he was out the door buttoning his blue tunic. She could hear his boot heels on the stairs from the ell's second story. Then the garden gate opened and closed.

She rolled away from the door, placed a pillow over her face and wept.

On the 20th of the month Sergeant Quick appeared at Balthazar's log hut in civilian clothing carrying a letter from Victoria. Smoot, Harris and Sergeant-Major Roarke sat in front of the fireplace with Quick talking about Washington and the Devereux kin. Balthazar stood to one side while he read the letter by the light of a lantern.

"What is it, sir? Not bad news we hope?" asked Roarke. The battalion's new first soldier had written from hospital in January asking to serve with the friend who had carried him off the battlefield, with a deep wound in the side. Balthazar moved quickly to bring him to the battalion. It had not been easy to arrange. The assignment was evidence of Early's continuing favor. General Hays was not happy with the loss of one more of his precious "Tigers," but had put the best face possible on the situation and yielded gracefully in the end, saying to Balthazar, "you owe me." Roarke now sat on a three legged stool with the yellow flames outlining him. His right hand cupped the still tender place where the bayonet had gone in at Rappahannock Station.

Balthazar's features lit as he turned to look at them. "They have decided to read the banns of our marriage in the parish church!"

They looked at each other, puzzled at his happiness with this seemingly superfluous bit of Catholic Church administrative business.

Joe White had just come in, his arms filled with wood for the fire. He smiled at the news, grasping its true significance.

Quick looked smug in his knowledge. "Your colonel is going to be a father!" he cried while raising his glass to the burly, mustachioed figure standing in the light of the lantern.

Raphael Harris crossed the room to offer his hand and congratulations.

They all did, one by one with Joe White the last.

After dinner, Balthazar wrote a reply while his friends drank and talked before the fire.

"Boys!" Smoot finally interjected to stop the stream of repartee. "We need to talk about something. You fellahs know something that you should not."

Harris nodded. "We must all remember this! If captured we know nothing of these Devereuxs and their secrets, nothing!"

On the 27th of March Lee went to Gordonsville in the Piedmont country to review Longstreet's First Corps, just returned from five months away. Two of the divisions had spent the fall and winter in Tennessee where the great victory at Chickamauga had been in no small part a benefit of their presence. After that, they had been at Knoxville where things had not gone as well, but now they were back. The third division of the corps, Picketts', was still in Carolina rebuilding in strength since their near destruction at Gettysburg. Pickett's men were absent from Virginia but not from Lee's thoughts. The 17th Virginia Infantry Regiment was there with them. This was the "Alexandria Regiment" and his hometown friends and neighbors were never far from Lee's thoughts.

The troops at Gordonsville knew well in advance that General Lee was coming to look at them. They drilled for days, shined whatever there was to shine, and mended their disintegrating tents and canvas wagon covers. They tried to make some improvement in their appearance with rough haircuts and repairs to clothing.

Many of them joked about "Marse Robert," his odd looking hat, and the grey horse that was the same color as he looked to be. With the shyness of a display of their feelings so common to their kind, they tried not to seem too eager for him to come.

On the day of the inspection, they formed in a big field outside the town. The two divisions of infantry and the corps' artillery were drawn up in long, straight lines of ragged, faded men. The browned and bearded faces peered out from beneath floppy hats. The difficulty of their lives showed in the hollow eyes, sunken cheeks and the bagginess of their clothing. Only the weapons looked new, bright and shining with the long bayonets making a hedge of steel. Behind the infantry, the corps' trains were aligned in ranks of wagons, the drivers standing by their animals talking and soothing against the unexplained presence of so many others. The artillery waited at one end of the line. The guns, teams, and wagons were arranged by battalions as they stood in the early spring sunlight.

Lee rode out of the trees, and they fell silent. The whispering leaves were the only sound on the field. The grey old man halted Traveler in the middle of the grass in front of them.

Stillness covered the multitude, for there was between him and them something extraordinary. Generals are seldom loved by their men. This is particularly true of generals whose fate it is to send so many to their deaths. Some are respected. Some are hated. Some are despised, but few are loved.

When Lee looked at his 10,000 veterans, come back to him, the men of Malvern Hill, Sharpsburg, and Manassas, he wept.

As they looked at him, sitting there on the grey horse, the men wept, wiping their eyes on their brown sleeves. Then they began to cheer, and cheer and cheer as he rode down the line holding the funny hat outstretched to them.

Chapter 14

The Wilderness

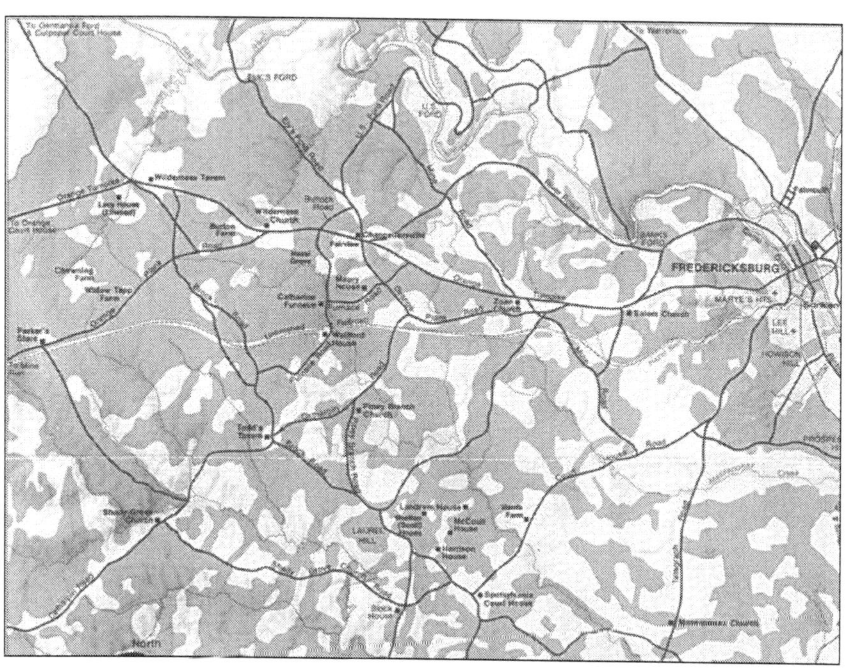

Figure 1 - The Overland Battlefields

-2 May, 1864-
(Clark's Mountain)

The height of land stood 600 feet above the south bank of the Rapidan River. Dense green covered it except for a small meadow at the northeastern end. In this space the high command of the Army of Northern Virginia gathered to see the enemy spread across the land to the north. Lee, his generals and the staff sat their horses in the bright sunshine and spoke of the omens.

The tent camps of the enemy were stretched out before them. They reached in some directions to the horizon. The smoke of cooking rose in the blue sky. The Rebels thought they could smell the wood fires. Miniature blue men lounged around the tents. In one opening in the forest a brigade review was in progress. The troops stood at "Present Arms" while a band played. The music reached to the mountain top.

Lee waited quietly, listening, watching.

"Oh say does that star-spangled Banner yet wave
O'er the land of the free and the home of
The brave?"

Lieutenant Colonel Charles Marshall glanced at the army commander's back, wondering what was in his mind. At moments like this, Marshall always felt sympathy for the former United States officers among the Southern leaders.

There had been a great deal of talk in the last hour. The conversation had circled and worried at the subject of Grant's plan. To the east and west the forest of The Wilderness extended to the several fords which made the rivers passable.

At the same time, the Union army spread so far across the landscape that its disposition gave no real hint of the probable direction that an advance might take.

Would it be to the left or the right of Clark's mountain?

Does it matter? Marshall asked himself. *Surely we all know what the end will be. Surely he knows. Perhaps it does not matter any longer. Something odd has happened to us all. No reasonable man would have any doubt about our fate. Ah, that is it! We are no longer reasonable men. We have 45,000 men here. There must be 100,000 over there, and how many behind?*

Lee shifted in the saddle, feeling in a pocket for a handkerchief, wiping his face.

It is all about him now, Marshall thought. *He has become our father, the chief of our clan, the best of our people, the best a man can be. So long as he continues, we will continue. So long as he stays we will be at his back, to the last man.*

Lee pointed to the right. "They will cross there, over the Germanna and Ely fords. He will seek to march past us to the open ground beyond the Wilderness, to Spotsylvania, to bring us to battle where his numbers will bear, but it is too far. He will have to spend at least one night extended along the roads in the forest. We will march to him from Orange and Gordonsville. We will strike him in the flank in the forest. We will break his line into pieces, and destroy him."

Longstreet was at the army commander's right hand. He looked unhappy. He cleared his throat. "Sir, perhaps he will see the danger and hurry through the jungle in one day."

Powell Hill spoke in agreement. He looked better than usual today. His long auburn hair framed his pale face. He looked almost healthy. "Yes. It could be done if he marches his infantry and guns straight through and sends the wagons around by Fredericksburg."

Lee pondered this, chin on chest. He shook his head. "No. General Grant is filled with the confidence of his victories in the west. He thinks the reports of our powers of resistance are over drawn. Because he does not fear us, he will wish to bring his trains with him through the narrow roads. Perhaps he will have them march to the east, away from our approach. They will slow him." He pointed. "He will halt just along there, along the Brock Road."

Behind his back the generals looked at each other.

A hope, Marshall thought, *a wish, or maybe more. God knows he has been right so often.*

Lee turned the horse's head away from the enemy, turned the animal so that he could face his officers. "Gentlemen, prepare your commands. Those people will move soon. Pray for your country." With that he rode down the mountain, back to the tent in which he would wait for Grant to move.

- 3 May –
(The Headquarters of the General in Chief))

Devereux arrived at Grant's Headquarters near Brandy Station to find that with the exception of a few officers whom he had met in the last month in Washington, nearly all were strangers. They had all come from the west with the new General in Chief. They did not seem to know how to deal with someone like him. Clearly the western commanders had been held on a much longer leash than those in the east.

Devereux had tried without success to be sent to the front throughout April, but the problem was solved when "someone" remembered that he had been with the Army of the Potomac in Pennsylvania and had reported from the field to the War Department. This had made Stanton and Halleck real participants in what was happening there.

Devereux had always suspected that his "ring" was not the only Confederate "apparatus" in Washington. This new and mysterious intervention increased his belief that this must be true.

The trip up the railroad line from Alexandria to the front was depressing. From his post in the War Department headquarters on 17th Street in Washington, he had known intellectually of the vast strength of the force that Grant had at his disposal, but to know this was one thing. To see it was another. Despair settled in his heart, gripping him in a fist of iron, and raising the level of his desperation.

Sergeant John Quick watched this mood settle on him and tried his best to lift it, joking privately of the big but useless Yankee Army. This did not have much effect. He had returned from Balthazar's camp most unwillingly, having seen in the Frenchman a leader to his taste. It was only Claude's many difficulties that had kept him from refusing to return to Washington.

One of these difficulties weighed heavily on Quick. He had responded to a question from Balthazar by joking about Claude's way with the ladies. Smoot asked what he meant. He told them of the amount of time that Devereux had been spending with Amy Biddle. He had not become close to the family as Smoot had, and it had not occurred to him that Smoot might not find this story and his innuendo amusing.

Smoot rose and spoke with Balthazar in a corner. Quick watched with growing unease as Balthazar stood with his back to the room, hands behind his back, shaking his head as his second in command whispered to him.

The next day Smoot took Quick aside after breakfast. "Hope Devereux is ten times the woman that prune faced Yankee biddy will ever be," he began. His face was red with anger.

For Isaac Smoot, Hope's origins in Boston no longer had meaning.

"You tell him," he said, as his face darkened steadily, as the terrible scar throbbed with his anger. "You tell him, that if he hurts her..."

He had not seemed able to complete the thought, but John Quick grasped the idea. In Ireland he had seen men so enraged by insult to a sister or sweetheart that they were incapable of speech. He held up a hand to hold back this strange officer who knew the Devereuxs so well. "But, Lootenant, I don't rightly know that he has touched her, much."

Smoot stared for a moment and then walked away.

Quick watched him go with mixed feelings; admiration for his loyalty to Hope and worry at what would happen when next the two men met.

In his first meeting with Grant, Devereux presented his credentials, and hoped for an enlightening conversation, hoped for a talk that would tell him something significant about this new opponent.

The general was living in a regulation tent. There was a field desk in the tent, a cot, a few chairs and a wash stand and basin in a corner. An aide de camp waited outside, waited for a signal as to what to do about this unexpected newcomer.

Devereux looked Grant over, inspected him, seeking clues to the riddle of his success. There was nothing much to see, just a thin little fellow with a sandy beard dressed in a private soldier's uniform. There were three stars on the shoulder straps. The general looked at the papers, handed them back and asked where he intended to be during the advance.

Devereux said that he would follow the lead corps across the river.

Grant looked at him for a moment, chewing on a cigar the while. He finally took it out of his mouth and spoke. "Colonel Sharpe thinks there is something funny about you. Do you know that?"

Devereux was angry, frustrated and fearful, and all at the same time. The desire to lash out was strong. He shoved the emotions back down into the place he thought of as a "strongbox," locking them in with so much else that disturbed his peace. "I thought it was Baker who believed me a Rebel spy," he responded with a smile. "We went through that last year. He had me investigated extensively I believe. We discussed it at the War Department. That was before I took a commission."

Grant grimaced in what was supposed to resemble a smile. "Oh, yes. I have heard all that, colonel, and I know about your many friends and admirers, including the most important ones. Please don't believe I am in any way prejudiced against Southern men. My wife is Southern. My closest friend on earth is Pete Longstreet, over there somewhere." He pointed with his chin. "He was an usher at our wedding. I have owned a few slaves..." He waited for Devereux to say something.

"I have not," Claude replied, "but then I have always lived in my father's house, and never in the country."

Grant twitched slightly and stared at him through the cigar smoke, obviously irritated at the reply.

Devereux thought how stupid it had been to needle him in that way. He expected some sharp answer.

The little man from the west looked at him for a while longer, not saying anything, then replied. "Well, come by and have supper with me and Meade tonight. I'd like to hear what he has to say about your assignment here. You know him?"

"Yes, sir. I do. I should be happy to join you."

Outside the tent, Devereux took a deep breath. Having spoken to the man, he could see how dangerous Grant must be. He saw something of himself in the enemy commander. Pain had taught the Union general to conceal his hurts and move on. Devereux's thoughts went to his brother, his cousins, and his friends waiting across the river. He wondered just how much pain Grant could take.

At dinner, Devereux learned that Winfield Scott Hancock's Second U.S. Corps would lead the way, crossing at Ely's Ford before dawn the next day. This was welcome news. It gave him an excuse to leave dinner early. It was clear that the senior officers' mess would be happier without him. He would make it easy for them as soon as possible.

There was an elderly civilian dressed in black seated at the table.

After a moment Devereux realized that it was Congressman Elihu Washburne, Grant's patron in the House of Representatives. Washburne acknowledged Claude's presence with a polite question about his father's health. The table listened silently to this indication of Devereux's connections in the capital.

As host, Grant could not avoid talking to Devereux but was non-committal in his replies to questions and definitely on guard. This was not a surprise. Next to him sat Colonel George Sharpe, the Army of the Potomac's chief intelligence officer. Sharpe had the courtesy to recall the last time he and Devereux had met. It had been behind Cemetery Ridge at Gettysburg.

"Ah, I remember," Meade said from Grant's other side. "I met your brother in the little building we were using for the staff. He was helping with the information files..." He looked at Sharpe hopefully.

Devereux's previous encounters with Major General George Gordon Meade had reinforced in his mind the man's reputation for irascible nastiness. This concern for another human being's feelings was something new. Looking at Meade's sharp profile and bald head, he began to see why Meade's Old Army friends in the Confederate Army still liked him.

Sharpe took the hint. "Yes. Yes. He was a great help. I don't know how we could have managed without him... I saw you up on the hill after the Rebel attack failed. I saw you with him, after his death...

Meade cleared his throat and said, "May I offer my condolences?" He offered his hand across the table.

Grant watched with interest.

Devereux took the hand and held it. "Thank, you," he said.

"I didn't see you up there, Sharpe," he said while continuing to look at Meade. "When did you arrive?" He released the hand.

Meade looked confused. He was not accustomed to having a man hold his hand. The embarrassment at physical contact which was so common in Northern people usually amused Devereux, but not now.

"Just as Hays rode down the line with the flags... Just then."

"What's this?" Grant asked sharply.

Meade looked even more troubled. "I was... occupied at the time," he said.

The general in chief waited. A stubborn rigidity appeared in his features as he waited.

"Alexander Hays," Meade continued.

"He was at West Point with me," Grant said. You could not tell from his face if that was good or bad. Finally, he made up his mind to say something, "I have always been his friend but he can be..."

"Well," Sharpe said, lacking a cue as to how to proceed. "He rode down the line dragging an enemy flag behind him..."

Grant's face was unreadable.

Meade looked away.

"His staff rode behind him. They each had one..." Sharpe said in a near whisper.

26th North Carolina Volunteer Infantry. Sharpsburg, Manassas, Savage Station...

The black embroidered words from the regimental color were burned on the inside of Devereux's skull. He could see it dragging in the dirt. The fresh, wet stains of the Carolina color sergeant's blood were caked with the billowing dust of a hot summer afternoon in Pennsylvania.

Henry Burgwyn, Devereux thought. *That was his regiment. He must have been all of twenty five that day. Do you all have colonels that young? His body must have been in that wall of guts and broken bones in front of your line near the clump of trees. Second Corps, I believe...*

"And what is General Hays doing these days?" Devereux asked.

They all looked at him.

"He has the same brigade in Birney's division... Why?" Meade asked.

"I haven't seen him since that terrible day..." Devereux said.

"This should not have happened," Grant said. He was evidently not much interested in his old schoolmate. They all knew what he meant. "We would not have done this in the west. To dishonor their flags is not good. They will retaliate if they know. Do they know?"

Meade was pale and quiet at the rebuke.

"You were more accustomed to winning," Sharpe said. "These men were astonished at their own success in stopping Lee. Of course they know. Men escape. There have been prisoner exchanges."

"Let's drop the subject," Grant said. "There won't be many more prisoner exchanges. We are going to stop fighting the same men over and over..."

Watching them, Devereux knew that Sharpe would not be working for Meade much longer. Grant had chosen not to remove Meade from command of the Army of the Potomac. Instead, he was "accompanying" Meade in his role as General in Chief of the armies of the United States. This was a decision for which Devereux had urged acceptance in Washington believing that it inevitably would lead to friction between the two.

Damn! He will take Sharpe for his own staff. We don't need that! We don't need to have Sharpe working for Grant...

"Do I understand that your brother was killed while serving with this army at Gettysburg?" Grant asked.

"He was actually a civilian," Sharpe answered for Claude. "Colonel Devereux was there representing the War Department, and the Sanitary Commission, somehow... His brother was with him, and volunteered to help us. He was quite good at the work."

"Did the Army give its sympathy to your family?" Grant asked.

Why do these bastards have to be so civil? Devereux asked himself. He said nothing.

"The president attended the funeral, as did General Halleck and half a dozen members of Congress," Sharpe answered for the silent blue coated figure seated across the table.

An awkward moment passed quietly as this reminder of the political importance of their "guest"" sunk in.

"By your leave, sir" Devereux said. "I shall go now. Ely's Ford awaits and I would like to find General Hancock to inform him of my, my presence..."

"Certainly," Grant said, nodding in agreement. He held a cigar in one hand, and felt his lip for shreds of tobacco with the other. "Give Hancock my regards. Why don't you ride with Hays...? He will be thrilled with your, associations... Maybe you can keep him from doing some other fool thing. Good luck."

Standing outside in the cool May night, Devereux listened to the conversation inside.

"What do you think?" Sharpe asked.

"I don't know. Keep him away from me, for now... George, read to me again the last part of that order you sent your army."

Meade's dry voice cut through the fabric of the tent,

"...Actuated by a high sense of duty, fighting to preserve the government and the institutions handed down to us by our forefathers, victory, under God's blessing, must and will attend our efforts."

"Has this sort of proclamation been usual before an offensive?" Grant asked.

"Yes."

Why didn't you say anything about the Constitution?" Grant asked. The voice waited for the answer that would not be given. "Well," Grant finally said. "We will see how well these men of yours fight, George. We will see."

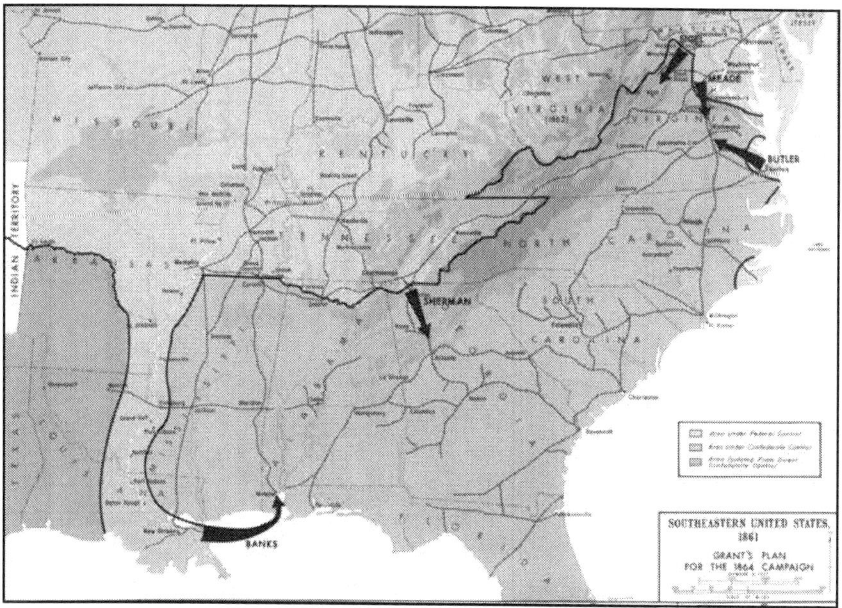

Figure 2 - Grant's Overall Plan

-After midnight, 4 May – (North of the Fords of the Rapidan)

The tents were already broken down when Devereux and John Quick arrived at Alexander Hays' bivouac. Wagons were in the final stages of preparation for their journey to join the field train of David Birney's Division.

Hays commanded one of the two brigades in the division. He had commanded the same brigade at Gettysburg. Hays welcomed Devereux with a display of hearty, masculine camaraderie. The hand-written note from Meade that arrived with the visitor insured the welcome.

The corps commander, Hancock, had added his own words at the bottom of the page, asking Hays to take special care of their guest. Devereux's official orders, drafted by him, but signed by the Secretary of War may have had something to do with the reception as well.

Hays poured Devereux a drink from a battered flask as they sat together watching the brigade's infantry regiments march past on the road to the southeast.

The night was clear and chill. Bright stars crusted the black sky above. Sergeant John Quick sat on a third stump a few feet away with their saddle horses and the led pack mule. Quick had tied them to a sapling.

Hays' staff hovered in the background respectfully. Devereux sipped the whiskey.

Not bad for some sort of Yankee swill, he thought.

"Pennsylvania?" he asked the big, square outline beside him.

"Why, yes!" Hays exclaimed in a rumbling baritone. "It's from my cousin's distillery outside Pittsburgh, the best Pennsylvania rye whiskey, not at all like the syrupy mess these people around here drink."

Hays' adjutant separated himself from the staff group, whispered in his chief's ear, and then rejoined his colleagues. There was a short pause while the general tried to manage his recovery from the news that Devereux was one of "these people."

"Alexander Hays, is it, general?" Quick asked from his stump. He had seemed absorbed in rubbing his horse's nose, and his words were a bit of a surprise.

"Yes, yes!" Hays replied turning toward him, glad of an interruption in his impossible task.

"Would it be County Monahan? I know some Hays there. Would you be one of them?" This was malicious, for Quick knew well that the Hays of Monahan who looked like this man were all Anglo-Irish Protestants. He and Devereux watched while the Union General decided what to say to this obvious "Paddy."

"Why, yes," he said. "Did you know them well? They are my cousins, every one."

One is Lord Lieutenant of the county. Another is the sheriff. May God curse the Sassenach swine!

"Yes, sor! And a luvvlier group of men ye've nivver seen! Ye're the spit ov'em."

My God! thought Claude. *Were they so bad that you talk to him like that? I wish Bill or Jake were here to listen.*

"Perhaps we should be going, General," Devereux suggested. "Your staff looks impatient." It was true. The young men had taken note that their proper place in the column of march had passed them by and were looking nervous."

Hays tore himself away from an inspection of Sergeant John Quick. "You're right of course! Colonel Devereux, please join us. I would like nothing better than to hear from you of the "inner workings" of our masters' houses in Washington. And you, Sergeant Quigley? Was that it? I would like to hear more of my kin..."

"It will be our pleasure, sir," Claude said, reaching to take the reins of his horse from Quick who was already in the saddle.

"I remember that one of the ladies of your house was named "Maude," Quick said somewhere from the darkness.

"Yes. That would be my cousin... You knew her?" He sounded incredulous, as well he might. "One of my sisters has that name as well..."

Devereux smiled in the dark behind the mask that covered his hatred.

Alexander Hays' Brigade passed the remaining hours of the night in the approach march to Ely's Ford on the Rapidan. Beneath a cloudless sky, the brigade's infantry moved down the road to the south, passing into history, passing into the folklore of the two peoples. This thought may have come to some among the marching infantrymen and gunners but few among them would have held that thought for long. They were more absorbed with the fit of their boots and the weight of their loads. Thoughts of home and the women they had left there filled their minds as they always fill soldiers' minds.

Dawn found them across the river. It was eight o'clock before Devereux focused enough on his surroundings to know that they would soon reach a crossroads where the Orange Turnpike crossed the track they had followed from the ford. He knew that at that point they would see the ruins of the Chancellor House hotel. It was gone now, burned in the midst of the battle which had taken its name from the house the previous year. Claude remembered the daughters of the house. They were pretty girls, smiling, blonde and flirtatious in the sweet, seductive way that Virginia girls often were. He wondered where they might be now.

Hays fell silent after the river crossing. Perhaps their entry into the forest of the Wilderness depressed him. He had talked all the way to the river. You could see that he wanted to take advantage of the presence of someone from the War Department to curry favor on high. This forest was not a good backdrop for the effort. The Wilderness was a remnant of the primeval wilderness itself. It extended twenty miles or so along the south bank of the Rapidan-Rappahannock River system and at some points stretched as far as ten miles south of the rivers. It was a sprawling tangle of mixed coniferous and deciduous second growth timber tied together with deadfalls and Virginia creeper. German iron workers had been brought to the area by colonial government in the eighteenth century. Generations of them stripped the woods of first growth trees to feed the fuel needs of their "puddling furnaces." The result was a nearly impassable barrier of vegetation in which only the local people had any chance of finding their way. It was a place that inspired silence.

Devereux was grateful for the quiet. He found Alexander Hays to be no more or less annoying than other extroverts, but the unfolding drama of Grant's offensive called for mental effort to grasp its meaning. The prattle of yet another ambitious general did not help with the needed concentration.

Scouts from the cavalry and an engineer officer from Second Corps headquarters waited at the crossroads by the Chancellor House to make sure that the brigade crossed the turnpike and continued to the south.

Devereux understood from the discussions at Grant's mess that the Fifth Corps under the command of Major General Gouverneur Warren had crossed the Rapidan at Germanna Ford to the west of Ely's Ford and was advancing southeastward on a parallel road a few miles away. By this hour, they too, should have reached an intersection with the Orange Turnpike. There, they would also continue straight across, marching down the Brock Road through the tunnel of trees and tangled underbrush toward Spotsylvania Courthouse.

To the east of Devereux's position with Hays' brigade and Hancock's 2nd Corps, the Army of the Potomac's massive trains were marching in parallel toward the southeast, also moving towards Spotsylvania County Courthouse and the edge of the Wilderness forest.

As Lee had predicted on Clark's Mountain, the trains could not move fast enough to reach the open ground in one day and for that reason the whole army would camp for the night along the roads in the woods, spread out as though waiting for the Southern army to arrive.

On the evening of the Third of May, Tom Barclay, a Virginia boy in the Stonewall Brigade wrote his parents a long letter from the Second Corps' camps west of Mine Run on the Orange Turnpike. Among the things he wrote that night appear these sentences.

"..our cause we believe to be a just one and our God is a just God, then why should we doubt? ...The struggle will be a bloody one, but it is noble to die so with one's friends."

The Stonewall Brigade led the advance to the east the next morning. It was the point of the spear that Lee was flinging into the Wilderness aimed at the side of Meade's army. In the Second Corps column of march, Johnson's Division led with the Stonewall in front, then came Early's Division, followed by Rodes.

All that day Jubal Early's men hiked eastward on the Orange Turnpike in the dust of Johnson's Division. It was a beautiful spring day in Virginia. The winter had been cold and the trees were mostly still in bud, but the roadside glowed with early flowering Redbud and the white Dogwood had begun to open its cross shaped blossoms.

Early's riflemen trudged along, grumbling about the horses in the artillery battalion that followed Johnson's troops. "I thought these damned nags were short of food, if that's so, how can they be so full of crap?" would have been a typical sentiment.

Balthazar's men felt no differently, and it was with relief that they received news just after the halt at dusk that Dick Ewell, the corps commander, had decided to reinforce the advance guard with their battalion.

Wearily, they reformed their column of fours in the road.

Balthazar stood among them. He seldom rode Victoria's mare. That seemed odd to them at first, but now they expected it.

A soldier led the animal at the end of the battalion column.

Balthazar chatted with Lieutenant Harris and Sergeant Major Roarke while they waited for Smoot to return with a wagon full of rations for the next day.

Balthazar held the Sharps carbine by the muzzle. The trigger guard rested just behind his left shoulder with the weapon's butt sticking up in the air behind. He often carried long arms this way, believing that it was more comfortable on the march. Looking back, down the column, he realized that nearly all of them were carrying their rifles the same way. He turned away to conceal his enjoyment of the moment, and saw Smoot approaching with the wagon.

"Forwaard! March! Route step! March!" The battalion went east to join the Stonewall Brigade at the point of the advance.

Far away, the two Presidents worried away the hours until dispatches could be expected from the front.

In Richmond, Jefferson Davis waited in the upstairs office of his home. In his hand was the telegram he had received from Robert Lee that day. It contained the sonorous words,

"I have set the army in motion..."

In his heart the Southern leader could not help but hold foremost the image of his small son who had died in the last week, the victim of a fall from an upstairs window. He could not help but think that now he shared the misery of all those other parents whose children he had sent to their deaths.

Away to the north, in Washington, Abraham Lincoln also knew the pain of the death of children. He had lost his own son, Willie, this past year. He had many personal problems. There was something unstable and terribly wrong in his wife. Her mental state was becoming more and more unpredictable and capricious. He, himself had been chronically ill for many years with a sickness that never seemed to leave him fully.

In his hand he held a copy of a letter he had sent Grant.

"I am most pleased with your arrangements until now...what I know of them..." Why can't these damnable generals tell me what they are doing? Well, that's all right. What is it Meade's officers say of Grant? Ah yes! `He hasn't met Bobby Lee and his boys yet...' We will see if it is different this time.

What is it I heard one of Meade's officers saying last month, something about "Bobby Lee and his boys?"

*If only **we** had Bobby Lee and his boys….*

At their bivouac that night, Devereux shared a meal of canned beef, biscuits and coffee with Hays and his staff.

John Quick sat nearby meditating on the broad back of the federal commander. He, too, could still see Hays on his big black horse riding in triumph along the crest of Cemetery Ridge.

A dog walked through the trees towards the smell of Quick's ration. It was a big dog. It stood a few feet away, uncertain of a welcome from this strange silent man. Quick held out a piece of bully beef from his tin mess plate. The dog approached, smelled his hand and took the meat. After a few more pieces of meat the dog lay at his feet.

Devereux looked over and seeing the animal asked to whom it belonged.

A captain on the staff replied that it belonged to no one, that it had haunted their winter quarters and followed them on this march. He picked up a stick to throw at the animal to drive it off.

“"Don't do that," Claude said in a tone that commanded attention. "Don't do that..."

"An animal lover," Hays commented in a way that made it clear that he was not and that he thought those who were to be sentimentalists.

Claude laughed and looked at the dog. It looked back at him. After a moment he said, "I'll take him. Give him a name..."

Quick had been examining the dog. Now he scratched between its ears. "Some sort of hound, sor," he said, "and it is she, not he. Looks almost like a wolfhound, almost..."

The captain with the stick nodded, "She started following us when we were settled in near the Irish Brigade. It must have strayed from them."

Devereux and Quick awoke the next morning with the wolfhound bitch snuggled up to Quick's back against the chill.

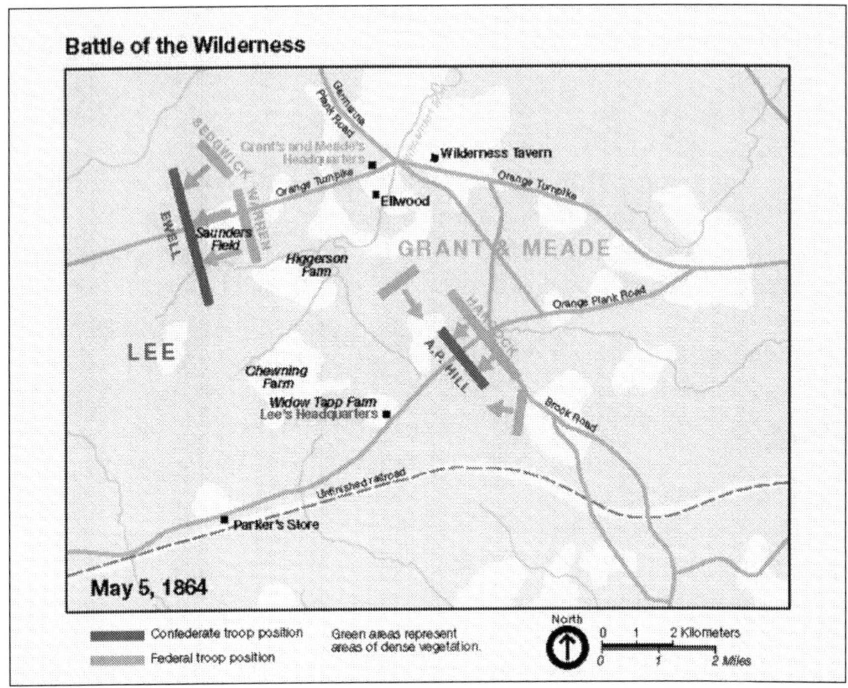

Figure 3 - 5 May

On the Orange Turnpike southwest of Wilderness Tavern, Major Robert Stiles, commanding an artillery battalion in Ewell's Second Corps, came upon General Ewell himself.

It was six o'clock and the sun was rising.

"Old Bald Head" was standing by the side of the road, watching his troops go by in the growing day. His skinny little body was propped up on crutches, and the buggy he used to get around was parked in the edge of the forest. Staff officers stood near by, but Ewell ignored them as was his custom.

"Mornin' Gen'ral," Stiles said in greeting, touching the brim of his kepi to show respect. His twelve guns continued to roll east and he knew he had only a minute to talk to this august figure.

Ewell took his eyes off the troops and looked at him. "Good morning, Robert," he replied. "Heard from your mother lately?"

They were distant cousins, related by blood or marriage as were nearly all the Virginians in the army's command structure.

"Yes, sir. She sends her regards to you and Mrs. Ewell," Stiles lied gallantly. His mother would never have taken notice of Mrs. Ewell, whom she thought to be "an upstart."

Dick Ewell nodded, unimpressed.

Stiles decided to risk a reproach. "Might I ask, Sir what sort of orders you have today?" He held his breath.

"Hah! Hah!" cackled the general. "Just the sort I like. Go right up the road and hit'em, just what I like... You'd better hurry, Robert. You wouldn't want your boys to go in without you. You'd better hurry." He was smiling at the incongruity of the thought.

Major Stiles saluted, and spurring his mount to a trot went down the road to catch up with his last gun. It was just disappearing around a bend in the road.

Chapter 15

Sander's Field

- 8:00 A.M -

One mile away to the northeast, a mounted Union infantry colonel named David Jenkins watched Confederate infantry deploy in line across the grassy meadow in front of him. They were coming out of the woods on either side of the point at which the turnpike crested the rise in the far side of the little valley. As he watched, the formation grew wider and wider as the brown figures emerged from the trees farther and farther from the road.

He could imagine the process of deployment that had happened after the Rebels came over the rise to see Gouverneur Warren's Fifth Corps in front of them. The leading regiment had gone from a column of fours to a "line of battle" formation as he had watched. Then the word had been passed back down the Confederate column and all the following regiments had fanned out into the woods on either side. Succeeding brigades went farther and farther out to the flanks and now they came out of the greenwood at a trot, unslinging rifles as they ran.

Something glinted on the left flank of the enemy formation. The colonel raised his telescope to look. A stocky Confederate officer with a big mustache stood behind the fighting line just inside the trees looking in his direction through binoculars. As he watched, the man swung his free hand from side to side over his head.

My God, he's waving at me, the colonel thought. As Jenkins watched, the whole long Rebel line turned and walked back into the forest.

Looking for shade. Maybe we should do that, he thought.

- 12:55 P.M. -

Behind Balthazar, the battalion waited in the wood. The men lay on the forest floor in the cool, shady, dimness. They lay in their fours, chatting with messmates. As became the veterans that they were, they had no desire to see out of the wood. They were acutely conscious of the possibility of a stray bullet or a sharpshooter. Balthazar would come for them when it was time.

Standing near the road, Balthazar watched the Yankees' seemingly aimless activity across the meadow.

What a lovely day, he thought. *A shame to die today.*

It was about a quarter of a mile to the other side.

They do not seem to know what to do next. Timid, that is the word, he thought.

He could not know that this was the same word that Sam Grant was applying to the inaction of Warren's Corps. Grant had ordered an attack to clear the enemy force from the Orange Turnpike. The order was issued at nine o'clock. Three hours had passed with no result. He let it be known that either Warren's Corps would attack or he would take charge of the situation personally.

As a result, activity on the Federal side of the clearing suddenly increased. A mounted officer rode out of the trees. The horseman turned in his saddle and said something to an aide. He ordered something in a voice that Balthazar heard as an unintelligible sound and then his men stood up, towering above the knee high green of the meadow grass.

Zouaves! Zouaves! Look at them! Balthazar thought.

The Northern soldiers were magnificent. They wore short blue jackets adorned with orange piping along the seams. Baggy pants of the same blue and red Fezzes with a long tassel hanging to one side completed their dress.

Balthazar could see that they were part of a column of regiments. Looking closely, he could see that the front ranks of the Zouaves wore a darker shade of blue than those behind.

Different groups, he thought.

To the left of the Zouaves, other Union units dressed in standard uniforms were appearing, more every minute. The Zouaves carried New York colors. Balthazar could read the word "Excelsior" on the flags though his binoculars.

He turned his glasses to the Federal troops to the right of the Zouaves. He looked first at the national color of the nearest regiment and then at the blue regimental color beside it. There was no state named. As he watched, a breeze bellied out the flag. "Second Infantry Regiment" was written in gold across the material beneath the national eagle emblem. You could clearly see the arrows in one claw and the olive branch in the other.

Regular Infantry, this should be interesting, he thought.

There were seven more units of regulars lined up to the right of the "Second Infantry."

The enemy colonel's voice was strong and it carried well now across the clearing as he ordered his men forward. "Brigaade! Second Infantry is the Battalion of Direction! Forwaard! Maarch!" The mass of soldiery lurched into motion.

They started down the slope that led to a dip in the bottom of the valley. The grade was so gentle that the Union troops were under continuous rifle fire from the waiting Confederates as soon as they started forward. Rifle bullets knocked men down in the ranks. Arms and legs flailed in the midst of legs. The green grass was so high and dense that it actually slowed the advancing front rank. Clouds of grasshoppers flew up.

Behind the infantry, two artillery pieces rolled out of the woods and halfway down the slope. The teams circled to point the muzzles up the slope toward the Confederates. The gun crews dismounted hurriedly as the gunners ran to the limbers for ammunition.

As he watched, Balthazar saw that a gap was developing between the right flank of the Zouaves and the left flank of the regular infantry. The regulars were moving obliquely away to the left and the Zouaves were not moving with them. Instead, they came straight up the slope, directly at the trees in which the battalion lay hidden.

The two Napoleon guns opened fire with solid shot. One projectile went high, passing over the Zouaves, missing them by a few feet and flying on to smash and crash its way through the trees to Balthazar's right. The other shot tore a hole right through the two New York Zouave Regiments in front of the gun. Several gaudily colored bodies lay in the path cleared by the ball.

One man screamed and ran to the rear holding his intestines in one hand. With the other he grasped the rifle he was using as a crutch.

Seeing that, the New Yorkers ran uphill as fast as they could. They wanted desperately to reach the trees on the Confederate side of the meadow... There was nothing in their minds but an immediate desire to get out of the valley and out of sight of the men shooting at them from both front and rear.

With a roar the Southern infantry burst from the trees, running forward to meet them. The Confederates halted once to fire a volley.

With clubbed muskets and bayonets the two lines closed.

The two cannons fired again, killing friend and foe indiscriminately.

The weight of the Northern attack pressed the Stonewall Division back into the woods. The Federal advance threatened to pass Balthazar's own position by the road. "Roarke!" he roared, looking around for the sergeant major.

The black bearded figure appeared at his elbow. "Ask Captain Smoot to bring the battalion up, please. I would like a line formation just here and there..." He pointed with his walking stick, indicating a line along the turnpike and another facing the meadow, "We will fire into the flank of the attack and at the guns. You see?"

Roarke disappeared into the trees.

Bullets slapped the trees with the "thwack!" sound that tell an "old hand" just how much speed the bullet has behind it at impact.

"Colonel! Why don't you stand behind that nice tree to your right!" Joe White's voice was insistent.

Balthazar moved, and, remembering that this was White's first fire fight, looked for him.

Joe stood behind a nearby oak. He looked anxious, but not unduly so. He cradled a .577 Enfield rifled musket in the crook of one arm. It was the model with which the battalion was armed.

Balthazar watched the gap between the New York Zouaves and the regulars widen.

Nature abhors a vacuum, he thought. *Someone should fill that one!*

As if in answer to his summons, a double line of Confederate riflemen trotted out of the forest, into the grassy field between the two bodies of Northern troops. Balthazar watched with satisfaction as the column placed itself between the two Federal forces, and at a word of command, faced in opposite directions into the flanks of both the Zouaves and regulars.

Well, well. Someone has been listening to me, or perhaps watching.

He spied the major of the 33rd Virginia Infantry standing hatless between the two brown ranks and smiled.

"At my command! Fire to your front! Fire!" the major cried. The roar of the rifles nearly deadened the mind, but not quite. Confederate bullets from the volley buzzed around Balthazar.

How stupid it would be to be shot by our lovely Virginians across the way.

The billowing smoke from the volley could not conceal the terrible effect of the fire on the Zouaves. Blue and Orange bundles littered the ground everywhere in front of the woods.

The Zouaves rushed forward to close with their tormentors and put a stop to the murderous volley firing.. The fight became hand to hand. The Rebel infantry generally preferred a close fight. There were few in the Northern army who shared this appetite for personal mayhem. As a result the Northern soldiers often sought to use their bayonets in the "fencing" techniques taught in the drill manuals. The Southerners had no use for such "niceties." They preferred to swing their rifles by the barrels like axes.

Through the smoke, Balthazar could see the gun butts as they rose and fell. *They won't take this much longer,* he thought. He was trying to guess the breaking point of the Zouaves.

Maybe a little push? "Joe?" he called."

"Colonel?"

"Do you see the tall officer waving his sword over there? The one in the middle of the fight?"

Joe peered through the smoke. "The red cap?"

"Yes, shoot him, if you please..."

If Balthazar thought that this order might prove a severe test for Joseph White, he was mistaken.

I wish I had my own rifle, but this will do, Joe thought. He braced the weapon against the tree trunk. The range was about 100 yards.

The report startled Balthazar. He had not expected Joe to fire so quickly.

The Federal officer pitched to one side, driven down by the heavy bullet.

Smoot and Roarke arrived at Balthazar's side panting from running in the afternoon heat. Smoot leaned against a tree. "Where do we go?" he rasped.

Sergeant-Major Roarke looked exasperated. "Over there!" He yelled over the noise. "I told ye, over there." He pointed to the area Balthazar had indicated to him.

"Thwack!" A bullet hit the tree trunk between them. Smoot felt the force of it through the living wood.

Balthazar was watching them both. He nodded, and turned back to watch the collapse of the enemy attack. He hardly noticed the column of his men as they jogged toward the position he wanted them in.

The collapse came all at once as the Northern men realized that there was no longer a driving force urging them forward. Heads turned seeking the voice that had become part of their lives. Their colonel lay broken on the green grass. Two men knelt at his side. One of them fell across the body, struck by another bullet.

Forward motion stopped. The soldiers in blue and orange began to drift backward, away from the murderous brown figures at the edge of the wood, away from the killing fire into their right flank. The two Northern guns spoke again from behind them, tearing wide holes in the faltering mass of Zouaves. Then, suddenly, it was over and the Union troops fled down the hill leaving behind bloody heaps of flesh and bone that only a few minutes before had been healthy young men.

Balthazar was momentarily disappointed. He had looked forward to setting the battalion at the task of chewing the left flank of the Zouaves even as his friend the Virginia major was destroying their right. Smoot, Roarke and the other leaders had just gotten the men into position for this when the Yankees fled, disappearing suddenly from their front in a stampede to the rear.

This left the two cannons behind, standing in the open, surrounded by their crews, naked to the Rebel infantry.

Balthazar blew his silver whistle for attention, extended his arms straight out from the shoulders and swung his body to show what he wanted. That was enough for the company commanders. The battalion began to swing in imitation of Balthazar's signal. "A" Company on the left marched forward and "D" Company's men faced to the rear and walked that way until they had established the orientation that the Frenchman wanted. In their new formation the two lines faced downhill aimed at the two Yankee guns.

The whistle blew again. The arm rotated through a circle and pointed at the cannon. "Fix! Bayonets!"

From the adjutant's position behind the lines, Lieutenant Raphael Harris watched Balthazar's battalion perform. He counted silently to himself as he had been taught at West Point.

One, the right hands went to the grips in the scabbards,
Two, the long bayonets came shining into the light of a lovely day,
Three, the weapons fit with a click into the sockets on the muzzles of the rifles,
Four, the right hands came back smartly to rest alongside the right leg.

Amazing, he thought. *Cadets couldn't do it better... Who would have thought it possible.*

He looked to his left at the 33rd Virginia. They seemed dumbstruck at what they had just seen.

"Chaarge! Bayonets!" Balthazar roared. The rifles came up into fighting position presenting a hedge of steel to the front.

"Bat-talion! Forwaard! Maarch!" The troops stepped off together, headed for the prize. They marched down the hill with lines as straight as a yardstick. The enemy had not yet recovered from the defeat of the Zouave attack and there was little fire to interfere with this demonstration of Balthazar's methods. Halfway to the cannon, he gave his assault order.

"Guide Centerr! Double Time! Charge!"

As he started to run, Harris glanced to his left to see what the 33rd Virginia was up to and saw that they had faced away and were firing into the rear of the regular Union infantry still trying to fight their way forward into the trees.

He looked to his front. Balthazar, Sergeant Major Roarke, and Joe White were ahead of the front rank running in a group with the color party.

Smoot was on the right. Someone was running alongside him.

Must be his "runner." Harris thought. *Good, I told that boy to stick to him like a burr!*

The man in front of Harris jumped over something and looking down he saw that it was a wounded Zouave. "Get down!" he yelled as the lines swept by. Glancing back, he saw that the man was watching them go.

The guns were close now. Harris could see fear on the faces of the gunners. They had been slow in focusing on this oncoming threat.

Target obsession, bad thing boys! You're going to pay for it today...

The red-legged artillerymen began trying to swing the two pieces and load them at the same time.

Harris guessed that they would not have enough time to bring their weapons to bear on the approaching battalion.

The Union Army gunners were looking over their shoulders at the oncoming Confederates as they tried to finish loading. Fear and duty warred in them for supremacy. Fear won. With the assault fifty yards away, they bolted for the far side of the meadow leaving the section's horses, limbers, and caissons standing alone in the tall grass.

The battalion's lines swept past the two cannons, past the caissons and the horses. The animals looked around wildly, startled by the infantry lines as they passed. As he went by the horses, Raphael Harris, artilleryman that he was, marveled that they were all alive and unhurt.

They ran so fast that no one shot the horses, not us or them...

Balthazar blew his whistle to halt them. The blue tinged forest ahead seemed to heave and surge with the human mass gathered inside. The battalion halted and stood in an arc, its face to the forest, to the fleeing Zouaves and to the departed artillery crews.

Harris heard Balthazar call his name. Balthazar pointed at the Napoleons.

It took a minute for Harris to understand what was being said. He shook his head to clear the fog that the charge had brought. "You want the guns?" he asked to be sure he understood.

"Get them limbered up, and moved to the rear!" the Frenchman yelled back over the noise of battle. "Take men from each company," he added. "You have five minutes, don't leave anything! He turned back to watch for signs of life from the enemy troops across the field to the north. "Give Lieutenant Harris the men he needs," he yelled at the company commanders.

They waved back.

The artilleryman in Harris came suddenly to the surface.

The troops in the ranks knew something interesting was going to happen now. A number of them were looking back at him. Harris recognized faces from his old battery in the Louisiana Guard Artillery. He beckoned to several, knowing they would be happy to return to their old arm of service. "Jones, Fredericks, Robichaux! Pick enough men for two crews! Pick our old gunners first, hurry! We are taking these two pieces. Get enough drivers for everything."

The federals had left behind half a complete four-gun twelve pounder Napoleon battery. The two smooth bore bronze guns stood silent on the grass. Behind them were two wheeled limbers, each with an open ammunition chest on top. Behind the limbers were two caissons, each with its two ammunition chests. Between the two stood a wooden contraption on wheels called a "battery wagon." The five six-horse teams were nearby; left behind and staring about, looking for men they knew.

A cannon fired in the Union held wood ahead. A shell from a three inch ordnance rifle *whizzed* in to bury itself in the dirt near one of the teams. Providentially, it did not detonate.

The bastards are going to kill the horses. Harris thought.

"Hurry, up, damn you!" he screamed at no one in particular. "Get your asses moving before they wipe out the teams!"

Behind each company a little group was forming.

The men Harris needed ran to the guns and teams. The horses looked at them in distrust, trying to pull their heads away.

More shells struck the ground nearby.

The first team was hitched to a gun, then the second. All at once, everything was ready.

More shells screamed in, searching for the animals, hoping to hit an ammunition chest.

"Come on, lets do it!" Harris yelled, and turning his back on the Yankees ran up the gentle grassy slope in the direction from which they had attacked a few minutes earlier.

Smoot and Balthazar watched as soldiers slapped some horses on the flank and dragged others into motion. Somehow everything started moving uphill.

Another shell from a rifled gun whistled in. This one struck a soldier in "B" Company who happened to have his back turned so that he did not see it in flight. It hit him in the torso, cut him in half and threw blood, intestines, and other inner parts all over the men around him.

They looked down at what was left of their friend. They looked at each other. One picked up the man's rifle and threw it away when he saw the damage done by the shell. Another picked up the dead man's hat, and put it on.

Once again, the shell had not detonated.

The teams were almost to the trees now.

Balthazar ordered a retirement by alternating companies.

The fight between the Stonewall Division and the regulars had ended. The Rebel troops were busy in the edge of the forest digging in with whatever came to hand. The Federals had mysteriously disappeared.

"A" and "C" Companies went back up the hill a hundred yards, then stopped and faced the enemy. "B" and "D" Companies passed back through their lines to take up a position behind them and three quarters of the way to the woods.

Harris stopped in the trees from which they had attacked. He was wondering how far back he should take the guns and what an infantry battalion would do with them when Joe White passed him at a dead run.

"Got to get the Colonel's mare," he sang out as he rushed through them.

The skittish horses tossed their heads and pulled away. One reared.

"God damn it, Joe," someone yelled! "I'll kick yur black butt, you scair these husses agin!"

Joe just waved and ran on into the forest.

Harris was facing to the rear watching Joe run through the trees when cheering started in the woods to his left.

Everyone stopped doing whatever it was they were doing to listen to that sound. It was distinctive, Southern soldiers did not bellow out "huzzah" in this way. The sound got louder and louder, moving closer and closer.

Harris got his group moving again. He went back farther into the trees and stopped to listen. The cheering kept getting louder. The ripping, tearing sound of a hard infantry fight at close quarters began to fill his ears. He suddenly realized that the loudest part of the noise was moving away from him, *toward the Southern rear.*

Confederate soldiers ran out of the noise, coming through the trees, fleeing the fight.

Harris drew his revolver and stepped in front of one. "And where would you be going?" he asked the man.

Unfocused dread filled the big, brown bearded face. "Yankees ev'rwheer! ev'rwheer!" the soldier gasped. "They killed Gen'rul Jones. Shot him thu' the head. Shot him dead!"

Raphael Harris listened to the fight. Clearly, the Rebel line had broken in Jones' Brigade.

Someone will counterattack... There must be some reserves back there, surely...

Balthazar came up behind him. Harris gave his opinion on the situation while the French soldier inspected the military refugee. His attention wandered from the receding fire fight in the woods on the right to the soldier and back. "Lieutenant Fagan," he called.

"Sir! Yes Sir!" came the reply from nearby.

"Please take charge of our guest, and any others, like those over there!" Balthazar pointed at two more coming through the brush. Major Smoot!" John Balthazar had his own schedule for promotions. "Take a detail from the companies, and get these prisoners under control, and their arms collected."

There were defeated Zouaves everywhere. They were standing aimlessly in groups, glassy eyed at the moment but apt to recover their senses and sense of duty at any time. There were abandoned rifles scattered over the ground. "Get them out of here and back down the turnpike."

Smoot started picking men for the guard detail.

"Harris, unlimber your two guns and face them into the brush over there in the direction the stragglers are coming from."

It had not seemed possible to Raphael Harris that he would actually have the opportunity to fight these two guns. The idea must have been somewhere in the back of his mind. That was clear in the way he had selected men from the rifle companies, but it had seemed unlikely.

It took ten long minutes to get the section into battery facing in the desired direction. This was complicated by uncertainty as to how far the previous owners had actually progressed in trying to reload before they ran. This issue was resolved by firing the two Napoleons into the trees at the highest possible elevation. It made a satisfying roar, and branches fell to the ground for quite a long way in the woodland.

To everyone's surprise, five Union Army enlisted men then stumbled out of the brush with their hands raised. They were a mixed group from the 83rd Pennsylvania and 20th Maine Infantry Regiments. They were quite willing to talk in return for a small increase in their personal level of safety. They said their brigade commander was someone named Bartlett, that their whole division had attacked, and that a division from another army corps had attacked farther to their left.

Balthazar sent them to the rear and then put the battalion into an "L" shaped formation with "A" Company forming the cross bar facing into what someone said was "Sanders Field," while "B," "C," and "D" Companies faced into the woods where Bartlett's Brigade had overrun the Confederates. He told Harris to put a gun between "B" and "C" and another between "C" and "D."

Once in place the men sat down to rummage in haversacks for rations, clean rifles or sleep.

Harris took the opportunity to go through the contents of the "battery wagon" and to inspect in detail his new equipment. The new gun crews were in place by the Napoleons and the gun captains, both experienced men began to practice the crews, putting them through the gunnery drill that some already knew.

The forest was on fire. Smoke came drifting through the tops of the hardwoods, wispy at first but then thicker with the acrid sting of old, damp wood burning in a bed of dead leaves. Rabbits and a fox ran out of the wood escaping from the flames. At the sight of the troops they turned and ran around the ends of the line. One rabbit ran between the wheels of a cannon. A soldier swung at it with a ramming staff, but missed and the little beast scampered away behind the battalion's lines.

Harris and Sergeant Robichaux looked in wonder and admiration at the "battery wagon." It was brand new, freshly varnished, and without a speck of rust. It was immaculately lettered "U.S. Army" on the sides. It had a hinged round wooden top, and was hooked to its own limber. At the tail end there was a hinged "tail-gate" loaded down on the outside with fodder for the horses. Harris gestured to this and Robichaux nodded.

"We'll feed and water the horse soon, mon lieutenant" he said. Robichaux was Cajun from the bayou Teche.

In the wagon was a chest containing carriage repair and sadler's tools, awls, planes, saws, and other riches. The wagon body itself held oil, paint, grease, axes, shovels, spare parts for the guns and a mass of extra harness for the teams. "My, my, too bad they didn't think to bring the battery forge as well," Harris remarked with a smile. "We are in luck, eh, *mon vieux lapin*?" With that, he went to tell Balthazar of their good fortune.

The smoke was getting steadily thicker.

As he approached Balthazar, Harris began to hear a strange noise out in the woods. It was a steady, if irregular "pop, pop, pop" sound. After a minute he knew what it was. The fire was igniting cartridges in the pouches and pockets of fallen men.

Chapter 16

The Brock Road

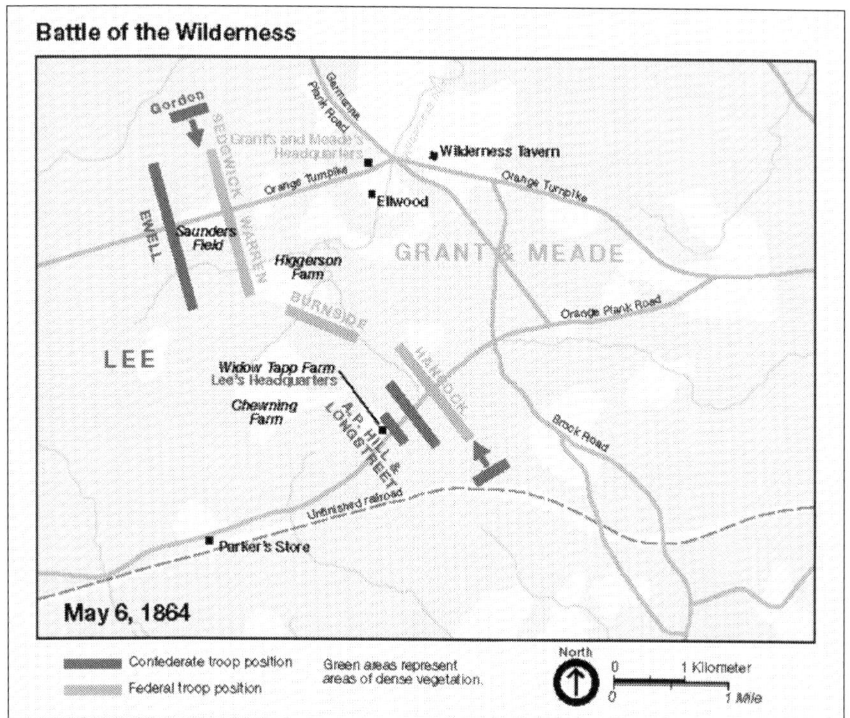

Figure 4 - May 6

Major General Charles Griffin rode his lathered horse into the crossroads clearing where Meade and Grant had set up a field headquarters. He climbed down and handed the reins to a junior officer of the staff. He ran, red faced, across the clearing to Meade, who stood not more than ten feet from Grant, and began to upbraid the Army commander on the subject of the lack of support his men had received in their attack across Sander's Field. In particular, he charged Sedgwick and his Sixth Corps with a total failure to be where they were supposed to be. "God damn it, George!" he said. "Why don't we just shoot these men ourselves, and save the Johnnies the trouble?" With that, he ran back to his mount and departed the crossroads in a cloud of dust, headed for his division.

"Who the hell was that?" Grant bellowed, recovering from his shock at what had happened. "Who was that general? What is his name? I want that bastard put under arrest for insubordination! Maybe mutiny! Who was that?"

Meade came to stand close to him and began to button up Grant's uniform coat as though he were a small boy on the way to school. "Now,

now," he said calmly. "That's Charlie Griffin, you remember him. A better man is not to be found. He's just a little upset right now. Now what were you saying about the pontoon bridges?"

"I want them taken up."

Meade's buttoning fingers stopped. "All of them?" he asked.

"Yes." Grant saw the look on the other man's sober face. "No. Leave one down for ammunition re-supply and evacuation of wounded."

"All right, Sam, I'll take care of it," Meade replied.

Grant remembered what he had been about to say when Griffin arrived. "Send a courier to Hancock. Tell him to put his people in line facing west on that road down ere." He pointed south. "What's the name?""

"The Brock Road," was the reply.

At three o'clock that afternoon, Devereux was standing beside a dusty road in conversation with Winfield Scott Hancock and Alexander Hays when a galloper arrived to inform Hancock of Grant's desires with regard to his corps.

The continuous sound of rifle fire to the west had been a companion to the discussion from its beginning and it was growing louder.

John Quick, the horses and the dog stood to one side watching Hancock's men pass by on the road. Everyone and everything was moving south.

Devereux kept looking at the dog, wondering if it would lose interest in them and wander away. He half wished it would. That would be one less thing to worry about, but the dog sat next to Quick looking at him and sometimes turning to Devereux as though seeking something it needed.

Quick talked to it occasionally and it stared up at him when he did.

A small, country church was visible down the road through the thicket.

The noise to the west became louder. That meant the fighting was moving toward them.

Hancock read the order and sat on a stump to write instructions for his divisions. When he was finished, and had sent couriers, he called Hays to him. "We are going to form front to the west and move forward to tie into Warren's people on our right. By my map, we are about a mile from them. They have been fighting along the Orange Turnpike to the northwest of here. It seems that it might be Ewell's Corps. If that is so, then the rest of Lee's army should be coming straight east along this other road right in front of us." He pointed on the map and squinted. "It says here that it is a plank road." He looked up from the map.

His staff and that of Hays' brigade had crowded near to hear what they could. It was warm and over the distant sounds of fighting and the nearby sounds of marching men and animals you could hear birds in the trees and the insect buzz so common in summer.

A soldier who had wandered off into the woods to relieve himself now stumbled out of the thickets into the dusty road. He was still buttoning himself up and looked surprised to see all these officers gathered at the spot where he had left his company. His regiment had moved while he was in the woods and now he trotted off in pursuit of them. He was carrying most of his equipment in his arms, eager to escape the gaze of so many colonels and generals.

The dog looked at him as he ran off, and stood up. Then she looked at Quick and sat down.

Hancock pointed in the direction of the noise to the west. "Hays, I want you to go straight west through these woods until you find Warren's left flank, then deploy into line on his left. I have written to General Birney that you will do that. There is a north-south road over there," he said pointing, "where General Meade's note says you will find Warren's people." He looked at the note. "It is called the Block Road."

"Brock Road," Hays corrected. He was looking at his own map.

"Yes," Hancock replied, but the main thing is to extend Warren's line to the left." He and his staff rode south in the direction of the church.

The infantry moved to the sides of the road to let them through.

It took Hays forty-five minutes to get his collection of undersized veteran regiments disentangled from the woods along the road and spread out as a line of regiments in columns with the heads of the columns facing roughly west. As he placed them, the colors of each regiment were not more than fifty yards apart.

A staff officer from David Birney's division headquarters sat his horse nearby fretting and muttering that the process of deployment was taking too long.

The noise to the west continued to grow in strength. Smoke was beginning to drift through the trees from that direction.

The dog sniffed the air.

It was clear that the woods were on fire.

Devereux and Quick watched in amusement as Hays ignored the staff man and went on with his methodical preparations. Finally, around four o'clock he was satisfied and told the staff man that he would advance in fifteen minutes. He then walked over to a tree and urinated against its trunk.

The dog looked interested but kept its place with Quick.

Standing in the road, Hays raised his voice.

"Brigade will advance! Guide Center! 17th Maine is the battalion of direction! "Forward! March!"

He said something inaudible to a bugler who rapped out the short call for "the advance."

The notes were repeated over and over as each regiment's bugler repeated them.

The troops walked forward into the woods, going west through the thick brush in regimental columns four men wide at the front and hundreds deep. Drummers struck up a steady beat to provide a sound to guide on in aligning the move through the tangled brush and second growth timber. It was slow going from the moment they left the road.

Hays's staff party inserted itself into the space between the 17th Maine and the regiment to its right.

Devereux and Quick followed Hays. They led their horses. The dog followed Quick, sniffing the air and looking fearful but unwilling to leave its new friends.

The tangle of underbrush pulled and tore at clothing. It was so thick that detours around deadfalls and hanging Virginia Creeper were frequent. The smoke was thick enough to conceal the features of men only a few yards away. A rifle bullet hit a tree somewhere. It struck the trunk above the height of a man, carried to that collision by the ballistic curve of its trajectory. The horses shied from the sound, but the dog plodded on behind Quick.

After that first bullet, the number of unwelcome arrivals from the territory of the unseen enemy increased steadily. They began to hum and sing through the scrub, buzzing like bees or cracking like a whip if they happened to pass directly overhead. Men went down, struck by random lead. For the most part these wounded men could not be seen, but their cries of shock and pain were heard on every side. The brigade moved forward through the wood for half an hour.

Devereux began to see orange clumps of flame in the dry leaves of the forest floor. The fires were spread by sparks carried on the steady breeze from the west. As the fires multiplied and merged it became more and more difficult to see anything more than the nearest trees. The sound of men breaking through the brush became more scattered as the formation inevitably spread.

Devereux and Quick were soon isolated from the mass of moving soldiers.

The volume of Confederate fire coming through the trees grew until it became a continuous menace.

Claude began to think of his options. Did he really want to walk straight forward with these Yankees into the "maw" of this inferno of fire?

He emerged from a clump of trees in a small clearing and looked around.

Hays sat his big horse in the middle of the open space, standing in the stirrups and peering to left and right through the smoke. The general was unhappy. His careful deployment of the brigade had broken into fragments as soon as the line entered the forest. He had sent messages up and down his line of troops, but the enemy fire, the growing flames, the smoke and the resistance of the thickets had made a mockery of his careful arrangements. He had never seen a wood like this one and would not see another.

Devereux stopped, looked down at his clothing and saw that his beautifully tailored tunic had been ripped open by the stunted hardwood trees and that he was bleeding from scratches across his chest. He looked around and could see that he, Quick and Hays were alone in the smoke. He thought of the blood wet red Carolina color that Hays and this horse had defiled at Gettysburg.

Time for retribution, he thought. *Time to act...*

He tied his mount to a tree, drew the beautiful Colt revolver and walked up next to Hays' bay horse. He grasped the reins. He looked around once more to be sure...

Quick was grinning at him.

Alexander Hays looked down at him and snarled "What the hell are you doing?" Devereux smiled at him. "Do you remember Gettysburg, Alexander? Do you remember the flag you dragged down the ridge?

Hays stared down at him. He tried to pull the horse's head away.

"Listen to me, Alexander! I want you to remember that flag now! Do you see it? I do!"

"What? Let go, damn you!" Hays tried again to pull the horse away from this threatening figure. He moved to draw his pistol.

Quick raised his voice from behind. "The dog's name is Maude, jinrul, Maude like yer bitch relatives." He looked down at the dog. "Maudie, don't yeh think the jinrul makes a fine figure on the byootiful horse, Don't yeh, Maudie?" He was petting the dog now and laughing from deep in the chest.

Hays twisted in the saddle to stare at Quick.

"This is for my brother," Devereux said.

That was the last thing Alexander Hays heard. Devereux's bullet hit him in the temple. He fell heavily from the horse and lay gasping on the leaves while smoke eddied around him.

Claude leaned over him. "I said you would pay, Alexander. I said it on the ridge at Gettysburg. And now, you have."

Hays' mouth opened and closed like a dying fish. There was no sound that rose above the crackling of the woodland fires around them and the distant musketry.

Quick walked up, stared down for a second and then spat on Hays who was now comatose.

"Take the two horses and "Maude" and go home," Devereux said, never taking his eyes from Hays. "Your papers will get you there if you leave now. I am going in with the attack to see if I can get across."

Quick looked unconvinced.

"I didn't ask your permission. Maybe my wife would like the dog…"

Maude sniffed Hays body. She lost interest. She had seen many dying men. Her attention turned to the west again. The noise was growing closer by the minute.

Sergeant Quick looked down once more at General Alexander Hays.

The big man's face was now the blue grey of impending death.

Turning away, the Irishman held out a hand in farewell and without a word gathered the reins of the horses and walked toward the east through the trees.

Maude looked back once and then followed him into the smoke.

Hays' horse stood by the dying general. Devereux went through the saddlebags, and retrieved the bottle of Rye whiskey. He took the bridle off the animal, pushed it around until it faced east and slapped its rump hard. Startled, it departed into a new and harsh world in which it would fend for itself.

There was a creek nearby. Devereux carried the bridle to the bank and threw it in. It sank nicely. He could hear voices out in the smoking woods somewhere and fearing that they would find the clearing with him in it walked away from them into the underbrush. He stopped twenty yards inside the forest to listen.

The cries behind him soon indicated that Hays' body had been found.

He walked back into the clearing. Soldiers were gathered by the prostrate form. Their surprise and grief saddened him and after a few seconds he told the senior officer present, a major, that they should send the body to the rear and get on with the movement to the Brock Road. The silver eagles on his shoulders and the severity of his presence carried the day.

After an interminable and protracted struggle with the undergrowth, Devereux and the men with him walked into the back of the brigade's main line.

It was halted for some reason. Men stood around coughing and spitting in the gloomy smoke. Some sat on the ground.

"What's this?" Devereux shouted. "Get moving, damn you! Where's the road?"

"Right in front of you, colonel," a private said from somewhere in the line of men. "Right in front of you." The soldier hacked and rasped in the acrid smoke. Even so, the accent of northern New England was clear in his voice.

Devereux peered through the drifting haze and saw that the light brightened sharply ahead in a way that always meant an open space.

Bullets still clipped bits of greenery in their passing overhead but the Confederates seemed to be shooting high today.

Devereux would normally have been unhappy with that, but in this case could only thank whatever god he still believed in. "Get up," he yelled. "Get moving you damned Yankees..." It had been instinctive, but he realized instantly what he had said. They did not seem to have noticed.

The color party of the 17th Maine was fifteen or twenty yards away.

He pushed his way through the color party and grasped the national color's staff. "Come on, damned you. Follow me," he cried. He tried to wrench the flag from the color sergeant.

The color sergeant would not surrender it to this strange, wild looking officer. Every man in view now watched him.

Devereux looked back at them and the old hunger came over him, the hunger to be accepted as the leader of men who saw him as their chief. Suddenly, he saw them as his, his alone... All rational thought of what he was committed to doing left him. The blood hunger that had been fed by Hays' death was still strong in him. "Come on, then," he cried, and ran towards the light in the west. As he went, the federal infantry rose and followed him. He came out of the trees and jumped down from a little bank into the ruts of the road.

There were Southern skirmishers in the trees on the far side of the dirt road when he reached it.

The 17th Maine came out of the woods on either side of him. That probably saved him from a wound or death. The grey sharpshooters in the trees automatically fired at the color party without focusing on the idea that the blue officer with a revolver in his hand was probably a better target. The color sergeant of the regimental color went down with several bullets in him. The sergeant major grabbed for the falling flag and fell himself across the first man's body. They bled and writhed on the ground for a second and then the sergeant major crawled away towards the wood line.

"Volley fire!" Devereux yelled "At the woods!" He pointed with the hand that held the Colt. "Fire!"

The rifle muzzles rose. A sheet of lead slashed at the unseen Southerners. A cloud of powder smoke suddenly threw up a screen that hid the confused scene along the little road.

Time slowed down for Devereux. He looked at the brushy forest twenty yards to his front. There were shadowy figures behind the flashes of red. His vision narrowed and the old, hot, sweet, intoxication of the battlefield descended on him. He fired at one half seen silhouette in the smoke. It disappeared, but above the noise he heard the liquid gurgle and cough that meant a hit in the chest.

He picked up the blue regimental color and started across the road. The man with the national color followed him. Devereux began to shout at the men to either side. What the words were, neither he nor they could have said, then, or later. The line surged forward into the brush behind him.

Sounds of breaking branches retreating from the advancing line made it clear that the Rebel skirmishers were running for their lives.

Devereux stepped across a prostrate brown form. He had both hands full with the flag.

An officer of the Maine regiment caught up with him and asked for the flag.

Devereux gave it to him and then bent over the fallen Confederate. Rolling the body over, he found that the wounded man was a lieutenant and that he had been hit in the face.

The soldier mumbled something through the confusion that had been his lower jaw. Bloody bone ends and broken teeth prevented him from speaking.

Still swept up in the fight, Devereux hardly looked at him. What he wanted was the wounded man's sidearm. Holding it in his hand he saw that it was a Navy Colt and that it had four unfired cylinders. He looked at the man on the ground.

The infantry officer stared back at him and then began to scream through his injury. Bloody foam was blown out of his ruined mouth. It speckled Devereux's blue tunic.

Ignoring the ruined face, he rose to his feet and looked around at the 17th Maine. Many of them were looking at him, waiting to be told what to do,

My men are waiting...

He remembered the order given by General Hays. The objective of the attack came to the front of his mind. "Let's go," he yelled. "We have to find General Warren's left flank! Keep moving! Keep going!" He walked toward the regiment's right flank intent on being on the scene when Warren's men were found. As he pushed his way through the jungle and bitter smoke, he found that he had to walk around fires burning in more and more places. He found several men cowering behind trees. These he dragged to their feet and shoved toward the line that was steadily if slowly moving to the west.

Unexpectedly, the forest ended to his left and he walked out into a big clearing with the moving line all around him.

The sun was shining in the field. The sky was blue with a few fluffy white clouds high up. It was meadow land. Several cows stood looking at them stupefied by this apparition come from the forest as if from another world. In the experience of the cows, men came from the forest to bring them home for milking. The cows looked hopeful.

Devereux yelled at the nearest officers to get their men back into line. He was thinking that a company should be sent to the right to find Warren's flank.

In the vacuum created by his killing of Hays, he had seized effective control of the brigade. It was the role that he was born for. By nature he would lead men in battle if he had the chance, and by nature they would obey him.

He turned to the left to find an officer in one of the other brigade regiments to yell at, and saw about ten men standing or sitting around a tree on the left side of the field. The men sitting were all in grey. Those who stood by the horses wore brown. While he watched, the seated men rose to their feet and one of them walked rapidly away from the Union soldiers.

Even at seventy yards, Devereux recognized the straight back, short legs and white haired head of Robert Lee

Lee's staff was transfixed by the sight of hundreds of federal infantry close enough to hit with a thrown stone. They seemed paralyzed. None moved.

Devereux knew that a volley from Hays' brigade would kill or wound everyone standing by the tree. The horses would go down as though harvested by a giant scythe. Lee would die.

The world came back into focus for Devereux. He waved an arm toward the woods behind the line and walked away from the cows and General Lee. The blue soldiers already accustomed to the idea of obeying him turned and followed him back into the forest. Fifty yards inside the wood, he stopped and the line stopped with him. A lieutenant colonel from Hays' staff arrived from farther down the line to ask what he thought the brigade should do.

"Well, I think you should find whoever is now in command and persuade him to send a force to carry out General Hancock's instruction to tie the flank to Warren. I am going to sit down somewhere..."

The staff man saluted. He looked uncertain. "Colonel, who do you think those Johnnies were… out there in the meadow?"

Devereux had found a comfortable tree to sit by. He was settling his back against the tree and looking around at the nearest fires. He glanced up. "I have no idea. They must have been some cavalry scouts… There were a lot of horses…"

"We're really grateful, sir at the way you took charge when General Hays was killed." The officer did look grateful. "God knows what would have happened if you hadn't been there to get us moving again. The division commander will hear of this I am sure. We thank you."

Devereux laughed, thinking about how far astray he had gone in leading this advance. Then he remembered his manners. "Kind of you. I am going to stay here for a while and then make my way back to Meade's Headquarters. Don't you worry about me…"

The staff man nodded. He was one of the people that Devereux had shared a couple of meals with at Hays' field headquarters.

"Sorry about Hays. You all liked him. I saw that."

The man blinked back tears, saluted again and walked away to find the new brigade commander.

Devereux smiled to himself and tried to settle his bad leg in a more comfortable position. The day's walking had created a great aching ball of flame in his right knee.

I need Hope or Amy here to massage that. Actually… Combat generally made him want a woman and this experience was no different.

The firing line was halted where he had let them stop. He closed his eyes, determined to rest until nightfall.

He dreamt of Hope seated in the parlor window seat of his parents' home on Duke Street. The dog, Maude, sat at her feet with its chin on her knee. His wife was beautiful in the amber light of late afternoon. Her golden hair framed her perfect oval face. The dog turned its head to look at someone else in the room. He realized now that Hope was talking to Amy Biddle. She was seated across the room in his favorite chair. They were talking about him. They were discussing his faults. His grandfather came into the room...

He awoke unhappy. His grandfather was often in his dreams. He always came to defend Claude, but rarely was given the chance. Claude's father was there at times as well. He had not spoken in a dream for a long time. Perhaps it was better that way. Blinking his gummy eyes, Devereux remembered where he was. Night was coming on quickly in the late twilight. A small, leaf fire had burned its way to him and one of his boots was smoking. He beat the flames into extinction. The burned leather made an unpleasant smell in the surprising quiet and dimness. There was no one in sight. He could hear soldiers talking somewhere nearby but the voices were too faint to be understood as speech. He found the two pistols and re-loaded the fired cylinders in both. Luckily, they were both .36 caliber. Loading the cap and ball guns was difficult in the dark, but Claude had always been good at the skills of the soldier. Banking had been his father's idea of a career for him. He had always wanted the uniform as something to lose himself in, something in which he might find shelter... He settled his own revolver in its beautiful, handmade holster and then put the other one under his leather belt in the small of the back. The memory of the day swept over him. He remembered the Southern soldier whom he had shot. The man must be lying somewhere nearby. He thought of looking for him. He thought of the men who had been in the clearing. He thought of Lee.

We might have killed him. My God, I might have killed him.

He shoved that thought down into the hole into which he had shoved so much else.

Time to go.

He climbed awkwardly to his feet using the rough tree trunk for support in getting his aching legs under him. It had become very dark...

West, I have to go west. Where the hell is west?

He stood with his back to the tree and tried to remember it as a point of reference.

Did I turn around getting up?

He looked up at the sky, searching for the North Star.

A man walked near him.

"Soldier," he said in a calm, subdued voice.

The sound of the other man walking in the brush stopped suddenly.

"Who is there?" the man asked.

"Colonel Devereux, from the War Department."

"Ah, yes, sir. I remember you today," the man said in a Maine accent. "We all do. Thank you, sir."

Devereux was hungry for this, hungry for acceptance by "his" soldiers. He fought that down, thinking that he should kill this man. "Which way are the Johnnies?" he asked. "I fell asleep here. I don't want to walk into them in the dark..."

The man came closer.

Devereux felt the air move as the soldier waved his hand, feeling for him. He reached out and found the hand.

The man touched his chest to know what direction he faced. Taking one of Claude's hands he pointed it in the darkness. "That way, they are over that way. Our pickets are about fifty yards in that direction. The password is 'Grant," and the countersign is 'Meade.' I'm Caleb Moulton. I'm the senior officer left in 'B Company, 4th Maine.' We moved sideways while you were asleep. I saw you here, but thought to let you sleep."

Claude relaxed his hand on the pistol in the small of his back.

Not this one. Not tonight.

"We have a little fire back on the Brock Road," Moulton said. "Coffee. We'll attack again in the morning. That's what brigade says..."

"I'll be along in a minute. Have to answer a call... Save me some coffee."

Moulton moved away toward the fire and the coffee.

Devereux had not been lying. After he finished, he buttoned his pants, and wiped his hands on the tree and some leaves. That done, he walked in the direction of the Union picket line, feeling his way with his toes to prevent noise he might otherwise make. He was soon challenged but the signs that Moulton had given got him past the picket with nothing more than an exhortation not to wander farther forward. He walked to the right, paused, and then got down and crawled away from Moulton's pickets toward the unknown country where the Southerners must be. The crawling was interminable but he was patient. He knew from protracted experience that infantrymen in the front line are quick to shoot and unrepentant about it. He crawled for what seemed a long time and was still crawling through thick, high grass near the place where he had seen the Confederate officers when a whisper stopped him.

It was close and to one side rather than in front.

"Who're you?" it asked.

Devereux lay still for a minute, knowing that his life depended on the answer. "I want to surrender," he responded.

"Are you armed? The whisperer enquired.

"Two pistols and a clasp knife."

"Is it a nice knife?

He smiled in the dark, reassured to hear evidence that the slightly mad humor of his own army had not changed. "Hand made in England."

"Hmmm. What's your rank?"

"Colonel."

A silence ensued and then another voice whispered at him, "All right, you crawl straight ahead until you reach the trees. We will be right with you. You know the rules. Anything we don't like and we shoot you or whatever..."

Ten yards into the trees rough hands were laid on him. One set of hands relieved him of his weapons and another felt his uniform, dwelling on the shoulder straps with their embroidered silver bullion eagles.

"Damn! He really is a colonel, or dressed like one at least."

Devereux smiled invisibly.

They dragged him another fifty yards and then let him stand to have his hands tied behind him. Five minutes later, he was introduced to a harried looking colonel who inspected him by the light of a match behind a clump of evergreens.

"What's your name?" the colonel asked after the match went out.

"You don't really want to know. I lied to your outpost line. I am not a deserter. I am a Confederate scout, impersonating a Yankee colonel just now."

"And you decided to cross the line to report?"

"Precisely."

"How do I know that is true?"

"Who is your division commander? You might as well tell me. You have me now. What could I do with the name?

"Heth. This is Heth's Division."

"Harry knows me well. Just take me to him and he will vouch for me."

"That's reasonable. Sergeant Willis…"

"Sir?"

"You heard him. Go find General Heth, and deliver this man to him…"

"Any idea where he is? "

"He was here five minutes ago. Go find him"

"Yes, sir, come on cunnel, or whatever you are…"

Chapter 17

The Prodigal son

It would be inadequate to say that Charles Marshall was surprised when Devereux appeared at Lee's headquarters. The shock was so great that he almost forgot to offer his guest a place to sit, but, always the gentleman, recovered quickly to find a chair into which Devereux sank in exhaustion.

"My God, Claude," Marshall asked, "what on earth are you doing down here among us common people? And you are a colonel as well? I had heard of that, but the sight is... disturbing."

"Where is he?"

"You haven't come to see me? I am wounded. He is out looking for Ewell. Longstreet is just down the road. Want to talk to the "tycoon, do you"? Well... They will both be back shortly, I hope. Any idea where we are in this damned jungle? I don't think I have been here more than once or twice in my life. I had a cousin who lived over near Zoan Church, but I think the Yankees ran him out a while back..." At this point, Marshall realized that he was talking to an unconscious man, and looking around found a blanket with which to cover the man.

-6 PM, 7 May, 1864 –
(The Left of Ewell's Second Corps Line
In the Wilderness)

It was a long and wandering path through the woods that brought Devereux to Balthazar's Battalion the next day... He went first to Dick Ewell's command post on the Orange Turnpike, then east on that road to find Jubal Early's division. A courier from Lee's little staff took him to Ewell and then another brought him to the slope just west of Sander's Field where Balthazar's men had fought the first day. A brigade commander sent him northeast from there through the forest to the far left of the Confederate line where he found Early almost at the Rapidan.

Devereux was dressed in old, rough, civilian clothes that came from the bottom of someone's knapsack. None of it fit very well and it smelled bad when he put it on. He had found another knapsack in a stack next to a pile of Union Army bodies. He carried his U.S. uniform in that.

After he had worn the old clothes for a day and had walked ten miles in them, they did not smell at all.

Early shook his head at the sight of him. "You are a spy, our spy. What are you doing here? You are supposed to be over there." He pointed east towards the Union position along the Germanna Ford Road.

"He's one of our spies in Washington," Early said to Brigadier General John Gordon who happened to be standing next to him. "He is one of our best spies. You will have to forget that..."

"I was there, yesterday" Devereux said after a moment's thought, but I decided to come to tell Robert Lee what they are going to do, and here I am, for the moment... Lee was not happy to see me either. You people are not very hospitable. I want to visit my cousin for a few days."

Gordon was annoyed and puzzled by this intrusion on his attempt to convince Early that the Union right flank did not reach to the river, was in reach of a night turning movement and that something should be done about that.

Devereux held out his hand, "I would introduce myself but... He is right. I am a spy, and a Confederate officer on detached duty." He felt compelled to justify himself to the Georgian. He felt foolish about this.

Gordon shook hands in silence.

"Are your parents well?" Early asked in the inevitable response of any Virginian to meeting a family friend. "And that lovely woman, who tolerates your trifling ways, how is she?"

Devereux flinched at that. "They are well. Thank you. "Since my father is one of your few friends on earth, I will remember you to him, if I can. I want to go visit with my cousin Balthazar for a few days until a chance comes to send me back, or Lee gives me a command." Just thinking of that second possibility was like turning a knife in his guts. The prospect of that had been his only real aspiration since the beginning of the war. If he had his own regiment, there would surely be friends there who understood his merits. Unhappily, he knew that Lee might like to give him a regiment or perhaps even a brigade, but no longer had the power to do that. The matter was no longer in his hands. Devereux had somehow become a "public benefit," the "property" of larger interests in the Confederate government than those of General Lee. It was clear from their meeting the previous evening that the army commander would have sent him back across the lines without delay if he had known a way to do it. Lee was appreciative of Claude's information concerning Grant and his plans but also distracted and eager for his "guest" to depart the Army of Northern Virginia. Seeing that, Devereux pleaded for the chance to visit his French cousin nearby and Lee agreed to be rid of him.

Having disposed of the necessity of common courtesy, Early, too, was weary of Devereux. Like Lee, he was busy, and unlike Lee had never liked Claude much, believing that Charles Devereux's judgment on his son's character was correct.

He was preparing himself for the unpleasantness of telling Claude that he wanted him out of his division's area when there was a commotion in the brush which announced the arrival of a "galloper" from Lee with a message for Early. He read it in silence, chewing, spitting and scratching reflectively while Gordon walked up and down, impatient with the interruptions.

Early finished and looked around. "Hill is sick again. He is relieved, and I am to take over Third Corps tomorrow at noon. We are going to move to the right, to try to block Grant against a move he might make towards Richmond." He looked at Gordon. "Sorry, John, I have other things to think about now. You come with me," he said to Devereux. "I don't want you to be wandering around without somebody knowing where you are.

John Balthazar and Joe White were glad to see Devereux.

The men in the battalion had no idea who Devereux might be. His mysterious appearance in the woods was of no particular interest to them. There were local people about. They wandered in and out of Southern positions without hindrance rightly convinced that they would be welcome there. Devereux's disguise made him look very like one of them unless you saw the eyes. The eyes had always frightened some people. Now they frightened most people.

Smoot was gone away to pick up the battalion's rations. His opinion about Devereux's arrival was not yet available.

Balthazar's Battalion was in a wood a hundred yards behind the low crest in the Orange Turnpike where Devereux had earlier turned left to find Early. If he had turned right at that point he would have found them.

"I went right by here this afternoon," he said. Several chairs had been found in the battery wagon that the battalion had captured. Devereux, Early and Balthazar had tin cups of whiskey in their hands. The rain had stopped. The spring evening was pleasant. The battle was quiet at the moment. Everyone listened "with one ear" for outbreaks of firing, but there was little to be heard. The line of contact between the two armies was some distance away in the east and southeast. There had been some firing earlier in the afternoon but it was dying away with the light.

Early told Balthazar of his new appointment to temporary command of the III Corps and warned him to be ready to move south with him.

Impatient with the lack of attention he was receiving, Devereux mentioned that it had been in that area that he had crossed the lines and that he had been present there the day before when Longstreet tried to turn Grant's left flank.

"What?" Early snapped, startled by the interruption. "What did you say?"

"We heard the noise about noon," Balthazar said. "What happened?" He would be in that area soon. Knowledge of the situation would be a good thing.

Claude was pleased. He needed to be the center of attention. "The engineers found Hancock's left flank," he began. "That was the left end of Grant's line. There's a railroad cut that leads in behind it from the road Longstreet's corps used coming up from Orange. Longstreet's arrived at the right time in just the right place to be put in there, just behind Grant's left flank. I listened while Lee and Longstreet decided what to do. Moxley Sorrel, Longstreet's chief of staff is from this area. He guided the head of the column up the railroad cut. Longstreet had them all together, the whole corps. They were headed for the "hinge" behind the flank, the spot where they could "lift" Hancock's "door" off its hinges if they struck all together. But, before they got far enough forward of our lines, someone in Jim Lane's brigade shot Longstreet through the neck by accident. Lee tried to keep the attack moving by leading it himself but with the Dutchman gone it all fell apart. What a shame it was. We might have destroyed that wing of Grant's army... We really might have done it this time. We have been so close, so many times..."

"Longstreet?" Balthazar asked.

"He may be dead by now," Early answered. "I was gonna tell you..." He glanced at Claude. "Lane's men shot Stonewall last year on almost the same ground. There was less excuse this time. It was dark when they shot Jackson. Something should be done about them. It's a big mess in the woods down there, a lot more fires, men trying to crawl away from the flames, a mess."

"What will Grant do?" Early asked Devereux. "Do you have an opinion?" What he really believed of Devereux's ability to answer the question could not be judged. The curly, brown beard was too good a mask and the growing darkness hid much in his face.

Claude sensed the subtle mockery. "I had dinner with him and Meade, before the river crossing. George Sharpe was there..." He named several others.

Early and Balthazar looked blank at the mention of the names.

Devereux began to glow with inner anger.

I risked my life for this? I risk my family every day. I crossed the lines to bring this information and to be with them, and they do not care? Lee was not interested... He thanked me, but, then, he would thank anyone for the most trivial thing.

Devereux remembered Alexander Hays' face as he lay dying and gasping in the smoking forest.

Early was still waiting for an answer. He looked impatient.

Thinking of Grant, Claude knew what the man's reaction would be to the events of the last few days. "He will shrug off whatever you do to him," he said suddenly. He will bring up more troops from the rear and move on towards Richmond, moving away to the southeast, knowing you will have to fight him over and over again if he keeps moving in that direction. He has about 130,000 men available to him for this line of advance. He will accept his losses and keep feeding those men to you. Lee's Army is his objective. He means to destroy you by making you fight for Richmond until you are all used up. He will succeed unless a major part of his army can be destroyed before you are ruined. I have read everything in Stanton's office and I have met Grant. That is what he will do..."

Early stared at him in the fading light. He was thinking of Devereux in blue, reading army papers in Washington. Then, without turning from Devereux, he said to Balthazar, "I'll send orders for the move." With that he walked back out of the trees to the Orange Turnpike where a soldier waited with his horse.

At that moment, three or four miles to the east, Grant finished listening to reports of the day's fighting. The ferocity of the struggle to keep Lee from cutting his army in half was something not often seen in the western theater from which he had come. Grant now knew why Union officers in the east spoke with something approaching reverence for Lee and his men. He tried to sort out the mass of details.

The returns say that I have lost at least 18,000 men in the last four days. I wonder how many Lee has lost. I will bring up more troops, Burnside's corps first. Ferraro's division of blacks is with them. Good. Let them have a taste of this. I must not go to the field hospitals. I must not think about that. That man today who walked out of the trees with his clothes on fire... His face was gone, just raw meat. I must not see too much of that. I will tell Meade to pull Warren's corps out of the line on the right and pass it down the Brock Road behind the rest of the army, then the rest of the army one corps after another the same way. Lee will see Spotsylvania Court House as my goal. I must meet him there. I must destroy him there. This must end soon. I must remember the election in November...

Half an hour later, having given his instructions for the morning, Grant went into his tent, lay down on the bed and sobbed until he slept. The men in the headquarters and those passing on the road could hear it.

From the point of view of the Confederates, Grant's resolution in pressing on to the south without regard to casualties was unfair, a violation of what they had come to see as the rules of the game. Grant's predecessors, including Meade, had all tried their luck south of the Rapidan and then, mauled by "Lee and his boys," had retired with a decent speed to their side of the river to lick their wounds and wait for a new commanding general. As they came to understand how differently Grant thought of war, "Lee's Miserables" would always think him unfair. They were always badly outnumbered. Was that not enough of a handicap in the game? One of Grant's predecessors, George B. McClellan, had helped in overcoming that disadvantage by believing that they were far more numerous than they truly were.

The men in brown and grey were particularly envious of US Army rations and always looked forward to the prospect of emptying the knapsacks of dead men. They were starving in the Wilderness that spring, the victims of a system of government so decentralized that it could not force the states or the railroad companies to adequately support them.

Eighty or ninety miles away and in opposite directions, the two presidents waited and brooded on the prospects for themselves, their peoples and their countries.

Devereux's two women brooded, united in two things, their feeling for him and their confusion over what to do about each other. They spent more time in each other's company than was healthy. Perhaps they found solace in the presence of someone with whom it was unnecessary to discuss him...

Balthazar was confused by the tension he had seen between his cousin and Jubal Early, a commander whom he had come to respect deeply. "You should not annoy him," he said to Claude. "Early is a good man. He has been a great friend to me and to the battalion.

Devereux said nothing. He seethed with bitterness born of disappointed hopes, hopes for so many things important to him, but he was a guest in Balthazar's camp and could say little.

He had left Lee's headquarters without permission after witnessing the fiasco in which Longstreet's corps attack failed. He had found a courier headed for the Second Corps and had taken advantage of the opportunity. He expected to find Balthazar and Smoot. Claude had the gift of persuasion and used it ruthlessly.

He expected that someone in Lee's headquarters would be looking for him by now. He relished the thought.

Yes, I will abide with these folk for a few days.

The fighting would not end soon, and his soul needed the solace of this kind of companionship.

"Let them look for me. I am not their servant."

Lee's staff was already looking for him. The army commander had found a few minutes to renew his conversation with the spy and asked after him. The inability to produce him created the occasion for one of the rare but much feared outbreaks of Robert Lee's temper. His cold rage was impressive. He never cursed, but this time seemed very close to doing so.

After some enquiry the sergeant who took Devereux to Ewell's headquarters was found. At first the man was bewildered by the commotion. Then, he was terrified when confronted by Lee who wanted to know why he agreed to take Devereux with him. From the look on the soldier's face, Lee knew the answer to his own question.

Claude is someone they always accept as a leader. They always will. I should have given him a regiment. Perhaps I could still persuade Benjamin to give him up. He hates this work. It is destroying him.

Focusing on the man in front of him, Lee thanked him and mercifully let him escape. "Charles," he said to Marshall. "You find him, and soon! I don't want him to die in some thicket here!"

There were reports that Grant would withdraw to the north behind the shield of the Rapidan River. Lee thought that this was largely wishful thinking. His impression of Grant was that the man's bulldog heart would be hurt by the shock and trauma of Confederate attacks through the forest, but that he would persist. Looking at the maps, the beautiful old man traced the roads towards Richmond and put his finger down firmly at the crossroads village of Spotsylvania Court House. Looking up from the table, he searched among the faces in the twilight. "Martin... Where is General Smith? Where is the 'Army Engineer?'"

"I am here, sir." The tall thin faced man stood by his side.

"Martin, show me where the track of the road is, the road you marked for me in February. It must be very close to where we are now..."

"Yes, sir. It crosses the Plank Road right over there..." The New York born officer turned and pointed west on the road."

"Where?" Lee asked again.

Martin Smith picked up a rock and threw it at the trees. See the blaze on the trunk? Right there, it starts up on the turnpike about two miles north, runs through here, and then on down to the south until it comes out of the Wilderness near Spotsylvania. It is blazed, all the way, and we took out some of the bigger trees and rocks. It is ready..."

"Good. Good, a fine job. Have the engineers start cutting the road from the turnpike to here and from here to Spotsylvania at the same time. Use all the colored pioneers, as well, all. I will tell Ewell and Anderson to give you all the infantry you need to help. Start Now! We must be at Spotsylvania Court House before Grant!"

Having said that, he looked around for Walter Taylor, his chief of staff.

"Right here, general, right here," Taylor murmured, order pad in hand.

Devereux woke slowly in the bed of the battery wagon. He was stiff in every joint and his leg hurt badly. The floor boards were uncompromising, but he was tired of sleeping on the ground and a tarpaulin had kept the drizzle off. He had crawled into the wagon bed, pulled the canvas over him, moved a few hard and angular objects in the bottom of the wagon and was instantly asleep. It began to rain about eleven and the random, halfhearted showers were just enough to soak everyone, including Devereux. As he came to his senses, he lay quietly, wondering where he was, and then remembered. He needed to urinate, but the half sleeping state that he was in did not allow movement. There was a lot of noise somewhere in the distance. He could not identify it at first. It could have been artillery, but perhaps it was thunder. If the noise was that of artillery, it was a long way off. There were voices nearby. He listened closely. After a few minutes he was sure he recognized one of them. Climbing awkwardly out of the wagon, he staggered to one side of the dirt roadway and unbuttoned. Shivering in relief, he heard Isaac Smoot speak from just behind him,

"Hello, Claude, how long has it been? Last September, maybe? How is everything at home? Everyone well?"

Devereux turned to see two men standing within a few feet. Smoot's stocky silhouette was easily recognized. "Isaac, good to almost see you. Mighty dark right just now. My parents are well. Victoria is well. Hope is well… I understand that you are major of this battalion, congratulations! I would shake your hand, but…"

"No, not yet. I am still a captain." Smoot remembered the man standing with him. "I am sorry. This is Raphael Harris. He's our adjutant and now has the guns that we captured two days ago… He knows who you are. Most of the officers here know who you are. That's a bad thing, but John Quick showed up in winter camp and ran his mouth before we could stop him. He said a lot, much too much. The soldiers don't know who you are…" He stopped for a moment. The noise was growing louder.

"The engineers are cutting a corduroy road through the woods from here to Spotsylvania," he said. "The colonel has gone to see how they are doing.

He'll be back soon." There was a pause and then he continued. "Are you going to be here for a while? I think we will move tonight."

There was something in the man's voice that had not been there in the long period in which they had worked together in Washington. Smoot had risked much as a part of Devereux's team.

What is this? Claude asked himself. *I will have to ferret this out.*

Balthazar walked into the conversation. "Ah, you are awake. Good. We will move now, down to the head of the road cut. The engineers are making good progress. They want some infantry with them in case they suddenly find themselves to be guests of the enemy. Claude, please step over here for a minute I would ask you of Victoria and the boys."

By two in the morning, the battalion was strung along the rough new road watching and listening as the engineers and pioneers chopped and cursed their way forward ahead of them. The crude path through the forest ran in a patternless way around the larger rocks and over little gullies that the engineers filled with earth and new logs. General Smith's winter survey parties had done well and the work went forward through the night. At four o'clock the officer in charge asked Balthazar for help. He had been given soldiers from Ewell's Corps. These men were now exhausted and he pleaded for more help. Balthazar gave him half the men in each company. Their excess belongings would be carried by their comrades. The ability to do that marked them as fit to be members of Balthazar's battalion and their willingness to do so was the unspoken token of their commitment. Balthazar made his way to the front of the construction project, and after listening to what was wanted put his infantry to work. He and Claude worked side by side with axe and shovel in the flickering light of the torches.

"Smoot seems to be well," Devereux remarked as they stopped for a momentary break. The blackness of the wood was beginning to disintegrate as dawn approached. The trunks of trees could now be seen twenty or thirty yards away.

A shout went up at the front end of the road, the end where the axes rose and fell continuously. Balthazar picked up the axe he had been leaning on and walked forward without answering. They emerged from the walls of vegetation into an open space where the gathering light of the coming dawn made the world seem a more encouraging place.

Looking around, Devereux knew the place. "This is where I came across the lines," he whispered turning to the left apprehensively. "Grant's people must be just a short way off over there!"

An officer from Lee's engineers, who had been waiting for the road to open into the clearing, spoke from nearby. "No, they pulled back last night.

We went looking for them but they are moving away from us towards the south."

He saw Balthazar's two stars and pointed to the far side of the meadow." There's where the road continues, colonel!"

The sun was rising steadily.

The engineers and black pioneer troops who had led the work thus far from the Orange Turnpike moved out of the line of march, and by the time that Balthazar's column passed them were already building fires for whatever passed for coffee. Many were already asleep in the tall grass.

General Lee stood in the middle of the field to greet the soldiers as they passed. There were a few people with him, but he was really alone and stood within a few hundred yards of the enemy's main force.

Balthazar saluted and stopped for a word as the battalion's column began to enter the dark path ahead.

The two artillery pieces with their horses and wagons were something new to Lee. "Where did you get these?" he asked Balthazar.

"Good morning," the Frenchman said cheerfully. "We captured them."

Lee smiled. "Congratulations. Put them to good use. I suppose you have artillerymen?"

Balthazar nodded.

"I continue to hear nothing but good of you and your men…" He was looking past Balthazar at Devereux. "I see that you have a guest."

Claude said nothing, sure that this chance meeting would be the end of his visit to the Army of Northern Virginia.

"Yes, my cousin came to visit us. I do hope it will be possible for him to stay a few days. We have much to talk of, concerning the family…"

Lee looked thoughtful. "Claude," he said. "You are troublesome. I do not have time to deal with you in the midst of all this… Your lack of self-discipline is… disappointing. You are not to be captured. Do you understand?"

Devereux nodded, strangely pleased at the provisional sentence of death that had just been passed on him by a man whom he had known from boyhood. Lee's irritation was less important for him than the assurance that he derived from it that at least he had been missed.

Lee looked at Balthazar, who nodded. *"Oui, mon general, je comprends…"*

Lee held out his hand to Devereux. "You should not be here. Your place is with *those people*. That is your duty."

Claude knew instantly that Lee meant that he should be with the Union Army, that his duty called him to that place and task. The words re-opened the wound of loneliness.

"Try not to kill your mother with your foolishness," Lee said softly. "One dead son is enough. Be on your way, gentlemen, on your way. Come and see me," he told Claude. "If we have some time, come to see me. I have to get you back to their side of the line or at least out of here."

They ran a quarter of a mile to reach the head of the battalion column. It was already far down the track. The distant end of the road was now two miles south of where they met Lee and the work moved forward fast in country that opened up as the marching column moved into open farmland.

All day long the Army of Northern Virginia marched south at a pace that the long gone "Stonewall' would have praised in his silent, solemn way, passing up and down the line of march, nodding and bowing to the men as he went. His spirit went with them.

Jubal Early's new command, the Third Corps was last in the order of march. They had been left astride the Plank Road facing east to cover the army's rear as it moved away from the ground on which it had fought Grant for three days. By the time they began their long walk, Balthazar had halted his men a few hundred yards beyond the hole in the forest wall through which everyone emerged.

They were Early's men and they would wait for him to arrive. Balthazar sited his battalion in a half circle facing east with the two guns in the middle. The digging began. There was no way to know how long they would be in this position. Balthazar made them dig themselves into the ground like voles at every stop. He would wait for Early and, while waiting, he would block the chance of the Union Army's accidental discovery of the new road.

Far ranging cavalry on scout were always a danger.

Devereux had no duties to keep him busy. Inactivity raised his level of frustration. Too much idle time in which to think of real or imagined slights affected him badly. Left to himself, his feelings of loneliness grew. He tried to talk to Smoot and found that his perception of coldness in the man was persistent. Smoot answered questions if they were asked, but that was all.

Devereux asked Balthazar what the problem was. This time he demanded an answer. His cousin looked at him for a moment. "Your man Quick has a big mouth," he said. When he came in March he made it clear that you are deceiving your wife, your lovely Hope. I thought you had made amends to her..."

"Did he say with whom?"

"Someone named Biddle..."

Claude cursed. "God damn him! But what is that to Isaac?" Even as he said this, the scene in the kitchen of his parents' home the night of Balthazar's arrival came back to him.

She reached up and held his hand. He looked down at her... Of course, what a fool I am.

"He has good taste," he said. "She is very lovable, very devoted and unfortunately for him, very faithful." He said this to Balthazar with a grin. "Yes, he has very good taste. What about his own family? He has a wife and children I believe?"

Balthazar looked at the ground. He was beginning to see why many people disliked Claude Devereux. He was not pleased to find himself discussing the personal life of one of his men. "He has moved on from that. The children..." He shrugged. "I don't know about that, but to say that he is in love with your wife is simply the truth, and you have wronged her. You can not deny that. You really deserve this. You have wronged the woman he loves and can not have. He may kill you. A duel is likely if time permits. It is between the two of you. You should leave as soon as possible. As Robert Lee said, your place is with the people across the way... Your duty lies there. Ours is here."

"I never wanted this. I never wanted this work... Benjamin forced me into this!"

Balthazar shrugged again. He fished the red beads out of a pocket.

"I will not fight him in a duel," Claude whispered. "I did that once. It was once too often. I killed a friend, for nothing, for nothing..."

The beads clicked. "Yes, you will fight him. There will be no choice. Unfortunately, I will be compelled by family obligation to act for you. We will all be court-martialed if it comes to that, those of us who are still alive... For now, stay away from him." He laughed. "Ask Lieutenant Harris to find you a rifle. It will be needed soon." With that, the French officer walked away. There were many defensive arrangements to make.

Devereux spent the Tenth of May, talking to the men of the army as they came from the mouth of the woods road.

Joseph White followed him as he wandered from unit to unit.

Claude had known Joe since he was a baby. The relationship was too strong to be broken by Devereux's philandering and misbehavior. In Joe's experience Claude had always been the same man. He was what he was, and Joe accepted that, however regretfully. In any case, the family tie was too strong to be abandoned.

As units came out of the woods, they were dispatched by waiting staff officers to whatever part of the line around Spotsylvania Court House that Lee wanted them to be in. There was a lot of line to extend. It ran away to the southeast following the contours of the ground.

Devereux judged that troops would still be arriving after dark.

In his roving, he found some troops from the First Corps. Pickett's Division belonged to them. The 17th Virginia Infantry Regiment was with them in Corse's Brigade. His brother and Bill White were with the 17th Virginia, as he had once been. According to Union Army reports that he had read in Washington, the division was in North Carolina. They had been there all winter training recruits and trying to recreate what had been destroyed at Gettysburg the previous July. He asked if Corse's Brigade was with them. He was told that they were somewhere around New Bern on the coast, bottling up the Union garrison in the small coastal town. He thought of the reports from New Bern, from the federal force there.

It has been quiet there for months. Jake and the others should be all right. I wonder what has happened in the last week. Grant planned to land a force south of Richmond and north of Petersburg at the same time he attacked Lee frontally...

He asked a colonel in the 1st Corps headquarters if there was any news from the New Bern area. "My brother is there," he explained.

"Ah," the man said. "The Yanks are stuck down around Petersburg. They landed from the sea, but the Petersburg and Richmond Home Guard pushed them back into the Bermuda Hundred peninsula, and there they are, caught in that swamp. Beauregard is moving troops from all over to handle them.

Yes. Beauregard is in charge down there. I wonder if he can find enough men to deal with this. I wish I were there, anywhere but here.

Chapter 18

John Sedgwick

Devereux was present that day in the 1st Corps lines when one of their sharpshooter teams killed Major General John Sedgwick, the US Sixth Corps commander.

The three sharpshooters, with their heavy barreled English hunting rifle had been busy scrabbling at the ground with mess tins and biscuit box boards to make themselves a hole. Along the line, the veteran Confederate infantry were sinking into the ground like moles as they dug rapidly, seeking protection from enemy fire. The day was clear. Birds sang in the hardwood trees. The rain had temporarily stopped and the cloud cover had blown away. The refreshing coolness in the air after the rain made this May day seem almost festive. This same sharpshooter team had been shooting at the Union line before beginning their excavation. They had fired as much as seemed necessary to keep the federals from becoming too comfortable as they dug their own line. The Union men did not seem to have anyone with them who could come close to hitting a mark at this distance. The range was a thousand yards. Every minute or so, a rifle bullet had passed over from the blue line. The sharpshooters in butternut had listened to the passage of each shot to make sure the fire was inaccurate, and satisfied, they had begun to dig their own hole.

Claude was chatting with the first sergeant of an infantry company near the sharpshooters when a fuss in the distant blue haze along the wood line attracted attention.

Men with good vision, like Devereux, could see that some of the tiny blue men stood up for a minute and then lay down again.

An officer pointed at that part of the enemy line and ordered a halt to the digging.

The leader of the sharpshooters looked at the distant tree line through a short telescope. "Ah," he said, 'there's a fool sittin' on a box or sumpthin'.

The officer asked if he could see the buttons on the sitter's tunic.

The shooter stared for a bit and then announced that the buttons were shiny and in two rows.

"Shoot me that man," the officer demanded.

The marksman lay down, settling himself among the tree roots and stones, removing a few from strategically inconvenient spots where they hurt his bones.

His assistants fired the rifle in the air to clear the bore and then reloaded it to make sure that they were satisfied with the load that would be fired against the seated Union officer.

The shooter took the gun as they knelt to hand it to him. Looking through the long telescopic sight, he studied the prey. "He's talkin' to'em some," he eventually pronounced. "The're tellin' him to leave. He's laffin."

"Shoot him now," the Confederate officer ordered, "before he gets smart and listens to them..."

At that moment, Uncle John Sedgwick, the well liked commander of the Sixth US Army Corps was telling the enlisted men lying on the ground around him that "the Johhnies can't hit an elephant at this range."

The bullet hit him just below the left eye, knocking him backward off his seat on the upturned box. It passed through the brain and killed him instantly.

Claude knew Sedgwick well and liked him. He learned of the man's end some time later and felt guilty for having been present at his death.

"I hit his Yankee ass," the marksman reported and while his men reloaded the rifle, examined the place of Sedgwick's death to see if another target would present itself.

More than a little unhappy at the immediacy of this death, Claude wandered away from the front line and found his way back to Balthazar's newly entrenched position.

Charles Marshall waited for him there. He smiled at Devereux but did not offer his hand.

Smoot stood to one side listening.

"Claude, you are a lot of bother," Marshall said. "We sent word to Richmond that you are here and now we have a message brought from the rail depot at Orange that we are to send you to them there at 'our first opportunity.' But, alas! There is no opportunity just now. General Grant's Army is still here and we are busy with them. If they would be reasonable and go back, then all would be well, but, here they still are... To make matters worse, the damned Yankee cavalry is running around in strength all over the countryside between here and Richmond. We would like to send you but... can not." He waited for a reaction.

There was none. Devereux was looking at Smoot who watched him from a few yards away. "Anything else?" Claude asked turning back to Marshall.

Marshall approached him to whisper, "Yes, I have some very bad news. Your father has suffered a severe heart crisis.

Devereux stared at him. "How do we know this?"

"The Signal Corps courier brought word across the river a few days ago. I have to get back, and you are going with me, but take a few minutes. I will wait."

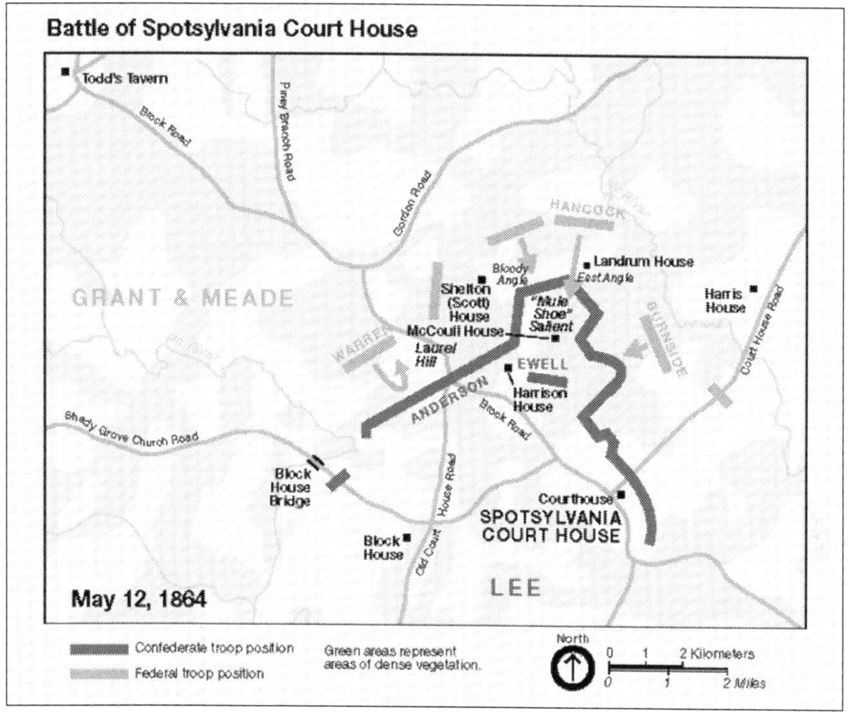

Figure 5 - The Mule Shoe

All through the 8th of May the two armies extended themselves farther and farther to the southeast, probing for the enemy's presence, digging in when the hostile force was too close to allow progress. The process continued into the night.

By the morning of the 9th, Ewell's corps was in position to the right of the troops Claude visited the previous day. Officers had groped their way forward in the darkness struggling to tie flanks together so that units would not discover in the dawn that they were exposed to Federals unseen and silent in the night. The tentative and probing nature of this process resulted in men halting along the forward edges of rambling bits of insignificant terrain. The edge of patches of trees, gullies, fences and small streams, all loomed large at midnight, but what the coming of the sun revealed was that this fumbling around in the blackness had caused the creation of a large bulge in Lee's line. It was a half mile deep in its projection into the federal position and over a quarter mile wide across its open end on the Southern side... Once the shape of it was clear, some wag quickly named it the Mule Shoe.

Early's Corps continued the line to the southeast and physically stood between the federal army and the county court house. As Early's headquarters' reserve, Balthazar's little battalion took residence in the village itself. The battalion headquarters moved into the court house. A solid roof was welcome. Spring rains had been sporadic for days. The rain was growing more persistent and intense. Balthazar believed that "misery does not require practice" and so he occupied most of the buildings in the crossroads hamlet, tied them together with trenches and settled in to wait.

Lee was so distraught when he saw the Mule Shoe drawn on a map that he could hardly be restrained from visiting it. He knew that it was a fatal weakness in his defenses and that it must be eliminated. Grant and Meade would see this bulge as vulnerable to an attack from both its sides with the opportunity to "pinch out" and destroy a major part of his small army. He ordered another line to be constructed across the "shoulders" so that Ewell's troops in the salient could be withdrawn to safety behind it. The men in the Mule Shoe were the "Stonewall Division" and their artillery. "Allegheny" Johnson was still their commander.

The work on the new line began slowly.

Lee was ill. The long illness that would someday kill him was now evident to those around him. The pain deep in the chest made him cross. He was usually kind and the change disturbed the staff and distracted them in their work. He hurt badly and it was hard to think, even harder to keep pushing the men when they were so tired and hungry.

The engineer troops were exhausted after their labors on the forest road and the new entrenchments.

As a result, nothing much happened that day as the Army of Northern Virginia sat down in a weary hope for a little rest.

Fortunately for them, Grant and Meade were slow to realize what had happened on the ground. The 18,000 casualties suffered in the previous week took its toll on the collective mind of the Union Army's leadership on the Wilderness front. The strange shape of Lee's line was not at first apparent. It was only late in the day on the 9th that the slowly accumulating reports of his own army's locations began to form a picture for Grant of what Lee's line must look like. Colonel George Sharpe would generally have done a better job of "seeing" that, but that day he did not.

The weather had been mixed for days. Now it seemed to be raining more with showers lasting longer and longer. The ground was becoming a sea of mud, red in places but more often the kind of sandy soil in which conifers grow well.

In a shoddy roadside building, Grant, Meade and Sharpe stood over a little table. Sharpe's disintegrating paper map lay on it. Water dripped on it from the rubber rain capes. The colors were running together in little streams.

"He will withdraw as soon as he can," Meade said as soon as Sharpe finished explaining the two positions.

Grant nodded in agreement behind a screen of cigar smoke.

"If he does not…" Sharpe began.

"No. He will. I know he will," Meade said firmly. He was filled with confidence in his colleague from the old army.

Grant looked at him. He knew that Meade must feel very differently about him than he did about Lee. Grant's failures in life were always close to the surface of his mind.

I wonder if I can ever have their respect. I wonder…

"If Lee is still in the salient tomorrow evening, have someone push him hard to see if he can be broken there. A brigade would be about the right size. Pick one with some young devil in charge, someone looking to make a name…"

"Upton," Meade said after a second's thought" "Emory Upton"

"Whatever you think best… I need to get some sleep." He left the building, mounted his shivering horse in the cold rain, and rode down the track toward his tent camp.

His cavalry escort followed. They hoped for some shelter themselves.

The 10th of May passed uneventfully in the rain as soldiers tried to make themselves as comfortable as the mud and bugs allowed. The Southern chigger had made an early appearance this year because of the wet weather. This tiny red arachnid swarmed over the two armies, wandering on their bodies and burrowing into their skin. Once entrenched in the epidermis they inspired endless scratching and cursing. On the Confederate side, the shortage of rations wore down patience and strength. Men began to look at the army's animals with hunger and desire.

Chapter 19

Emory Upton

At 6: 30 in the evening on the 10th, an oversized brigade of Union infantry waited quietly near the northwest corner of the Mule Shoe. The front ranks were in the Union trench line and the rest stretched away to the rear for two hundred yards.

Emory Upton, an 1861 graduate of West Point, waited with them for the artillery barrage to begin. He was 25 years old and a full colonel of volunteer infantry. His instructors at the academy had noted that he seemed a particularly bright and intense prospect for an officer's commission.

Three years later, he reached the apogee of his creative life in the Army. To achieve that height he made an imaginative leap that would have surprised his teachers. Having survived two years of experience with failed frontal attacks conducted in extended order, he decided that the way to breach entrenched Confederate positions was to mass artillery fire for a short but intensive barrage on the section of trench to be attacked, and then to charge with a column of massed infantry straight into the momentary "hole" in the enemy's defenses that had been created by the artillery. A key part of this tactic was that the infantry would charge without pause until they broke through the enemy line and that they would not fire their rifles until that was accomplished.

There was nothing very original in this method. Bonaparte would have been comfortable with it, but, in their relative ignorance of the military art, the Union Army high command thought it was radical.

Emory Upton and Claude Devereux had something in common. They did not seem to feel fear on the battlefield in the way that most men do. Their soldiers feared this. Soldiers tend to dislike officers whose recklessness threatens their own chance of survival. The fear of needless death or wounds wars in soldiers' hearts with their desire to follow a brave leader. The net outcome of that struggle between competing emotions often decides the officer's own chance of survival.

The artillery opened with a roar.

Upton walked to the color party of his leading regiment.

Now or never he thought. *The artillery will stop while we go forward. If they do not, they will kill us and none of this will matter.*

"Brigade will advance!" he roared over the noise of the guns. "Forward!" he yelled and ran toward the Confederate lines. After a moment he looked back and saw that the front ranks were pressing on his heels. The color party of the 121st New York Infantry was ten yards behind him and a solid phalanx of men stretched back as far as he could see. They cheered "huzzah! huzzah! as they went forward.

It began to rain again. The ground was soft everywhere.

Upton splashed across a little stream with Confederate bullets singing around him. The artillery stopped as he ran past the last trees. The muddy *glacis* of the Rebel field fortifications was twenty five yards in front of him…

An hour later, he was carried out of the "hole" in the Mule Shoe that his men had made. They had swarmed over the front line Confederates with the power of the depth of their column carrying them forward. The Southern line did not so much fall back as simply cease to exist in the section they captured. He was shot in the leg in the moment of his triumph. He went down with men hovering over him. There were dead and wounded Rebel infantrymen everywhere. The light of day was dimming.

A Confederate surgeon, captured in his brigade's field dressing station applied a bandage and tourniquet to Upton's leg. "Thank you, doctor," he said through the pain.

The prisoner did not respond at first, and then said, "I hope you bleed to death." He was hustled away.

Upton laughed through his pain.

Oh, well, would I feel differently?

He refused to be taken to the rear until reinforcements arrived. He very nearly bled to death waiting. Reinforcements never came in spite of the personal assurances he had received. It had not been believed that he would succeed, and so preparations had not been made to support him.

As night spread its shadows, John Gordon's Confederate division drove hard through the fields and woods to reach the breach in the "wall" of the Mule Shoe. With a collective roar they swept through the woods striking Upton's force at a moment when exhilaration was giving way to emotional exhaustion. The Federal infantry went reeling back in confusion, back all the way to their old line. Upton was carried out with them, his leg bleeding badly as he slipped into a state of wound shock that could easily have ended him. He did not die. The resilience of youth saved him. Grant promoted him to brigadier general the next day. Lincoln confirmed the order over the new-fangled field telegraph line that was laid into Grant's headquarters as it moved forward. Promotions in the war time volunteer service were easy to do. Upton would live to become the foremost theoretician of the US Army in the 19th Century. Many years later, like so many of his old comrades and foes alike, he became more and more mad. At the end, while stationed at San Francisco, he found a soldier's death with a pistol in his hand.

Grant and Meade reluctantly understood that somehow, unbelievably, Lee was not reacting to his danger in the Mule Shoe. Why that would be, they knew not. They had no way to know that the marble man's time on earth was beginning its last act. The two men most in charge of the Union's fate decided that if there was any chance at all that Lee would not act to eliminate the salient, then they would take advantage of his negligence.

Winfield Scott Hancock was summoned and told to put his whole II Army Corps in against the nose of the Mule Shoe in a massed attack.

Hancock's reaction was to look at the headquarters map and ask to be allowed to attack at night.

They did not like that idea. It was an uncommon proposal. There was fear of disorganization, fear of masses of men being lost in the darkness. There was even more fear of innovation.

Hancock pointed on the map at the fixed position he would attack. He insisted that if given until four or five in the morning the next day, he could reproduce Upton's feat on a much grander scale.

"So, you would be inside the enemy position by first light?" Grant asked. He was fascinated by the thought.

Why haven't we done this before, he asked himself? *Even if the Rebels can hear the men coming they won't be able to aim at them.*

"Any thoughts on how many guns Lee has in his front line?"

Hancock knew what Grant was thinking. Artillery firing canister at assaulting troops would be the biggest hazard. "No idea," he replied, "Sharpe has been questioning prisoners and deserters, but the location of the artillery is unclear. Nevertheless, this is still the best plan."

Please God, please. Make them let me do it this way. We can't do this many more times. We are running out of men who will do this. Let me break them now...

Grant looked at Meade. "I think you should let him try."

And so it was decided.

Devereux spent the night of the 10th of May at Lee's forest headquarters. He sat alone with Lee in the general's tent for a meal hardly worthy of the description. The old camp furniture was familiar. Claude remembered the chairs from hunting trips with his grandfather and Major Lee, as he had then been. The familiar camp sounds and smells were comforting. The noise and chaos of the last days' fighting seemed far away. There was talk of home and Alexandria. There was talk of family.

Lee was intrigued by the intimacy that had developed between Claude and President Lincoln and disturbed by Lincoln's persistent enquiries about himself.

"I think you should feel complimented, sir," Devereux commented. "He has made it clear that he considers you and he to be the principals in this struggle and wishes you had chosen the North…"

Lee stirred uncomfortably in his chair.

Devereux knew that the old man was ill. The present inactivity of the army spoke volumes about that.

The general looked at him. "I had no choice… You know that, and now we must fight it out to the end, the bitter end."

Devereux nodded. "Let me come back," he pleaded. "I detest this work. I can't manage the life I have been forced into. There are too many demands, too many people pulling at me… I need to simplify my life. I used to think that I enjoyed playing with these Yankees, but it is too much, too much. Let me come back to the army, to this army, with you and my brother, and cousins. Please."

Lee rose and walked to the front of the tent, looking out into the dim light of a fire a few yards away.

An orderly officer broke away from a group by the fire to start toward him, only to be waved away.

"Do you want Herbert's regiment? Do you want the 17th?" he asked after returning to his seat.

"Yes."

Lee considered that. "They are down in North Carolina at the moment…"

"I know they are," Devereux said.

Lee laughed silently, "Yes, you would know, colonel. Unfortunately, the enemy's knowledge of us has improved. Do you have anything to do with that?" There was sharpness in the voice. Claude had never heard that before. "No," he quickly replied. "it is all George Sharpe, all Colonel Sharpe. My brother…" He thought of the help Patrick had given Sharpe at Gettysburg.

We paid for that. God punished us for our weakness. He wanted to belong. Will God punish me as well if I help them?

Lee shook his head. "No, Claude, you are going back to Washington City if we can get you there alive and still seemingly one of their own... That is what Benjamin thinks best and I am now convinced as well. If you are seen here by someone who reports your presence with us, there is no explanation that could be made without causing a massive search for more of our people. Think of your family… No. You must return. Whether or not your duty there will bring some good is a mystery, but the die is cast in this matter. We will send you to Richmond as soon as we can see a path that is cleared of federal cavalry. Benjamin can find a way to get you home."

Devereux recognized defeat. He had hoped, but not believed that escape from secret service work was possible. His feet had been placed on this path long ago. No escape had ever been possible. He had tried to fool himself, but the self deception had never been convincing. He thought of home. He thought of the women who waited for him there. "I should leave you to rest, sir," he said to Lee.

"There is one more thing," the grey man said in the reflected fire light. "I thought it best to tell you myself..."

Devereux looked at the wall of the tent. "My father..."

"Yes. He died last week. The report of his heart crisis... We lied to you."

"That is understandable. Good night, sir." As he walked into the night and the darkness that would shelter him, he heard Lee's voice behind him.

"I will ask Benjamin, Claude. I can not accept seeing you like this. Would you take a colored brigade? We will have to begin with that soon. The army knows that. Would you?"

Devereux looked back. "Whatever you think best." He nodded once and went to find somewhere to spend the night, somewhere he could be alone to think of a father who had never loved him, and whom he knew he had never really pleased.

Charles Marshall tried all day on the 11th to find a way to send Devereux to Richmond. Small parties of cavalry from the army commander's escort rode southeast out of the bivouac. They tried three times and in each attempt turned back after meeting much larger Union cavalry forces. Several men and horses were lost in the resulting skirmishes. A prisoner was taken in the third effort. He was a captain from Pennsylvania.

He was not afraid of the Rebels. "You are finished this time," he laughed. "Grant is going to crush you here and everywhere else."

"Here, and where else?" Claude asked, intrigued by the man's poise in view of his present circumstances.

"We are going all the way to Richmond down this road and Butler is coming from the south. We will meet him in front of your capitol building. If you like, I will accept your surrender..."

One of the North Carolina troopers drew his revolver and held it up to the man's head. "Maybe I'll just shoot yeh now, loudmouth. How do yeh feel about that?"

In the end, common sense prevailed and the Union officer rode meekly back to camp where he was astonished to meet Lee himself standing hatless by the side of the road reading reports. He saluted automatically.

Lee looked up, nodded to him and then returned to his reading.

Devereux waited patiently until the lieutenant who had been trying to get him through the lines, explained his lack of success to Lee and Marshall. The battlefield was surprisingly quiet. Birds could be heard in the trees. Insects hummed in the grass. After the prisoner had been taken away, Lee beckoned. "Claude, I am very busy trying to get Johnson's division out of the salient over there." He waved vaguely toward the north. "I can't worry about you now. Stay with the staff until we can send you…" He seemed to be pleading.

"Yes. I will wait here," Devereux replied.

Chapter 20

The Mule Shoe

That night Lee removed his artillery from within the Mule Shoe and ordered Edward Johnson to withdraw the Stonewall Division to the new line across the "jaws" of the bulge into Grant's lines.

Somehow, knowledge of the artillery's early movement never reached Johnson. He waited in the darkness and rain for the dawn when he would leave the salient.

The wet was affecting the neuralgia that crippled his wounded ankle. He welcomed a few hours sleep and time off his feet even if he slept propped up in a corner of the canvas covered dugout that was his division command post.

Across no man's land in the territory of the blue army, Winfield Scott Hancock worked all night to move the twenty thousand men of his Second Army Corps into position a mile from the "nose" of the Mule Shoe. He moved them several miles in the dark to reach the starting points for the attack that Grant and Meade had committed him to make. He was finished by three in the morning.

The vast column of dripping, miserable men sat down in the drizzle to wait for the word to go forward.

The men who would make the attack tried not to think about what would happen. They were veterans of many lethal fights. They knew there was no use thinking about what might be.

At about the same time, Johnson was shaken awake by his staff and learned two things.

The first was that his artillery support had disappeared. That was discovered by an officer who went looking for the gunners to make arrangements for the general withdrawal in the morning. Where they had gone, no one knew.

The second was that the men in his forward trenches believed the enemy had been moving somewhere to their front for most of the night. These sounds had suddenly stopped in the last half hour.

Johnson was upset that no one had told him these things earlier. From his point of view nothing had gone well in several days. He cursed for a while, and then sent a courier to Lee demanding the immediate return of the guns. Then he left for the front line with an aide and a bugler.

In the lines of the Stonewall Division, the silence of the false dawn was broken by the cry of "Hurrah!" "Hurrah!" that reached the men resting behind earth walls and barriers built of tree branches. Some of them heard it first while they were in the woods where they had gone to relieve themselves. Others remembered being awakened by comrades who shook them and then held up a finger so that they would listen. Everyone knew what the sound meant. The Yankees were coming, and they were coming in the dark.

The order to bring the artillery's guns back into the Mule Shoe arrived in the battalion bivouacs around half past three. Fifty guns were formed in "march order" columns. The difficult night movement began. Drivers led the teams through the forest. As they crossed the ditch in front of the new line of defense, heavy firing began a quarter mile ahead.

At that moment, Francis Barlow's Division of Hancock's corps swarmed out of the dark against the dirt wall in front of the Stonewall division. In what seemed limitless thousands they poured over the wall and into the rifle pits where they swiftly disarmed hundreds of soldiers still trying to rouse themselves from sleep.

Edward Johnson was captured thirty yards behind his front line. The big man was astonished to find himself suddenly surrounded by blue infantry. He was enraged and stood in a circle of Federal soldiers swinging his cane at men armed with rifles and bayonets. "God damned artillery. God damned artillery!" he muttered as he swung the cane. The light was growing and his captors could see him well enough to know that they had a Rebel general in their grasp. He kept swinging.

A Federal officer told him that if he did not stop they would shoot him.

At that, he walked to the man and said "your prisoner, sir." For him the war was over. His captors let him keep the cane and marched him off to the rear.

Blue troops pressed forward in a flood of men through the meadows and clumps of trees behind what had been Johnson's front line.

Most of the guns of the Confederate Artillery were seized while still in battery columns. In the dim light of dawn they were "easy meat" as they made their way towards the positions from which Lee had withdrawn them the previous evening. One minute they were moving forward and the next they were prisoners.

In Carter's Virginia Artillery Battalion one battery succeeded in getting its four twelve pounder Napoleon smoothbores into battery before the blue multitude reached them. A volley cut down gunners and horses alike.

A lieutenant, shot through the abdomen with a disemboweling wound, knelt next to one of the guns. With his left hand he gripped the iron shod wheel of the gun for support. With his right he struggled to hold his belly together. His eyes were on the ground.

A corporal standing by the breech of the gun stared in alarm at the blue shadows moving steadily through the mist and trees. They were everywhere. "Where shall we fire, sir," he asked.

"At the Yankees," was the whispered reply. With that, the young man fell forward and the gunner raised his hands in surrender.

Claude woke to the sound of the guns. He heard the cheering typical of the Union Army. He was sleeping in a clump of trees away from the hooves of passing or hobbled animals. He pushed off the strip of canvas which he had found to cover himself against the dew, rose and walked around to restore feeling to his legs.

The headquarters was waking up around him. Men stood, half dressed, listening to the roar and the cheers.

Devereux pulled his boots on. His feet had swollen and they went on hard. He had expected that to happen, but he had not had his boots off in days and had been worried about the condition of his feet. His joints ached from sleeping on the ground. He decided that he would not obey Lee's orders any longer. Something bad was happening in the Mule Shoe. He would not stand by while it happened. He checked the loads in his pistols, rubbed his unshaven chin and walked across the camp in the direction of Balthazar's battalion half a mile away.

Several people noted his departure, but none thought to stop him. They were busy.

He found the battalion. The men had gathered their personal equipment and now lounged around their fires waiting for orders. The wagons filled with their baggage were ready. The horses looked around in empty curiosity.

Smoot stood by a fire. He watched Devereux approach. He looked friendlier than he had recently. "Coming with us?" he asked with a smile.

The noise from the salient grew steadily louder.

"If you'll have me…" Claude replied.

"We'll have you, cousin," Balthazar said as he came out of the courthouse. "Stay with me. We are attached to Gordon's command. He is going to counter-attack to clear the penetration. We are to go in on his right flank."

The Union Second Corps swept on. Its twenty thousand men filled the space between the "shoulders" of the Mule Shoe.

Rebels on the left and right watched in dazed surprise as the blue mass pushed past them in the new day. Commanders began to pull their men back on the flanks of the enemy force to form a new front that would have some chance of keeping the sudden shock from turning into a general rout.

Gordon's division of Virginians, North Carolinians, Georgians, and Louisiana "Pelicans," went forward once again and met the Federals half way down the length of the Mule Shoe. They went forward that morning in the sure knowledge that if they could not push back this mighty force, then Grant would break Lee's line and that would be the end of all their hopes. There were only two thousand of them. Gordon's men drove through the morning mist. The rain stopped.

Gordon soon met the broken remnants of the Stonewall Division streaming to the rear in the first shock of their defeat. They had been awakened by the sound of cheering as the Federals poured over the breastworks. Many of their leaders were lost in the confusion of the first minutes. There had been no choice but to run or be captured. Now, a realization of the calamity that had befallen them was settling on their minds and they searched for a way to rally.

Gordon sat high on a brown horse squarely in the center of his advancing line. Enemy bullets cut branches and leaves around his ears. He did not seem to hear. The "zzzzz" of rifle bullets in the air was everywhere, but his attention was on the crooked lines of infantry to either side of him.

The Stonewall division looked at him and saw what they were looking for. Many fell in behind his lines and went with him.

On the right of Gordon's line, Balthazar's men called out to the retreating men. There was a Louisiana brigade in Johnson's division.

Raphael Harris saw people he knew among those falling back. He shouted at them and hearing him speak in French, other soldiers pleaded in the language of bayou and home for these Pelicans to come with them. *"A nous frères, on va frapper les sales Calvinistes. Aidez nous!"* Fifty men joined the attack.

Balthazar was on foot. He would never risk Victoria's mare in such a desperate moment. His line of battle came out of the trees into the clearing where the artillery lieutenant had died. The Yankees had already dragged the two guns away, but the young officer's body lay face down in the grass. Captain William Fagan's company walked over him, the men stepping carefully so as not to tread on his corpse. Fagan noticed that the men were looking away from the body, and then saw that the young officer lay in a pile of his own guts. Grey loops of intestines, just starting to lose the sheen of life lay on the ground near his torso. *"Poor lad."* "Steady, boys, ye've seen worse. Steady. Just keep goin' forrard and watch yer dress. Jones! God damn it, pay attention!"

Firing grew heavier and heavier over on the left flank. Balthazar's men felt forward movement slow as the line, dressed to the left became progressively engaged in that direction.

Devereux and Joe White were side by side. Claude wore a collection of old clothing that made him look like a private soldier of the battalion. He had left his Union Army uniform in Lee's camp.

If I am killed, no one will know..

Wild cheering came from the left. The whole line began to move rapidly.

Claude remembered the day at Manassas when he had led his company forward in Dutch Longstreet's grand attack into Pope's flank. It had felt like this.

Two deer that had been hiding in the forest jumped to their feet and ran away from the troops.

The battalion came out of the forest and Devereux could see the backs of thousands of Union Army troops. Some were running. Some had lost their hats. He guessed that they had been caught at the moment of uncertainty that comes when an attack has succeeded beyond expectation and men look around hoping to be told what to do next.

The shock of Gordon's sudden appearance and the forbidding character of his relentless advance had thrown these freshly victorious soldiers back on their heels. They would recover their equilibrium but not until they found the chance to sit down somewhere to think about what had happened. For now, they were moving away. More and more of them were running.

In the distance, Devereux could see the red soil behind the trenches that the Confederates had lost three quarters of an hour before. Re-occupation of that line was the goal.

Half way there a body of blue infantry stopped and faced to the rear to confront the Rebels.

The battalion halted.

Devereux would have been mildly surprised to know that this was the 17th Maine Infantry, the regiment in Alexander Hays' brigade that he had led forward against the Brock Road a few days before.

Unaccountably, these lumbermen from the far North decided to make a stand to hold a space through which the rest of their brigade could escape. In the ranks were men for whom Claude had seemed an apparition sent from heaven to bring them to victory in the smoke and fire of the Wilderness. Now, he would kill and maim some of them.

A ragged volley from the Maine men *whizzed* through the ranks knocking down several and sending two to the rear with blood on their clothing.

"Battalion! At my command!"

Balthazar's deep voice could be heard among the Maine infantry across the way. They were loading their rifled muskets but in their guts they knew that the Rebels would fire before they finished.

"Present!"

The muzzles came up

"Fire!"

The scythe swung. Dozens were knocked back or to one side. Their falling bodies and grasping hands added to the disruption of the regiment's ranks. Men on the ground reached up for help. An officer shouted that they should fire at will. Muzzles came up. Single shots crossed the space through which Balthazar's men advanced. Through the noise on the field, he could be heard.

"Battalion! Charge! Bayonets!"

The brown line swept forward. At first they stumbled across tree roots and stared to left and right to be sure that all would go forward. Then, as their hearts filled with pack cohesion, their focus shifted to their collective enemy. Soon, men were running forward, racing away from control. Rifles reversed along the line and were carried as clubs. The screaming started half way to the blue line.

Among the Maine soldiers a sudden conviction took hold that each would be left alone to face these faceless beasts. The Downeasters turned to flee and found their route to safety blocked by the old Confederate trenches and beyond that by an earthen wall.

This ditch was filled with other Union soldiers seeking the safety of the far side of the wall of dirt. Men scrambled everywhere to reach the top and escape the likely end of those still there when Balthazar arrived.

Maine soldiers jumped down into the ditch and tried to push their way among the others to gain the top of the earth berm.

The battalion arrived at the lip of the ditch. Most stood on the rim firing into the surging blue backs. Some jumped down into the ditch and swung wildly at the heads and backs around them.

Devereux was one of the first into the trench with a pistol in either hand. He had not fired in the charge and had ten shots in the two Navy Colts. At this moment, he was not the man whose cultivated charm won so many in polite society. Now, he was his own self, a berserker who would kill until the enemy was gone and then sob convulsively while rage ebbed away.

White put himself at Claude's back. Their shoulder blades touched.

Devereux looked back for an instant, saw Joe and then turning away shot a Union Army corporal in the back as he tried to climb the dirt embankment to safety.

Behind him Joe swung his rifle. The steel shod butt had a deadly effect

Devereux's revolvers were quickly empty. Blue soldiers scrambled over the top of the wall trying to reach safety. He chased them up the dirt slope swinging with both pistols at available heads.

At the top, bullets buzzed past his head.

Joe heard this and pulled him back down into the trench.

Twenty yards away, Captain Isaac Smoot leaned back against the trench wall clutching what remained of his left hand. He had seen Devereux in the ditch and impulsively had followed... A Maine soldier tried to bayonet him there and failed because Smoot grabbed the muzzle of the rifle to keep the sword bayonet out of his chest. The soldier had fired, blowing away most the hand wrapped around the opening in the end of the barrel.

Now he held the wrist, pinching the vessels to slow the bleeding. Looking at the chaos that had been his hand, the old soldier expected to die of blood loss before anything could be done for him. He looked down the trench at Devereux and smiled. His wound did not hurt yet. Perhaps it never would.

O'Brien, the A Company commander lay at his feet, his head crushed on one side. He was dead.

Dead and wounded were everywhere in the trench. The Northern wounded moaned and clutched at themselves. Some tried to crawl over the dirt wall.

Devereux reloaded his two revolvers and then walked up and down the ditch shooting enemy wounded in the head. He said nothing.

Joe White followed him, watching but not interfering,

Balthazar's soldiers watched him.

Balthazar watched as well. He said nothing. There would be an enemy counterattack. It would be massive. What would they do with the Union Army's wounded when that came? Nonetheless, he saw the madness of the battlefield in his cousin. It was a familiar madness.

Balthazar's men began to follow Devereux's example.

A handful of prisoners and ambulatory enemy wounded stood nearby under guard, watching. At a gesture from Balthazar, Sergeant Major Roarke sent a few men with them to the rear and out of the fight.

The enemy had not left the scene. Some of Hancock's men clung to the outside of the earthen breastworks over which they had just escaped. The meaning of the random shooting was unmistakable for them. They cursed and screamed their hope of revenge. At the moment there were only a few of them on the far side of the wall. They could not leave. They were trapped with an open field behind them...

Fagan, the "C Company" commander went to Smoot. He laid his black roll of oil cloth covered medical instruments on the edge of the trench. "Let's see that, Captain" he demanded.

Smoot held out his arm. Fagan whistled. "The rest of that should come off and the blood vessels tied until a surgeon can make it into a stump, but I can't do that." Smoot was still gripping his wrist. He shook his head.

John Smith, the "D Company" commander spoke from beside Fagan. "I can. I am a surgeon." He had seen Smoot holding his wrist.

Balthazar stood above them on the bank. "I thought you were a cook..."

Smith spoke without looking up. "I took that up after I lost my medical license." He turned to Fagan. "Is there chloroform or ether in that collection of yours?"

"Yes, both."

Smoot listened with interest to that. He knew that he would be in a lot of pain soon. He was beginning to feel dizzy. Even so, his responsibility as a leader still ruled him. "What do you see?" he asked Balthazar.

After one more look from his elevated position, Balthazar jumped down into the ditch with the others. He sank to the top of his brogans in the soupy mud.

Rain was falling steadily, soaking everyone again. Bullets whizzed across the top of the dirt wall.

Northern soldiers continued to yell from beyond that wall. "You better run, Johnnies... You better run! Our friends will be here in a few minutes and then it'll be your turn! Run now!"

Balthazar's men looked for openings in the log breastworks. When they found them they fired through the holes or stabbed with bayonets. Then they filled the holes with mud. There were occasional screams from the unlucky on the other side.

"What else is in there?" Smith enquired.

"Basic surgical kit," Fagan said. "I have a bottle of brandy as well."

"Suturing?"

Fagan nodded.

Smith looked at Smoot, "You are turning very white... You'll be in shock soon if we don't get you wrapped up in something. The rest of that must come off. I'll tie the blood vessels to stop the bleeding and make a flap over the end where the ends of the arm bones are. Someone will have to take you to the rear..."

Smoot managed to smile at the man who was going to cut his hand off. The world was starting to revolve.

Joe White looked up at Balthazar.

The Frenchman nodded. "Get on with it, gentlemen," he said. "We are going to be busy soon. "Sergeant Major!" he roared.

"Sir!" Roarke answered from a few feet away.

"Go back and tell Captain Harris to bring our guns forward! I want them right over there." He pointed to a slight rise in the ground twenty five yards behind the trench. Behind the rise were two horseshoe shaped revetments from which Confederate guns had been withdrawn the night before.

In the old gun position they spread a rubber rain cape on the ground.

Smoot lay down on this still holding his left wrist in his right hand.

Smith knelt beside him with Fagan and Joe White. After looking through the contents of the black rubber pouch, Smith said he would need something hollow with which to make a drain.

Joe searched in his shoulder bag and found a clean, new, clay pipe. It was quite small and the stem was hollow. "I don't smoke," he said. "My brother's wife gave it…."

Smith broke off the bowl and the flared mouth piece and laid the shank on the black bag. He then removed his belt and made a tourniquet of it, tying a knot around a stick he found on the ground. Fitting this around Smoot's left forearm just below the elbow he turned the stick until satisfied with the color of the arm, and then handed the end of the stick to Joe. "Hold that tight until I tell you to let go. If you do not, he will bleed to death right here."

Joe nodded, grasping the stick while Smoot smiled at him.

"You don't want that, do you, Joe?" he said. "Your momma would be unhappy with you over that, Fine woman, your momma. Maybe Miss Hope would be sorry too…"

By this time Smith had made a pad from a fairly clean pocket handkerchief, and sprinkled on it a small amount of chloroform from a can in the pouch. He handed the cloth to Fagan who held it over Smoot's nose and mouth.

The wounded man was still talking about Alexandria. He said something about beauty too great for a real woman, something about blond hair, and suddenly he was asleep.

Fagan looked at Joe. "His wife?" he asked.

Joe shook his head. "No, not his wife. It is a family matter,"

Smith took the knife he wanted out of the bag.

Fagan poured brandy on it as well as the surgeon's hands.

Smith cut through the flesh on the palm and the back of the hand and laid back the red, bleeding meat so that he could see the shattered bones and the blood vessels. He cut the bones out of the mess. The thumb and fingers dropped on the ground. The round, white ends of the arm bones were clearly visible.

Fagan poured more brandy on surgical gut from the bag.

Smith tied off the blood vessels using a "surgeon's knot" as he always had.

Fagan reached over and cut the ties leaving an inch or so of loose end.

Balthazar stood over them, watching the amputation.

Only a few minutes had passed since the battalion captured the trench.

Smith poured brandy into the wound and then made a flap of tissue from the palm of the hand. He folded it over neatly covering most of the wound. He then folded the flesh and skin from the top of the hand over that.

He looked through the pipe stem and then fit it into an opening he had left between the flaps. He then sewed the whole thing together.

Joe had a clean cloth in his knapsack from which they made a bandage.

Smith wrote a note on an old envelope with a piece of pencil. The paper was bloody but the writing could be read. He gave Joe the note. "Give this to the doctor. Tell him an old *eleve* of the Medical College of Virginia did this. The drain should come out after a week." He looked up at Balthazar. "If it does not inflame too much he will live…"

Balthazar nodded. "You are appointed Battalion Surgeon. If we live, I will take care of the details." Smith grinned at him, opened his mouth and then said nothing...

"Fagan. Find a man to help Joe take Captain Smoot to our bivouac."

In a few minutes the three disappeared into the sodden forest.

John Smith walked back down the trench line to his company. He wiped his sticky, bloody hands on his pants. Soldiers patted his arm and back as he passed.

Soon, there were dead men floating everywhere in the thigh deep water of the trench. Some bodies were only partially concealed. The mud seemed alive. Some men drowned in the mud because they happened to lie face down. Their wounds and exhaustion kept them from rolling over and that killed them

The Confederates began building low walls between the rifle pits behind the berm. This was to keep hot pieces of artillery shells from hitting them in the sides or back. To build these walls they used the only materials available, dead bodies. If a body hoisted out of the mud for placement in a wall made a sound of life, that body was thrown as far back out of the immediate line of fire as exhausted men could manage. The rain poured down, a rain that soaked and dripped from clothing, hair and beards.

Balthazar's battalion held their little section of the line for several hours while Lee poured every man and gun he could find into the job of preventing another breakthrough. After a time they pulled back to the gun positions where Smoot's hand still lay in the dirt. Raphael Harris' two bronze Napoleons stood within the revetments. The section's animals were hidden in the woods. Harris hoped to save enough of them to avoid pulling the guns out by hand.

Grant's Army counterattacked the trench line all day long. There were so many attacks that they could not be remembered as separate events by the survivors of either side.

The attacks were all the same. A new group would form beyond the works and then would clamber across the barrier while hurling rifles and bayonets like legionary javelins. In the rifle pits the sodden, wretched scarecrows in brown grappled with the blue men in innumerable little combats.

During each attack, Balthazar waited next to Harris' guns to know when the big weapons should be used and when his rifle companies should be committed to the fight. When that was clear, he would blow his whistle and point. The company commanders needed no more than that. The advance into the imperiled section of the line took only a minute or so. Rifle butts, knives and fists were effective. The bodies of the Union soldiers who died in these attacks were thrown back over the barrier for the emotional effect that this had on those who had held back.

Harris's two guns fired all day at irregular intervals. The shots were aimed to pass just above the wall as another message to those crouching beyond. This harassment was useful but the main task of the two-wheeled killers was to break any assault that could not be stopped at the rifle pits. When that happened the gunners swept the space in front of them with canister, canvas bags filled with one inch lead spheres. The bags burst when they left the muzzle and the mass of balls spread in a lethal cone as they traveled away from the gun.

There seemed no end to this calamity. The day and the rain appeared to be eternal. The fire was so heavy that a large hardwood tree that stood in front of the dirt wall was cut down by rifle bullets and fell, crashing across a sector of trench.

After several hours, Hancock's men were exhausted and Grant knew from the lack of progress that more troops were needed. He was unhappy with the performance of many of the commanders of Meade's army. These men had the habit of defeat by Robert Lee. For that reason alone Grant did not trust them. Now, after a week of trauma and misery in the rains of springtime Virginia, most of the generals showed the effect of exhaustion and exposure to the elements. Grant thought that the only corps with enough fight left in it to deal with looming failure in the Mule Shoe was the Sixth Corps. This was the army corps which had lost its commander, John Sedgwick, to an English hunting rifle even as Claude stood by and watched

Obedient to his wishes, these men moved back from the line on Grant's right and "slid" to the left. Brigade by brigade they moved through the woods and fields until they reached the circle of death outlined by the dirt wall. There, they gathered in their multitude, prepared to make one more grand effort.

Lewis Grant's all Vermont Brigade attacked first.

The fallen hardwood tree lay across their path.

In the brigade, the 2nd Vermont Infantry Regiment was thought to be the hardest core of fighting spirit. Accordingly, the brigade commander decided to attack in a column of regiments with the 2nd Vermont at the head of the column.

The column of attack struck the tip of the salient. The Vermonters came across the top of the mud wall in silence. Their attack was only sixteen men wide, and they did not fire their weapons until they were already in the muck of the Confederate rifle pits. The ferocity of their advance overwhelmed the forward defenses.

The South Carolinians among whom they suddenly appeared had thought until that moment that they had the situation in hand. Suddenly, they found themselves grappling with men who were unmoved by the carnage in the watery trenches.

Balthazar's soldiers watched this from the holes they had dug around Harris's two guns. They gathered themselves up emotionally for the charge they knew to be inevitable. The Vermonters continued to pour over the wall. Their officers yelled and screamed at them, trying to pull them around to face the Confederates to either side. More and more blue soldiers came over the wall.

The whistle sounded in the rain. The battalion ran to the gap through which the men from the far north were still coming.

Devereux ran beside Balthazar. He expected to die and the prospect of an end was welcome.

The collision of the battalion with the Vermonters was heard up and down the line. The surging, heaving struggle rolled up the inside of the earthen wall and over the top. On the far side Confederates were dragged down and clubbed into submission or death.

Devereux stopped half way up the slope.

An officer on the far side came to the very top. He had a rifle and bayonet in his hands and lunged at the first man he saw on the other side.

Claude took the blade through a shoulder and fell back into the muddy, bloody water.

Balthazar saw him fall and picking up a rifle tried at first to fire it. When that failed, he threw the weapon at the Yankee who had struck his cousin.

The captain fell back and out of sight.

Suddenly, there were no more Vermonters coming over the wall.

At three in the morning, Lee began to vacate the Mule Shoe.

Balthazar's battalion was among the units left to cover the departure. Harris' guns went first, then the infantry. As they crossed the new trench lines in the misty night, Balthazar found Jubal Early waiting.

Early shook his hand, thanked him and handed him a flask of whiskey. "Any idea how many men you lost?" he asked anxiously.

"Oui, my general, we counted them just now. We lost perhaps thirty men dead, a miracle…"

"Thank God. We are going to need every one of these madmen of yours. Was that Devereux I saw on a limber?"

"Yes. My cousin is a brave man, foolish even for this army, but a brave man. He is wounded but would not be taken out until all came out. My surgeon thinks he will mend, somehow."

"Your surgeon? Is that who took Smoot's hand off? Never mind. Explain later. Go back to your bivouac. Your wagons and packs are still there. Get some rest. The Old Man thinks that Grant will start to move around our right again once he recovers from this… Another army is trying to seize Richmond from the south, from Petersburg. God knows what will happen there… Get some rest."

Chapter 21

Flat Creek

- 12 May -
Sixty Miles Away, South of Richmond

The cavalry raid rode northwest, two thousand three hundred men, three thousand horses, four regiments in all.

A dark faced, brooding man led them in a country of cavernous woods and imposing silences, a place full of red clay roads, deep forests, and staring farmers. Through these forests ran two railroads. They stretched away to the south and southwest, fragile vessels of steel through which food, ammunition, and hope flowed to the capital of a dying country.

The raid rode into the forest to break the railroads.

The regiments carried the standards of Pennsylvania, New York and the District of Columbia. The Pennsylvanians and New Yorkers were veteran volunteer cavalry of the line, weathered and blooded in the long years already past.

The "1st District of Columbia Cavalry Regiment" was different. Only rarely had they fought anyone able to fight back. Bar room brawls, and midnight arrests in the Irish slums of the city of Washington had been their portion until now, a strange regiment. The men were almost all New Englanders, the majority was from Maine. Lafayette Baker, their colonel, had recruited them there. He was also "Chief of the National Detective Bureau," the counterintelligence office of the War Department. Baker found it useful to have nine hundred cavalrymen consecrated to the work of compelling acceptance of his will, and that of Secretary Stanton.

Nothing in Washington could remain hidden very long from Baker and his friends. The search for traitors and spies extended throughout the government. Stanton wanted to know what was said in the Senate cloakroom, in the chambers of the Justices of the Supreme Court and in the headquarters of the general-in-chief. The plan of campaign devised by Grant had been easy to obtain. The immense power enjoyed by Baker seemed eternal to ambitious but fundamentally unimaginative young officers of the army staffs. Flattery and a hint of future favors insured cooperation.

Baker was in the room on the occasion when Grant explained his conception of the spring campaign to the Secretary of War. In Stanton's pocket was a much handled copy of the document from which Grant read. A week's possession of this information had allowed the secretary to closely critique the scheme to his face even as the commander of all the armies of the United States presented it. Gratitude was not an emotion that Stanton often felt impelled to act on, but in this instance he found the time to ask if there might be some matter in which Lafayette Baker required assistance.

The colonel's response was to volunteer his regiment for the envisioned amphibious landing south of Richmond. This operation would complement Grant's drive straight south from the Rapidan River.

This request had brought the 1st D.C. Cavalry to Bermuda Hundred on the James River. The officers of the regiment debated their chief's motivation in offering them up. In the end, majority opinion held that it was largely a matter of wounded pride. The sneers and condescension of cavalry officers who let it be known that "kicking in doors" was not quite the same thing as facing Jeb Stuart had finally proven to be more than he could endure.

There was also the influence of that irritating colonel from Stanton's personal staff, the one who smiled when he noticed that you were looking at him. His personal and public mockery of the regiment had a crescendo in the weeks before they were sent to the front...

Colonel Baker usually did not find the time to command his men in person. His many duties prevented this. A younger brother led them to Bermuda Hundred.

This collection of untried Maine woodsmen had the very best of weapons, the Henry lever action repeating carbine. Troopers of the other regiments in Kautz' Division often came to the bivouac just to see these arms.

General Kautz himself, the dark presence commanding the raiding force, had doubts about Baker's men. Their high bred horses, unfaded uniforms and Washington society officers all troubled him, but the fierce talk at their camp fires was the most unsettling. He told Major Baker that the horses were too fat, that the heat would kill many. He told him that any horses which broke down on the march would be shot immediately to keep them out of enemy hands. Baker was shocked, instinctively leaning forward to rub the neck of his mount, a pretty Thoroughbred mare.

"The rebels don't kill off their animals the way we do," said Kautz. "They can't afford to do it. We are going through the horse and mule population faster than they can be bred. We're bringing them in from Canada now you know. Is she yours?" he said referring to the mare.

"Yes." Baker still had his hand on the animal's neck.

"Leave her with our trains. She'll never stand the march. Draw a troop horse, something heavy in the chest, and big in the ass, and don't make it a friend! We leave at four tomorrow morning."

By nine A.M., the long column of his division had moved up behind the infantry entrenchments which defined the northern perimeter of the Federal lodgment in the Bermuda Hundred peninsula. They halted while barbed wire obstacles and *chevaux de frise* were removed from the roadway. The long lines of dusty, snuffling horses shifted from foot to foot, swatting flies with their tails, and seeking the most comfortable stance in which to carry their burdens. Finally the obstacles were cleared, and with a creak and jingle of horse furniture the march resumed.

Infantry filled the trenches to either side of the road. They watched in silence as the horsemen passed.

Kautz' men stared back, superior beings mounted on steeds of fire, passing into a world of adventure unknown to plodding dullards content to sit in holes in the ground.

"They're gonna' kick your ass!" someone yelled from the trenches to the right of the road. "Say hello to my brother, captain," cried another. "He's in Libby Prison!" "That's right," said a third. "You won't have far to walk when they bag the lot of you!"

A sergeant of the Third New York Cavalry held up a gauntleted hand, middle finger extended, as he rode through the lines.

Gales of laughter swept the infantry, rolling and resounding from the surrounding trees.

A mile down the road the advance reached the site of Terry's battle on the 10th. The smell of decaying men hung over the scene. Bloated, dismembered carcasses littered the way. The horses sniffed fearfully, shying away from the bodies. Soldiers averted their eyes, not wishing to confront their fate.

In preparation for their passage into the enemy's country a brigade of riflemen had moved forward to create space into which Kautz could advance. To their front the horsemen heard scattered shots, and the odd, high pitched noises that the rebels made in battle.

The road angled off to one side drifting toward the left end of the unseen firing line ahead. The shooting trailed off. Silence fell in the forest. Acrid, dirty white smoke drifted in the trees, rising toward the tops of the loblolly pines, swirling wraithlike in the crowns. The column marched on in a strained, unnatural hush. The buzz of insect life in the brush began to fuse in men's heads with the resinous odor of the trees themselves.

A volley exploded in the woods to the right rear. What must have been Confederate rifle fire answered. "We're beyond Weitzel's left flank," Kautz remarked to the officer riding beside him.

The other man stood in his stirrups to see farther through the trees. A slim, and elegant figure, he rose ramrod straight to peer through the forest. The bay gelding held between his thighs waited calmly for a signal from above, as contented with his master as Americans were sometimes uneasy with him.

The unease had to do with his strangeness. Major Marco Aurelio Farinelli wore about him an indefinable quality marking him as European. There was something subtly different in his behavior and dress, in the way he arranged the load of field supplies that he and his mount carried. His horsemanship itself had something about it of the riding academy. In moments of impatience with the inevitable waiting of army life, Farinelli had been known to teach army remounts the "Spanish Step". His fanaticism in the drudgery of stable call was legendary. These things collectively spoke of a different world, a place apart from this army of amateur volunteers. Perhaps it was just the newfangled field glasses always hung on his chest.

A crackle of musketry erupted at the head of the column. Bullets whirred through the leaves and branches in the underbrush beside the road. Connected clumps of leaves drifted to the earth.

General Kautz' charger shied from the sound. He gripped the beast with his knees, pulling the animal's head around to face the erratic firing down the road. The shooting died away.

A lieutenant thundered back along the column, galloping his horse through the pines. "Reb cavalry vedettes, sir!" the pink cheeked, bright-eyed officer reported, saluting the while. "Maybe five men. They're gone now. Colonel Spear sends his compliments, intends to press on!"

Kautz nodded his assent. "Tell him to do that. Young man!" His voice rose to stop the galloper, already pulling his horse away.

"Sir?"

"It may be that you do not like the way the world looks, but that horse does. If you go through the thickets at that speed, one of you is going to lose an eye."

The lieutenant flushed red, saluted again, and turning, jumped the horse across a small, muddy ditch onto a low bank covered with honeysuckle. The big animal scrambled with its feet among the vines and finding them drove forward through a screen of creeper.

Kautz listened to the sound of the courier receding in the forest. A growing anger disfigured his bearded features.

"He is very young, *Generale,* and he goes more slow."

Kautz listened for a minute, then glanced at the smiling, mustachioed, olive face.

"Hmmm. It appears to be so. Marco, I'd like you to go hold Spear's hand. He's as jumpy as a rabbit. I don't want him to fight any body of troops big enough to slow us down. We go straight for the railroad at Coalfield Station, understand?"

"Yes! The Colonel Spear is a trifle too eager to make his argument before San Pietro. I will hold his hands." The professional soldier touched the gelding in the flanks with his heels.

The animal leapt forward at once, its gait an eccentric combination of some of the features of both the trot and the canter. In some unique way it appeared to have all four feet off the ground at times. Major Farinelli bestrode this strangely gaited creature as though he were the centaur of old.

As Kautz watched them go, a smile peeked through the foliage of his black beard.

From his seat in the boxcar's door Bill White watched the forest slide past.

The rich green of the trees made a wall divided haphazardly by the brown trunks. Birds flew in and out of the green. A cardinal flashed red almost to the open door of the car, banking away at the last moment, his mate close behind in her desire not to be left. The little bird's sharp cry carried over the engine's rumble and the metal ring of the wheels and rails.

Bill's legs hung out the door, his hands gripping the edge of the floor to either side of his knees. Straw padded the floor. The cool of a May evening flowed around him. Above the train sounds, the hoof noise of the teams vibrated the rough planks beneath him. The voices of the soldiers and drivers hummed in the growing gloom of the car.

A rifleman of the 30th Virginia sat beside him. The man's silhouette could just be seen as the swaying of the train caused him to lean in and out of the doorway.

Corse's Brigade had rolled north for days, north from Weldon, Kinston and other North Carolina railheads. No one seemed to know much about where they were going, not even the officers. A sergeant told Bill that he had heard Colonel Herbert say something about a Yankee army south of Richmond. That did not seem possible. Yankee armies lived north of the Rappahannock, many miles north of the Confederate capital. They periodically tried to march south from that river in the direction of the city. McClellan tried to go around by sea in '62, but he had always stayed east of Richmond, and north of the James. If Federal troops had come to this side of James River, then something strange and new had happened.

The engine's whistle blew shrilly in the dusk. Iron wheels clanked against track. They slowed, rumbling and rocking to a stop. The forest sounds grew stronger. Steam *whhshed* from the engine.

They arrived.

Bill and the man from the 30th hopped down from their seats, picking their way across the darkening ground to the wood line. They stood side by side, face to the woods. Bill unbuttoned himself, urinating into the gathering night.

An audible sigh escaped the soldier. "Much longer and I'd a pissed myself, for sure!"

Bill only half heard. The smell of the damp grasses and trees mingled in his head with the acrid odor of their water. He listened to the night in the trees. Behind them more and more men climbed down from the train.

An officer strode through the ballast alongside the rails. "Get 'em off, everybody off! 17th after the caboose! There's a road crossing there. 30th, leave the wagons and teams on the cars! We're gonna clear the track in front. Move! Let's go!"

"You know where we are, Bill?" the soldier asked.

He shook his head, genuinely puzzled.

"Mills! Where the hell are you, Mills?" a voice demanded in the dark. "Sing out, so's we can find you!"

"All right! All right! I'm comin'." Mills' nearly unseen figure brushed by. Having passed, Sam Mills stopped and turning, laid a hand on Bill's arm. "You take care, you hear! You still owe me money from that last round of poker." A squeeze and he was gone.

At the end of the train someone was lighting *flambeaux*, spreading the flame from one brand to another. The light began to walk along the side of the train toward his position. A bearded face coalesced beneath the shade of a broad brimmed hat, the chin illuminated by the fire. One fist held the torch aloft.

Bill could see the blond hairs on the back of the hand. "Captain Green[5], I'm right here," Bill offered from the shadow of the woodline.

"Ah, Good!

They faced each other in the smoky, wavering light.

"Get the drivers together, and start unloading. I'll send you help as soon as I find "G" Company. I believe it's their turn." He turned away, toward the front of the train.

"Begging your pardon, Captain," Bill said to his back. I do think it is "H" Company's turn".

The officer came back to stand before the lead teamster of the regiment. "You think so? The Gypsies?" He thought for a minute. "Ah, I remember

---

5 The regimental quartermaster.

now. "G" loaded at Petersburg. I need more sleep. Thank you, Bill. I'll go get them. They are back two or three cars."

"Sir, before you go, two things. May I ask what we are doing"?

Green took off the hat. His bald head shone sweaty in the light. He wiped his forehead with a doubtful looking cloth normally stored in the crown of the hat. "Why?"

Bill stood his ground. "I just want to know."

The supply officer thought about that for a few seconds. He put his hat back on.

Bill could no longer see the eyes.

Green spoke. "I don't know how I would run this lash-up without you... The 30th is going to defend some big bridge up in front of the train. We are going back down the line a couple of miles where there are smaller bridges. They're ours. Yankee cavalry is coming. What was the second thing?"

"For loading and unloading, generally, I'd rather have some men from the brigade pioneer company."

Green thought about that. The pioneer company was a black construction gang under command of a white engineer officer. "Why?"

"It's easier for me to organize the work than having to use the soldiers. I can't tell them what to do."

The man with the torch thought about how many things he had to do to get the regiment's trains moving. He sighed and then spoke slowly and carefully, wanting to avoid hurting this man's feelings. "Bill," he said. "Most of the men in the 17th will do what you ask them to do as long as you ask them polite, and you're always polite. Hell, the way they know you, from home and all. Herbert and Corse would skin them alive... But I accept your point. I accept it. I'll talk to Major Taliaferro[6] the first chance. But for now, it's the Gypsies."

"Yes, sir."

Green walked away into the night.

"Hoss! Snake! Jim! Over here!" Bill yelled, calling the drivers to him.

"We here, honey," a soft voice answered from nearby. "We all here."

The raid struck the railroad ten miles southwest of Richmond. Vedettes of the 3rd New York Cavalry Regiment crossed the tracks on both sides of

6 The brigade quartermaster.

Coalfield Station at 11:00 P.M. in a driving rain. In spite of the weather, the city made a golden glow beyond the invisible horizon.

The telegraph operator was looking out a dirty, rain streaked window and thought he saw something moving down the right of way, believed it had been a mounted man. He was nearly certain he had seen this apparition in the flash of the lightning all about. He stood staring through the glass. The flickering light hid more than it revealed. He looked back at his desk. His telegrapher's key lay there. The wires trailed across the dark surface. He rubbed his face, pulling at the ends of the long moustaches. The railroad's general offices in the city had a poor opinion of employees who thought they saw Yankee raiders in the night.

A horse whickered somewhere in the rain.

Three strides took him to his seat.

The line was dead.

"Open the door!" a voice said firmly from outside.

"Who are you?" he asked.

"Don't fool around! We're gonna fire the station!" An orange glow appeared in the window, small at first, but growing steadily.

He emerged from the doorway, hands held high to stand among the dripping, rubber clad figures and steaming horses.

The New Yorkers burned the station.

The District of Columbia troops were brigaded with them. They watched in awe as the veterans piled tar soaked ties on the wreck of the depot. Colonel Simon Mix, commanding the brigade, yelled at them. "Get off your dead asses and help!"

Three New York companies had dismounted their men, and were using the horses to pull up track for a hundred yards on either side of the fire. The troopers heaved the rails onto the roaring blaze. The rain danced and spat like a cat in the white hot embers of the building. A dull redness spread and grew at the center of the rails.

A squad of New Yorkers picked up a rail from the heap and carried it to a nearby telegraph pole. They lined up the white hot middle section with the pole and wrapped the whole thing around the wooden upright, crossing the ends. "There!" a lieutenant said to the watching D.C. soldiers. "That's how you make'em!"

"Make what?" A hulking captain enquired.

"Yellow Leg[7] neckties! We adorn the landscape with'em!"

---

7 Union cavalrymen wore a yellow stripe down the seam of their pants.

The captain waved his men forward. Each squad gingerly lifted a glowing rail from the pile.

They left the telegrapher standing next to the ruins of his station. He shivered alone a long time in the wet misery of the false dawn.

At 5 o'clock Confederate cavalry arrived.

The telegrapher pointed southwest along the track. He gave the officer in command a note from Kautz. The dripping, bearded figure held up the note to the growing light to read. "On the advice of one of my officers, I have refrained from igniting the coal pits in the vicinity of this place. He maintains that if lit, they will burn forever. August Kautz, Brig. Gen. USV, Commanding." The Rebel officer looked up from the note. "What's the next bridge?"

"Mattoax, Solid iron."

The soldier smiled. "There's a regiment of infantry sitting right behind it since last night. We shall see how friend Kautz deals with that!"

The long column of horse rode down the rails. Spears' brigade led the way. Kautz let them rest for two hours in a muddy field beside the tracks. The men huddled together in the drizzle in clumps of dripping rubber. The horses stood apart, nuzzling each other, instinctively seeking a leader.

To Powhatan station they rode, a jingling, sodden, grumbling crowd of men and horses. They left the station there a mass of glowing embers, but they found several wagons full of bacon, hardtack, and fodder behind the tiny building. The troops carried off what they could, and burned the rest.

They came next to Mattoax Bridge. The advanced guard of the 5th Pennsylvania clattered out onto wooden planking laid alongside the rails of the metal span. Heavy rain had made the wood slippery.

A corporal's big mount slid on the boards. The animal fell heavily on its side, screaming in pain as splinters in the rough boards pierced its flank. The fall saved its life.

A well aimed volley of rifle fire swept the bridge. The sphero-conoidal .577 caliber Enfield bullets moaned and buzzed in flight the length of the trestle.

A trooper, placed by fate just behind the fallen horse, went over the side into the water when his wounded horse reared in pain to throw itself over the iron rail at the side of the bridge.

The Pennsylvanians scrambled to get off the bridge and out of the line of fire.

An artillery piece fired from concealment on the far bank. The projectile, a solid shot, ricocheted off a structural girder at the Yankee end of the bridge.

The 12 pound ball whipped over the Pennsylvanians' heads, decapitating an old locust tree behind them.

Kautz arrived on the scene, his horse laboring through the foot deep mud.

Colonel Samuel Spear and Major Farinelli sat their horses astride the red clay road on which they had approached the bridge. Farinelli's back was to the river.

Bullets occasionally cut a leaf from the trees that lined the road.

Farinelli did not appear to notice. Streaks of red mud clung to the legs and flanks of the Italian officer's bay.

It did not escape Kautz that Farinelli's horse blocked Spears' path to the bridge. Kautz looked around and saw that the underbrush was full of dismounted soldiers.

They stood in skirmish order, their lines perpendicular to the road, carbines in their hands. Most of them faced the river. A few looked up at him, with an odd, wistful hope in their rain wet faces.

Spear saluted the division commander. He turned from Farinelli to look full into Kautz' black bearded face. Anger showed in the tight lines that surrounded his pale eyes. "General Kautz, I propose to attack the bridge on foot. I would have already if..."

A cannon ball passed over them from the Southern side of the stream. Its passage was felt rather than heard. The heavy iron mass bored a tunnel of lower pressure into which the surrounding air pushed with enough force to make a breeze that could be felt by the three mounted figures.

Kautz glanced up, and deflected the fall of a small tree branch with his free hand.

"What's your plan?"

The noise along the river interrupted the discussion.

Kautz waited for it to die away.

"'E' and 'G' Companies will rush the bridge while everyone else gives covering fire," Spear said during a lull. "I will lead the assault!"

While Kautz watched, Colonel Spear's nose began to run heavily. Watery mucous streamed down his lip.

Kautz remembered that Spear had been nursing a cold when the column left Bermuda Hundred. He looked closely at the handsome young man. The nose was red and raw.

Sick, he's sick as hell.

Spear wiped his blond mustache with one buckskin covered fist. It left a darker patch on the tan leather.

Kautz looked again at 'E' and 'G' companies and back at Spear. "Yes, you would, you certainly would... Marco, what do you say?"

Farinelli looked embarrassed.

Kautz knew that Farinelli disapproved of disagreeing with any officer in front of those he commanded.

The Italian turned his horse to point down the road to the bridge. "Just there, *Generale*, there is a small path, a trail to the south. It has a sign, to Goode's Bridge." He gestured at the enemy. "There are many here. We can take them in reverse. It will be better for us."

The division commander glanced at Spear, then away. "5th Pennsylvania will hold these rebels here. 11th Pennsylvania will lead the advance on Goode's Bridge. Colonel Spear, you will command the advance. Proceed."

The young man saluted and turned away.

Kautz and Farinelli looked at each other.

"*Generale*, I would prefer not to..."

"I can't relieve him."

"I know, *Generale*, his uncle..."

Kautz watched his friend follow Spear's into the looming forest to the south.

"What was all that?" Bill White asked.

Captain William Fowle stood atop the high end of a fallen log, hat off, straining to hear. "Beats me!" he said at last. "It sounded like an attack on the 30th up at the iron bridge. Either they beat it off, or the Yanks broke through, and will be along shortly."

Bill White and Lieutenant Jake Devereux stood to either side of the log holding his pants legs.

"Who's between us and them," Jake asked?

The log teetered and swayed, threatening to drop "H" Company's commander into the bushes. "Oh, the colonel put "A" back there half a mile to announce visitors."

"What's this look like, Bill?" Jake asked for them both. "It was dark when we came in here."

Fowle climbed down to sit on the log's half rotted stump. Picking up a stick, he drew in the damp earth. In his sketch, the Richmond and Danville crawled down from the northeast. Mattoax Bridge, where the line jumped the Appomattox River, was indicated by two little cross hatches. Six inches to the southwest, another smaller set of signs showed that the railroad crossed another stream.

"This is our bridge," Fowle said. "They may think..."
"To come around behind," Bill White finished.
"Yes."

- 4:35 A.M, 14 May - (Chula Station)

The engine crept along in the dark, a towering, inky presence, its running lights unlit.

Small animals watched it pass. They had long become accustomed to the nearness of the railroad.

This train was unusual. It moved so slowly that a watching rabbit was tempted to cross the track just as it went by. Only the oily, hot smell of the metal prevented the attempt.

The locomotive dragged a long chain of rickety wooden boxcars. Down the tracks it rolled, down to the southwest. From high in the cab, the three men inside could see a long way up the track. The rain had stopped in the night. A half moon shone down, making shadows among the silent trees lining the right of way. An orange glow that had been Chula Station came into view around a long, gentle curve. As they watched the light grew nearer, and then without warning the engine ran off the tracks, its front wheels riding up and over a pile of gravel and extra rails. The cowcatcher struck the right rail a ringing blow in passing. A series of bumps and jolts shook the cab's floor as the road wheels ran across all obstacles into the gravel ballast. Inertia carried the great weight of the train along the curving shoulder of the road bed until a front axle struck a stone culvert. The locomotive pivoted around the point of impact with a grinding sound, sliding forward on its side, pulling the string of overturned cars behind it.

The cavalrymen bivouacked in the woods to either side lay in their bedrolls listening in awe to the terrible noise, and wondering what it might be. Their mounts reared and kicked, frustrated at restraining hobbles, seeking to flee from the sound.

From the hissing hulk of the dead locomotive, three dimly seen figures appeared. Two bolted back along the track, climbing spryly over broken pieces of train to disappear into the darkness. Their feet were heard in the gravel for a moment or two. The third person stumbled forward along the track toward the burning building.

"Dey leff me, dam 'em! Dey leff me!" The fireman shook his head in sadness. "I been de bes secesh niggah in Virginny, an' dey leff me.."

"Well, here's your chance to pay them back," Kautz interrupted from behind him.

The fireman turned to see who had said this. In the light of dawn he could see the single star. "Mawnin', Genrul, please to meet yuh! Dey shouldna' leff me".

Samuel Spear's irritation at Kautz' intrusion into his conversation with the Negro showed in his face. "Come now, Mister Washington! We must know their strength at the bridge! You were about to tell me?"

The fireman stared at Spear, straining to understand the strange words and intonation. He turned back to Kautz. "Whut he want, Genrul? I cain't rightly unde'stand de funny talk."

August Kautz lit his pipe. "What's your Christian name?"

"Plato."

"Like a pet dog!" Spear exclaimed in anger.

Kautz pointed the bit of his pipe at the other officer in a gesture which left no doubt as to its meaning. "Plato," he said. "How many Rebs at the bridge?"

"Mattoax?" The black man's features took on a peculiar impassivity.

Kautz considered him. "Are you a slave?"

"Yassuh!"

"Who owns you?"

"Mistuh Charles Talcott, de debbil what leff me here".

"No one owns you now, Mister Washington," interjected Spear. "You have been liberated by us. You are free!"

"I'se free?" He inspected the circle of white faces.

"Yes. How many enemy troops at Mattoax Bridge?" Spear demanded.

"Hund'ed fifty, two hund'ed.. Sumthin' in that region. Cain't say fuh shuah. It wuz dark as hail."

"Did you see any cannons?" Farinelli asked from the man's elbow.

"Naw suh. Jus' sojers".

"Where will you go now?" Kautz questioned.

"To see my woman! I'se free."

"Where is she?" Farinelli asked.

"Shockoe Bottom. She dere."

"You can go now," the general told him.

They watched him slip away into the forest.

"Colonel Spear, take two regiments and move up to the next little stream to the north where my map shows a wooden bridge. Burn it. We'll finish up here and wait for you."

Spear's face showed deep confusion. He wiped his nose on his sleeve. "But, sir, what about the enemy force at Mattoax farther north?"

Kautz still faced the woodline into which Plato Washington had gone. "Shockoe Bottom is in Richmond, Colonel," he whispered. "That man is going home now. Be very careful."

Behind Flat Creek, Colonel Arthur Herbert's men waited.

The aforementioned Talcott, as well as a man named Morrow who had been driving the engine, stumbled into their lines just before dawn. They were out of breath, and Talcott babbed incoherently of "Poor Plato, crushed to death in the wreck..."

Herbert heard him out, then ordered the regiment "to stand to under arms, ready to move at a moments notice."

Talcott, Morrow, Herbert, Major Robert Simpson, and Bill Fowle were seated together on a group of stumps a short distance north of the railroad bridge when firing started on the picket line beyond the creek. The railroad seemed to have cut the trees belonging to these stumps for some purpose of its own. What that might have been did not immediately come to anyone's mind.

The early morning air was aromatically bracing. The sky had that luminous quality that sometimes comes after a rain. The trees still dripped a bit from the ends of branches, but the soldiers were accustomed to being wet and so long as it was not cold they were content.

The group of officers and visitors were in "H" company's bivouac area. Herbert had the habit of spending a good deal of his spare time with "H" company. They were the "Old Dominion Rifles" of militia days and he had been their first commander.

Snake Davis, the company's head cook, stood a respectful three yards away watching his reaction to the food. The rain, and the general shortage of provisions made this morning a challenge, but Davis managed hominy, stewed venison, and biscuits. Steaming tin mugs of whatever it was that they now called "coffee" sat on the ground. They had begun to eat when the first scattered shots were heard.

A number of soldiers stood by the cook fires, their tin plates and cups held before them. The motley brown and tan clothes hung loosely on skinny young bodies. Short jackets, round, broad brimmed hats, and crude, but sturdy brogan shoes were their common dress.

Herbert inspected them as they waited in patient good humor for their food. There was so little fat on them that a visiting civilian doctor had recently told Herbert that he was concerned for their health.

My, God, Herbert thought. *I know their mothers, nearly every one. Their fathers are my friends. If I lose many more, how can I ever go home?*

The pop! pop! pop! of distant rifles froze them in place, heads up, listening to the sound.

The colonel sat, fork in hand, judging the moment. The shooting died away. He looked at Simpson. "That would be the men in the lead backing away until the main body comes up?"

Simpson nodded. He was eating fast, mopping up the stew with a biscuit.

The two civilians were ashen faced, immobilized on their stumps, resembling nothing so much as oversized garden dwarves. All thought of breakfast had deserted them.

A few more shots came to them on the cool morning breeze from the south.

The resumption of firing seemed to cause the riflemen around the fire to make up their minds about what would happen. Some hurriedly ladled food onto their plates. Others tossed their half eaten rations into the bushes and searched for their belongings.

"That was our picket line," Captain Fowle commented, lowering his mug.

Simpson finished eating, stood, and after handing his plate to Davis, climbed into the branches of a nearby walnut.

The volume of fire suddenly increased, spreading in both directions from an area directly across the stream from the railroad bridge.

"Their line of battle," Simpson offered from his elevated position.

A bullet hummed over them, cutting leaves as it went.

Snake Davis called up into the tree. "Majuh Simpson! You come down now, you heah! You don't need to be standin' up on that place like that". He was outraged, and spluttering.

Simpson shaded his eyes with a hand. "I can see them! They have a couple of companies dismounted on line. The rest are somewhere back in the trees." He glanced down at Herbert. "They're going to charge mounted. I can see the horses."

The colonel grimaced thinking, *well, here we go again.* He looked up at his second in command. "Robert, you do what Snake says, and come down now. Bring the reserve companies up behind our line as we discussed. I want a line of company columns, centered on the tracks. I'll be at the bridge."

An artillery piece spoke from somewhere to the south. Its message of death sighed across the sky.

Snake cocked an ear to the sound, shook his head and began to gather up the debris of the hastily abandoned meal.

The hard task of tearing up and bending track started in earnest after Colonel Spear's departure. The oversized District of Columbia regiment put its men to the work of destruction while Pennsylvania troops stood guard in the surrounding forest. In the warming sun, most of the men worked shirtless, sweating around the bonfires and piles of glowing rails. The horses stood in long, silent lines guarded by those lucky enough to have been overlooked by first sergeants.

Kautz watched the work from nearby. At dawn he had sent a scouting party further to the south to know if it would be possible to continue in that direction. Now, he waited for their return.

Farinelli's activities attracted his attention as a diversion from the scene of demolition. The Italian had assembled a group of officers, including Major Baker, for a talk. He drew pictures on the ground and spoke to them in a soft voice of things they had seen, of things they would almost certainly see. He told them what they should think of in cases that might arise in the course of this expedition. He taught them.

Kautz had brought Farinelli into the division for this very purpose. A German by birth, a West Point graduate by education, the general had a poor opinion of his officers. It was not that they were not willing, or fervent for the cause. They were certainly that. Kautz wished that some of them would temper their zeal with common sense, or perhaps some measure of humanity in their dealings with Southern civilians. No, the difficulty lay in their collective ignorance of the military art. They lost men when it was unnecessary. They made mistakes that must not continue. There was nothing basically wrong with them. They had been given too much authority, and too many men too fast. Kautz had inquired at the Cavalry Bureau in Washington seeking a European officer of experience and reputation; he was given Farinelli's name. He had lured him away from the 2nd New York Cavalry with the promise of a majority.

The original idea had been to acquire a peripatetic military schoolmaster, a tutor for citizen soldiers. What had developed had been unexpected, but welcome. Marco Farinelli was a soldier's soldier, someone whose presence made it possible to sleep at night without fretting over the details of basic soldiering. Kautz would not have traded him for a battalion. The two of them were the only professional soldiers in the division. Kautz was impatient for an opportunity to give his friend a regiment to command.

The wind blew from the southwest. Because of that, the first shots announcing that Spear's force had made contact with the enemy came to the general as a distant sputter, an almost inaudible rattle. He paid little attention.

Farinelli was struggling with his English as he tried to explain to the officers the criteria by which one decided to fight dismounted.

Kautz half listened to this, and half watched the progress of the track wrecking. His big, black horse pulled hard at the small tree to which the general had tied him. The animal yanked again and again at the thin leather straps. Kautz found hobbles in a saddlebag and released the horse to forage in the deep grass.

Five minutes later the dull thud of the mountain howitzer he had sent with Spear echoed in his skull.

"Marco!

The Italian looked up.

"Go remind Colonel Spear that it is not my intention that he should become decisively engaged, that we are, in a word, in a hurry." Sarcasm colored his words.

The junior officers around Farinelli stared at the heavy browed, black bearded figure with fear and surprise.

He hated their awe. He was a man who did not worship idols. He had no regard for those who did. He knew how much they wished to please him. He hated that too and for the same reason. It diminished them as men in his eyes.

Careful, he thought. *Much more of that and they will start avoiding you. We can't have that.*

He wrote out an order on the message pad he carried in a coat pocket.

He carried the little piece of paper to Farinelli. The circle parted before him like the waves before Moses.

"Give this to Colonel Spear, at your discretion. It directs him to withdraw to this position."

Farinelli stuffed the paper into the cuff of his blouse. He saluted, perfectly erect, his uniform improbably neat. "By your leave, *Generale*."

Kautz returned the salute.

Mounting the bay, the cavalryman rode to the north.

It was little more than a mile. The sound of the action grew in volume with his progress. The gelding had good legs, and a sound wind. Farinelli could feel the animal's barrel swell with the fullness of his breathing. He would go the distance. The horseman heard cheering, and frowned. Of the troops in the division, only the 11th Pennsylvania had the habit of cheering in action. An early commander had taught them to do this in the charge.

The trees flashed by. A riderless horse passed him headed away from the sounds of battle. Two more crashed out of the underbrush fifty yards away. A fourth horse dragged a bloodied, limp blue figure down the track toward a collision with the Italian. The bay swerved from its path. The crazed horse fell to its knees and then onto a side. There was a gaping wound in its flank.

Farinelli pounded past, driven onward by the sound of the guns. The mountain howitzer spoke from nearby. Turning in the saddle, he saw the little gun, surrounded by its crew. It stood in the center of a small clearing, smoke still drifting in the space forward of the muzzle. Crew drill went on; sponge! load! ram!

The bay carried him past the gun into the dense forest. The mixed noise of cavalry carbines and infantry rifles swelled rapidly. The piney woods smelled of gunpowder and horses.

At the top of a tiny rise, he found Colonel Spear's orderly. The soldier waited in the road with a pack mule and the extra horses of Spear's saddle string.

"Where would I find the colonel Spear?"

The man pointed forward down the road in the direction of the fighting. "There! He went in with the 11th! They charged the highway bridge. The Secesh drove 'em back. So, the Colonel went back in with both regiments on foot. They're gonna push 'em off the bridges and then burn 'em! Like always!" He grinned confidently. "Like always."

The intensity of the firing to the front rose steadily. It began to sound like cloth ripping, one continuous tearing noise.

The blue soldier frowned slightly, worry wrinkles appearing between his eyes, just visible behind a lock of yellow hair hanging below the bill of his kepi.

Farinelli dismounted. "Keep him good!" he told the orderly. "Good horse! You keep him. I come back for him. Understand?" He handed the soldier the reins. "You keep him no matter what! Yes?"

The trooper looked at the sweating bay, then at Farinelli. "I'll have him, major, no matter what."

With a brusque nod, Farinelli strode away, going downhill into the trees. He drew his revolver as he went. He went down, and down into the shallow valley of Flat Creek. To his left he saw the dirt track which led to one bridge. To his right lay the right of way and ballast stone of the Richmond and Danville. Along both lines of advance dead and wounded men and beasts were scattered. Here and there injured soldiers had managed to take shelter behind the bodies of their mounts. He had done his best to teach them to kill the horses to make a barricade if they must.

A gut shot sorrel raised its head on top of the highway grade to stare at him with pain filled eyes. He shot it in the forehead and walked on through the brush and pines. Walking wounded passed him on their way to the rear. He stopped counting them after twenty.

He heard Samuel Spear bellowing orders in a high pitched voice. The sound guided him to a small rise in the ground on which the brigade commander stood, his red and white swallow tailed flag planted nearby.

Twenty yards of bog to the front, Flat Creek flowed past. An insignificant stream, dignified for history only by the two bridges, it ran sluggishly north toward the Appomattox.

On the far side Spear's men clung to the three foot bank which held the rivulet in check when flood water came. They fired their weapons across the ground beyond at someone unseen. Several blue clad bodies lay in the water.

Farinelli stepped up on the mound at Spear's side. Rifle bullets hummed overhead, passing above them by some accident of topography.

Spear turned to look at him, staring coldly for a moment before returning his attention to the action before him. "Get moving! Push the damned militia out of the way!" he yelled.

A sergeant that Farinelli recognized turned from the bank. "God damn you!" he roared. "If you think these are militia, come try them yourself!"

High pitched cackling laughter reached them from the unseen enemy.

Farinelli considered the number of dead bodies in sight. He looked at the men on the bank.

Far too many were looking behind them, judging the distance to the nearest tree.

The volume of fire from beyond the bank was very steady.

He decided. "Colonel Spear!

The blond young man swiveled toward him, anger in his face.

Farinelli pulled the folded message form from his sleeve, saluted, and handed over the order.

Spear's features twisted in frustration and humiliation as he read. He turned from Farinelli to the bugler standing beside his standard bearer. "Sound Recall," he snarled.

Farinelli raised a hand to stop him, to counsel a withdrawal by bounds, but the first notes flashed out before he could say anything.

Soldiers immediately turned away from the firing line. Some broke back across the run.

In the unknowable territory of the foeman, drums began to beat the charge. The command "Forward!" ran up and down the hidden line of battle beyond the stream.

The shrill, keening war cry of the Confederate Army ripped through the forest. Grey brown shapes hurtled through the underbrush into the recoiling cavalrymen.

A man bearing a square red flag splashed down into the water.

On the far side of the creek, a tall, dark haired officer appeared. He held a pistol in one hand, and a straight, basket hilted sword in the other.

Arthur Herbert had followed the color bearer through the brush, knowing the distance was not far to the stream. Behind him he could hear the reserve companies tearing vines apart as they ran forward. Suddenly he was on the bank. Men fought in the hip deep water at his feet.

Jesus! We are going to bag the lot, he thought.

Across the creek, a little knot of enemy troops stood on a rise in the ground. A cavalry flag was planted among them. He looked right and left. His men fought with clubbed muskets and bayonets for as far as he could see. As he watched, they surged forward again.

The Rebel infantry stabbed, butt stroked and screamed their way across Flat Creek. Farinelli watched, astonished as the earth colored figures killed all who could not escape. Federals who fell were bayoneted repeatedly by all who passed.

Immediately to the front, a small group of blue troopers grappled in the water with the madmen.

"Take the flag!" the bearded Rebel officer roared.

The charge rolled toward the high ground. The wings of the assault passed the little knoll.

Farinelli emptied his revolver at a group closing from the right.

Spear yelled "Standard to the rear!"

The soldier with the banner backed off the rise with Spear..

A bullet hit the bugler in the neck. Dark red blood bubbled out in a pulsing stream. The man fell to his knees clutching his throat with fingers through which there was a steady flow.

Farinelli grabbed him by the arm, intending to drag him to safety.

The bugler continued his collapse, losing consciousness as he fell to the ground.

His empty revolver in one hand, the dying man's arm in the other, Farinelli saw that the Union troops were falling back away from him.

The horns of the Confederate attack were now far beyond his position.

The fight in the creek ended. Wild eyed warriors in brown swarmed up over the bank. Some had lost their hats. The pale white of foreheads contrasted sharply with the weathered tan of their cheeks.

His back to the Rebel advance, Farinelli shook his empty weapon at Colonel Spear's retreat. Federal wounded lay thick on the earth around the swell in the ground. Passion filled him at this abandonment.

"*Che cazzo fa*!" he screamed in his wrath.

He had cheated death many times, and now he knew the time had come to settle his account. He thought of Solferino, of his father's house in Rome, and waited for the end.

Nothing happened.

Heavy breathing behind him interrupted his wait.

He turned slowly to look.

Three riflemen stood in a semi-circle surrounding him and the wounded bugler. The two on the flanks still held their weapons at the ready. The man in the middle stared at him. "*Tu sei Italiano?*" he rasped.

The shock of the moment clouded the ability to respond. "*Si*", he managed at last.

The bugler moaned.

"Help me, please help with him." Farinelli entreated them.

The fire began to ebb in their faces.

The soldier in the middle handed his rifle to another, then went down on one knee beside the stricken man.

The counterattack whirled out of sight up the slope across which Farinelli had reached this spot.

The bugler died quickly. They looked in his pockets for his name, but could find nothing. His body lay on its side four feet away. They covered the side of his face with his cap.

The Southern infantrymen gathered their prisoners near the mound. Perhaps they were unwilling to make the Yankee major move. They had seen him stay for a wounded enlisted man. He had been willing to die for one such as they. That made him worth considering.

After a time, a prisoner asked to see the body on the hillock. "Israel Cook," he said. "He's from Albany". He went back to the dejected group of men sitting on the ground.

Farinelli wrote the dead soldier's name and put it in one of his pockets.

The sound of fighting died away. He knew that August Kautz would not repeat Spear's mistake. The division would move farther south seeking a return to the Bermuda Hundred lines.

He was alone on the mound with the dead man and the three Rebels. "How is it you speak some Italian?" he asked one of them.

"My father and mother are from Venezia, and you?"

"Roma, and what are you when you are not soldier?"

"I work on the docks with my father, and my uncle. In Alexandria," he added as an afterthought.

"My name's Kemper," a big, blond soldier announced without being asked. "I'm a farmer, down near Mount Vernon. You know, Pres'dent Washinton's place. You should go home, Major. You got no business in our war. This isn't no game."

"Alexandria, Mount Vernon, you are far from home."

"You don't want to remind us of that," interjected the third, yet another giant blond man. "We might stick you yet."

"Sir, Private Colonna was most good to me. Nothing would have save this poor fellow." Herbert had come to talk to him. He was still sitting next to the bugler's body.

"Would you like to wash?" Herbert asked. He was looking at the sticky brown mess that coated Farinelli's hands.

They walked together to the creek. The Union officer knelt upstream of a corpse not yet removed from the sluggishly flowing water. Farinelli wanted to get the bugler's blood from under his fingernails. Herbert watched him for a moment and then found a piece of soap in his haversack.

A steadily lengthening row of Federal bodies grew on the gravel ballast of the railroad nearby as the Confederates lined them up.

"How many you think, Colonel?" Farinelli asked from his crouching position in the stream. He pointed with his chin at the dead.

"Thirty five, maybe forty. It was very lucky for us that you blew "Recall" like that. I had just about made up my mind, but that made the timing..." Herbert watched him closely; curious to know what had happened.

"Some things not a matter of luck."

"Our surgeon is doing what he can for your wounded. I am going to leave the less serious cases here on the track with several unwounded prisoners and a horse. They ought to be able to find help. I presume that General Kautz will not have gone very far?"

Farinelli raised his eyebrows in surprise at this heavy-handed attempt to get him to reveal something of value. "That was impressive attack, colonel," he said. "These men have something strong in them."

Herbert frowned slightly, and then crooked his head a little in acknowledgment of his failure to learn what he wanted to know. "We are fighting for our independence, major. We want to be free of people who yearn to tell us how we should live. We are not children."

"Where you learn all this?" Farinelli's sweeping arm took in the whole scene.

"I could ask the same of you."

An arrogant little bastard, aren't you, the colonel thought to himself.

Farinelli shrugged expressively. "Ah! Me! I was born to fight someone's war. I am sure you know that my poor Italy has been cursed by war these past fifteen years." He glanced at Herbert to be sure he knew. "I was officer in the Papal Army. Then, I was officer in Garibaldi army. After, I served Savoy. Now, I am here. Perhaps I will stay here."

Herbert stared at him, his features hardening in disapproval. "You will be welcome in their country I am sure."

A stooped, black bearded major walked down the hill from the south. Beside him strode a short, slender man with the three bars of a captain on his collar. "Sir, Kautz' force has gone south, away from the railroad. We pursued these fellows until they reached the main body."

"Thank you, Robert." He turned to Farinelli. "I won't ask you where they are going."

The Italian bowed from the hips.

"A train will come tonight to carry my men to Richmond. We have an old score to settle with your General Butler. Captain Fowle has the best cooks in the regiment. I presume that he will invite you to dinner."

Fowle said nothing.

At least I won't have to eat with you, Herbert thought with amused satisfaction. *Bill will have that privilege.*

."We'll take your wounded to Richmond. After all, that's where they wanted to go."

Farinelli bowed again.

Herbert turned and walked away.

The rickety, neglected string of freight wagons and flat cars rolled on and on in the perfumed air of a Virginia spring night.

Farinelli sat cross legged with his back to the open boxcar door smoking a blackened, knobby briar that his grandfather had given him while he was at cadet school. Clouds of bluish smoke enveloped him in the dim light.

The Rebels more or less filled the large space within the car. They sat in small groups. Some played cards, dealing hands of poker from worn, brown, well weathered decks. Others slept with their heads propped up on blanket rolls. He marveled that the sleepers persisted in spite of the engine noise and the rowdy commotion of their comrades.

It did not escape his attention that only one officer had chosen to enjoy his company in the passage to Richmond. This was the blond lieutenant who had watched him so closely at dinner in Captain Fowle's mess, saying nothing, merely listening to their somewhat strained conversation.

Farinelli studied the men. He had never seen this enemy so near before. They were subtly different from the Union soldiers he had known so well. There was about these men a quality of loose jointedness, of playfulness. In America, he had become accustomed to his own veterans, the dour, faithful citizens of upstate New York and western Pennsylvania. These were different. They had about them a natural gaiety, a relaxed openness which showed in their brown faces, and which made their shabby, dull clothing seem appropriate, a reflection of their relationship to the soil. Their horseplay and lively talk had little calculation in it.

In his mind's eye, he compared the atmosphere of relaxed companionship in the freight car with the wild charge cross Flat Creek. There was something wrong about this juxtaposition in his mind, something he must understand.

The lieutenant sat at the far end of the car between two colored men. One was so light in skin and hair color that Farinelli had not at first understood the difference. The other was much older than either of the others, and dark. The three bent together, enjoying what seemed to be a long, perhaps unending, joke.

Looking at them, he was troubled. He was sure he had seen the two blacks before, but could not remember them as individuals. In Europe, Africans were such a rarity that they always stuck in the mind. In the North, they were really more of an abstraction than anything else. There were few in the cities, except Washington, of course. The Negroes that he had seen with the army in the field had nearly all been "contrabands," men and women who understood the precariousness of their position and who typically kept their eyes away from his. This was quite different. The Rebel infantrymen paid no attention to the two blacks, did not seem to be aware of them.

Colonel Herbert had brought the 17th Virginia's combat train[8] forward to carry the wounded back a mile to a place convenient for loading the cars. Farinelli noticed that the wagoneers were all blacks.

Unexpectedly, he remembered the older Negro as the man who had handed him a plate and his supper.

A short, heavily bearded corporal detached himself from a card game and rising stiffly made his way the length of the car toward the lieutenant. He limped on feet gone dead from sitting cross legged on the straw.

The floor of the car swayed and bumped over the rough roadbed. Two hanging lanterns made weak patterns of shifting light on the floor and walls.

The lieutenant and his Negroes raised their heads to watch him approach.

The corporal bent beside them to say something.

The three searched their pockets.

The dark man found a twist of tobacco.

Returning, the corporal seated himself in the doorway next to Farinelli. He cut himself a plug, and turned to the prisoner. "You don't chew, do you?" he asked.

"No."

"I didn't think so. I never saw any French or Italians who did chew. Some English, but they'd been here a long time."

Farinelli was intrigued by this statement. "And you know some Italian and French men, *caporale*?"

The soldier glanced at him from the corner of an eye. "I wouldn't be laughin' at us..."

"I meant no offense."

The corporal nodded. "I was bo'sun in a three masted schooner belonged to the Devereuxs." He looked embarrassed. "If we had more navy, that's where I'd be..."

"The Devereuxs?"

---

8 The collection of wagons and impedimenta which sustained the regiment's life in the field.

"Yes. That's Jake Devereux over there with Bill and Snake." He pointed with his nose at the lieutenant.

Farinelli saw that the three were watching him now.

"The 'Elizabeth Mayo', a sweet little ship, tender beatin' to windward, but fast as hell!"

"And where did you voyage in this vessel?"

"Cherbourg, Genoa, the West Indies. Mostly we went to Europe, bringin' back fancy goods for the big stores in Washington and Baltimore. Those were good times."

Farinelli thought for a minute. "The Devereuxs are rich?"

The corporal laughed aloud, causing everyone in the car to turn and stare. "Good God, Yes! Jake over there could buy and sell you and me with pocket change. Ain't that right lootenant?" he yelled across the car.

Devereux cupped one ear.

"I was tellin' the Yank that you're filthy rich!"

The lieutenant grinned. "That's right! I'm thinking of buying this whole company champagne and oysters as soon as we get to Richmond," he called back.

The soldiers hooted at that. A general discussion of methods of oyster cookery began.

"Banking, shipping, merchandising. The Devereuxs are in all that. They even have a farm around somewhere. I forget where, maybe out in the Shenandoah Valley. They're half French, the Devereux boys, Jake, Claude and Pat. Their ma's French. Pat's dead now. We heard that a while back. Claude used to be our comp'ny commander. He's gone. We don't know when he's comin' back..

"And the Captain Fowle? Is he rich as well?"

The soldier mumbled something inaudible to himself.

"I am sorry," Farinelli said, "but I did not hear."

"I said he's the richest of all. His daddy, William, owns a piece of everything around; the water works, the gas works, the railroad to Washington City, just about everything, or did before all this." He began to look suspicious. "Why do you want to know?"

"I try to understand... You are not what I thought..." The Union officer felt oddly awkward. He had felt this way as a boy when forced by his parents to contemplate something which demonstrated the inadequacy of his views. "Who are the black men?" he demanded, rather more forcefully than was required by the moment.

The corporal turned to look at the three.

They stared back.

"Snake Davis, the one on the right is our comp'ny cook, a damn good cook. He doctors us some too. I've known him all my life. The other one's Bill White. He isn't really in the comp'ny anymore. Runs all the drivers for the reg'ment. He's Jake's..." The soldier stopped himself in the middle of a thought.

"Jake's?

The man shook his head slowly. "I don't believe you'd understand." With that he moved away, rejoining his messmates in a game centered on a small pile of Confederate bills of large denomination.

The Italian thought about the possibilities, looked at the three men again, pondered one possibility while watching them talk and decided against it. After an hour he began to see something in two of the faces. Thinking about the circumstances of Southern life, he decided that he did understand. With that he rolled over on his side, facing the board wall of the car to seek sleep. He had almost reached that blessed state, had almost found release from a day that would never end when he felt someone sit down behind his back. He rolled over to peer upward through sleep-blurred vision at Jake Devereux who sat cross legged beside him.

"Yes?" he said in surprise. "I have made the impression that you gentlemen do not wish to speak with me..."

Jake cocked his head and nodded in agreement. "That's right. We don't want to be your friends. Why should we? On the other hand, courtesy demands..."

Farinelli sat up and looked at the other man, looked at his face. In spite of the weathered tan and worn field clothing, the lieutenant looked every inch the gentleman that the corporal had implied. "I am told that your family are big people in your native town."

Jake was pained by that, embarrassed by the custom among his people that such things may be known but are never referred to in the presence of the fortunate themselves. His discomfort did not show in the face. "Well, Charlie has always liked to talk..."

The corporal sat nearby listening.

"It must be that he misses the chance to pass the time with interesting foreign folks..." The eyes regarded Farinelli with a mildness that hid some secret purpose.

"And you have not been abroad?"

"Not too much, England once..."

The corporal turned his head, looking out the boxcar door at nothing in particular.

"You are Captain Fowle's second in command?"

"That's right. These men were foolish enough to elect me to be lieutenant a while back. I used to carry a rifle in this company. Charlie was my squad leader..."

Farinelli was now really interested. "This is not a difficulty?" In the Union units he had served with the same practice prevailed and he had always marveled at its existence.

Jake shrugged while pulling his knees up and wrapping his arms around his ankles. "No, not for me, but I don't think I'm anyone special. They just elected me. Actually, life was easier before...

What are we playing at? Farinelli wondered.

"I am told that you have lost a brother," he asked looking for a conversational opening.

The red-blonde beard twitched.

God damn you Charlie, Jake thought, *we need a muzzle for you.*

"Yes, he was killed at Gettysburg."

The Italian tried to remember what Charlie had said. "And he was commanding of this company before?"

Jake Devereux willed himself into impassivity, resisted successfully the urge to look at Charlie Bowen. His guts had turned to ice.

Bowen kept his gaze riveted on the black rectangle of the car door. He saw now that he had placed Claude Devereux in danger.

I knew Claude was on Secret Service duty in Washington. Why did I say that? Why?

He kept his eyes on the door.

"My brother? Oh, he must mean Claude. Claude was in charge when this was a militia company before the war. That must be it... Is that what you mean, Charlie?"

Bowen glanced at them. "That's right, '59 or '60 it would have been." He looked away.

"Actually, Claude inclines toward the other side." He grimaced, "a family tragedy, but so common these days..."

The Italian sensed that something in this was untrue, but had no method available to separate the wheat from the chaff.

"And Bill White?"

This was truly a surprise. "What about him?" An edge showed in the young man for the first time.

"*Caporale* Bowen said you were related." By that the Italian meant connected in some way.

Jake swung around to face Bowen.

"No, I never," he protested.

Farinelli saw that all the nearby soldiers had stopped to listen.

Jake turned back to him. A smile slowly suffused his face. "Bill's mother was my nurse, what the Yankees call a 'mammy'. She is a second mother to me, and Bill is like an older brother, or perhaps a cousin." He started to get to his feet. "You need some sleep, major, as do we all. Another long day tomorrow I fear. Good night." He went back to his own end of the car and resumed his place between the two Negroes, pulling his hat down over his eyes to shut out the light.

Farinelli watched for a minute, then lay back down with his face to the wall resolved to think all this over at some later time.

The engine pulled them onward through the darkness. It took them almost to the James, then paused at a junction just south of the river while linemen threw switches and started the string of cars running south toward Petersburg. Early in the morning, before the first light of false dawn, the train stopped at a siding.

Farinelli stood by the side of the road and watched the regiment disappear into the darkness and mist. The long column of fours slouched forward, the men uncharacteristically quiet in their sleepiness. Their faces were hard to see in the shadow thrown by the broad brimmed hats.

Corporal Bowen touched his sleeve as he passed. "You be good, now, major!" he said. Don't you be givin' these boys a hard time!" His eyes glowed brightly in the smoky half light of the torches.

Behind the marching riflemen came the wagons. They rolled along in the night, a continuous procession of horses, mules and rumbling iron tires.

Bill White walked into the light and stood beside Farinelli as the surgeon's three ambulances went by.

Doctor Lewis led the little caravan on his old buckskin mare. His soldier assistants rode high on the seats beside the teamsters. Safe from the need to walk, the medical contingent had wrapped themselves in issue ponchos and captured Union Army rubber raincoats.

The ammunition train followed, each board sided wagon stacked high with rough wooden boxes of cartridges.

"Are these your people?" Farinelli asked loud enough to make his voice carry over the road noise. He was thinking of the drivers.

White turned abruptly toward him. "Yes, they are!" Are the Yankees yours?" he asked with some heat.

Farinelli saw his mistake, but could not immediately find the words to change what he had said. "In European armies, there are many, men of color," he offered lamely.

"In the colonies mainly," White replied. His eyes held Farinelli unblinkingly. "I hear you are from Rome."

"Yes, yes. Our house is near the Villa Borghese[9]." He realized how pointless the last words were.

White said something.

Farinelli lost most of it in the clatter of a wagon. "What? Did you say 'zoo'?" he asked incredulously.

Snake Davis and his wagon approached leading the company kitchens.

White held up a hand encased in a coarse work glove to stop the wagon. A black man riding beside Davis climbed over the seat, and into the back to make room. White stepped on a front wheel hub to lift himself onto the seat beside the cook. He looked down. "Gazellus Gazellus Arabicus" he said.

"What?"

"The Arabian peninsula gazelle, Major. That's what it says on the sign by the pen. They were always my favorites. You should visit them if you get back. Let's go."

The dark, elderly, cook clucked to his team, slapping their backs with the reins. The wagon rolled on.

Farinelli watched them go, confusion filling his head. He heard a chuckle behind him, and pivoted to look at the guard detail and wounded prisoners.

Stony amusement filled most faces.

---

9 The principal park of Rome.

Chapter 22

Drewry's Bluff

- 16 May, 1864 -

If the Union Army had prepared adequately for the spring campaign, the general officer who commanded Confederate forces south of Richmond would himself have been considered a major factor.

Pierre Gustave Toutant Beauregard was always a man to take seriously and thus far he had endured a frustrating war. Handsome, dark, Catholic, Creole and perfectly fluent in English, Beauregard had always been a symbol of the absorptive capacity of the American republic. First in his class at West Point, he had risen steadily in the elite Corps of Engineers in what could only be called a "distinguished army career." His old friends called him "Gus". Their awareness of any real "difference" in him was largely limited to their appreciation of his ability as a cook. In 1861, the world had seemed open to him for all things. Nevertheless, in the time of decision he relinquished a newly achieved dignity as Superintendent of West Point to offer his sword to his native Louisiana. When she chose to join the Confederacy, he found himself catapulted to high rank as her most militarily experienced son. At Montgomery, the new government was creating an army, and his name was brought forward early by his friends. Jefferson Davis remembered the man well from his days as Secretary of War.

Samuel Cooper, the Adjutant General, remembered him as well, but then, he remembered everyone.

Perhaps that was enough, or possibly the need to placate the New Orleans political fraternity had some effect, but in any case, Beauregard received command at Charleston and the fame of having accepted Major Anderson's surrender of Fort Sumter. Joe Johnston and he then shared the laurels for the First Battle of Manassas, and the Southern people took them both to their hearts.

He was named in the first appointment of full generals.

After that, the trouble began. He had always believed in his own intellect. Now he considered it his duty to advise the president. He told him that they should concentrate the available force to fight this terribly strong enemy. He told him that it would be impossible to hold all the ground, everywhere, in all the states.

Davis was not receptive.

For his pains Beauregard was exiled to the west. There he planned and conducted the campaign which ended in battle at Shiloh Church, Tennessee. Albert Sydney Johnston had commanded there, and died, but Beauregard had held the reins. In that fight, he had come within a "gnat's eyelash" of destroying Grant forever. At the end of the first day, the Army of the Tennessee had stood with its back to the river with nowhere to go. Only Don Carlos Buell's unexpected arrival with the Army of the Cumberland had saved them.

It had not mattered to Davis. The chief executive correctly saw him as the military leader of the political opposition, the "Western Concentration Bloc."

His next exile was command in the Carolinas where he held Charleston against all comers, held it against overwhelming odds, held it for a year and a half.

When Ben Butler landed his Army of the James around City Point, Virginia, on 1 May, it was intended that he would operate directly against Richmond from the south. This would nicely complement Grant's drive straight south from the Rappahannock. His chance of doing that seemed increased by the South's own organization of its forces.

In accordance with the system of command which Beauregard had once fatally protested, Confederate Virginia was strangely divided into several military departments. Robert E. Lee's Department of Northern Virginia did not extend farther south than Richmond. Beyond that limit the great Creole's military fiefdom extended to Georgia.

In the midst of the emergency, it may have occurred to someone in Richmond that a change of boundaries was a possibility, but Lee was wholly occupied from the 4th of May onward with the situation before him.

Grant crossed the Rapidan that morning. It was out of the question to saddle him with more responsibility.

Major General George Pickett happened to be in Petersburg when the Army of the James came ashore nearby. He wired Beauregard for instructions.

"Hold the town. I am coming," was the reply.

Always the man to follow orders, Pickett assembled a force of Virginia Reserves and militia,[10] and with them kept Butler out of the city for several days, thus saving Richmond from quick occupation.

In fulfillment of his promise, Beauregard stripped his department of every man and artillery piece that could be spared and sent them north, following close behind himself.

He and Pickett then halted the forward momentum of Butler's movement inland from the James in a series of sharply fought and bloody little battles. Within a week they had caused him to draw to the shelter of his entrenched

---

10 Old men and boys.

bridgehead at Bermuda Hundred. Having watched Butler's reactions, Beauregard decided that the commander of the Army of the James was not capable of dealing with an aggressive enemy. With that conviction as basis, he acted to destroy Butler's army. The plan was simple. He would crush the Army of the James in the jaws of a giant nutcracker.

The interruptions of railroad service caused by Union cavalry raids launched from Bermuda Hundred by August Kautz could not keep the lines closed between Petersburg and Richmond for long against determined resistance and relentless repair gangs. In spite of the damage, regiments, brigades and whole divisions moved steadily northward on the rails and roads into assembly areas.

The jaws of the nutcracker steadily grew teeth. One force gathered at Petersburg, another came together astride the roads south of Richmond near the great river defense fortifications at Drewry's Bluff.

Ransom, Hoke, and Colquitt brought their divisions there in preparation for an assault from the north. Another force was prepared for a strike from the south, from the vicinity of Petersburg.[11]

As a part of Pickett's Division, Corse's Brigade assembled two miles south of the railhead at which the 17th had unloaded. The five infantry regiments had been separated for a week. The 30th and 17th had been busy with Kautz along the Richmond and Danville. The others had come straight north from Weldon and Petersburg to help keep these Yankees out of the capital. Now they were coming together again, massing for the fight.

As the night neared its end, the long snake of 17th Virginia riflemen strode forward in near silence. So many men, marching in route step, could not help but make some noise. The music of harness, shoe leather, and whispers filled the space around them. Nevertheless, they were remarkably quiet. They had soldiered so long now that the habit of discipline kept them still, and the damp earth of the forest track muffled the sound of their feet.

The head of the column reached a crossroads. Beneath an ancient sign General Corse waited for them. The regiment halted for a moment.

---

11 13,500 Confederate infantrymen would face 19,000 Union men in this action.

The leading "fours" of "A Company" listened attentively to the words of welcome and commendation given to Herbert for the Flat Creek affair.

Men farther back in the formation knew only that they had stopped and then unexpectedly moved onward. At the crossroad, Montgomery Corse stood by the side of the road, his round hat in hand. As each company in the column passed he leaned forward to murmur greetings.

It was an open secret in the brigade that the Alexandria Regiment was his favorite. As a major of militia, he had commanded them in the last year before the death of the old Union.

Guides led them on in a cavernous darkness filled with ominous shapes and the sound of confused forest beasts. Twigs broke underfoot. Muffled expressions of frustration occasionally disturbed the stillness as soldiers tripped over roots in the dark.

The night had just begun to pale into day as the regiment changed formation from column to line while moving forward in the piney wood.

Colonel Herbert stalked forward through the dead leaves, his arms held out straight to either side.

The color sergeant followed him closely, the stiff, red flag erect by his side.

The captain of each company doubled forward to establish the reference point upon which his company would form to left or right of the colors. The gloom of the false dawn and the swirling, tattered ground fog enfolded the movement. The widely spaced line of officers kept moving onward.

In front of them the flanks of the 30th and 29th Virginia could now be seen where they waited in the woods. A hundred yard gap between them beckoned.

The veterans fanned out, each unslinging his rifle as he went. They fell in on the guides with hardly a glance to left or right. The long brown line advanced, its two ranks were perfectly straight and centered on the color bearer.

The soldiers of the waiting regiments watched them approach. A captain at the right of the 29th's line lifted his hat in silent welcome as they grew nearer.

The flank companies came even with the brigade's line of battle. They halted. The men knelt, continuing to peer ahead for a minute, then relaxing in the expectation that they would not go forward yet. Knowing that they must, they dropped their horseshoe bedrolls by their feet. Some sat on the ground. Some lay flat in the utter repose so natural to old combat men. On the flanks, a few were lucky enough to spy friends or relatives in other regiments.

The light grew. The length of the line into which they had inserted themselves could now be dimly seen. The brigade's five, square, battle flags were there and beyond them the lines stretched on in the mist. The forest had little underbrush in the area immediately around them. If you looked hard enough you could see several thousand men on either side.

Behind the 17th's line, Major Robert Simpson stretched his arms and back, crossing his arms across his chest without bending the elbows. He retrieved his watch from a vest pocket. It was 4:30. He closed the cover and rubbed the old silver with his thumb.

Birds were stirring in the trees.

Along the back of the line, officers and staff sergeants were gathered in small groups to whisper.

Simpson listened closely to be sure no one spoke aloud. He buttoned his jacket against the pre-dawn chill.

It was very quiet in the wood.

Simpson knew that the enemy picket line was less than a quarter mile ahead. He glanced at Herbert who stood behind the other end of the formation with the sergeant major. With some pleasure, he saw that his friend was smiling at him.

4:30, fifteen minutes to wait...

Simpson drew his sword slowly from the scabbard. The dull grey blade emerged quietly, coming into the world as though reborn. There was a small spot of discoloration alongside the blood runlet. He rubbed the metal on his brown sleeve, watching it run back and forth on the faded braid of the Austrian knot that showed him to be a field officer. He stuck the point in the earth to stand the weapon on end, and drew his revolver to check the loads and caps. The sword drew his attention back to itself. It was quite old-fashioned, his great uncle's sword from the Revolution. The old man had carried it at Saratoga in Morgan's Virginia Riflemen. Thinking of the original owner, he remembered the day he had received it. His cousin had given him her father's sword, saying that he must use it well...

Bill Fowle walked over from his company to wish him luck. It was a ritual they found themselves engaged in each time they went into action.

Simpson extricated his fingers from his beard to grasp the other's hand.

The captain looked down at the antique saber. "The knights are dust," he whispered.

"Their good swords rust," the major returned.

"Their souls are with the saints we trust."

Simpson grinned. "Old Millner would be proud," he said. "But then, he said you were his favorite cadet, ever." He felt, rather than saw, the regiment rise.

All at once, the men were on their feet loading rifles, and fixing bayonets.

Herbert pointed at the brushy wood line in front.

A part of each company moved forward as skirmishers. They stopped just short of the jungle. Some looked back; others peered into the vines and brambles.

It was now light enough to recognize individuals, but the fog still rose from the damp earth.

He looked at his watch again. *"4:45."*

Time to go.

"Bri-gaade! Att-ten-shun! Caar-ry! Arms! Skirmishers for-waard, March! 29th the battalion of direction! Bat-talions for-waard! Guide center! March!"

The brigade's line of battle lurched into motion. The center moved first, responding to Corse's word of command. As the advance spread toward the wings like a wave, the somewhat bow shaped line glided toward the enemy.

The skirmish line vanished into the unknown.

Five hundred yards to the front, a private soldier named Baxter lay behind the meager shelter of a rail fence.

The fence ran around the kitchen garden of a farmhouse. Beyond the fence was the crest of a ridge and a meadow that sloped down to a wooded creek bed.

The night had been long, damp and unnerving. Only half awake, Baxter thought for a time that he heard a voice far away, but stillness rested so solidly in the air that he decided he must have dreamt, and returned to an inner contemplation of the memory of his last furlough. He rolled back and forth, wrapping the rubber ground sheet more snugly around his legs.

Sixty yards behind him, his company commander sat at the farmhouse kitchen table thinking about the injustice of his position. He was as sure as he was about anything that this damned farm was too far forward to be a good outpost. He had tried to tell his superiors that, but as usual, no one listened to him.

Three of his men were busy brewing coffee for the company on the big, wood burning range.

The captain moved his legs so that one of them could get by with an arm full of sticks for the firebox. The fire made a very satisfactory place of the kitchen. It burned hot enough to keep the damp wood blazing with a pleasing sound of crackling and hissing.

After a while, Private Baxter began to doze, secure in the belief that his sergeant would be along shortly to rouse him. In the warmth of his bedroll, the sound of feet in the long meadow grass did not reach him. His head lay on the ground, protected from the wet by nothing but the crown of his crushed blue forage cap. Over a period of twenty or thirty seconds the level of reverberation in his skull slowly grew louder.

"Jesus!" someone yelled. "The Johnnies!"

Baxter snapped his head around to peer under the bottom rail.

The ground fog was lifting. The bottom of it was a foot off the ground in the meadow. Pairs of brogans were visible beneath the cloud. Ten feet apart, they were halfway across the field and coming fast.

Trapped in his wrappings, Baxter flailed wildly, seeking escape from the grip of his bedclothes.

Around him, his comrades opened fire in a ragged volley. The clank of ramrods sounded with a particular frenzy he had not heard before.

He shook off nearly all his bonds, and rose to his feet one hand on a fencepost. His feet were nearly loose. One more kick... The thought of escape back across the farmyard was firmly in his head. He could see it so clearly in his mind that it stayed with him for an instant after the point of the bayonet hit him in the back.

It went in hard with the full weight of an "H" Company "Gypsy" behind it. The tip glanced off a vertebra, tearing cartilage as it wrenched two ribs apart. The rigid sharpness of it drove on through a lung and ended its travel embedded in the left side of his heart.

He fell to his knees, and then on his face with a great, searing agony in his chest.

George Latham, shoemaker by trade, put one foot on the fallen enemy's back alongside his blade and pulled it out with a twist of his wrists.

Firing was general around the house.

Rebel riflemen converged on it from three directions.

The door flew open. Four blue uniformed figures hurtled from the house, headed for the rear. A ripple of firing dropped two. Fifteen or twenty more soldiers from the outpost could be seen in flight across the open ground behind the farmhouse. The rest stood with their hands in the air, or lay where they would stay.

Latham stepped over the Yankee and strode across the yard, passing by the open door of the brick house.

Motion in the house turned him that way, ready to fire. A woman in gingham stood in the kitchen door, a child peeking from behind her.

"You stay in the house ma'am!" Latham called. "Get in the cellar!"

She said something unintelligible, waved and went back into the kitchen.

The skirmisher saw that he was dropping behind. He trotted away from the house to fill his place in the moving line.

The brigade's line of battle came out of the creek bed at the foot of the meadow, and started uphill. General Corse stepped through the ranks and walked out in front of his line. He turned to face them and strode backward up the hill. His sword swung parallel to the ground in his right fist. In his face shone the pride in them which suffused his being.

"Bread! Bread!" chanted the men. Laughter rippled along the front. This had started in the Peninsula two years before when they had gone into the assault at Frazier's Farm without rations. They served that up to Corse on every possible occasion.

"You'll have all the bread you can eat soon!" he yelled back.

The formation swept over the hilltop and around the farmhouse, "H" Company of the 17th passed through the yard between the house and the barn. The brigade line started down the reverse slope headed for the distant wood line.

In the house, Caroline Middleton stood at a window and watched them go.

The skirmishers had dwindled to tiny figures. Puffs of smoke drifted across the trees at the edge of the forest.

She could just hear sounds which she knew must be shots. Uncomprehendingly, she watched the Confederate skirmishers maneuver forward in groups of four, two soldiers firing at a time to help the others move ahead.

A brown figure threw up its arms and fell, its back arched and reaching for the sky.

She cried out, holding one hand over her mouth as though someone might hear. Falling to her knees, she prayed for her unknown protectors.

The three quarters of a mile from the crest to the wood was divided into two well-defined bands. There was a quarter mile of slash, stumps and felled logs in what looked like a recently cleared field. Beyond that, the ground sloped gently down to the Yankee breastworks.

The regiments marched steadily forward, picking their way through the maze of treetops and deadfall. The formation opened and closed like a concertina as men climbed over and through obstacles. At last the fallen trees were passed, and they emerged into the silver light of a sun glowing low on the horizon as an indistinct and pale disk.

Corse led them down the slope. He and the colonels, lieutenant-colonels and majors had come forward from their usual posts behind the line.

The veteran infantrymen knew what that meant. The attack would be pressed home with the bayonet. A murmur of anticipation swept the ranks. Emotion swelled across the field.

Out in front the skirmish line had gone to ground, keeping up a steady fire against the enemy entrenchments.

Incoming rifle bullets droned around the battle flag of the 17th. One cut the cloth itself.

300 yards to go. From his place at the right of the front rank of his company, Fowle could now see the *abatis* in front of the trench.

Major Simpson began to distinguish white faces through the tangled branches.

In the midst of the color party, Sergeant-Major Hart spun in his tracks, shot through the mouth.

"Close ranks!" bellowed the regimental quartermaster sergeant.

The color party pressed together, filling the empty place.

They reached and passed their skirmishers. The men fell in on the rear rank.

The enemy's face could be seen through the obstacles.

Suddenly, a private in "B" Company ran forward, beyond the colonel, raised his rifle in one hand and gave voice to the shrieking, trembling, melody of the Rebel Yell.

Another did the same in the 29th.

Up and down the brigade line, the raw emotion of feral, blinding rage raced from man to man. White hot murder filled up their souls leaving room for nothing but the vision of the trench line before them.

The pace picked up.

Montgomery Corse looked at them, then at the colonels. "Wade in, my bullies, wade in!" he shouted.

The riflemen filled their lungs. "Whup! Whup! Whup! swelled the sound, a hunting call summoning the dogs to the kill. "EeeeeeeHaah!" it continued, transformed by tribal fury into something very like the sound that rang in the ears of Caesar's legions.

The men broke into a trot. Their war cry ripped through the air, filling their heads, and filling their enemies' heads.

Across the ranks bullets took their victims, pitching them backward in the spasm of nervous tension which meant an ending, or just dropping them in a sodden heap of misery.

A .58 caliber Minie ball hit Bill Fowle just below the knee. As is common with serious wounds, it did not hurt at all. The leg collapsed under him, and he fell to the ground.

The soldier behind stepped over him and kept going.

Fowle lay in the dirt clutching his calf. Blood flowed into his boot. "Ah, Sweet Jesus, Emily!" he muttered through clenched teeth.

Bayonets shone beneath a newly risen sun. The howling charge rushed onward.

In the Federal position the conviction of impending, senseless doom grew suddenly, and became a force that could not be denied.

The brigade raced in through the *abatis* behind their leaders.

Smoking musket barrels protruded in the embrasures made by the small spaces between head logs and revetments.

The front rank ran up the earthen *glacis*, leaping the obstacle of the head logs to land in the ditch behind. They sought their enemy.

Only a few Union infantrymen were there. The rest had vacated the trench at the last moment and were now 50 yards away headed at a run for the rear. Scattered fights swirled around those Northern soldiers who had not left with their comrades. Gun butts and bayonets decided the outcome. More and more hands stretched into the air.

Arthur Herbert looked about for his officers; sure that Corse would quickly order continuation of the attack. "Simpson! Major Simpson!" he bellowed. Men looked left and right in search of the familiar, stooped form.

"Back here! He's here!" a voice cried.

A thousand faces turned to the rear, seeking the speaker.

On the *glacis*, among the fallen treetops and piled brush two soldiers knelt beside a bloody mass of clothing and boots that only slowly resolved itself into the form of the major of the regiment.

Herbert climbed back out of the ditch to reach his side. "My God, Robert... What has happened to you?" His voice shook as he looked down.

Simpson grinned at him with eyes that betrayed his agony. "Itripped on this goddamned wire, and they shot the devil out of me..."

His left leg bent at a right angle above the knee. White bone ends stuck out of the torn remains of his trouser leg.

"I felt them all hit me," he said, looking down at the carnage. "Funny, after all this..."

Herbert looked around. Now he saw the telegraph wire wrapped tight around pieces of stump and buried tent pegs. It was all about six inches off the ground, running in crazy, patternless patterns in all direction.

A number of his men were stretched on the ground in the band of obstacles. Lifting his eyes to look back along the line of advance, he spied the brown bundles scattered across the hillside. Behind them, wagons had come into view, following a logging trail down the slope from the farmhouse.

"Here you are, Robert," the colonel said. Doctor Lewis and our people will be along shortly. A month in hospital and you'll be back..."

The man on the ground held up a hand.

The colonel took it, held it in both hands.

Behind him the regiment climbed out of the trench. The earthen figures formed their two ranks.

A driven enemy must not be allowed to rest.

"Go on, now, all of you... They'll be here in a minute. Go on."

"Dunn, you stay with him. Get the doctor!" He squeezed the hand, and then turned to pick his way through the obstacles.

On the ground, Robert Simpson looked at the sky. It would be a beautiful late spring day. A few billowing white clouds were coming in from the west. Birds sang in the edge of the woods.

A cardinal chirped above him. The little bird was easy to see in his scarlet pride against the green leaves. Peering about, the tiny creature seemed to watch him.

He tried not to breathe deeply. It hurt too much. For some reason he saw himself for an instant standing at the blackboard, chalk in hand.

"Forwaard!" Corse's voice resounded. "Maarch!"

Over the top of the dirt wall in front of the trench, the wounded man could see three of the five red flags. As he watched, they started forward.

The soldier, Dunn, stared at the backs of his comrades.

"Go with them," Simpson ordered.

The man shook his head. "You just lay there quiet. I'll find help." With that he walked off toward the wagons.

Simpson covered his eyes with the back of a hand. The sun had grown so bright...

Chapter 23

Going Home

- August -
(Richmond, Virginia)

Harry Jenkins tied his horse to the back of the carriage. He stood on the sidewalk in front of the old house waiting for Devereux. Claude was a relative of Joseph Mayo, the mayor of Richmond, and often stayed with the mayor when he was in the city. Jenkins remembered waiting in front of the mayor's house once before for Devereux. That had been in the winter of 1863. On that occasion, Lieutenant Franklin Bowie had waited with him. Now Bowie was dead. He had died trying to take Devereux across the Potomac so that he could begin his mission in the North. That was sadly ironic since Bowie disliked Devereux and had made no secret of it.

The front door opened. Claude walked down the steps, nodded to Jenkins and the coachman, and entered the carriage.

The day was warm. Jenkins' uniform jacket was wool. Sweat would soon run in streams down his back. Summer haze had arrived and the city seemed indistinct and slightly out of focus.

Jenkins and Devereux seated themselves on the same bench seat facing forward.

"Personally, I think you should not go back," Jenkins finally said. The red headed intelligence officer, like Bowie, had never liked Devereux. He disliked him for his self assured manner, for his obvious assumption of class superiority and paradoxically, for the ease with which he mastered tasks given him, tasks that would have crushed most men. There was also the matter of Patrick Devereux. Jenkins resented Claude Devereux's survival of his brother's death. He knew that was grossly unfair, but.... Jenkins knew he must speak to his unwanted companion. Some official business needed to be settled before they reached their destination. Chimborazo Hospital was less than a mile from the mayor's house. "We could hide you here in the War Department," he began. "We can hide you until the end of the war and then you can decide what to do. They may already know you have been here with us, and not as a prisoner. Perhaps we could send you back to Europe... Not to France, that would be too difficult. They have been searching for news of you there. Perhaps you could go to Rome. There has been talk of sending a permanent envoy to the pope..." He looked at Devereux who seemed fascinated by something in the street scene. "There are many uncertainties about the people involved in all this," Jenkins continued. Just as an example, do we really know everything there is to know about this driver?" He stopped for a moment, thinking of the black coachman on top of the vehicle. "It is true that he drives for General Cooper, but how do we know who has "gotten to" him?"

This reminded him of the question he had been itching to ask since the previous day. "How was your talk with Cooper?" He turned to watch Devereux closely for answers that might not be contained in his words.

Claude's arm was still immobilized by the bandage and sling that covered the holes where the Yankee captain's bayonet had gone into his shoulder in front and come out behind below the shoulder blade. The lung was untouched. He had always healed well, and his recovery from this latest damage was no exception. Months in hospital had seen the wound close and some mobility was returning to the arm. His uncle's house had been a good place for convalescence.

Devereux smiled slightly. "Cooper reminds me of all the good times we had together at home in Alexandria. My grandfather and he were close friends, similar men, really. I went fishing with them often when I was a boy, fishing on the Potomac in Cooper's little boat with his coachman rowing. That's him up there driving..." Claude knocked on the ceiling.

The driver's access hatch opened to reveal Sam Watson's face peering down. "Yes, Mr. Devereux? You need sumfin?"

"No, Sam we're fine. How's your family?" "Jus' fine sir, jus' fine." Having decided that this was just friendly talk, Watson closed the little sliding door.

This little exchange gave Jenkins one more thing to dislike. The mockery had been unmistakable.

Devereux concentrated on the previous thread of the conversation. "Ah... Cooper... He doesn't know what to do with me any more than you do. You people in the War Department value my group's information, but you are fearful of Benjamin's connection with us. You are worried about what he might have us do, or what I might do with his support. No? Is that not so? Why are we coming out here today?"

Jenkins did not answer.

The carriage slowed on the cobblestones as it turned off the street and into the grounds of the hospital. The old trees and the big brick house that was the headquarters were so familiar... The better parts of Richmond resembled each other in the comfortable, solid way that their inhabitants often resembled each other. Beyond the brick house were many rows of one story clapboard buildings connected by covered walkways.

Jenkins told Sam Watson which of these was their destination.

The low, white building looked like all the others. Patients in loose fitting hospital clothing sat in wooden chairs outside. A few were reading newspapers or books, but most either talked to neighbors or slept in the sun.

A black hospital orderly in white clothing held the screened door open for them as they went inside. There was an open ward with a nurse's station by the door. A doctor was leaving as they entered.

Devereux nodded to him assuming that he had been doing morning "rounds."

They walked the length of the ward to Captain Fowle's room at the other end.

"Mornin, Bill," Jenkins said as they entered. "How are you today? Have they decided about that leg?"

Fowle had been watching the clouds go by. He smiled at Jenkins, an old school friend, but went blank when he saw Claude come into the room as well. Devereux had served in "H Company" of the 17th Virginia Regiment with Fowle before he had been sent on secret service duty. He had preceded William Fowle in command of the company.

"Claude, if you want the company back, there's a vacancy," he said without looking at him. His unhappiness with that thought was in his voice. His ruined leg, still immobilized on a board and heavily bandaged was obvious under the sheet. There was no need to be more specific about his injury. "You know Simpson is dead, don't you?" he asked no one in particular. There was no reply. "He died a few days ago…"

"Hurt much?" Devereux asked standing across the bed from Jenkins.

Fowle turned to Jenkins and grinned. "Only when they insist on getting me up for a trip to the outhouse or some such thing… They don't seem to like bedpans here…"

He looked at Devereux. "It seems the knee is pretty well gone. It will always be stiff. It has been a struggle to keep them from taking the leg, but it isn't infected, so they are going to let me keep it I believe. Nevertheless, I would like to get out of here before they change their minds. I am permanently through with field duty, permanently…" This pronouncement of the end of a big part of Fowle's life triggered a response from Devereux.

"We are in the same position. They won't let me go back to the regiment, not ever."

"They?"

Devereux waved a hand in the general direction of the red headed major. "He and his colleagues, all the way up to Samuel Cooper."

Fowle shook his head. "Cooper… I always thought you were one of his favorites. You and your grandfather…"

"He says I am not his "property" anymore. I am still in the army but I belong to Judah Benjamin. He says he is sorry about that, but Benjamin has the president's ear... I am sorry as well. There is nothing I can do about this just now, but we will see what can be done... What are you going to do if you can't go back to troops?"

Jenkins was not happy with the general tone of self pity and alienation in this conversation. "Claude, your previous wounds should have kept you out of the field. Your right leg is almost as bad as Bill's. I don't know how you got around up at Spotsylvania. It must hurt like hell."

Devereux ignored him.

Jenkins sighed. "We have decided that Captain Fowle is going to be in charge of your group from the Richmond end." He watched the spy for a reaction.

A slight narrowing in the eyes was the only indication that Devereux's response might be unpleasant for the creators of this plan. "Ah," he said at last. "I see. It is all worked out. I go back to Alexandria, somehow, and Benjamin assumes complete control of our effort there. Harry, I thought you said that you did not think I should go home, that it was too dangerous..."

"My personal opinion, only that... I really have no choice," Jenkins said quietly. He seemed interested in some indeterminate point in space between them. "I could go to General Lee with this if you wish. Cooper and Benjamin would be angry, very angry. Benjamin has some grand scheme in mind in which you pay a role."

"Will you still be involved with us?"

"A little, but, Bill here will be your man in Benjamin's office. I will keep track of what they are doing with you to make sure the army agrees."

"This whole thing was your idea in the beginning was it not? The whole idea of sending me to Washington?"

"Yes. I knew you through Patrick. Your family is obviously an important means to the end of doing secret service work in Washington City."

"That makes you responsible for what has happened to us. You and Bill here and my brother were classmates at the military institute, the VMI. You were, are, his brothers. You owed him. You owe us."

Jenkins looked directly at him. Anger showed for the first time. "Why do you think we have argued our way through a thicket of indifference and bull-headed inertia to have him made responsible for your case? Why do you think we did that? We have been working on this since the day I knew that Bill would not go back to the field. We asked Robert Simpson what he thought. We asked him a few days before he died... Why do you think we did all this?"

Devereux decided. "I think you can tell the U.S. War Department that I was captured unconscious near the Brock Road. Tell them that I was out of my mind in a hospital for a while and then recuperating. Tell them that you were not notified of my capture until recently. They will believe that. They want to think you are stupid and inefficient. Tell them that. If I am going home, I want to go soon. There are people waiting for me there."

The slight smile made his meaning clear.

Jenkins frowned. His Calvinist sexual morality was offended by Devereux's behavior with women, especially women whom Jenkins knew. "It is none of my business, but…."

"Yes. You are right. It is none of your business. Ah, I have forgotten to ask. How is Captain Smoot? I last saw him when one of Balthazar's men had removed his hand."

"He is Major Smoot now," Jenkins replied. "He was in hospital in Lynchburg when Early and Balthazar passed through there headed for the Valley. They took him and your man White with them…"

"How do I get back to town?" Devereux asked.

"General Cooper's coachman will take you wherever you like, just leave my horse. I have other appointments here."

"All right, boys, have a nice chat. Remember, Harry, I want to leave quickly! See you soon, Bill!" With that, Devereux turned and left. His echoing boot heels could be heard in the ward, followed by the slamming of the screen door. The sound of the carriage wheels faded away.

Jenkins realized that he had been holding his breath as the sound receded. He moved a chair next to the bed and sat. "If he had asked I would have tried to find a way around Benjamin. I would have tried to keep him here…"

Fowle moved uncomfortably on the narrow hospital bed. "Get the nurse, would you?"

Jenkins came back after a minute with two black women in white aprons.

"Could you prop me up, somehow?" Fowle asked. "I have to talk to this man. He's a pest, but there is no avoiding it."

They looked doubtful, confused by his attempt at humor. He grinned through the pain of his still unhealed wounds. When they were convinced that he was joking, they piled up pillows behind him and under his leg.

"Does Claude know that Benjamin wants to use him against Lincoln?" Fowle asked.

Jenkins rested his elbows on the bed, holding his head in his hands. "He has been suggesting it to Benjamin since the beginning of the year. Cooper and I tried to divert his attention to something else, anything, but he knows we are losing everywhere. He knows it better than anyone else. He reads the enemy's own documents and papers every day. He knows that Lincoln is the soul of the forces that are destroying us. He knows. What he does not know yet is that they have asked if we captured him or have his body. They refer to him in the correspondence as 'Claude C. Devereux, Brigadier General, United States Volunteers.' We will have to tell him soon.

"They have promoted him?"

"Yes."

"They are not going to kill him, are they?" Fowle asked. "I mean Lincoln. That would be a terrible thing. We could never recover from the effects of that. If we lose... If we lose..."

"Benjamin is talking about capturing Lincoln, talking of holding him until they accept our 'departure," but I am not sure Devereux will accept restrictions on his action. I am not sure that he accepts anything anymore. You see the change in him, don't you?"

Fowle shook his head. "He was always headstrong and certain of himself. Now there is a bitterness in him that is worrisome."

"Will you take the job?"

"I have no choice," Fowle sighed. "None of us has much choice any longer. You caused this Harry. You never knew how much was too much. Now, go away. I need to sleep."

Harry Jenkins untied his horse and mounted for the ride back to headquarters in the Mechanics' Building...

He tried to remember. What was it Cooper had said last year after Gettysburg?

Ah, he said that Claude would "take us where we fear to go..." What have I done?

The End

- Some of the People of the Book in Alphabetical Order-

Anderson, Major General Richard Herron, CSA. Commanding General of an infantry division of Lee's army.

Babcock, John. Colonel George Sharpe's civilian deputy.

Baker, Colonel Lafayette, USV. Chief of the National Detective Bureau and colonel of the 1st D.C. Cavalry Regiment.

Balthazar, John, also known as Jean-Marie Balthazar D'Orgueil, Major, Army of the French.

Benjamin, Judah Philip. Secretary of State of the Confederate States of America.

Biddle, Lieutenant Warren Knowlton, USV. Amy' Biddle's nephew.

Biddle, Amy. An official of the U.S. Sanitary Commission Lodge at Alexandria, Virginia. A native of New Hampshire.

Booth, John Wilkes. Actor.

Bowie, Lieutenant Franklin, CSA. An officer of the Confederate Army Signal Corps.

Braithwaite, Commander Richard, US Navy. Brother of Frederick.

Braithwaite, Elizabeth. Wife of Lieutenant Colonel Frederick Braithwaite, United States Volunteers (USV).

Browning, Major Charles, USV. The Provost Marshal of Alexandria, Virginia.

Butler, Major General Benjamin, USV. The Federal commander at Fortress Monroe on the Virginia coast.

Butterfield, Brigadier General Daniel (Dan), USV. Chief of staff of the Army of the Potomac. The composer of "Taps."

Cooper, General Samuel, CSA. The Adjutant and Inspector General of the Confederate States Army. The most senior officer by rank of that army.

Corse, Brigadier General Montgomery, CSA. Commanding a brigade made up of the 15th, 17th, 29th and 30th Virginia Infantry Regiments. Another banker.

Corse's Brigade, CSA. Confederate Army brigades were usually named for the officer who had first commanded them. An exception was the "Stonewall Brigade" which was named by act of the Confederate Congress and who claimed that the general had been named for them. He agreed. Corse's Brigade included the; 15th, 17th, 29th, and 30th Virginia Volunteer Infantry Regiments.

Davenport, William. An Assistant Secretary of War.

Davis, Jefferson. President of the Confederate States of America.

Davis, Varina Howell. His wife.

Devereux, Charles Francis. Banker and father of Claude, Patrick and Jake,

Devereux, Major Claude Crozet, Confederate States Army (CSA). In civilian life a banker at Alexandria, Virginia. (Hannibal). Also Colonel, US Volunteers.

Devereux, Hope Prescott. Wife of Claude. A native of Boston, Massachusetts

Devereux, Lieutenant Joachim Murat (Jake), CSA. Brother to Claude and Patrick. In civil life a classics scholar at the University of Virginia, currently serving with the 17th Virginia Infantry Regiment.

Devereux, Patrick Henry. Claude's brother, also a banker of Alexandria, Virginia

Devereux, Marie Clotilde. Wife of Charles and mother of his sons.

Devereux, Victoria. Patrick's wife.

Early, Major General Jubal Anderson, CSA. Commanding General of an infantry division in Longstreet's Corps. Lee's "Bad Old Man," and one of the most underrated men in either army.

Ellis, Jefferson. A clerk in Major Browning's office.

Farinelli, Major Marco Aurelio, USV. A foreign volunteer officer. A professional soldier.

Ford, Major Wilson, Artillery, USA. A Regular Army officer assigned because of a disabling wound to the National Detective Bureau.

Fowle, Captain William H., Jr. CSA. Yet another banker from Alexandria, commanding Company "H" (the gypsies) in the 17th Virginia Infantry Regiment.

Galbraith, Lewis. Mayor of Alexandria under Union Army occupation.

Grant, US. Lieutenant General, US Army. Commander of all United States ground forces.

Hays, Alexander, Brigadier General, USV. An infantry brigade commander in the Second Corps, Army of the Potomac.

Harrison, Lieutenant James, Signal Corps, CSA. An actor and also a scout.

Herbert, Colonel Arthur, CSA. Commanding the 17th Virginia Infantry Regiment. A banker.

Jackson, Lieutenant General Thomas Jonathan, CSA. (Stonewall) Commander of the Second Army Corps of Lee's army.

Jenkins, Lieutenant Colonel Harry, CSA. A staff officer of the Confederate War Department Secret Service Bureau in Richmond, Virginia.

Jourdain, Colonel Edouard, French Army.. The French military attaché at Washington, D.C.

Kautz, Brigadier General August, US Army, Commander of a cavalry Division in the Union "Army of the James."

Kennedy, Lieutenant Frederick, CSA. Signal Corps

Kruger, Father Willem, S.J. The pastor of St. Mary's Catholic church in Alexandria and Claude Devereux's confessor. A native of the Netherlands.

Lee, General Robert E., CSA. Commander of the Confederate Army's District of Northern Virginia and the army of the same name.

Lewis, Jim, CSA. A free man of color of Lexington, Virginia. Stonewall Jackson's camp cook.

Lincoln, Abraham. Sixteenth President of the United States.

Longstreet, Lieutenant General James, CSA. Commanding General of the First Army Corps of The Army of Northern Virginia. (Lee's army). An Army Corps was made up of three or more infantry divisions.

Marshall, Major Charles, CSA. An officer of Lee's staff

Mayo, Joseph. Mayor of Richmond, Virginia.

Meade, Major General George Gordon, USA. Commander of the Army of the Potomac at Gettysburg.

Mitchell, Major Johnston, USV. A volunteer officer assigned to Baker's National Detective Bureau in New York City. A newspaper man in civilian life.

Mosby, Major John Singleton, CSA. Partisan Commander of the 43rd.

Neville, Major Robert, 60th Rifles. Assistant military Attache in the British Legation at Washington and an officer of British Intelligence.

Pickett, Major General George E., CSA. Commanding General of an infantry division (about 5,000 men) in Longstreet's First Corps.

Quick, Master Sergeant John. (Johnny), US Army. Claude Devereux's enlisted aide.

Renfroe, Judge Caleb. An assistant Secretary of War in Washington.

Ruth, Samuel. Superintendent of the Richmond, Fredericksburg and Potomac Railroad..

Seventeenth Virginia Infantry Regiment, CSA. This is the "Alexandria Regiment", an unusual Confederate army unit in that most of its members were urban people from the City of Alexandria, the District of Columbia or nearby Maryland. At full strength it would have had more than nine hundred riflemen formed into nine companies. The companies came from the pre-war Virginia militia or were created for the war. They included two companies raised from among the Irish immigrant parishioners of St. Mary's in Alexandria. Their priest blessed their flags at the altar there.

Sharpe, Colonel George, USV. Chief intelligence officer, Federal "Army of the Potomac" and later of all US Army forces.

Simpson, Major Robert, CSA. Second in Command of the 17th Virginia Infantry Regiment.

Smoot, Sergeant Isaac, CSA. A soldier of Mosby's Rangers.

Stanton, Edwin. Secretary of War of the United States.

Stuart, Major General J.E.B., CSA. Commanding General of the Cavalry Division of Lee's army. Stuart's men usually numbered about 6,000 sabers.

Venable, Major Charles, CSA. An officer of Lee's staff.

White, Bill, CSA. A member of the Devereux household now serving as lead teamster of the 17th Virginia Infantry Regiment.

White, Betsy. Cook in the Devereux household and wife and mother to all the Whites.

White, Sergeant George, Jr., United States Colored Troops (2nd USCT Cavalry Regiment). Bill White's older brother

White, George. Butler of the Devereux household, and father of the White brothers.

"Snake" Davis, CSA. An Alexandria man serving as head cook of Company "H", 17th Virginia Infantry Regiment.

Made in the USA
Middletown, DE
14 July 2018